A Death on Crooked Lake

By Robert W. Gregg

ISBN 0-7414-3007-X

Cover photos courtesy of Steve Knapp,
www.keukaview.com

Published by:

INFI∞ITY
PUBLISHING.COM

1094 New DeHaven Street, Suite 100
West Conshohocken, PA 19428-2713
Info@buybooksontheweb.com
www.buybooksontheweb.com
Toll-free (877) BUY BOOK
Local Phone (610) 941-9999
Fax (610) 941-9959

Printed in the United States of America

Printed on Recycled Paper

Published March 2006

To my grandchildren

May they continue to enjoy Crooked Lake summers
for many years to come

PART I

THE BODY ON THE DOCK

CHAPTER 1

Kevin Whitman's summer had been quiet and uneventful, full of lazy, mostly sunny days, miles away from the crowds and noise of the city and weeks away from boring faculty meetings and uninspired student papers. Never had the decision to buy the lake cottage seemed so right. August, like July before it, provided respite from the academic wars—of not having to worry about anything more challenging than what novel to read next or what wine to have with dinner. But Kevin's idyllic summer changed suddenly and dramatically on the third Tuesday of the month when he came face to face with death on his own dock.

———

From where he lay on the bed, Kevin could see no sign of morning light. He turned toward the window, a rectangle of black on black, and concentrated on a thin sliver of space between the bottom of the drawn shade and the sill. Was the sky slightly less black, a dark gray that heralded the approach of morning? Whatever the exact time, it was certainly much too early to be so wide-awake. He rolled over onto his side and made the effort to go back to sleep, an effort he knew would be unsuccessful. Some inner clock was sending a different message. After trying several positions and stalling for ten minutes or so, Kevin resigned himself to the inevitable and got up to face the day.

He collected his bathrobe from the chair beside the bed and made his way out into the hall, where it became obvious that it was indeed very early. The door at the end of the hall opened onto a screened porch, and through the branches of the large cotton-wood tree on the beach he could see the sky, still dark but with the barest hint of the new day on the horizon. Not yet five o'clock, he decided. Maybe no more than 4:30.

Coffee would help. Kevin descended the narrow staircase and went to the kitchen, where he filled the percolator from the tap, guessing at the proper level because he couldn't bring himself to turn on the light. He located the coffee can from memory, and spooned enough for two cups into the basket.

The pot plugged in, Kevin went out onto the deck to contemplate the lake. On this particular morning it was nearly calm, a dark mirror. The cottonwood leaves, so often in motion, were barely stirring. No sound from man or nature disturbed the silence. The frustration he had felt at waking so early ebbed away. He decided that he would enjoy a swim in this quiet hour while he had the lake to himself.

Swimming was the one form of exercise he indulged in, and he usually managed to test the cold waters a couple of times a day during the summer months. Not usually before sunup, but why not? In another few hours the lake would come alive as it always did with fishermen and boaters and, of course, the Brocks' grandchildren, who never slept late and seemed to spend the whole day in the water, emerging only when called for meals. So Kevin retrieved his bathing suit from the clothesline which stretched between the two old oak trees behind the cottage and quickly changed. He found himself thinking, not for the first time, how lucky he was to have a profession that allowed him the luxury of a prolonged summer vacation. Well, not entirely a vacation, because he always brought his briefcase and laptop to the lake with him. It was an ideal place to ruminate and write, and academics were, after all, expected to publish. But whereas most of his city friends could only manage two or three weeks before returning to their professional routines, he could enjoy this change of pace until Labor Day. The coffee would stay hot; Kevin headed for the water.

Poised at the end of the dock for his dive into the lake, he noticed with a small twinge of annoyance that Mike Snyder was loading fishing gear into his boat a few cottages away. It was too dark to recognize him, but it couldn't be anyone else. Mike went fishing almost every morning, and always at an hour when just about everyone else was asleep. Nonetheless, some of the magic went out of the morning with the knowledge that the lake would have to be shared with another. No, with two others. Some distance down the beach in the other direction, he now realized, were a man and a dog. It was impossible to see them clearly, but the dog seemed to be running back and forth along the water's edge and the man, if indeed it was a man, appeared to be skipping stones out into the lake.

Too much activity for such an early hour. It made it seem less like his lake, a swim less like the little adventure he had been looking forward to only moments before. But Kevin quickly brushed that thought aside and, reminding himself of how much he treasured these summers, he dove into the still, dark waters of Crooked Lake.

He surfaced and began swimming vigorously, combating the shock from the cold water. He always swam purposefully; the lake was too cold for leisurely paddling about. Using the crawl, he swam some thirty yards out from the dock and then turned to follow a course parallel to the shore. His goal was a raft a third of a mile and as many as ten cottages down the lake. It was a manageable swim, well within his capabilities, and it also took him around a bend in the shoreline of Blue Water Point to an attractive cove which he could not see from his own cottage. Kevin settled into a comfortable, steady stroke.

As he passed the spot on the beach where he thought he had seen the man and the dog, he looked toward the shore. But there was no sign of life anywhere. The cottages had not yet emerged from the dark cover of hemlocks and cottonwoods that surrounded them, but the beach was now visible. The man had disappeared, the dog with him.

Kevin swam on, his muscles alive with the exertion. As he made the turn into the cove, the raft came into view, a low dark object in the still dark lake. He heard the cough of an outboard motor in the distance. Mike had presumably started his boat and would now be heading across the lake to one of his favorite fishing spots. Unlike Mike, Kevin was no fisherman. He felt no envy, but he was reminded that different people have different skills, and that his city-bred accomplishments were of very limited utility in this world of outdoorsmen.

Kevin pulled himself up onto the raft and surveyed the lake. Although many cottages hugged its shores, most had been constructed with respect for the woods, which came close to the water's edge, so that only a few lacked a natural canopy of green. Several of the cottagers had coaxed flowers into bloom, and when the sun rose above the hill across the lake, the shoreline would burst into color. Crooked Lake had never known the disciplining hand of zoning ordinances. The result was a great variety of cottages, large and small. Some were occupied the year around, either by retirees or by local families who earned their livelihood in nearby Southport or Cumberland or from the vineyards that flanked the lake. Others were owned by city dwellers who made their appearance after Memorial Day and packed up and left on Labor Day weekend. The lake people Kevin knew were an interesting mix of professionals and blue-collar workers. Such neighborhoods were virtually nonexistent back in the city, where the people who shared this point would have been segregated by occupations and income. Here, in this rustic democracy, they met and interacted on a daily basis, the attorney and the grocer, the pharmacist and the laborer, swapping fish stories and pictures of grandchildren and occasionally sharing hamburgers from their grills on a warm summer's evening.

The sound of Mike Snyder's boat grew fainter as it moved across the lake toward some remote shelf where the trout fed. Soon all would be silent again and the lake Kevin's private pond, at least for another hour or so. At the latest it could not be more than 5:30, probably still closer to five. The coffee would stay hot. But Kevin didn't feel quite right about sitting on someone else's raft, even if the owner were still in bed. There were certain unwritten lake rules; one didn't use a neighbor's facilities without permission. Respect for privacy was the other side of the coin of informality, which characterized life on Crooked Lake. Later in the day, he would have swum to the raft, touched it to satisfy himself that he had gone the full distance, and then returned to his own dock. Today he had taken liberties.

He slipped back into the water for the return swim and shifted to the breaststroke after a hundred yards or so. He could see his destination better that way, and it gave him a chance to practice one of his weaker strokes. The sky was gradually getting brighter. The beach was still deserted, but it appeared that someone else must be up because light smoke was drifting along the water's edge. As he closed the distance between himself and his cottage, it became apparent that the smoke came from the chimney of his neighbors, the Morgans.

Kevin smiled to himself. He wasn't the only one who wasn't sleeping well. But then he spotted something which was much more interesting. There was something—or was it someone—on the end of his own dock. He couldn't tell from his vantage point in the water just what he was looking at, but as he drew closer it became apparent that the something was a man.

The man was stretched out lengthwise of the dock, his feet dangling over the end. He was fully dressed and soaking wet. Kevin could not see the man's face, which was turned the other way and buried in the crook of his arm. There was something decidedly awkward about the way he was lying. He did not look as if he had decided to stretch out to dry off or catch his breath.

"Hello. Are you all right?"

Kevin's words sounded foolish in his own ears. He was pretty sure that this man was not all right. Quickly he swam closer to shore where he could more easily haul himself out of the water, then went out to the end of the dock and knelt beside the still figure. He rotated the body slightly in order to get a look at the man's face. It was then that his concern turned to shock.

It was immediately clear that the man was dead. His eyes stared sightlessly at the brightening sky. His skin had a distinctive pallor that even to Kevin's untrained eye did not look natural. The sense of pleasure which his private swim had kindled drained rapidly away.

The shock came in three waves. The first was the realization that there was a dead man on his dock. The second came quickly on the heels of the first. This was no stranger; this was John Britingham. While Britingham was neither a friend nor an acquaintance, he was a prominent member of the Crooked Lake community whose recent arrival had touched off considerable controversy. A wealthy man, reputedly both brilliant and arrogant, John Britingham was now lying dead before sunrise on Kevin's dock. How had he gotten there? Had he fallen into the lake, suffered a heart attack and crawled onto the dock, only to die before help arrived? Had he been in a boat? If so, where was it? Had he been the man with the dog he had spotted earlier? If so, where was the dog?

It was while he was trying to order his thoughts, to regain some control over a day that had suddenly gone awry, that Kevin experienced the third shock. As he shifted the weight of the body and eased it down onto the dock, he saw that the cardigan Britingham was wearing was badly torn across the front. He pulled the sweater and shirt aside. The man's abdomen was an ugly sight. There was little sign of blood, but the wound was large and deep, as if a knife had been plunged in and then pulled across the belly.

Britingham had almost certainly not died of a heart attack. It was hard to believe that he had inflicted this wound on himself. Kevin looked across the lake to where the sun would soon appear and drew a deep breath. It was very likely that murder had been committed on Crooked Lake.

CHAPTER 2

It had been more than ten years since she had stopped taking lessons, at least seven since she had even touched a piano. Like many another adolescent girl, she had discovered boys and could no longer find time for practice. Her mother had coaxed and cajoled, lectured on talent wasted, and ultimately resigned herself to the fact that Dolores would never be a concert pianist.

Perched on the front edge of the piano bench, she picked out "Fur Elise," at first tentatively and then with more confidence. The casual listener might have been impressed. But there was no one else in the room, and even though she was able to recall the music, Dolores herself was not impressed. Her fingers would not respond as she wanted them to; it was a ragged rendition, and she brought it to an abrupt end, banging angrily on the keyboard.

If she was angry with herself, she was even angrier with John. Where in hell was he? They were to have met at his house at seven to go over some reports; he'd promised her an omelette and a croissant, although she suspected that when he had suggested a working breakfast, it was the bedroom rather than the kitchen that he had had in mind. She had been surprised upon arriving to find his car gone. Letting herself in with the key he had given her back in June, she had called out his name and, getting no answer, had searched the house. It was readily apparent that he was not at home and that he almost certainly had not been home all night. The bed had not been slept in; the coffee pot was cold.

Puzzled and increasingly resentful, she had returned to the big, bare living room that he had not yet gotten around to furnishing. The grand piano would have been conspicuous in any room; it dominated the room in which it was the only piece of furniture. The only place to sit, other than the floor, was the piano bench, and Dolores had sat there. Through the large bay window she could see the circular drive in front of the house, and she fully expected to see John pull in at any minute.

That had been at seven o'clock. Half an hour later he had still not arrived, and she no longer expected him. While she was waiting, she had played a little and thought a lot. How strange that

8

she should be sitting here at this early hour in the morning, in a nearly empty house, miles from what she considered civilization and a continent away from her home in San Francisco. And waiting for a man who was twice her age, a man who had asked her to his house to work on business that could as well be conducted at the office and with whom she had expected to go to bed that morning.

———

She had been both surprised and pleased to hear from him that Sunday morning in May.

"Dee! Glad I caught you at home. What are you doing these days?"

He hadn't needed to identify himself. The voice was unmistakable, and no one else called her Dee. She had made no effort to conceal her excitement. She had been taking a psychology course at San Francisco State, but she had lost interest and dropped it rather than risk a failing grade. At this rate she would be past thirty before she finished her degree. While she still kept her name on file with an agent, she had nearly given up making it as a model. She had no plan, no real idea what she wanted to do. There had been two jobs in less than two months since John had left for the east, and both had bored her. There had been another man, although he had not remained in her life long enough to be called a significant other, and she wasn't quite sure who had been responsible for breaking off the relationship. Dolores Weber was a woman without a purpose in life, drifting from job to job and bed to bed, attractive, intelligent, and a classic underachiever. John Britingham's call could not have come at a better time.

"I need you, Dee. I really do." He was asking her to drop everything and come east to help him run his new company. Little did he know how little there was to drop. While he rattled off the reasons why she should say yes, she was already mentally packing her bags.

Dolores was not so naive as to believe that she was essential to the success of John's new venture. She knew very little about the wine business, and had limited secretarial skills and experience. What she did have was a commanding presence. Seated behind a desk, she looked and sounded like every executive's idea of a perfect keeper of the gate. A bit young perhaps, although that was a matter of taste. Her manner was brisk. Her voice was deep for a woman, and she spoke with authority. People paid attention.

She recalled the day they had met. It had been late in the previous fall. A receptionist at his winery north of the Bay had gone into labor early, and the supervisor had placed a call for a temporary while the woman was on maternity leave. Had they needed a skilled secretary, the firm would never have sent her. But she had impressed the manager of the firm with her front-desk manner. So she had been sent and soon found herself dealing with the public at the Britingham Winery. It had been unbelievably easy. Within a day she had mastered the essentials of the job, and the hours were such that she could still make her class at the university. And then he had come into her life.

"I'm sorry, sir. You can't go in there. There will be a tour in twenty minutes if you'd like to wait here." She had risen from her desk to intercept him and steer him back to the reception area.

"I beg your pardon. What did you say?"

He later told her that it wasn't that he hadn't heard her or that he was trying to make her uncomfortable; he had simply wanted to hear that voice again. When he explained that he owned the winery, she had not been embarrassed or fumbled for an apology, and he had been impressed. Before the week was out, he had stopped by her desk three times to talk, and by week's end he had asked her for dinner. And for the next three months they had dated, if his polished aggression and the alacrity with which she had agreed to share his bed could be called dating.

The job at the winery had lasted only a few weeks, but the relationship with John continued until he moved east in March. Dolores, whose expectations in this as in other aspects of her life had been modest, took his announcement of the move in stride. It had been a pleasant interlude, a welcome and occasionally exhilarating experience, but she had never believed it would last. He had promised to stay in touch and to see her whenever he returned to California on business, but she was convinced that it was over and had quickly slipped back into her old lifestyle. She had not expected his call.

Dolores had come east, rented an efficiency in one of the few garden apartments in the area, and assumed the position of executive secretary at the Silver Leaf Winery. The apartment was a thirty-minute drive from the winery, but it was an easy trip over country roads, nothing like commuting in the Bay area. The job was less demanding than the title suggested; in effect, she was expected to intimidate people on John's behalf. Everything else was incidental. Except, of course, the sex. She had assumed that the real reason he had sent for her was that he wanted to resume their affair. Perhaps he really missed her. Perhaps there was a dearth of attractive women in the small town where Silver Leaf was located. She preferred the former explanation, but either way she was once again sleeping with him. And she liked the job. It gave her a sense of power she had never experienced before. It was obvious that everyone at the winery was fascinated by her— and afraid of her. They were afraid of her because they were afraid of John, and it was very clear to even the casual observer that she enjoyed his full confidence. She was a mystery, an outsider, an attractive woman with a mesmerizing voice and a relationship with the owner that was inevitably the subject of endless if uninformed speculation.

At the moment, that relationship was being strained by his failure to meet her as planned and by the fact that he hadn't even been home all night. There might be some perfectly innocent explanation, but Dolores's experience with men had taught her to suspect another woman.

She decided that no purpose was served by waiting longer. She would leave him a note and go on to the winery. The message she was drafting in her mind was sarcastic, and she planned to leave it on his pillow, an appropriately ironic touch. First, though, she needed to find a sheet of paper, so she climbed the stairs and went to his desk in the study.

The desk was nearly as bare as the house, so Dolores started looking in the drawers for paper. What she found instead jolted her and convinced her that she had been right. There was another woman.

"God damn magpie!" Dolores said it aloud to the empty room as she surveyed the contents of the drawer. There were two champagne corks, a pair of ivory and gold earrings, a gem-studded and obviously expensive brooch, an elegant monogrammed pillbox, and a pair of woman's panties. And the panties had been worn since last being sent through the wash, of that she was quite certain.

She slammed the drawer shut. But as she started to get up from the desk, she paused, sat down again, and reopened the drawer. This time she gathered up the things she had found there and shoved them into her purse. Then she closed the drawer and went down the stairs, her note unwritten, and out to her car.

Dolores followed the gravel driveway down to the West Lake Road, turned right, and gunned the engine for the short trip along the shore of Crooked Lake to the winery, set on the hill above the lake on the outskirts of the village of Southport. There were only six cars in the parking lot when she pulled in at 7:45, and none were John's.

She let herself into the building, said a perfunctory good morning to the watchman on duty, and took the stairs to her office, her anger just barely under control. She plugged in the coffee maker and got herself a yogurt from the small refrigerator in the corner. Unless he outdid himself, John would not arrive until at least 8:30. Rarely did he come in before nine. There would be time to see if there was any clue to his plans for the previous night. Dolores made sure that the door to the corridor was locked, and, leaving her yogurt untouched, she went into the inner office and began going through the papers on John's desk. His calendar told her nothing she didn't already know, inasmuch as she kept his schedule of appointments. Nor were any of the files or papers on the desk helpful. She had already seen most of them, and in some cases had herself drafted and typed the papers.

Then she turned her attention to his desk drawers. She wasn't sure what she was looking for, and when she found it she almost didn't realize its importance. Tucked away in a corner of one of the drawers was an envelope addressed to John at his home address, a folded sheet from a lined yellow pad, and a blank card, which had been torn off the Rolodex. She turned the card over, going through the motions of a search that she now was convinced would tell her nothing. The back of the card contained numbers— telephone numbers by their appearance. There were four of them, three with area codes. She was about to close the drawer when she realized that one of the numbers had been hers in California. She had almost forgotten it, but there it was, at the top of the list. The second number carried the same Pacific coast area code; the third, an area code she didn't recognize; the fourth had no area code—a local number?

Dolores took the things she had found in the drawer back to her desk, poured herself a cup of coffee, and tackled the yogurt. It was obvious to her that the numbers on the card were not business numbers. Her old California number on the list seemed to make that point. And the cards weren't in the Rolodex, with names identified and properly alphabetized. This suggested a private agenda, personal relationships which John had wanted to keep hidden. Women? One of the numbers surely belonged to a woman. Why not the others? And one of them apparently from the immediate area.

She had no illusions about John's sex life. But she had assumed that he was at least serially monogamous. Had she pulled up stakes and moved to the wine country around Crooked Lake only to share John Britingham with another woman? The evidence in the desk drawer of his study at home suggested that she might have done just that. The phone numbers from his office desk might tell the same story.

And the letter? She extracted it from the envelope and read its message, which was brief and said simply that the letter writer was working on it. On what? But it was a man's name, Tony, so she picked up the yellow paper. It proved to be a hand-written note addressed to no one in particular. And not a very neat hand at that. If the letter was brief, the note was even briefer. It consisted of four crudely scrawled words: "Youl pay for this." There was no signature.

A grim smile crossed Dolores's face as she added the cards and the letter and the note to the collection in her purse. Then she began organizing her office for the day ahead.

CHAPTER 3

The white car, its dome light off, crested the hill above Cumberland. The road behind it had been full of large, sweeping curves. The road ahead stretched out more or less in a straight line across a gently rolling landscape. The sun had not made its appearance, but the eastern sky was suffused with light and the fields and trees and scattered buildings had acquired sharp definition in the clear, early morning air.

There were no other vehicles in sight, and the white car picked up speed. Carol Kelleher, the sheriff of Cumberland County, usually enjoyed this drive, and she would have preferred to take it at a more leisurely pace. But there was a dead man on a dock on Crooked Lake, and the sheriff felt obligated to get there in the shortest possible time. She could feel the butterflies stirring in her stomach as she pushed the Chevy five, then ten, miles over the speed limit. Unless there was some innocent explanation for John Britingham's death, she could look forward to much the toughest case in her brief seven-month tenure as sheriff. And the man who had called to report finding Britingham's body had left the strong impression that there would be no innocent explanation.

Well, hell, she thought, this is when I find out if I'm really cut out for this line of work. Carol had gone off to bigger and what she had hoped would be better things after high school. First a college degree in political science, then law school, the bar exam, and for seven years a position in a law firm in the state capital. The practice of law had had its moments, and the firm had treated her well. But on balance it had been a disappointment. Her colleagues had been a driven, humorless lot, and only rarely had she found that the long hours produced a commensurate sense of fulfillment. They had certainly made it difficult, and for weeks at a stretch impossible to get out into the clean country air.

All of that had changed suddenly and unexpectedly the previous year when Big Bill Kelleher, her father and longtime sheriff of Cumberland County, was felled by a massive coronary. Carol was still nursing her grief over his death when a delegation of old family friends and influential citizens from her home town had arrived one day to urge that she come back and stand for election to fill her father's post. It seemed that the man who might have been expected to step in had been indicted on a charge of passing bad checks. Although she had agonized over it for quite a few days, it was an invitation she couldn't refuse, and the result was that Cumberland County now had the first woman sheriff in its history, as well as the youngest.

While there were those who were uncomfortable with what they regarded as a sheriff of the wrong sex, the family name and the infectious enthusiasm which she brought to the job had made her transition to a career in law enforcement a relatively easy one. The pay was but a fraction of what she had been earning as an attorney, but the cost of living was considerably less and her tastes were modest. For the first time in years she did not feel office-bound, and on the whole she found herself enjoying her new job. Carol was well aware that the violent death of the county's most prominent citizen could quickly change that.

But even at sixty-five miles an hour, and with what might be a very serious crime awaiting her attention, the sheriff experienced some of the pleasure she had always felt when driving these hilltop roads, especially just before sunrise and just after sunset. Carol had never quite understood the feeling, and had never tried to explain it to anyone except her father. Part of it, she supposed, was simply the peacefulness of the place. For many of the miles between Cumberland and Crooked Lake there was little habitation. There were a few working farms, but some of the houses and barns had been abandoned and were now in disrepair, weathered wood collapsing, bushes and weeds taking over. An occasional piece of rusting farm equipment stood sentinel beside a barn. Fields that had not been tilled in years flanked the road on either side, divided here and there by the remnants of fences, now barely visible. In places the open fields gave way to stands of second and third growth timber, creating a patchwork quilt of dark greens and softer greens and browns.

Many would have described the area as desolate, but not Carol. She knew that the soil was poor and that it had largely defeated the efforts of generations of farmers to raise profitable crops. Those who stayed did little farming. Most worked in Cumberland or Southport or in the vineyards which covered the slopes around Crooked Lake. But if the hill country of Cumberland County had not always been kind to those who tried to farm

15

it, it had become a very special place to Carol Kelleher. She wondered whether others felt the same way—whether they treasured the sight of the darting swallows that had taken over the old barns, or the hawks circling over the fields, or the varied colors of the wild flowers that grew so profusely along the roadside, or the stark beauty of her favorite farmhouse, the victim of a long forgotten fire and now but a pair of chimneys rising out of a foundation overgrown with brush.

After several miles, the hill began to slope downward to the east, and when it did, another hill came into view. Crooked Lake lay in the valley between these hills. As hills go, the hills in this part of the country weren't much. Eons ago, the region had consisted of one broad, extensive plateau, devoid of distinguishing features. During the Ice Age, glaciers had cut through the plateau, scouring out valleys, which had become lakebeds. Most of the lakes resembled elongated fingers. Crooked Lake, however, had a distinctive Y-shape, and in Carol's view, was the most beautiful..

She calculated that she was only about two miles away from Blue Water Point, and she was very much of two minds about what lay ahead. On the one hand, it promised excitement. But she found it hard to believe that there wouldn't be lots of publicity, and publicity meant scrutiny of her every step—or misstep. She hoped that the case would be neat and tidy, that there would be some perfectly simple explanation for the death of John Britingham.

The phone call from Officer Barrett had come at 5:52. A man who had identified himself as Kevin Whitman had called 911 and reported finding a dead man on his property; the dispatcher had contacted the sheriff's department, and Barrett, the officer on duty, had talked with Whitman and decided that he'd better wake the sheriff. It appeared that Whitman had been swimming from his cottage, that his dock had been empty when he entered the water, and that a body was on the dock when he returned at around 5:30. The body was that of John Britingham, of that Whitman had been sure. As she crawled out of bed, splashed cold water on her face, and began dressing in the uniform which was the thing she liked least about her job, Carol had begun to digest Barrett's news: Britingham dead, and almost certainly not of natural causes. The body discovered by a man who had been swimming in Crooked Lake at five o'clock in the morning. She had not been sure which was the more improbable piece of information. Sans makeup, Carol had grabbed an apple and headed for the lake.

It was 6:38 when Carol turned onto West Lake Road. She didn't anticipate a problem finding Whitman's cottage, nor was there one. A gravel road branched off from West Lake and wound down toward the water, circling in a wide arc behind the cottages on Blue Water Point until it swung back away from the lake to join up again with West Lake a little more than a quarter mile to the south. Barrett's instructions had not been necessary; his car was parked behind a white clapboard cottage with blue shutters at the windows, right next to a recent model Toyota that presumably belonged to Whitman.

Sheriff Kelleher had no sooner pulled in behind the Toyota then three people appeared from around the corner of the house. The trio stood, somewhat uncertainly, several yards away, as if posed for a group picture they weren't especially happy to have taken. The woman was still in her dressing gown, and she clung to the arm of a tall gray-haired man who, like her, appeared to be in his 70s. His clothes hung loosely on his thin frame. The other man looked as if he had showered and then forgotten to comb his hair; his legs were bare between a blue beach robe and a pair of white canvas beach shoes. As if aware that his appearance left something to be desired, he self-consciously ran his fingers comb-like through his straw-blond hair. If this was Whitman—and it seemed likely—he certainly didn't match the mental image the sheriff had formed on the drive to the lake. She had imagined a robust physical culture nut. Who else would be swimming before dawn? But this man looked soft, and his skin was the light pink of people who fear exposure to the sun. She guessed that he was around forty. Of course all three of these people might look a few years older at this hour than they would later after they had dressed for the day.

"Mr. Whitman?" She stepped forward, hand extended to the man in the blue robe. "You're the one who reported this?"

"I am." He took her hand, then quickly withdrew it to pull his robe together and tighten the sash.

"And who are these other people?"

"Neighbors. The Morgans—George and Edna. They heard all the commotion. I guess it would be difficult not to notice."

Yes, the sheriff thought. It's been more than an hour since you found the body, probably close to an hour since Officer

Barrett arrived. Why aren't there more people here? Your wife, your family, your other neighbors? Maybe they'd be around front gawking at the body on the dock.

"I'll want to talk with everybody," she said, motioning toward the older couple. "But first I want to see the body. Let's do it now."

The small party trooped around the house. Officer Barrett had positioned himself where the first section of the dock rested on the shore. He looked ready to resist an invasion, but to the sheriff's surprise the only person in the vicinity was a small boy, sitting with knees drawn up to his chin, about fifty feet away along the shale beach. The boy was staring impassively at them, a silent observer of the tableau on and around Whitman's dock.

"Hello, Jim." The sheriff acknowledged her young colleague, and then gestured toward the boy. "Would you please talk to that kid over there? Find out where he lives, and escort him back to his folks. He shouldn't be here."

She beckoned to Whitman, and the two of them walked out to the end of the dock and the dark bundle that had been John Britingham. Squatting beside the dead man, she studied his face, the awkward position of the body, the clothes that were still damp, the raw wound in the gut. It wasn't her first encounter with death since her election as sheriff, but it could well be her first with murder. And Whitman had been right. The man was indeed John Britingham.

The sheriff looked up at Whitman, a scowl on her face.

"Is this how you found the body? Same position?"

"Yes—well, not quite. I had to roll him partway over to see if he was breathing. That's when I saw that cut on his stomach."

She looked again at the mutilated gut. It wasn't her duty, nor was it within her competence, to judge the cause of death. But it looked very much as if the cause of death would be a no-brainer. It was an ugly wound.

The sheriff straightened up and looked around, taking a mental picture of the area. To her surprise, not only was the boy still there on the beach, but another small companion had also joined him. Both were engaged in an animated conversation with Officer Barrett.

"Jim!" she called out. "What's the trouble? Those boys should go home now."

"I know. They're going."

He didn't sound very convincing, but the three of them began walking slowly in the direction of the cottage next door. The Morgans, she noticed, were still standing on the beach near the dock. She would need to put some questions to Whitman, but not with an audience present. Carol explained to the Morgans that she would come over to their place after she had finished with their neighbor. George Morgan realized that they were being dismissed. He said he would be around and, with wife in tow, drifted away in the direction of his own yard, where he could go through the motions of doing some outdoor work.

"Now," she said, turning to Whitman, "we need a blanket to cover the body until I can get an ambulance over here. Would you get one for me? And then I need to ask you a few questions."

Kevin dutifully headed back to the cottage on the sheriff's errand; Carol walked down the beach to meet Officer Barrett, returning from his mission.

"What took you so long with the kid?"

"You know how kids are—just curious. It's big excitement for them. Don't want to miss a thing."

"Sure, who does," Carol said, thinking of the Morgans, but also wondering why more people hadn't been lured out of their cottages by the presence of two police cars on the point. "Look, there's a lot we've got to do, and we'd better get at it. I want you to make some phone calls for me, and then I need you to scout around the beach, see if you can find anything that might account for that man's death. Like a knife, maybe."

But she shook her head as she said it.

"No, I doubt you'll find a knife, but just keep your eyes open for anything that looks out of place—anything that might have something to do with the situation we've got here. You know, places where the shale's been disturbed, anything that looks like it might be blood."

Carol wasn't optimistic. Quite a few people, herself included, had been walking around the area since Whitman's discovery of the body. And there was Whitman himself. She had no idea what he had done after he found the body. Or for that matter when he had found it. Indeed, she only had his word for it that he had found the body on his dock. For all she knew, he might have been responsible for Britingham's death.

She gave Barrett instructions that would set the wheels of the investigation in motion. The coroner had to be notified; the body, removed; the man's home and office and car searched for evidence of where he had recently been and where he might have been going. And there were many questions to be asked. She had just finished giving Officer Barrett his marching orders when the cottage door slammed. Whitman was coming down the steps to the beach, carrying the blanket he had been asked to provide. He had traded the blue robe for a pair of slacks and a polo shirt, and he had combed his hair.

Okay, the sheriff said to herself, let's start asking those questions. Beginning with a man who goes swimming before dawn and on whose dock he claims to have discovered the body of Cumberland County's most famous resident.

CHAPTER 4

By the time Sheriff Kelleher and Kevin Whitman had settled into wicker chairs on his deck, the sun was just making its appearance above the hill across the lake. The early morning chill was beginning to dissipate. Kevin had suggested coffee, and Carol, grateful for the offer, had been only too glad to accept. But in spite of the friendly gesture and the two steaming cups it had produced, there was an unmistakable air of tension on the deck.

"Let me begin," Carol began, "by asking you a question that's been bothering me ever since I got the call from Officer Barrett this morning. You said that you found Mr. Britingham's body around 5:30. At 5:30, most people I know are still sleeping. You say you were swimming—indeed, that you had been swimming for, what, more than half an hour? Do you usually swim that early?"

Kevin had anticipated the question, but it still made him uncomfortable to be asked. It suggested that the sheriff would not automatically accept his explanation of the morning's events. She looked as if she would expect nothing less than direct, unambiguous answers to her questions. He had no idea how experienced she was in law enforcement; having paid little attention to local politics and having had no run-ins with the law, he hadn't even known who the sheriff of Cumberland County was. But here she was, sitting on his deck and about to interrogate him about his swimming habits, John Britingham, and heaven knows what else. For all he knew, she suspected him of having had something to do with Britingham's death. Of having killed him? Kevin was unaccountably nervous.

"No, not very often. Not before sunup. But I swim a lot. It's one of the reasons we bought this place. It just happens that I was awake early, and I thought I'd take a swim while the lake was quiet."

Carol's face reflected her skepticism. She didn't trust coincidences, and she was now confronted with one: that Whitman had taken a rare predawn swim and that John Britingham had shown up dead on his dock on the same morning—and at just about the same time.

"What woke you up? Did you hear something outside? Someone moving around?"

"I don't know that it was anything in particular. I don't remember a noise. I just haven't been sleeping too well."

"And when you got up, did you hear anything? See anything when you went out to take your swim?"

Kevin had his first crisis of conscience over the Britingham affair. He started to mention that he'd seen Mike Snyder setting out in his boat, and that there'd been someone walking a dog further down the beach. But wouldn't that information stimulate the sheriff's suspicion of Snyder, send her off on a search for neighbors with dogs, to be followed by persistent questioning of people who'd had nothing to do with Britingham's death? But he could hardly lie and say he'd seen no one. These people could explain themselves. People do what they do. He'd decided to go swimming. Mike had gone fishing as he often did. A conscientious dog owner had responded to a pet's signal that it had to go out.

So Kevin told the sheriff what he had seen. Not surprisingly, she seized on this information.

"Have you seen this man Snyder come back yet?"

Kevin could see that the small boat Mike used for fishing was not in its usual place alongside his dock.

"No, his boat's not there. We'd have seen him come in anyway."

"Okay, we'll keep an eye open for him. You say you saw him getting ready to go fishing. Did you see him leave?"

"Well, no, not actually. But I heard him set off not long before I got to my goal. That'd be Mrs. Hess's raft, down around the end of the point."

"How can you be sure it was Snyder's boat you heard?"

"It had to be, didn't it? I mean he was obviously going fishing, and the boat I heard starting up was definitely back this way. There wasn't any other activity along the point. No, it had to be Mike."

Perhaps, Carol thought.

"We'll see," she said. "Now about the other man. Who on the point owns a dog?"

"Quite a few people, I think. I'm not sure I could give you a complete list. The Sandersons have one, and the Pierces own a beagle, I know. There's another family down the other way that has a dog that goes crazy when they're swimming. Oh, I almost forgot Mrs. Hess, down on Mallard Cove. She's got a handsome golden retriever."

Kevin was taking mental inventory, but it was clear that he hadn't paid much attention to the dogs in the neighborhood. He tentatively identified a gray cottage several places below his as the spot where he had seen the man and the dog, but the occupants were renters whom he didn't know. Nor was he able to be specific about the size of the dog. It had been dark, and he hadn't really paid much attention.

Carol tried not to show her frustration. Whitman hadn't known what had awakened him. He hadn't recognized the person walking the dog, wasn't sure where he had seen it, or even how big it was. He had noticed nothing during his swim. Was he always this vague?

"Tell me about yourself. Would I be right in assuming that this isn't your year-around home? The family just here in the summer?"

"Well, yes and no. I live down in the city—I teach at Madison College. And I spend the summer here, but there's no family. Just me."

"I thought you said *we* bought the place for the swimming."

"I probably did. That was a few years back. I was married then."

Carol digested this information, which meant that there would be no one else in the cottage with whom to discuss Whitman's movements during the night. Unless, of course, he had another woman in there, still asleep or prudently staying out of sight. She found herself surreptitiously examining the man in the wicker chair across from her. She was probably right about his age—forty, give or take a couple of years. He was still pale, but she revised her estimate of soft to wiry. Not handsome, but not unattractive. And he looked intelligent. Yes, there might be a woman in the cottage. She was prepared to bet that there was one or more in the city.

"And what is it that you teach?" Carol realized that this was almost certainly irrelevant to her investigation of Britingham's death, but inasmuch as she was likely to be seeing quite a bit of Whitman during that investigation, she really should try to find out what she could about him. Besides, she was now curious.

"Would it surprise you if I told you that I teach the history of music? And that my specialty is opera?"

For the first time, Carol detected a spark of enthusiasm in Whitman's voice. But opera? No, she would never have guessed it, probably because she knew nothing about it.

"Would it surprise you if I told you that I have never been to an opera in my life?" She immediately regretted the tone of her voice. It was as if she were back in the law firm, dealing with a lot of guys who respected her mind but probably felt sorry for her that she had grown up in a culturally deprived backwoods upstate area. This city-upstate thing had gnawed at her self-image for many years; they looked down on her, and in self-defense she tended to look down on them. It was silly, and unworthy of her. But it kept surfacing. Not now, she said to herself, and changed the subject.

"Tell me about Britingham. How did you know him?"

"I didn't really. I met him at a party over at the Morgans back in the late spring—said hello, exchanged a few pleasantries, and that was that. I never saw him in person again. But you see his picture in the *Gazette* quite a bit."

"So you had no relationship with the man, yet he shows up dead on your dock. Why your dock?"

It was a question Kevin had been mulling over in his mind almost from the moment he had recognized the dead man as Britingham, and he hadn't come up with a satisfactory explanation. Much as he didn't like it, the sheriff could hardly be blamed for wondering what might be the link between him and the county's most prominent citizen.

"No idea—none at all. All I can think of is that he got knifed, or whatever, somewhere else, got as far as my dock, hauled himself up out of the water, and died before he could go any farther."

The sheriff wasn't buying it.

"That doesn't seem likely, does it? How deep is it at the end of your dock, Mr. Whitman? It looked pretty deep to me. There's no ladder out there, and I have trouble believing a man that badly wounded could pull himself up out of the water and onto your dock."

"No, I guess you're right. I know I can't stand on the bottom out there, and I'm just about six feet tall." Kevin turned the puzzle over in his mind. "Maybe he could have climbed onto the dock nearer to shore, where it's a lot more shallow."

"But why would he have been out at the end of your dock? If he was hurt, wouldn't he have been looking for help? And he'd find it in the cottage, not on the dock. How long is your dock—

fifty feet or so? I'd guess that means Britingham not only didn't come to your house to get help, he went fifty feet further away. Now that makes no sense at all. Unless, of course, you moved him. Or someone else did."

"I thought we'd agreed I didn't move the body," Kevin protested. "I only turned him over enough to get a better look at him."

"No, *we* didn't agree. *You* told me what you did, so what I have is your word for it. Anyway, I was only suggesting that the body might have been moved. Maybe he didn't get onto your dock on his own. Maybe he was killed somewhere else and dumped there. And that brings me back to my question. Why your place?"

The sheriff had been very observant, and her logic was hard to dispute. The water was a good six feet or more deep at the end of the dock, which consisted of five nine-foot sections. Britingham had almost certainly not come out of the water at the end of the dock under his own power, and it was hard to imagine why he would have gone out to the end of the dock after leaving the water nearer to shore. None of this proved that someone had put Britingham's body on Kevin's dock, but it did make it a strong possibility. And that, in turn, made the sheriff's question more relevant—why Whitman's and not some other dock on the point? And, for that matter, why Blue Water Point?

Kevin was about to attribute Britingham's presence on his dock to random chance when two men, one in uniform, made their appearance. The sheriff was up immediately to greet them. The one in uniform was apparently another of Sheriff Kelleher's officers; the short, older man with an incipient paunch, he learned later, was the county coroner. The three of them joined Officer Barrett on the dock, where they huddled around the blanketed body. Kevin was relieved to be left alone for a few minutes. He found it hard to believe that the sheriff really suspected him of having played any role in Britingham's death, but for some reason he had not been comfortable answering her questions. And his discomfort bothered him. He had nothing to hide. The sheriff had not been officious or rude. Indeed, she had been professional and patient—and obviously smart. Kevin wondered what had brought her into the law enforcement business. An unusual choice. In spite of the uniform, she didn't look like his idea of a sheriff.

The lake was coming alive. Two or three of his neighbors were standing on their porches, staring at his dock and no doubt wondering what was going on. As he watched them watching the sheriff and her team, he heard the sound of an approaching vehicle with a rough-running diesel engine. The engine cut off close to the cottage, a door slammed, and the driver came around from the backyard, where now were parked three police cars, the coroner's Buick, his own Toyota, and an ambulance.

———

Twenty minutes later, Kevin and the sheriff had resumed their seats on the deck. Pictures had been taken of the late John Britingham; the ambulance had departed with his body; the coroner had returned to Cumberland, and the two officers were slowly walking up and down the beach, their eyes glued to the ground. The dock was empty.

The sheriff was once again pursuing the possibility that someone had put John Britingham's body on the Whitman dock.

"But isn't that improbable?" Kevin asked. "I was only swimming for a little more than half an hour, forty-five minutes at most, and for a good part of that time I was within sight of my dock. If anyone had wanted to dump Britingham there, he'd probably have seen me. He couldn't be sure I wouldn't see him. And where did he come from? I didn't see anyone—except Snyder, of course, and he was just going fishing."

"There was the man with the dog," Carol reminded him. "And it was dark, as you yourself said."

"Yes, but not so dark that you couldn't see someone moving around on the beach. Like the man with the dog. But he'd have had to wait until I'd gotten out of sight and then move the body before I came back. And he wouldn't even know how far I was going to swim—for all he knew, I might have turned back at any minute. Why would anyone risk that?"

"Damned if I know." Carol didn't hide her frustration. "There are a dozen angles. Maybe he didn't see you at all—who'd have expected someone to be swimming at that hour? Maybe he just got lucky, him not seeing you and you not seeing him. And maybe there wasn't another man." She paused for effect. "Just you."

Kevin was ready to mount another protest, but they both heard the sound of the outboard motor at that moment. The sheriff moved quickly to the deck rail and peered out at the lake.

"Snyder?"

Kevin, who knew Mike's fishing habits well, spotted the boat easily. It was still several hundred yards away, but it was heading for Blue Water Point.

"Right. It's about time Mike would be coming in."

"I'd better move about a bit and talk to some of your neighbors. This man Snyder, of course. And those other people who were here earlier. Morgan, isn't it?"

Kevin nodded. He waved in the direction of the two-story cottage that stood about forty yards further up the point, much of its lower floor shielded from view by a thick row of spirea bushes. George Morgan was bent over a makeshift worktable that had been set up next to a toolshed down near the water. From their vantage point on the deck, he seemed to be scraping or sanding a beach chair.

"By the way," the sheriff asked, "you said you met Britingham at the Morgans' home. Were they friends of his?"

"No. They'd invited him to their annual beginning-of-the-season cocktail party as a friendly gesture to a new neighbor. To introduce him around. You'll have to ask them, but I doubt if they've seen each other socially since."

Carol had been watching the approach of Snyder's boat as she listened, but she turned quickly at this apparently innocuous answer to her question.

"New neighbor? Britingham was a neighbor? I'd heard that he lived in the old Keighly mansion."

"I think he does. But he was going to build on this point. He'd bought some land down at the lower end of the point on Mallard Cove. You didn't know about that?"

Sheriff Kelleher hadn't known about it, and she was trying to digest the implications of this unexpected piece of intelligence. Her questioning of Whitman's neighbors suddenly took on new significance. She would almost certainly have to talk to more of them than she had first anticipated. The discovery of the body on this point no longer seemed quite so strange. There was a lot of work ahead, but Carol felt somewhat better already about the fledgling investigation. First Snyder, she thought, and then, one by one, the other residents of Blue Water Point, all of them now identified as neighbors of the deceased.

CHAPTER 5

Sam Bridges, the deputy sheriff of Cumberland County, fancied himself in the brown and gray uniform he was wearing. To his way of thinking, Sam looked the way law enforcement officers were supposed to look—gut in, hair neat and razor trimmed, shoulders back, shoes highly polished, pants sharply creased. It continued to bother him that the sheriff didn't look quite right in her uniform. Not that she was sloppy, but unlike Sam she hadn't been a marine. And, of course, she had a woman's figure.

It was 9:13 in the morning of the day John Britingham's body had been found on Kevin Whitman's dock, and the deputy sheriff had just pulled into the parking lot of the Silver Leaf Winery. He checked his appearance carefully in the rearview mirror, removing a small remnant of breakfast from between his teeth and adjusting his cap to the correct angle before stepping out of the car and heading toward the winery's administrative offices. This was going to be a big day, certainly one of the biggest he had experienced since leaving the Corps, and Sam was making a conscious effort to project an air of authority. The sheriff had phoned with the news of the winery owner's death; still tied up with people over on Blue Water Point, she had given him the task of checking out Britingham's home and office.

The voice behind the door marked 'John L. Britingham, President,' said to come in and Bridges did so, at which point his reflexes took over, as they usually did when he came into the presence of an attractive woman. He took a deep breath and added a half an inch to his height as he crossed to the desk.

If Dolores Weber was impressed by this uniformed specimen of the male animal, she gave no hint of it.

"What may I do for you?"

Sam, who didn't know that the woman behind the desk rarely favored anyone with a smile or that she had had a bad morning, was thrown off stride by the cool reception. He fumbled for the right words.

"I just wanted to ask you—uh, you are John Britingham's secretary, aren't you?"

"My name is Dolores Weber. I manage the office, yes."

"Well, okay, then I want to ask you a few questions." He paused, looking for some sign of acknowledgement. "You don't know about it, do you?"

"I'm afraid I don't know what you're talking about, Officer."

Bridges was of the school that believed nothing was to be gained by beating around the bush.

"Your boss, Mr. Britingham, is dead. We found his body this morning."

The sheriff later remembered Sam's description of Dolores Weber's reaction. "Damnedest thing. Never moved a muscle in her face, just looked at me with that same expression."

Actually, the news had given Dolores what was probably the greatest shock of her life. It was only with the greatest of effort that she managed the mask that Bridges had found so incongruous.

"No, I didn't know. That's terrible. He wasn't that old. What was it, a heart attack?"

"No, ma'am, I don't think so. He may have drowned."

Although she did not lose her composure with this revelation, Britingham's efficient, no-nonsense secretary did pale visibly. She pushed her chair back from the desk as if to get up, but seemed to think better of it.

"I see. You're investigating his death. And you're here because you suspect that it wasn't an accident?"

"We aren't sure," Sam replied. The sheriff had told him very little, and had asked him not to be drawn into a discussion of the possible causes of Britingham's death. "It might have been. I need your help with a few matters."

"Yes, of course." Dolores, quickly recovering from the shock of this unexpected explanation for John's failure to keep their breakfast appointment, resumed her role as the unflappable secretary. "You'll want to know what I can tell you about Mr. Britingham's schedule. I have his appointment calendar here. There's nothing listed after 3:30 yesterday afternoon, and I saw him leave at 5:15. I have no idea where he went or what he did after that."

Bridges had expected an interrogation like the ones he had seen on television shows. She would search her memory under the prodding of his questions, and before he left he would have learned something of importance with which he could impress Sheriff Kelleher. But it hadn't worked out like that. Britingham's secretary, or assistant or whatever her title was, had anticipated the questions he would ask. The precision of her brief report gave him little hope that he would learn more about the comings and goings of the owner of the winery just prior to his violent death.

Nor did he learn anything else. Britingham's calendar was as devoid of information as Ms. Weber had said it would be, and none of the correspondence or other papers on his desk gave any clue to his plans upon leaving Silver Leaf the previous afternoon. The secretary said she knew nothing of his after-hours habits or who his friends were, and when he left the winery at 10:12, Sam Bridges was a much chastened man. He had learned nothing that would help in the investigation of Britingham's death, and his ego had been bruised by the indifference of the Weber woman.

———

Thirteen minutes later, and after a trip of some ten miles north along the lake above Southport and then up a driveway which was well hidden from the road, Deputy Sheriff Bridges arrived in front of Britingham's home only to be confronted with another disappointment. The big old house was locked, and no one answered the bell or a series of vigorous knocks on the door. He kicked a car tire in frustration. He had half expected to find the house locked and empty, but he had hoped, in vain as it turned out, that his luck would turn. Now he faced a real impasse in his assignment. There had been no keys on Britingham's body, according to the sheriff, and Sam had no idea who, if anyone else, might have a key to the house. He hadn't asked Ms. Weber back at the winery, but she hadn't seemed to know anything about Britingham's private life, and he doubted that she would be able to help him gain entrance to the house. He'd go back to Silver Leaf and ask her in any event, but he had already concluded that they would eventually have to break into the place.

Sam steered his car down the winding drive and turned right onto West Lake Road for the return trip to Southport. He had gone only a hundred yards or so when the car he had noticed in his rear view mirror disappeared. It took a moment for him to realize that it could only have vanished by turning into Britingham's drive. Sam wanted to make a 180, but there was no shoulder on his side of the road, so he had to go another quarter of a mile before he was able to make a U-turn. He gunned the engine, wanting to get back to the big house before the driver of the other car, having discovered that no one was at home, left.

The car that was parked in front of the house was an old Ford that looked as if it might have logged 200,000 miles or more. There was no one in sight, but as he climbed out of the patrol car he thought he saw motion at one of the windows facing the wraparound front porch. Sam's luck had turned. Somebody held a key, and that somebody was going to let him in and do some explaining.

Whoever it was had stepped back out of sight as Sam mounted the steps and rapped on the door. For a long minute there was no response, and Deputy Sheriff Bridges experienced a surge of adrenalin as it occurred to him that he might have Britingham's killer trapped inside the house. But then the door opened, and he faced a woman of indeterminate age who looked as if she thoroughly disapproved of his presence.

"What do you want?" The voice was dry and totally lacking in inflection. This woman, like Britingham's secretary, was obviously unimpressed by his uniform.

"Who are you? What are you doing here?" Bridges asked, putting his hand on the door and pushing it wider open.

"I'm Sarah Washburn, that's who I am. I'm Mr. Britingham's housekeeper. What do you want?"

"You're here to clean the place?" he asked, knowing that he couldn't allow her to do that.

"Of course I am. What is it you want?" Mrs. Washburn was still barring his entrance, her feet planted across much of the width of the doorway. He wondered if she would really try to deny him entrance.

"Why are you here today? Did Mr. Britingham ask you to come this morning?"

"Would you mind telling me what this is all about, Officer? I clean the house every Tuesday. I'm here doing my job, like Mr. Britingham pays me to do. And pays me good. What's your business with him? He's not here. If you want him, you should go down to the winery."

"Mrs. Washburn, I think I'd better come in so we can talk. Mr. Britingham is dead. He got killed sometime last night or this morning, so I need to take a look around."

The housekeeper's reaction was much more transparent than Dolores Weber's had been. It would have been hard to feign the expression of shocked disbelief with which she greeted the news. She offered no resistance as Bridges stepped into the foyer.

"I'm sorry to have bad news; I really am," he said, trying to adopt a consoling tone. "But I have to do my job, and you can help me."

He looked around him. The foyer and what would presumably be the living room off to his left were almost entirely devoid of furniture.

Mrs. Washburn had recovered and spoke for the first time since Bridges had dropped his bombshell.

"I should have figured that the police don't come to the door with good news. Do you want to tell me what happened?"

"We don't know. It might have been an accident. It might not. Somebody found him up on Blue Water Point early this morning. The sheriff's up there right now, talking to people in the neighborhood. We'll know more soon. I need to take a look around. There may be something that will help us figure out what happened."

"I see. Well, look around all you like. You won't find much—there's not much here. I guess I'd better get on with my work. They say work takes your mind off your troubles, though I don't know who'll be paying me now that—that he's..."

The housekeeper who moments before had been ready to bar the door now looked ready to cry.

"I'm sorry, but I can't let you clean the house today. We may need to look for fingerprints and things, so the house has to stay as it is." Although the procedure had been part of his training, Deputy Sheriff Bridges had never had to check for fingerprints. But the sheriff had been quite clear that he was to handle things carefully.

"Good lord! Fingerprints! You think he was murdered, don't you?"

"Mrs. Washburn, I don't have any idea. I'm just doing my job."

In the end, neither his tour of the premises nor his questioning of Mrs. Washburn turned up any useful information about the late John Britingham. If there were any clues to his activities or visitors just prior to his death, Bridges was unable to find them in the man's house. The answering machine contained no messages; there was nothing of interest on or in his desk—no mail, no memo pad, no checkbook. E-mail was still something of a mystery to the deputy sheriff, so he didn't bother trying to log on to the computer. The sheriff would have to do that later. As for the housekeeper, she had been a great disappointment. She did convey the information that Britingham had lived alone, that she came in once a week to clean and occasionally prepare a meal, letting herself in with her own key, and that she rarely saw her employer. And that was all.

Not only had she not seen him on the day before he turned up dead or heard him mention any plans he might have had for that evening or the following day, but she also seemed not to have been the least interested in his habits or acquaintances. Bridges could hardly believe that a person so utterly lacking in natural curiosity existed.

"But Mrs. Washburn," he protested, "surely you must know something about Mr. Britingham that would help us. When you cleaned, did you ever see an appointment book? Did you bring in his mail—and maybe notice who corresponded with him? How about phone calls? You must have taken some calls. Were there any regular callers? Strange calls?"

She was a study in injured innocence. The expression on her sharp-featured face said more clearly than words that she found these questions offensive, that she was almost as disturbed by the suggestion that she might have pried into Mr. Britingham's affairs as she was by his death.

"I never, ever, poke into other people's business. I didn't take his calls, and I'm glad I wasn't expected to. It's a dreadful thing, his being killed like that. But I don't know a thing about it, not a thing."

And Deputy Sheriff Bridges was quite prepared to believe that she didn't. He also couldn't imagine why Britingham needed the woman as often as every week. The house was a large one by any standard, and especially for a man living alone, but it was nearly empty. To say it had been furnished sparely would have been an understatement. All the floors had been refinished, new windows installed, the walls freshly painted, the doors fitted with elegant new hardware; but except for the grand piano in the living room, the only rooms containing as much as a stick of furniture were a bedroom and a study on the second floor and the dining alcove in the kitchen. Britingham had invested a lot in restoration of this old house, but he either had not had time to decorate and furnish it or he had not intended to live there long.

When the deputy sheriff finished his fruitless search of the house, he pocketed Mrs. Washburn's key and saw her to her car. He promised that he would let her know if they learned anything about the death of her employer, and urged her to contact the sheriff's office if she remembered something that could help in their investigation. He did not know that she was already thinking about the little things that told her a woman had spent more than a a few nights in the big house.

———

Sheriff Kelleher brushed off Sam's apology for the paucity of useful information he had been able to turn up.

"I haven't done much better," she said into her cell phone. "But it's early, Sam. Hell, we just heard about this a few hours ago. Tell me, was Britingham's car out at his house?"

"No, why?"

"Well, it isn't over here. At least we haven't found it. We learned that Britingham was getting ready to build a place down at the south end of the point—thought the car might be down there at a construction shack he's been using. Barrett's been all over the area, and there's no sign of the car. It isn't likely that it'd be at the winery, unless he left it there last night. But why would he do that? Anyway, check it out. Find out what he drives, and see if it's parked at the plant. Maybe it's in some garage for work. For all we know it could be sitting in a parking lot in Cumberland, or maybe it's up in Maine or out in Kansas. Just get the make and license number and find it."

Carol rang off and took a deep breath. Yes, it was early, much too soon to be frustrated by developments in what she was sure the papers would soon be calling the "Britingham Murder Case." But she was frustrated. They couldn't find the dead man's keys. They couldn't find the dead man's car. No one she had talked with knew him well, and no one could imagine why his badly mutilated body had been found on Blue Water Point. Or on Whitman's dock.

CHAPTER 6

The sideboard by Kevin Whitman's kitchen sink contained seven used cups, testimony to a series of conversations over coffee, beginning with Sheriff Kelleher's interrogation several hours earlier. After her departure to question neighbors, her place had been taken by first one and then another of these neighbors. They had dropped by to satisfy their curiosity and to offer their theories on the death of John Britingham. The consensus seemed to be that Britingham's death was a terrible thing, the more so because it had occurred on their point.

It was eleven o'clock, and for the first time since Officer Barrett's arrival more than five hours earlier, Kevin was alone. He had had no breakfast, and he was tired. He popped two English muffins into the toaster, poured himself a large glass of orange juice, and sank into the living room couch. Although a part of him found this breakdown in his fairly well-ordered life distasteful and wished for an early solution to the crime, he realized that he was also discovering a perverse pleasure in the mystery of Britingham's death. Thinking about it, treating it as a puzzle to be solved, might be fun. The sheriff, he sensed, had been feeling her way over unfamiliar ground. But he had been impressed with her practical, commonsense approach to the problem, even if she kept reminding him that he, too, was under suspicion. He knew he had nothing to do with Britingham's death, and he was sure that the sheriff was too perceptive to cast him in the role of a killer. Or was she? He knew as little about her as she did about him. No, that wasn't true. She knew that he was a professor, lived in the city, was divorced, loved opera, swam a lot, didn't sleep well, had met the deceased once, and wasn't very observant. He knew nothing about her except that she was young and, yes, attractive. At least for a law enforcement official.

It was while he was examining his impressions of the sheriff that he heard a knock on the front door. The quiet interlude since the departure of his last visitor had lasted only ten minutes, and he still hadn't had breakfast. Reluctantly, he went to the door.

35

"Mr. Whitman? I'm sorry to bother you. Do you mind if I come in for a minute?"

"Mrs. Hoffman, isn't it? Please, come in."

He had immediately recognized his visitor, although he wasn't sure of her given name. She lived just two cottages away, and had been a neighbor for only a little more than a year since she and her husband had bought the Hathaway property next to the Morgans. But the Hoffmans had been reclusive neighbors. They rarely used the water for swimming, owned no boat, did not participate in the occasional beach party, and seemed averse to the friendly banter so typical of vacationing neighbors. Moreover, Mr. Hoffman was away most of the time. Whatever he did, it required his presence back in the city, so that Mrs. Hoffman was the lone occupant of the cottage for all but weekends.

Kevin didn't think he had ever spoken to this woman except for the perfunctory hello, but there was no mistaking her. Elegant was the word that came to mind. She was tall and slender, with an impressive mane of blond hair. She was probably in her late thirties. Her features were striking, although there was something a trifle hard about her mouth and no hint of laughter in her eyes. But it was her clothes that really set her apart from everyone else on the point. He had never seen her when it didn't look as if she were on her way to a modeling session or to the captain's party on a cruise to Bermuda. Her wardrobe was not that of the beach or woods. Kevin pictured her spending hours each day—luxuriating in her bath, brushing her hair, manicuring her nails, applying her makeup, selecting the right outfit. For what? She didn't seem to go anywhere or do anything. Today, however, she had come to his cottage.

He recovered from his surprise at her presence at the door and invited her to have a seat.

"Thank you. I'm Emily. I know we haven't been very social."

As she moved into the room, she dropped the apologetic tone and began to compliment him on the cottage.

"That's a beautiful fabric on the couch. The chairs, too. Oh, and what is this? Did you do it yourself? It's striking!"

Emily Hoffman had gone over to a long maple wood table in front of the picture window overlooking the deck and the lake and was admiring—or at least pretending to admire—a large, glass-encased ship model, which occupied much of the table.

Kevin was both puzzled and irritated by this line of chatter. The cottage was quite simple and undistinguished. The couch and two of the chairs were old, and the fabric was beginning to show its age; Susan and he had brought them to the cottage when they refurnished their apartment in the city. And the ship's model was not his handiwork. He had no interest in model building. It had belonged to an uncle and by some process of inheritance, and over a series of moves, had ended up in Kevin's possession. Susan had not wanted it in the city apartment, but had consented to putting it on display at the cottage. She had never cared much for the lake house, and after the divorce had let Kevin have everything in it except for a couple of prints and a few personal knickknacks.

Why was the Hoffman woman lavishing such praise on his home? He didn't believe her. He started to explain that he couldn't take credit for the ship model, but she had already passed on to something else. She wasn't listening. The torrent of words betrayed a bad case of nerves. What was her problem?—he wondered.

"Please, won't you sit down? May I get you some coffee? Or tea, if you prefer?"

His effort to put Mrs. Hoffman at ease was not having the intended effect. She did take a seat, but proceeded to cross and recross her legs, each time smoothing out the crease in her smartly tailored, white linen slacks. She bent down to adjust a strap that didn't appear to need adjusting on a silver sandal that had never been intended for beachwear. She was wearing a turquoise and black silk blouse that looked to be one of a kind, and carrying a small clutch purse, which she opened and closed twice before asking if he minded if she smoked.

"I know everyone is quitting these days, and I really should. I don't want to be any trouble, so if you don't have an ashtray handy..." But she had taken out a pack of Kents and a trim silver lighter, and before Kevin had a chance to reply or go for an ashtray, she had lit a cigarette. It seemed to help.

"Thank you for talking to me. And I would appreciate some of that coffee. Just cream, no sugar." Emily Hoffman studied her cigarette for a moment. "I hear they think that the man you found was murdered. Are they sure?"

It was her first reference to the morning's big news.

"The sheriff didn't say, but there doesn't seem to be any other logical explanation. If you'll excuse me, I'll get your coffee. Right back."

Kevin made a quick trip to the kitchen. It was the first time since they had become neighbors that the woman had been in his house. And although it might only be conventional curiosity, her manner suggested a more complex explanation.

"I know I must sound awfully morbid," she was saying as Kevin handed her her coffee. "But was it really bad? I mean I heard the man was stabbed to death. Is that true? Do you suppose he suffered much?"

"I don't know, really. He was dead when I found him. I suppose they'll have to do an autopsy to find out how he died."

She looked at her cigarette as if trying to decide whether to smoke it or put it out.

"Somebody said that he was dressed, but that he'd been in the water. What would he..." She paused in mid-thought and shifted her gaze from the cigarette to her coffee cup. Twice she started to say something, then thought better of it. There's something on this woman's mind, Kevin thought, and she's not sure what questions to ask or how to ask them.

"Look," he said, trying to put her at ease and fill in some of the blanks, "I don't know what happened. And the sheriff doesn't either. Not yet. All I do know is that when I found the body, it was fully clothed, even shoes. Nice clothes, too, except for an old sweater. And soaking wet, so he'd probably been in the lake after he got hurt and just before he ended up on my dock."

Emily Hoffman made an elaborate ritual of snuffing out her cigarette in the ashtray Kevin had provided. She fumbled with her purse and produced another before raising her eyes to look at him. She had developed a pronounced tic below her left eye.

Kevin decided that it was his turn to ask a question. "Did anyone tell you who this man is? Or was?" She had never mentioned a name or asked about his identity.

"Somebody—I think it was your neighbor, Mr. Morgan—said he thought his name was Britingham. Isn't he the one who owns that winery down in Southport?"

"Yes, and there doesn't seem to be any question that it was Britingham. Had you ever met him?"

"I may have been introduced at that big party your neighbors gave back early in the summer. I'm not sure—it was a large crowd, and I met a lot of people." As she spoke, she crushed out the cigarette she had lit only moments before and stood up to leave. "I'm sorry to have come barging in like this. You've had a rough morning. And I've got to get the house in order."

Kevin doubted that Mrs. Hoffman had to get the house in order. He pictured the Hoffman cottage as a page out of *Architectural Digest*, with nothing out of place, no dust bunnies anywhere, magazines and books casually but artfully displayed on the coffee table.

"Don't worry, you aren't being any bother. Won't you finish your coffee?"

"No, thank you. I really must be getting back. I'm sorry we're meeting under these circumstances. Perhaps we can get together again—with Alan, too, I mean."

Emily Hoffman backpedaled toward the door and was gone as suddenly as she had come. Kevin did not expect a return social engagement with the Hoffmans.

———

What was that all about? Kevin tried to make sense of the brief, puzzling visit of his neighbor as he added her coffee cup to the stack on the sideboard in the kitchen.

That Emily Hoffman had been nervous was obvious. But why? And what had she learned from their conversation that decided her to leave barely ten minutes after arriving? She had apparently already heard via the grapevine that Britingham had been stabbed. She had assumed, or had been told, that it was murder. And there had been her question—well, actually an unfinished question—about what he had been wearing. No, Kevin remembered, she didn't ask; I told her. And as he reconstructed what had been said and by whom, he realized that it was he who had been shaping the conversation before she made her hasty exit. He had asked her if she knew who the dead man was, and when she said Britingham, he had asked if she knew him. It was only then, after a vague and hurried reply, that she had extinguished the unsmoked cigarette and made a transparently phony excuse to leave.

The dishes could wait. Kevin wandered back into the living room and stood at the window, where he could see the dock, now empty and bathed in the sunshine of midday. Why?—he kept asking himself. What could explain the Hoffman woman's strange performance? Hers had not been the behavior of someone either saddened or titillated by the violent death of a stranger, even if the stranger had expired within sight of her home. No, she had behaved as if the news of Britingham's death had made her anxious. But anxious about what? Did she know something about his death? Had she seen something? Heard something? That was possible, and the sheriff would certainly be asking her, along with his other neighbors, those very questions. But another theory was taking shape in Kevin's mind. He was willing to bet that Emily Hoffman knew John Britingham better than she had let on.

CHAPTER 7

Sheriff Kelleher was sitting in her office in Cumberland, staring out the window and across the street to where a few people were going in and out of Mayes Pharmacy and the supermarket. She could count eight cars diagonally parked on the opposite side of State Street; on this, the main business block in town, there were spaces for as many as thirty cars. Cumberland, which could never be described as bustling, was especially quiet. There would, of course, be more people out at the mall on the western end of town, although Carol couldn't understand why anyone would prefer to do business in a sterile mall, surrounded by an unshaded parking lot, when they could be shopping on the tree-lined street outside her window. Sooner or later, though, everybody would be going to the mall for almost everything. Already there was a vacancy sign on what had been Emmett's Variety Store down the street, and rumor had it that Ida's Luncheonette would be closing. It meant that she would have to make new arrangements for her lunch hour, and she wasn't keen on driving out to the pizza place at the mall or down the road to the Rustic Inn, which wasn't very rustic and served lousy coffee.

That had been good coffee that Whitman had given her. It definitely had helped her to get through the morning. Now that she had finally put some food in her stomach, Carol was ready to get back to the Britingham affair. Not that it had been off her mind for even a minute since Officer Barrett's call, but she hadn't yet tackled it in a systematic way. She had been doing the easy things—sizing up the scene on Whitman's dock, asking the obvious questions, putting Cumberland County's modest law enforcement machinery in motion. Substituting action for thought. There were still many things she had to do. There were still people to be questioned, phone calls to be made. And there would be the autopsy report in due course, hopefully by the following morning. But right now she needed most to sit and think about the case.

Damn! What if Britingham really had been murdered, as seemed likely? She hadn't liked the look of things on Blue Water Point. The deceased was someone to be reckoned with. No weapon had been found. No one had told her anything, at least not anything that had sounded very useful. Wasn't there always supposed to be someone who came forward to say he'd seen something suspicious, or had overheard two guys arguing? That's the way it seemed to be with lesser crimes. The sheriff's experience had been exclusively with lesser crimes. She had found that in a small town people were usually only too eager to talk—even the culprit. But she had to admit that the culprits she had known were petty thieves, and testosterone-driven young men who'd sideswiped cars while driving under the influence, and an occasional wife-beater. They weren't murderers. In any event, the people on Blue Water Point had been singularly unhelpful, especially Whitman. What was she to make of this man who went swimming in the dark and who had discovered John Britingham's lifeless body on his dock? Or so he said.

Carol turned back to the pad on the desk in front of her. It contained the notes she had made during the morning, plus a few she had added over lunch at Ida's. Getting her mind into gear was not proving easy to do. She chewed on the end of a pencil and watched a kid come out of Mayes with an ice cream cone. The kid tried to get on the bicycle he'd left in front of the pharmacy, and in the process of juggling his cone and maneuvering the bike, he lost the ice cream onto the sidewalk. Life was full of minor tragedies.

The sheriff picked up a rough sketch she had made of Blue Water Point and its cottages. It did not come close to being a scale drawing, she knew, but it did show the relative locations on the point of the people she had talked to that morning, as well as those she had missed. She had learned that there were 16 houses on the point, 17 if you counted Britingham's construction shack at the southernmost end, the tangible evidence that the deceased had indeed been in the process of becoming a neighbor.

She had sketched in small squares to represent the houses, and was now using her pencil to shade in the ones where she had talked with the occupants. There were seven of these. Two of the other cottages had been vacant. She drew an X through these places, leaving seven blank squares. She would have to return to the lake and question the occupants of those seven cottages. Probably that same evening. But right now Carol was determined to review the morning's conversations and add to her notes while impressions of those conversations were still fresh.

———

The sheriff had begun with Mike Snyder. She had walked up the beach from the Whitman cottage, nodding at George Morgan as she passed and meeting Snyder as he brought his boat in. The fisherman had acknowledged her as he cut the motor and guided the boat onto the beach. He was apparently accustomed to showing off his morning's catch, and he had held up two beautiful specimens of the trout for which Crooked Lake was famous.

"Nice fish," Carol had commented.

"They're okay. Not the best fishing today, but I've had worse."

Snyder hadn't seemed surprised at the presence of the sheriff of Cumberland County on his beach. He had busied himself with pulling the lightweight aluminum boat out of the water, fastening it to an iron stake, and collecting his gear. Carol had admired the economy of motion with which the man performed these tasks. She had sized up the fisherman and concluded that he would be able to handle himself in a scrap. Snyder was about six feet tall and lean and fit; his dark hair was close cropped, and he sported a deep tan, at least over those parts of his body that had been exposed to the sun. When he bent over the boat, his shirt rode up above his belt, exposing a pale white back that contrasted sharply with the color of his face and his muscular arms. She guessed his age to be late 40s, early 50s.

Carol had decided to ask a few questions first, before conveying the information that John Britingham was dead and that his body had been found on a neighbor's dock. She wanted to know if Snyder had observed any unusual activity earlier when he was preparing to go fishing.

His reply had been direct and disappointing. No, he'd seen nothing unusual. Kevin Whitman had been up early to take a swim, but he was the only person he had noticed. Had Snyder found it surprising that Whitman would be swimming at that hour? Well, he supposed it was pretty early, but his neighbor swam a lot, and he himself was an early bird. Was it Whitman's habit to go swimming before sunrise?

This line of questioning had clearly puzzled Snyder, then alarmed him.

"Is something wrong? Is Kevin okay? What's happened to him?"

Carol had reassured him that Whitman was all right. Then, trying to present the news so as to elicit an unguarded reaction, she had informed Snyder that, unlike Whitman, John Britingham was not all right.

"Britingham? What's the matter with him?" It had been clear that, like Whitman, Snyder knew the deceased or at least knew who he was.

"What's the matter with him is that he's dead."

"Dead?" Snyder had stood there, looking puzzled and waiting for the sheriff to elaborate.

"Dead. He'd been in the water, but we found him on Whitman's dock."

There had been no mistaking Snyder's reaction to this information. He had seemed genuinely surprised. The man's death—well, not what one expects to hear, but something one could imagine. But dead on a neighbor's dock—that was shocking news.

"I'll be damned." Snyder had then repeated himself. "I'll be damned. Did he drown?"

Carol had offered no opinion on the cause of death.

"Now you see why it's so important to know what you saw this morning. Or heard. Did you see Mr. Whitman in the water—I mean, did you actually see him swimming?"

"No, I was concentrating on getting the boat off. You know how that is. Why? Do you think Kevin had something to do with Britingham's death? But that's..." Snyder didn't finish his thought; Carol suspected that the word unsaid was 'absurd.'

She had said something vague about it being too early to accuse anyone of anything, that she was just trying to figure what people in the neighborhood might know.

"So you didn't see anybody else, just Mr. Whitman, and you didn't pay much attention to him. How long before you took off— I mean, how long was it between the time you came out of the house and the time you left to go fishing?"

Snyder had wrestled with this question for a moment before admitting that he wasn't really sure.

"Hard to say. Probably three or four minutes—long enough to untie the boat, load my gear, you know, the kind of things you have to do. Not long."

Carol had considered this information. Hadn't Whitman said he'd heard Snyder's boat start up at about the time he reached the bend in Blue Water Point? How long would it have taken him to swim that far? Surely a great many more than three or four minutes. Was there a discrepancy in the two stories? She had decided not to pursue it at the moment, having already made up her mind to be careful at this stage of the game about asking questions that would imply that she suspected someone of wrongdoing.

Before she left, she had asked Snyder for his opinion of the deceased, and had gotten an answer much like Whitman's: he didn't really know him. They'd talked about who might have wanted Britingham dead, the sheriff stressing that his death could well have been accidental, but conceding that all possibilities had to be considered. Snyder had not been very helpful. He didn't know much about Britingham or his relations with others; maybe some people didn't like him—nobody in particular, just people— but you don't kill someone just because you don't like him. There may have been a hint of animosity, but it was vague and non-specific, and none of the sheriff's questions had elicited references to any particular person or grievance.

After half an hour, Carol had let Mike Snyder get on with the task of cleaning his fish and rushing off to work without a shower. It had been an unsatisfactory discussion, devoid of any hard new information that might be helpful in her investigation. She had the uncomfortable feeling that she hadn't asked enough questions. She knew that Snyder had been up and out of the house around the time that Britingham had supposedly made his mysterious appearance on Whitman's dock; he had freely admitted it, and Whitman had also placed him on the lake a little before five o'clock. But she hadn't pursued the matter of his movements before taking off across the lake in his quest for trout, and on reflection she wasn't sure that hadn't been a tactical error. She had also been disappointed to learn that there was no one else in the household who might have been awake and aware of what Snyder was doing. It appeared that there had been a marital spat and that Mrs. Snyder had gone to stay with her parents, taking their two daughters with her.

But the sheriff had gotten the feeling that Britingham was not liked. While this did not translate into a motive for murder, it did suggest that she would have to do much more than merely ascertain whether people on the point had seen anything out of the ordinary.

Carol's next stop had been at the Morgans. She had initially been surprised that they were the only neighbors who had gathered at Whitman's after the discovery of Britingham's body. She had seen their behavior as natural, that of those who stayed at home strange. Now she was more inclined to wonder about the Morgans. What accounted for their early morning appearance and George Morgan's continuing curiosity? And there was no question about it, he had not wanted to miss a thing. He had found something to do that had enabled him to observe just about every move the sheriff made.

"What's the project?" Carol had asked as she crossed the beach and approached the Morgans' boathouse.

George Morgan, who had been watching the sheriff with great interest as she made her way over from Snyder's, had feigned surprise at her appearance.

"Why, Sheriff Kelleher! Hello there! I figured you'd get back to me sooner or later. This? Oh, I'm just refinishing my beach furniture. Like a fool, I never did store it last winter, and it shows. Work just never gets done, does it?"

She hadn't thought it necessary to join Morgan in his lament about the hard life of retirees on Crooked Lake.

"Wife go back to bed?" she asked.

"Maybe so. Edna has a book going, and it's too early to be running errands. Want to go up to the house? Have some tea or coffee? I can fix it if Edna's fallen asleep."

"No, no," the sheriff had demurred. "Thanks anyway. Let's just sit here."

She had selected an Adirondack chair whose cracked and peeling paint meant that it hadn't yet undergone refinishing. Morgan brushed the dirt from his large, calloused hands and eased his long frame into another chair that still needed work; he'd been right, she thought, there was a lot to do here. And so for half an hour the sheriff and Morgan had discussed Britingham's demise while the sun slowly climbed further above the hill across the lake from Blue Water Point.

The sheriff's first question elicited a familiar response.

"How does it happen you were up so early?"

"Couldn't sleep. I don't seem to sleep well anymore. It seems to be one more curse of old age. Maybe the Lord figures we haven't got a lot of time left, and he wants us not to waste it sleeping."

Morgan had chuckled at his own wry humor. Carol wondered if everyone on the point had insomnia.

"When did you wake up?" she'd asked.

"I didn't look to see. We try not to run our lives by the clock up here. But it was beginning to get light—so when would that be, maybe six?"

Carol had been disappointed.

"So you didn't see Mr. Whitman go swimming or Mr. Snyder go fishing?"

No, Morgan had replied, seemingly unhappy not to be able to provide the sheriff with more information. Nor had he heard anything unusual. He had not realized that anything was wrong until he'd seen the police car. Then, of course, he had gone out to see what was going on.

Carol rapped her pencil on the desk, recalling her frustration that Morgan, like Whitman and Snyder before him, had claimed to have seen or heard nothing out of the ordinary. Incredible. All of these people, up at an early hour on a quiet morning, and none of them able to provide a shred of information as to how Britingham had gotten onto a dock that was within shouting distance of their cottages.

She had started to shift the subject to the Morgans' relationship with John Britingham when they heard the screen door of the cottage bang shut. Edna Morgan was coming down the path toward them, and her husband had not looked very happy about it.

"Good morning, Sheriff." She had joined them, taking one of the chairs, which had been sanded but not painted. "I don't think I ever said hello when we were introduced. I really looked a frightful mess, I'm afraid. But I suppose you see people in every condition imaginable."

Mrs. Morgan had improved her appearance somewhat since their first meeting. She was still not an attractive woman and probably never had been, but the garish plaid robe had disappeared; she was now dressed smartly in a subdued print dress, and her hair looked as if she had had a permanent within the previous few days. Carol had revised her estimate of the woman's age downward by a few years.

Like her husband, Edna Morgan had apparently been awake early, but had remained in bed and didn't get up until George had come to tell her there was a police car at the Whitman cottage. There was nothing remarkable about her recital of what she had done that morning, but it had gradually become apparent to the sheriff that there was a palpable tension in the air, that Edna was stepping carefully, with her husband monitoring every word. George had said nothing, but his posture and expression had seemed to suggest that he was willing his wife to get it right. And Edna had tried a bit too hard, Carol thought, to look and sound matter-of-fact. One could be wrong about such things, but the sheriff was prepared to swear that information was being withheld and that George Morgan had coached his wife on what to say but had limited confidence that she would say it.

Carol hadn't been sure how to deal with the problem. She still wasn't. In this case, she didn't need her notes to recall the conversation that followed.

"Mrs. Morgan," she had interrupted, "why do I have the feeling that something's bothering you, that there's something you want to tell me, but you aren't sure how to put it into words? We all have an interest in finding out what happened to Mr. Britingham. This really isn't the time to be shy about sharing information. If it's important, I need to know. If it isn't, I'll simply forget it. But why don't you let me be the judge."

If a woman of her years could be said to fidget, Edna Morgan had fidgeted. She had tried to avoid looking at her husband, but had ended up staring across the lake as if she were looking for something on the distant hill.

It was George Morgan who had replied to the sheriff.

"I'm sure Edna isn't hiding anything, Sheriff. This whole business has unnerved her, I guess you'd say. I've tried to calm her down, get her to look at it as one of those bizarre things that just happened to take place here. She'll shake it off, I know."

Carol found it interesting that Morgan had denied that his wife was hiding something. The sheriff had been careful to avoid inferring any such thing. Nor had she found Morgan's explanation of his wife's behavior convincing. Edna had apparently agreed.

"Don't mind George," she had said. "He thinks I'm in a dither over this thing. Well, I'm not. He started in on me right after we realized a man had been killed on Kevin's dock. He's very sweet, but he's really old-fashioned. Expects a woman to go to pieces when she's confronted by disaster. Well, as you can see, I haven't gone to pieces. It isn't my disaster, in any event. So I'd appreciate it, George, if you stopped being so solicitous."

She had straightened her back, as if to underscore this declaration of independence from her husband.

"I'm sorry, Sheriff," she had continued, "if this little disagreement with George made you think I was withholding information. I wish I could tell you something that would help you. But I can't, and neither can George."

Not only had George Morgan not taken offense at his wife's rebuke, he had visibly relaxed, as if a crisis had passed. It had been clear to Sheriff Kelleher that she would learn nothing more that morning from the Morgans; she had not been taken in by their little charade, but they had closed ranks, and there was no point in pursuing the matter further.

They had talked about Britingham, and the Morgans' assessment of their relationship with the deceased was very much the one Whitman had suggested. They had found him pleasant enough, but his lifestyle and obligations were very different from theirs, and he was of course quite a bit younger, so they had never expected a real friendship.

Carol had wondered aloud about Britingham's reputation. Hadn't she heard that the man wasn't very well liked? The Morgans really couldn't say. There might be some envy of his wealth and position. That was to be expected. But they didn't know of any reason why anyone would want to kill him. When the sheriff had finally vacated the unfinished Adirondack chair, she once again had the feeling that she hadn't gotten the full story.

The sun was now shining directly into the second-floor office where Sheriff Kelleher was reviewing the notes she had made earlier in the day while questioning Whitman's—and Britingham's—neighbors. She went over to the window and adjusted the blind until it blocked out the sun. Resuming her seat, she picked up her notes and leafed through them until she came to a page with the name Brock written across the top. The Brocks had been the fourth stop of the morning as she made her way from cottage to cottage, introducing herself, asking who had seen what and who knew what about Britingham. And she had learned almost nothing except that Whitman had underestimated the dog population and that the story of Britingham's death was already being embellished in the retelling.

It was at the Brocks that she had received the briefing on dogs and the first hint that misinformation regarding the morning's events was in circulation. Alice and Herman Brock were an affable if slightly harassed white-haired couple who lived on the other side of the Whitman cottage from the Morgans. They knew quite a lot about the big news of the day, much of it factually wrong. They had gotten their information from Billy and Darrell Keyser, who were temporary wards of the Brocks while their parents, the Brocks' youngest daughter and her husband, were traveling in Europe. It was these two young men, ages ten and eight, whom Officer Barrett had banished from the beach with some difficulty earlier in the morning.

The Brocks had known even less about Britingham than their neighbors. Unlike so many others on the point, they seemed to have no trouble sleeping and had not gotten up until well after eight, by which time all of the excitement was over. They had gotten their information secondhand, and the sheriff had to explain that, no, she wasn't planning to arrest Mr. Whitman, and, no, the fish had not been eating the victim's body. Where did these kids get their ideas?

The Brocks' information on dogs, on the other hand, had a ring of authenticity. With some prompting from the boys, they had positively identified seven dogs in residence on the point, all of whom were known by name and five by breed. She had even gotten some unsolicited anecdotes regarding some of the dogs and their habits, and had dutifully taken notes.

After leaving the Brocks, she had been able to see three other families—the McLarens, the Wilkowskis, and the Carlinos. They had all been equally unhelpful. Neither Debbie McLaren nor her son had been aware that there had been a death on the point. Sean McLaren had seemed like many other teenagers without a summer job; he was apparently used to sleeping in and then catching the sun's rays during most of his waking hours. The surprise registered by both mother and son at the sheriff's announcement had seemed genuine. The Wilkowskis, probably about the age of the Morgans, had been very gracious, and Carol had finally consented to have some homemade strudel and another cup of coffee. But in every other respect it had been a wasted quarter hour. They either knew nothing about Britingham and his death or were among the most accomplished dissemblers she had ever met.

The Carlinos had been marginally more interesting. They turned out to be the owner of one of the seven dogs. It had lain on their screen porch like a shag rug throughout the sheriff's brief visit; even before the Carlinos had denied walking on the beach with Ciao before sunrise, Carol was prepared to cross it off her list of canine suspects. More importantly, they at least were well aware of who Britingham was. Bernie Carlino worked for his winery, and in his own oblique fashion had implied that the owner wasn't exactly popular with his employees. They had talked about this, but the Carlinos had been carefully circumspect in their replies.

Even in death, John Britingham seemed to evoke something akin to fear.

CHAPTER 8

It had been a frustrating morning, but it had ended, rather surprisingly, with the first piece of truly interesting information—or was it misinformation?—Sheriff Kelleher had received during her questioning of Whitman's neighbors. And it had come from the young boys who had been so intently watching the tableau on Whitman's dock when she arrived at the lake so many long hours before.

She had worked her way down the point, following the shoreline. She had formed impressions of the cottages, considered the possibilities of their occupants being able to observe activities on the Whitman dock, and jotted down estimates of the distances between places, figures that might or might not prove helpful in reconstructing the events of the morning. She had only spoken with people in seven of the cottages, and they had given her almost no hard information. What she had found most intriguing was that so many people who lived so close to where Britingham had been found had been up so early and had observed so little. It defied the laws of probability. And there was that business at the Morgans. She had been going to say something her husband didn't want her to say, but in the end she had said nothing. Other than that, and it wasn't much, the sheriff had learned very little.

She had decided to return to her car by circling behind the cottages. A different angle of vision might yield a different perspective on what she was now thinking of as the crime, even if she had been careful not to call it that in her conversations with the residents of Blue Water Point. Emerging from behind a line of hemlock trees that served to define one of the property boundaries, Carol had seen a small green tent in the Brocks' backyard, their grandchildren sprawled on the grass beside it.

"Are you really the sheriff?" the bigger boy had called out.

"Yes, I'm afraid I am," the sheriff had replied. "You boys camping out?"

"But you're a girl," her young interrogator objected, ignoring the sheriff's question.

No, Carol thought, I'm a woman. And then, how sad that one so young should already be making assumptions about careers and gender. But there was no time this morning for the reeducation of the Brock grandchildren.

"You're very observant," she said with a smile.

"So, don't you want to ask us more questions?"

The sheriff had been thinking of doing so earlier, but inasmuch as the boys had been the source of the wild rumors she'd heard while questioning the Brocks, she'd decided that she wasn't likely to learn much from that quarter.

"Why, should I? Do you have something you want to tell me?" Two can play this game, she thought.

Billy Keyser had assumed an upright position and removed the earphones he'd been wearing.

"Maybe."

"Yeah, maybe." His smaller sidekick had spoken for the first time.

"We've been outside here, you know. You can see a lot from the tent. Do you want to know what we saw?"

Probably not, Carol had said to herself, but then no one else seemed to have seen anything, so maybe she should listen to what the boys had to say. Adopting her most serious, authoritative tone, she had asked them to fill her in, insisting on attention to details.

"Well, we saw the dead man—before he was dead, of course—walking that way." Billy had pointed south in the direction from which the sheriff had come. "In fact, we saw him a bunch of times. He went that way, then he came back, then he went that way again."

Carol had suppressed an urge to grab the boy by the shoulders and shake the truth out of him. This was very possibly critical information, but she had no confidence in her informant.

"Let's back up a minute, can we? When was it that you saw this man go by your tent?"

Billy looked at Darrell. The smaller of the two boys had shrugged, and his brother had then screwed up his face in what looked like a major effort to recall this important fact before replying. He studied his watch.

"It was about six o'clock," he finally said.

"Six?" The sheriff's eyebrows had gone up. "But that man was already dead at six. Your neighbor found him and called us before that."

"I don't care, we saw him, right out here behind the house!" Young Keyser's voice had risen as he defended his story.

"Okay." Carol had tried another tack. "You saw somebody. But maybe it was earlier, or maybe it wasn't Mr. Britingham. What did he look like, this man you saw?"

"Oh, it was the dead man, all right. It was the same man as was out there on the dock when you got here this morning. And it wasn't earlier. Well, maybe just a little before six."

Whitman's timetable could, of course, have been a fabrication, but Officer Barrett's call had come before six o'clock. Carol decided to focus on the identity of the man the boys claimed to have seen.

"Tell me about him. What did he look like?" She hadn't seen how the boy could have gotten close enough to the body to know what Britingham looked like, and she had already decided that Billy had probably seen someone else or had simply made the whole thing up to get attention.

"He looked just like that dead man. You know, kind of tall— not like Grandpa—and dark hair. And not as old as Grandpa. Maybe just a little older than my dad."

It was such a general description that it could have fit many people. Carol chose not to make that point right then.

"Did you notice anything special about him? What he was wearing? Was he smoking? Anything unusual?"

"No, he wasn't smoking. I didn't see any scar either. But it was the dead man, I swear. And when he came back the second time he'd put a sweater on."

No scar? Had the kid been putting her on? But it was the clothes she had asked about.

"He was wearing a sweater, you say. What did he have on when you first saw him?"

"Just the usual stuff—pants and a shirt, kind of brown. The same stuff he had on out on the dock, you know, when he was all wet and dead. Oh, and there was something funny. I forgot. He almost fell down. Would have, except he grabbed that tree over there."

Billy had started to point, but then in a burst of activity had jumped up and run over to a small mountain ash, apparently deciding that he could better convince the sheriff if he made an on-the-spot identification of the tree.

Carol had now been more interested. Suppose the Keyser kid was on the level and suppose he had seen Britingham? His wound could account for his trouble walking.

"You say he went that way?" She had asked, gesturing toward the southern end of the point. "Where did he go? Did he keep on stumbling?"

"You've got me. He just disappeared."

"Where? Did he go into a cottage? Or get in a car?"

. Billy Keyser had exchanged glances once again with his brother, and then dropped to the ground beside the tent.

"I don't know. We didn't watch him." And then, somewhat defensively, "We didn't know he was going to get killed, did we? Why should we watch where he goes?"

Sheriff Kelleher squatted down beside the two boys and gave them a brief lecture on the duties of citizenship.

"These things you've told me may be very important. There'll be an investigation of this man's death, and eventually we may have to go to court. You might be asked to come and tell the court—tell a judge and everybody else—just what you saw. And it's got to be right. Not maybe, but what you can be sure of. So think about it. Think hard."

Getting up, she had assured the boys that she appreciated their cooperation and then opted for a less formal exit line.

"Nice tent. Sleep out much?"

It had been Darrell, the silent one, who answered.

"Always. Unless it rains. Dad said we could, otherwise Grandma wouldn't let us. She thinks we fool around all night."

"Well, it sounds like fun. Now I've got to get back to work. Take care, both of you, and remember what I said."

"Sure, Sheriff." Billy had cuffed his younger brother and the two had become involved in a wrestling match as Carol walked away toward the Whitman cottage and her car.

Kids, she thought. And then, do you suppose they really saw Britingham? Or the man who killed him?

CHAPTER 9

Crooked Lake was capable of mercurial changes of mood, but week in and week out, and especially during the summer, it was a predictable body of water. In the early morning before the sun had begun to heat the air, and again in the early evening, after the sun disappeared behind the hills to the west of the lake, it was more often than not becalmed, a perfect reflection of the hills that rose sharply from its shores. And it happened frequently that by midmorning a moderate breeze would come up. It would first ripple the surface, turning the mirror-like reflections into an impressionist canvas, and later generate modest waves which would roll across the lake in endless succession to break gently on the shale beaches. Those who knew the ocean and had vacationed there would scoff when the locals spoke of waves, for rarely was the water turbulent enough to produce whitecaps.

There were exceptions. The lake could turn ugly in bad weather, and almost everyone could remember times when a storm had sent water cascading in torrents down ravines into the lake, carrying with it dirt and tree branches and even whole trees from the hillsides. After one of these storms, the lake would look swollen and brown for days, and debris would litter the beaches from Southport to West Branch.

But for most of a typical summer day, and for most of the summer season, Crooked Lake was benign. Large white cumulus clouds would often pile up over the surrounding hills during the day and then dissipate toward evening. But cloudy or clear, the water seemed especially congenial for those who liked to swim, water-ski, sail in small-draught sailboats, and, of course, fish.

The discovery of John Britingham's body on Blue Water Point did very little to change this. The rhythms of summer on Crooked Lake persisted, even on that unforgettable Tuesday in August, even in the face of violent death. By midmorning swimmers could be seen swimming as usual. Several young fishermen tried their luck with worms, hoping to catch a bluegill from the end of a dock. A steady breeze came up, providing wind for the colorful sails of three Sunfish having an impromptu race off the north end of the point. For a time the clouds threatened an afternoon thunderstorm, but by five o'clock the threat had passed, the lake had again become calm, and the hill across from Blue Water Point was bathed in the warm glow of late afternoon sunshine.

The only thing distinguishing this from almost any other summer afternoon was the subject of most conversations. From one end of Blue Water Point to the other, and indeed on most beaches and in most cottages on the lake, the topic of the day was John Britingham's untimely death. Sheriff Kelleher would very much have liked to eavesdrop on some of these conversations. That being an impossibility, she planned to be more direct. By six o'clock in the evening, she was willing to bet, most of the residents on Blue Water Point would be nursing drinks and lighting the charcoal on their grills. She would drop by, work her way along the point, and ask the questions that had come into sharper focus after a day's rumination on the death of the owner of Silver Leaf Winery.

There were still a number of cottagers whom she had not talked with that morning, and this would be a good time to catch them. A drink or two would hopefully have loosened tongues. She ticked off in her mind the names of the people she had yet to meet on the point; there were seven families in this category, and they owned six of the dogs, or so Billy Keyser had insisted.

As Carol climbed into her car, she found herself speculating on what Whitman and his neighbors would be doing. She pictured the professor sitting on his deck, and guessed that he'd be drinking a martini. Or perhaps white wine. The sheriff associated city people with drinks like that. Personally, she preferred beer. She had tried to enjoy an occasional glass of wine. In this neck of the woods it was practically a civic duty to drink wine, like buying American-made cars in Detroit. She'd tried, but hadn't developed a taste for it, and she felt mildly guilty. After all, this was the center of one of the East's largest grape-growing and wine-making regions, and every bottle consumed helped to sustain the industry and keep the locals employed.

It was ironic, she thought, that Britingham was now dead. The man had only recently bought the Silver Leaf Winery, the largest company in the area, and rumors were rife that he was planning to terminate many of the contracts for buying grapes from local growers.

The sheriff didn't understand the logic behind such a move. To her it was just one more piece of evidence that the familiar, established order she treasured was disappearing, the victim of unconscionable developers and outsiders who had no roots in the region or respect for its people and their needs and wants. In any event, this particular outsider had just been killed.

———

Over on Blue Water Point, Kevin Whitman was sitting on the redwood deck, much as the sheriff had imagined that he would be. She was wrong about the martini, however. He was enjoying a beer, as were his two guests. Barbecued chicken was on the menu, and Kevin knew that the coals were nearly ready. But Dan Milburn was talking about motives for murder, and no one seemed anxious to put the chicken on the grill.

Everyone knew that John Britingham was unpopular, but the Milburns could cite book, chapter and verse. Rachel Milburn was one of those people in whom others felt they could confide. She was totally unpretentious, plain in appearance, warm in a most unaffected way, and a wonderful listener. Behind the sympathetic face was a very quick and retentive brain. Rachel was no gossip, but she was an invaluable source of information on all manner of things, including events on and about Crooked Lake. Dan Milburn was something of a chameleon. In the city he was a professional to his fingertips, a very successful architect. At the lake he was the quintessential old-shoe type. He had built his own cottage, and was recognized from one end of the point to the other as the man you consulted about dry rot and septic tank problems, and as a neighbor who could help you fix everything from faulty wiring to a leaky roof. He had been in and out of almost every cottage on the point and, like his wife, knew the inhabitants fairly well, although hardly intimately.

"I can't imagine any of these people killing Britingham," Dan was saying. "But I can well imagine that some of them would have been delighted to see him get his lumps. Not dead, you understand, just cut down to size. It would be interesting to know how our neighbors reacted to news of his death. Shock, I would guess, but no regrets."

"I can tell you at least one person who's very upset. That's Emily Hoffman." Kevin filled the Milburns in on Mrs. Hoffman's brief visit earlier in the day.

"I'm not so sure her behavior was all that strange, considering," Rachel suggested. "I don't know it for a fact, but I think it's possible she was having some kind of an affair with Britingham."

"That would be something, wouldn't it? A lovers' quarrel. Or maybe a jealous husband. How do you know they were having an affair?"

"Like I said, I don't. But it was the way she reacted when I ran into her down in Southport a few weeks ago. She's not very sociable, but we were exchanging some casual chitchat when Britingham happened by. He didn't stop, just nodded his head as he passed, but she just stopped talking—sort of froze. You could almost feel the change that came over her. And when I saw her later that morning in the drugstore, she went out of her way to apologize for—for what, I don't know—for being distracted? For losing her train of thought when he happened along? She protested too much. I don't know much about such things, but it struck me that maybe they had some kind of relationship going."

Dan steered the conversation from the particular to the general.

"It may be. But Britingham had all kinds of relationships, if you could call them that, with people from around here. And some of them were pretty intense, not what you'd expect for someone so new or for a guy who didn't have the common touch at all."

"That's an understatement," Rachel chimed in. "The man not only couldn't relate to people, he positively antagonized them. Not that we knew him well. But I remember when he came by our place and asked if he could see the cottage—said it had something to do with gathering ideas for some building he was planning to do. There we were, being obliging about it, and he starts making critical remarks about Dan's workmanship. Can you imagine? Of course, I'm sure he didn't know that Dan had done the work himself, but that doesn't excuse him."

The simple act of recalling the experience was getting Rachel riled up. If Kevin's friend, normally so calm and so charitable to others, could display such a flash of emotion toward a man now dead, what might others have felt when he was alive? Dan picked up the narrative.

"Rachel overdoes her defense of me, but she's basically right. I suppose the biggest flap has been about his plans for Silver Leaf—the decision about renewing contracts with local growers. Of course, it's a business decision, and maybe, for all I know, it's defensible. But any damn fool could see how devastating it could be if your livelihood's involved. Why not hold open meetings, explain his plans, try to allay fears? Not Britingham. He sees— sorry, he saw—people up here as yokels. If they can pick grapes, they can pump gas or something. It's the 'let 'em eat cake' attitude. And I'll tell you, there are a lot of worried people around—some of 'em downright angry. Take my neighbors, the Sandersons. Larry and Chris—they're as nice as they come, but don't try to talk to them about Britingham. They're scared. If Larry loses his job, their home's in jeopardy."

They agreed that Britingham's assumption of ownership of Silver Leaf had already had a chilling effect on the area.

"And right here on this point, too," Dan continued. "He had a feud going with Grace Hess, you know. He was going to break up that beautiful wooded section beyond her place, create a whole bunch of small lots, clear the trees, put up saltbox cottages. She's been fit to be tied."

Kevin didn't really know Mrs. Hess, although he saw her frequently, usually jogging behind the cottages on Blue Water Point. Only that morning he had been resting on her raft, and he knew that one of the most attractive features of her property was the expanse of woods just south of her house. They created an idyllic setting, giving the cottage a picture post-card look. He could easily believe that plans to clear and build would have upset Mrs. Hess.

"I'd heard he was building himself a small place," Kevin said. "That's what the construction shack was supposed to be for, wasn't it? I didn't know he planned on putting up more cottages."

"Well, he lied to her about that. Her home will never be the same if those lots are developed. Anyway, he was going right ahead, to hell with Grace."

"Time!" Kevin broke in before Dan could add to his indictment of John Britingham. "Sorry, but if I don't put the chicken on pretty quickly we won't be eating tonight."

Dan Milburn was now well launched into the litany of grievances people felt toward Britingham. When Kevin went over to the grill to assume his role as outdoor chef, Dan turned his chair partway around so their host wouldn't miss what he was saying.

"So there's a few people up here who won't be shedding any tears over that man. Tell you who else—the guys who're heavy into fishing. You heard about this year's Charley's Cup, didn't you?"

Dan knew that Kevin didn't fish. But Kevin had heard about Britingham winning the cup this year, his first in the competition. Mike Snyder had told him.

"I heard," he nodded. "Can you imagine that kind of beginner's luck?"

"But we know he wasn't a beginner. Oh, sure, this lake. But he'd been fishing for years. All kinds—deep sea, mountain streams out west, Minnesota lakes—you name it. They tell me he has one of the most sophisticated collections of lures in the country. *Field and Stream* even did a feature on him a couple of years ago. I'm sure he had this lake well cased before he ever put a line in the water. The problem is he won't let any of the local boys forget it. So that's another wing of the John Britingham fan club."

"But surely no one is going to stab Britingham to death because he caught a bigger fish and bragged about it!"

"No, no. I'm not saying any of them killed him. But just look at all the people who didn't like the man, people he'd irritated—or worse."

The conversation shifted to the question of whether John Britingham's various insensitivities and threatening actions provided motives for murder. Kevin left the grill and headed for the kitchen to get the Milburns another beer, reminding them as he did so that they didn't know for a fact that there had been a murder. But he no longer had any real doubts himself, and it was clear from the animated discussion that the question was not whether there had been a murder, but who was the guilty party and what had turned a grievance into an act of violence.

Kevin was uncapping the beers when he saw a car coming down the drive from the direction of West Lake Road. It was Sheriff Kelleher, and she was turning in at the Whitman cottage. Kevin stuck his head through the door to the deck to announce that they had company, and then went out to greet the sheriff. She looks tired, he thought. And perhaps discouraged?

"Hello, Mr. Whitman. I just can't get enough of this place. Thought I'd see how you survived the day, and if perhaps you've remembered something you neglected to tell me this morning."

"I'm okay, and I already told you everything I know about this matter. How about you? Have you solved our crime?"

"Takes time." The sheriff sounded as if it might take years. "I didn't get to talk to all of your neighbors this morning, so I thought I might catch a few of them tonight."

"Come on around. There are some people here you missed this morning. The Milburns. Can I fix you a drink?"

"Truth is, I'd love a beer. But I'm going to pass, thanks all the same. I've listened to more wild rumors today than you'd ever believe—don't need to start another about a sotted sheriff."

Dan and Rachel Milburn rose to greet the sheriff, and, introductions concluded, they settled back in their seats while Kevin tended to the chicken.

"You're some of the people I came over to see. You must have been still asleep or already gone when I came by your place this morning."

"Hardly asleep, Sheriff. I don't know when you tried to see us, but we went to town early. In fact, we first heard about this mess over in Cumberland. Anyway, I'm glad we're not going to be left out. What can we tell you? That Britingham was an unpleasant man? That there won't be a lot of mourners at his funeral?"

"You, too? Doesn't appear Britingham had many friends," Carol observed.

"I wouldn't know about that," Rachel spoke up," but we can't think of many around here. We were talking about the man's penchant for making enemies just before you arrived. He wrote the book."

Sheriff Kelleher studied the Milburns. Were they really going to give substance to the veiled hints about Britingham she'd picked up during the morning?

"Had you and Mr. Britingham had trouble?"

"Nothing serious. I mean nothing I'd kill for." Dan smiled. Carol found the quip less amusing. "But he was a thoughtless man. No, let me take that back. It wasn't thoughtlessness. He simply had no regard for other people's feelings. Went about his business and just brushed you aside if you were in his way."

"What did he do to you?" Carol wanted to know.

Rachel repeated the story of Britingham's criticism of Dan's workmanship, leaving little doubt that she thought this the basest of canards. And for the next few minutes the Milburns reprised their recital of Britingham's offenses, sidestepping mere innuendo and focusing on documented cases.

The sheriff found this information interesting, but like the Milburns, she was having trouble with the notion that someone would commit murder over these slights and slanders. Unless, of course, the murderer was so precariously balanced that it had taken only a shove like Britingham's to push him—or her—over the edge.

The chicken was almost certainly done. Kevin even thought it was beginning to look suspiciously black. He didn't want to be rude to the sheriff, but he didn't want their dinner ruined either. Carol came to his rescue.

"Aren't you people famished? I'd better let you tackle that chicken. It smells awfully good. I didn't pick the best time to come around asking more questions," she apologized, while privately feeling very pleased that she had dropped in at the dinner hour. "But you've been very helpful."

Carol declined Whitman's invitation to stay and have some of the barbecue with them.

"I've got other people I have to see—other dinners to interrupt." She mentioned the names of residents on the point she hadn't talked with, and decided to get an opinion from the obviously knowledgeable Milburns on the most promising next stop. Dan was only too happy to oblige.

"I wouldn't think you'd get much from the people in the Sullivan or the Perkins places; they're just renting. Of course they might have seen something. That's a different matter. The rest? Well, Larry Sanderson would probably support what I told you about the way the growers feel about Britingham. And I'd talk to Grace Hess. She's a fine lady, and you ought to let her tell you about Britingham's development scheme. Don't just take our word for it."

"What about the Hoffmans? Their place is close to where Mr. Whitman found the body."

Neither Dan nor Rachel had mentioned her theory that Emily Hoffman might be having an affair with Britingham. There was no proof of such a liaison, and Rachel didn't think they should be sharing mere speculation with the sheriff. But studied avoidance of any mention of the Hoffmans would only arouse her suspicion, and that was not their purpose.

"Sure, I'd talk with them. Or with her, anyway. He's probably in the city—he works down there."

Sheriff Kelleher decided, reluctantly, that she'd have to talk with them all, even the renters, both of whom had dogs. It had already been a long day. It promised to be a long summer.

CHAPTER 10

Two hours and twenty minutes later, with the last vestiges of light disappearing in the Western sky and Venus clearly visible overhead, Sheriff Kelleher headed back toward Cumberland. She had talked with everyone except the Sandersons. And Dan Milburn's predictions had been accurate.

The family in the Perkins' cottage, the Dannings, had been puzzled by the turmoil on the point, didn't know any of their neighbors, and owned a small, noisy dog, which definitely was not the one Kevin Whitman had seen down the beach at five in the morning. The whole tribe—father, mother, four children under ten, and the vocal dog—had been away overnight, making the pilgrimage to Niagara Falls for the first time since Mr. and Mrs. Danning had honeymooned there. The sheriff tried to imagine the motel that would have tolerated the dog.

The other renters, a young couple named Bettencourt, were interesting only because they, too, owned a dog—two of them, in fact—and because it was on their beach that Whitman had tentatively placed the man and the dog early that morning. It had at first seemed like a highly promising interview, in spite of the Milburns' doubts. But it turned out that the dogs were toy poodles, house pets that were always walked as a pair, and then no more than absolutely necessary. The dogs were also, the sheriff observed, very jealous of the new baby, whom Mrs. Bettencourt was nursing when she arrived. If they hadn't been walking a dog that morning, Carol had suggested that perhaps they had seen someone else doing so. This brought a laugh from both of the Bettencourts. When little Hillary slept through the night, a relatively new and rare occurrence, they certainly weren't going to be up before sunrise.

The Bettencourts' neighbors, the Pierces, also had a dog—a beagle, one of the few Whitman had gotten right when he'd inventoried the dog population for the sheriff that morning. Helen and Walter Pierce had at least been residents of Blue Water Point for a while, and might be presumed to know their neighbors and something about John Britingham. Unfortunately, they proved to be both eccentric and irascible, and Carol had been relieved to escape from their claustrophobic living room. Such people might be capable of anything, she supposed, but they were so preoccupied with their own bickering and armchair misanthropy that she doubted that they would have taken notice of their neighbors, much less bestirred themselves to commit mayhem. She felt sorry for Poppy, the beagle. If it had been on the beach that morning, it had almost certainly not had either of the Pierces for company.

———

Emily Hoffman had been a rather different story. She was an undeniably attractive woman. Seated across from Carol, legs tucked under her and one arm trailing across the back of the couch, she had been the picture of casual, cool elegance. And she had quite obviously been sizing the sheriff up. Carol knew nothing of Mrs. Hoffman's visit to Kevin Whitman that morning, and hence nothing of the nervousness she had exhibited during their discussion of his discovery of Britingham's body. In any event, the woman had pulled herself together and presented a very different face to the sheriff than she had to her neighbor earlier in the day. She had seemed surprised when Carol mentioned that she had tried unsuccessfully to see her that morning.

"But I was here all day. I don't know why I didn't hear you. Never mind, you're here now. How can I help you?"

Carol had pursued the by now familiar line of questions: Had Mrs. Hoffman seen or heard anything that might help explain Britingham's death or the discovery of his body on the Whitman dock? Did she know Britingham? What could she tell him about the man and about who might have wanted him dead?

"I wish I could tell you that I know something about this terrible thing. But I don't see how I can. I have a back bedroom, you see, and I must have slept through it all." She had given a small gesture of helplessness. "Why is this such a violent society?"

"I wouldn't know, Mrs. Hoffman. But this isn't about a violent society. It's about the death of one man. Unless it was an accident, somebody didn't like Mr. Britingham—didn't like him enough to want him dead, enough to kill him. Why do you think anyone would have hated him that much?"

Emily Hoffman had carefully rearranged herself on the couch, all the time shaking her head.

"I can't even imagine. I just don't understand killing."

The sheriff's question had not elicited an admission that the woman knew Britingham, so she put it more directly.

"Did you know him?"

"We'd met, yes. But I didn't know him, not really."

"What do you mean, not really?" Had it been Carol's imagination or had color risen in Mrs. Hoffman's cheeks.

"You must think I'm a terrible recluse, but the truth is we keep pretty much to ourselves. I'm sure the neighbors will tell you the same thing. I don't even remember ever discussing..." She had balked at the man's name. "I don't think we discussed him with our neighbors. Was he disliked?"

"That seems to be the consensus around here. But I'm interested in what you think of him."

Emily Hoffman had turned her eyes away from the sheriff. It was a striking profile, but it had the effect of depriving Carol of a chance to study her face for her reaction to the question.

"He seemed like a nice enough person. He might have been a nice person to know." It had seemed at the time, and it seemed now as Carol thought about it, an unusual response, both detached and somehow wistful.

Nice. She turned the word over in her mind. Nice. Emily Hoffman's opinion of John Britingham was not that of the others she had spoken with that day. Why the difference? Because she did not know the man as well? Or because she knew him better? The woman was an enigma, a beautiful woman, living in a beautiful cocoon. What a waste.

———

The sheriff had finally turned her attention to the cottages at the other end of the point, the ones that faced Mallard Cove and were closest to the property which Britingham had purchased and on which he had placed his construction shack. One of these belonged to the Milburns. The others, one large and distinctive and the other small and conventional, had been her last stops of the day. She had parked in the driveway behind the smaller cottage, which belonged to the Sandersons.

The note on the back door had made it clear that she would not be talking with all the residents on Blue Water Point that day.

Bernie and Rose—We've gone ahead down to the field. See you there. Bern, I think you borrowed my glove. Bring it and maybe another six-pack. Larry

A softball game? Probably. Just as the sheriff had turned to walk over to the adjacent cottage to pay a visit to Grace Hess, she had been accosted by a large, exuberantly friendly golden retriever. It had bounded across the yard and leaped up, paws shoulder high, to greet the sheriff as if she were a long lost friend.

"Down! Down, boy!" Even as she fought off the dog's affectionate embrace, she had heard a surprisingly firm woman's voice calling the animal. The woman had appeared from behind the cottage to her right, moving purposefully in Carol's direction. The dog had promptly abandoned the sheriff and set off toward the other woman. She looked tough and wiry, and in spite of her years she looked as if she could handle the dog with ease. Carol had been sure it was Grace Hess who had saved her, and so it was.

"You mustn't mind Jeff. He's harmless, but he doesn't know his own strength. I'm Grace Hess, and I assume you're the sheriff. Have I got it right?"

She had taken Carol's hand with a surprisingly firm grip the like of which the sheriff had rarely encountered in a woman.

"Your dog just took me by surprise, Mrs. Hess. I was on my way to see you."

She had started to explain her mission, but Mrs. Hess had brushed the explanation aside.

"You want to know why anyone would kill John Britingham. And you're asking around. Now you've gotten to me—last house on the point. Well, I'd like to talk about it, so why don't you come over to the house."

She had marched off in the direction of her house, an attractive log cabin, Jeff cavorting at her side. Sheriff Kelleher had brought up the rear, no longer quite sure who was in control.

The interior of the house had overwhelmed her, and she had to pry her attention away from the stunning display of objets d'art so that she wouldn't miss what Mrs. Hess was saying. The living room in which she had taken a seat contained a museum quality collection of oriental art, but the owner of this unexpectedly elegant home was not interested in compliments. Grace Hess was the antithesis of Emily Hoffman, energetic where the other woman had been reserved, conversationally aggressive where the other had been extremely reticent. Carol had barely spoken twenty words since meeting her.

"What do I know about John Britingham? And what did I think of him?" Mrs. Hess had put the questions for the sheriff. "I knew enough about him to know that he was a despicable man. Other people will have known him in different ways, I've no doubt. My reasons for disliking him are quite personal. That man planned to turn this point—this perfectly lovely point—into a slum. Have you seen my woods?"

The sheriff remembered the license with which the woman had appropriated the wooded area beyond her home, as well as the way she had spat out 'that man.'

"Well, he was going to cut down all those trees and build cheap cottages there. Can you imagine such utter disregard for aesthetics? That's the kind of man who would tear down the Taj Mahal to make room for a parking garage. I detested him.

"Oh, I know it's all perfectly legal. It's people like Britingham who make the laws. And they're so sanctimonious. Pillars of society. Rot!"

Grace Hess had made no attempt to disguise her contempt for the Britinghams of the world.

"But did I kill him? No, of course not. The very idea is ridiculous. I was fighting his request for a variance on that property, and I'd have made his life miserable. But I don't kill people, Sheriff. And I expect you to believe that."

It was Sheriff Kelleher's business to take people's self-serving explanations for their behavior with a very large grain of salt. She was inclined to believe Mrs. Hess, however, and if she had killed Britingham, she didn't seem like the kind of person who would break down and confess if pressed. Carol had wanted to shift the discussion to Jeff's early morning habits, and had finally been able to get her word in.

"If I may, please. Just a question or two about this morning. Did you, by chance, take Jeff for a walk—I mean early, before the sun was up, say around five o'clock?"

There had been just a moment of uncharacteristic hesitation, as if Mrs. Hess were making mental adjustments to a new line of questioning, the purpose of which she did not know. But when she replied, the answer had come in the familiar firm voice.

"Walk Jeff? Sheriff, have you ever tried to walk a big dog like this? A retriever? No, I don't walk Jeff. He's very independent, has the run of the point. You can't keep this breed cooped up. I suppose he was out this morning—usually is. A real early bird. But not me."

"You're telling me that Jeff may have been running around on the point but that you weren't with him?"

"That's right. Why do you ask? What does this have to do with that man's death?"

Carol had decided that a little candor was in order.

"Someone was seen with a dog just shortly before Mr. Whitman down the point found Britingham's body. That person was spotted between here and Whitman's dock. I hoped I might find that person, and that he or she might have seen something that would explain how Britingham got onto that dock."

"Or that he or she might have had something to do with his death? Sorry I can't be more helpful. Jeff's friendly with everyone, as you've seen yourself. It could have been Jeff, making up to someone. Even to the murderer—he doesn't discriminate. Wouldn't it be something if my dog knows who killed Britingham and can't tell us?"

As she was driving back to Cumberland, Carol recalled Grace Hess's ready assumption that Britingham's death had not been an accident. And her rhetorical question. She decided that the woman would be secretly delighted with the thought that Jeff had romped on the beach of Blue Water Point with Britingham's killer. Jeff who would never talk. Jeff who would have showered the killer with affection.

CHAPTER 11

The following obituary appeared in the *Cumberland Gazette* the morning after Kevin Whitman's discovery of the body on his dock.

'John W. Britingham, 55, owner of the Silver Leaf Wine Company in Southport and internationally renowned sportsman, died August 16 of wounds sustained in an accident or an attack by an unknown assailant. Mr. Britingham's body was discovered on the west shore of Crooked Lake, ten miles north of Southport. The investigation of the mysterious death of one of the area's most prominent citizens is continuing.

'Mr. Britingham had moved to the area only recently, after many years as the owner of the Britingham Winery in California's Napa Valley. He announced upon assuming ownership of Silver Leaf that he believed that eastern wines could compete in the market with the best of those produced in California, and he intended to bring techniques developed there to the winery in Southport. Although Mr. Britingham retained a controlling interest in his California wine company, he had demonstrated his commitment to his new company by buying the old Keighly estate outside of Southport and beginning extensive restoration. He had also bought property on Blue Water Point on Crooked Lake and was planning to build a cottage there.

'In addition to his reputation as a vintner, Mr. Britingham was also widely known for his accomplishments in the sporting world. He was a highly successful big game hunter and fisherman, with many trophies to attest to his skills. This summer he won the cherished Charley's Cup for the largest lake trout taken from Crooked Lake during the annual June competition. Mr. Britingham was also a distinguished diver. In 1986 he led the expedition that discovered the wreck of the Spanish galleon *Salamanca* in the Caribbean and recovered a small fortune in gold pieces and jewelry. His business responsibilities made it impossible for him to play the game regularly, but at the time of his death he was still recognized as one of the country's top amateur golfers. As recently as 1990 he won the Sierra Open event on the PGA tour, the only amateur ever to do so.

'John W. Britingham was born on March 3, 1949, in Chillicothe, Ohio. He attended Ohio State University, where he lettered in football and golf and served as president of the Sigma Iota Nu fraternity. Following graduation from college, he moved to San Francisco and entered the importing business. In 1979 he established his own company and soon became one of the largest importers of oriental and oceanic art and specialty items on the west coast. In 1980 he married the late Sandra Laughlin, heiress of the Laughlin Wineries fortune, and became president of that wine company, which today bears his name. Mr. Britingham was actively involved in San Francisco and California civic affairs until his move to Southport. A lifelong member of the Republican Party, he served briefly in the California state legislature in the late 1980s. He was past president of the California Viniculture Society, as well as a trustee of the Napa Valley Community College, the Western Museum of Oriental Art, and the Omega Foundation. A world traveler, Mr. Britingham belonged to the exclusive One Hundred Nations Club and to the Safari Club. He contributed to various journals, including *Safari*, *Adventure*, and *Deep Sea Diver*, and had recently been the subject of a feature article in *Field and Stream*.

'Mr. Britingham's first marriage, to the former Dorothy Seeley, ended in divorce. His second wife, the former Sandra Laughlin, died in a boating accident in 1988. He is survived by a daughter from his first marriage, Linda Britingham Carson, of Sacramento, California, and by a son from his second marriage, John W. Britingham, Jr., of San Francisco. Funeral arrangements are incomplete.'

———

The man who wrote this obituary, Jack Hasbrouck, had not known his subject personally. His information came from a sketchy file someone had assembled when John Britingham had bought Silver Leaf and moved into the area, as well as from a telephone conversation with a spokesperson for the Britingham Winery in California. That person had unearthed phone numbers for Linda Carson and John Britingham, Jr., although she had been doubtful that the son's number was current. Mrs. Carson, he had been dismayed to discover, had not yet heard of her father's death, which made the conversation somewhat awkward. On the other hand, she had not seemed shocked or even much upset by the news, and had clearly not wanted to talk about it. She had told him nothing that had not been in the file at the *Gazette* or that he had not learned from the winery.

Hasbrouck had been even less successful with Britingham's son. The woman who had answered the phone at the number he had been given by the winery reported that the young man had moved about a month earlier. Fortunately, she had been able to give him the phone number at his new address, but unfortunately, his quarry had not been there either. The voice on the other end of the line had told Hasbrouck that J.B., as he called young Britingham, had left about a week before, taking only a small duffel bag with him and announcing neither his destination nor his date of expected return. Hasbrouck had not pursued the matter further, figuring that Britingham was living in a group house with relative strangers who would be unlikely to know of his plans. He had decided to go with what he had.

There would, of course, be feature stories as the investigation unfolded. A murder—even an accidental death—was big news in the area, and John Britingham's demise was very big news. In a part of the state where school board elections and a summer drought were good for page one headlines, this case was sure to keep most of the *Gazette*'s small staff busy for weeks. But the obituary was merely a brief profile cataloging the major accomplishments of the deceased. It told the reader virtually nothing about the man whom Kevin Whitman had discovered, dead, on the end of his dock.

PART II

A CANDIDATE
FOR MURDER

CHAPTER 12

Spring typically arrives late on Crooked Lake. The thermometer may occasionally climb as high as 65 for a day or two in March, but such false promises of an early spring are almost invariably followed by a protracted cold snap and even a snowfall or two after the first daffodils appear. By April the thin skin of ice on the lake will have disappeared for good, but even in May the water will still be much too cold for any but the bravest swimmer.

Although the solstice is still several weeks away and the weather still unpredictable, the transition from the long winter to the summer season on the lake takes place on Memorial Day weekend. It is then that most of the summer residents arrive to open their cottages, letting sunlight and fresh air into rooms shuttered since the previous Labor Day. The permanent residents on the lake will, of course, have been going about their business throughout the intervening months, but it is the influx of the transients that brings the lake alive. Boat traffic increases exponentially, and sales figures skyrocket at local paint and hardware stores as lake dwellers confront the task of putting their cottages into shape for another season in the sun.

The summer of John Britingham's untimely death began very much as many another summer on Crooked Lake. At least for most of its residents. There had been an unseasonable snow during the second week in April; barely more than an inch of the white stuff had fallen, but it was enough to remind people that winter has a way of outlasting its welcome. The lilacs came into bloom in May, finally putting an end to the last vestiges of cabin fever among the citizens of Southport and West Branch and points in between. Memorial Day had produced its annual surge in the area's population.

But this was not to be a summer like most others for some of the residents on Crooked Lake. Events which were to cast a shadow over the summer took place during the transitional weeks when the quiet of spring was beginning to yield to the bustle of summer. Seemingly unrelated, these events had one element in common: a protagonist named John Britingham. In each case, the relatively uneventful and generally pleasant lives of several lake residents would be thrown into turmoil by Britingham's presence, his plans, and his persona. And as fate would have it, the relationships set in motion in the late spring were destined to fester over the summer and ultimately become the most important focus of the investigation into Britingham's death.

When Kevin Whitman discovered Britingham's body on his dock, he knew very little about Cumberland County's most prominent citizen, and almost nothing at all about the difficult relationships which he had forged with a number of other people on Crooked Lake, many of them Kevin's own neighbors. Sheriff Carol Kelleher's knowledge of these matters had been even less. But in the days following the death of the owner of Silver Leaf Winery, it gradually became apparent to both that if ever there were a candidate for murder, John Britingham had been that man.

CHAPTER 13

The residents of Southport may have disagreed about many things—politics, religion, the relative merits of powerboats and sailboats, of trout fishing versus bass fishing—but they would have been very much of one mind as to the village's most popular citizen. He was Charley Mikkelson, and he would have been the mayor, unopposed and hands down, had he chosen to run. But he preferred to go about his business of many years, and his business was the Lake Hardware Company. The local residents were of one mind about that, too. Lake Hardware was the messiest, most chaotic store in three counties. Making a purchase at Charley's was invariably an adventure. Almost daily, someone would apologize to Charley for inadvertently knocking over one of his displays, and the proprietor would routinely wave off the apology and promise to put his store in order. It never happened. Charley, of course, navigated through the store without mishap, which was an amazing feat, considering that he ran his business from a wheelchair.

Lake Hardware was not the charming country store celebrated in American folklore. It was simply a large cluttered box of a building on Water Street, half a block from the town dock. A cast-iron bench had been placed on the sidewalk in front of the store, ostensibly for the purpose of adding character to an otherwise undistinguished commercial establishment, but even with the bench Lake Hardware did not present an interesting face to the public. It was, however, something of a local hangout. There wasn't much room for people to congregate, but dropping into Charley's was a habit for many, and on a slow Friday afternoon in mid June, three men were wedged between the cash register and a precariously balanced stack of paint cans, talking with Charley Mikkelson, who had maneuvered his wheelchair into the narrow aisle behind the counter.

"How many've signed up?" a large florid man in a striped polo shirt asked.

Charley consulted some papers on the counter.

"Hundred and forty-three. Seems a bit low to me. Maybe we'll get a flurry of activity before the deadline."

"That's way down from last year, isn't it?" one of the other men asked. "Didn't we get it up to two hundred?"

"Close," Charley agreed. "Hundred eighty-seven. Oh, well, it's been a late spring. We'll still have ourselves a pretty good pot of prize money."

"Suppose we end up with a hundred fifty. What's that make the winner's share?"

Charley busied himself with a hand calculator.

"Seven hundred fifty bucks," he announced, and the men at the counter nodded as if this were a respectable sum of money.

They were speculating on the likelihood of enough last minute entrants to push the top prize higher when a young woman in a business suit entered the store. All eyes watched appreciatively as she worked her way down the center aisle, past a large box of unopened merchandise and around the paint cans to the counter.

"Yes, ma'am, something I can do for you?" Charley gave the woman his best smile.

"I understand this is where people sign up for the fishing competition. Is that right?" Her voice suggested that she was no longer sure her information was correct.

"This is the place," Charley nodded. "You fish? Don't get too many women in the competition."

The men appraised the newcomer with interest. She was an attractive, dark-haired woman in her late twenties or early thirties, but her manner made it quite clear that she was not likely to engage them in banter or small talk, and she didn't.

"No, I don't fish," she replied. "I'm here to sign my boss up for the Cup competition."

She reached into her purse and took out a checkbook.

"I've got the fee here. What do I have to do to register him?" She tore out a check and stood poised to write it.

"Well, ma'am, people are supposed to register themselves. You should have your boss come by—this afternoon it would have to be. Deadline's five o'clock."

"You can't be serious," she protested. "What difference can it make? I'm here because he's busy. He shouldn't have to make a trip like this. So what's the registration fee? I hear there is one."

There was a moment of silence. Everyone at the counter looked uncomfortable.

"Look, I don't know what you men are doing here at 2:30 on a workday, but Mr. Britingham is very busy and so am I. I have to get back to the office, and I want to register him for the Cup."

"Britingham? The owner of Silver Leaf? Didn't know he'd be in this." Charley Mikkelson was suddenly more interested.

"Mr. Britingham fishes. You're sponsoring a competition, and he wants to enter. And he asked me to take care of it for him. If you don't mind, I'd just like to get it done. The check is good—call the bank if you like." Dolores Weber was making an effort to rein in her impatience.

And Charley Mikkelson was deciding that no great harm would be done by accepting her check and adding John Britingham's name to the roster of entrants for this year's Cup. There was no written rule that said that participants in the Cup competition had to register themselves. It was merely custom. In fact, there were only three rules that had been codified, and they were spelled out on a sheet of paper, which had been laminated some years before and attached by a magnetic clip to the refrigerator where Charley kept live bait behind his counter. One required a ten-dollar registration fee, another stipulated that the trout had to be taken from Crooked Lake, and the third declared that the fish had to be brought to the town dock for weighing by one o'clock on the afternoon of the day of the competition. Everything else was gentleman's agreement.

"Okay, I guess that's good enough, Miss—I don't think I caught your name."

"I haven't mentioned my name, and it isn't important. I just want to do what I came to do and leave."

"Sure, no problem. We're pretty informal here. I'm not sure your boss couldn't sign up in the morning if he had to. It's just that we do things by custom around here. We do insist on taking the ten bucks up front, though."

The other men chuckled at Charley's attempt at humor. The annual trout fishing competition hadn't always been his responsibility, but after the accident ten years ago, Charley had had trouble getting in and out of a boat and when he announced that he didn't plan to compete anymore, someone had suggested that Lake Hardware should be Cup headquarters. Charley had let himself be drafted for this one, and had been running the competition ever since. It gave him pleasure, and he was now so closely identified with the annual event that everyone referred to it as Charley's

Cup, this in spite of two pertinent facts: there was no Cup—it had disappeared mysteriously years before and had never been replaced—and the official name of the competition was the Tyler Cup, in honor of the Southport resident who had started the affair as an antidote to Depression blues in the 1930s.

Charley Mikkelson was not ordinarily impressed by the likes of John Britingham, but he rather relished the idea that the county's most distinguished and wealthy citizen would choose to compete with a lot of regular guys for the Cup. Must be a regular guy himself, he found himself thinking.

"Miss Weber," he said, reading her name off the check, "it's been a pleasure doing business with you. Tell your boss we're glad he's going to try his luck with us tomorrow."

"I'll do that." She snapped her purse shut, favored the men with a half smile, and left the store as quickly as the obstacle course in the aisle allowed. As Charley dutifully entered the name of contestant 144 in a ledger book, his companions observed with obvious pleasure Dolores Weber's legs as she stepped up and over the large box and out through the front door of the Lake Hardware Store.

————

The sun never made an appearance the following morning. It was a gloomy day, with intermittent drizzle stippling the waters of Crooked Lake. Had it been any other Saturday, the lake would have been deserted except for a handful of fishermen for whom the sport was an all-weather addiction. But the Charley's Cup competition had no rain date, and boats could be seen on the lake all the way from West Branch to Southport. The ledger in Charley Mikkelson's hardware store contained 162 names, and it was doubtful if any of that number had taken a look at the weather that morning and gone back to bed.

Most of the boats were moving slowly through the gray mist that had settled over most of the lake. Trolling, copper lines trailing behind and deep where the trout would be feeding. This annual competition was a test of knowledge and skill and patience. Everyone knew that the competition was also about luck, but the history of the Charley's Cup made a powerful argument that to be lucky one had to first be good. In the previous nine years, two long time Crooked Lake residents and experienced fishermen, Freddie Jonathan and Mike Snyder, had each won the cup twice.

Whatever their starting point—some of the entrants lived on the lake and some came from the surrounding area and used public launching sites—all participants in the competition came into the municipal dock in Southport to have their best catch weighed and recorded before heading home. Quite a few had checked in well before the one o'clock deadline, either confident that they had landed a trout that would put them in contention or discouraged as the morning wore on without a break in the weather.

By 12:45 the town dock was crowded. Many of the fishermen who had come in earlier had stayed around to see how later arrivals had done. All of the slips were filled, and at least two dozen boats were beached along the shore where bathers would have been sunning on a nicer day. A few boats rode at anchor offshore, their occupants huddled in rain slickers and exchanging small talk across the water. At the center of all the activity was Charley Mikkelson, oblivious to the weather and the slick dock, wheeling his chair about to talk to new arrivals, overseeing the scales, and having a thoroughly wonderful time. He had lashed a beach umbrella to a post near the scale so that he could keep the record log dry, and he had deputized a young high school boy who had been standing around to enter the weight of each fish as he read it off.

A few boats were now coming in, and Charley propelled himself down to the end of the dock to see who they were. This was the only part of the competition he didn't care for. Inevitably there were men who were having no luck and who would wait until the last minute in the hope that their luck would change. And then there was the occasional case where somebody had himself a trout, even a big one, but didn't get back until after the one o'clock deadline. Charley had over the years tried to be sensibly flexible in such matters, using the 'reasonable man' standard. But he knew that fishermen could be pretty competitive and that what might be reasonable to one would look like an unfair advantage to another.

Charley didn't recognize the man in the boat that was just then pulling alongside of the dock. No one else seemed to either. Instead of the friendly informality with which the people on the dock had greeted most of their fellow fishermen, this man's arrival produced a polite offer of assistance and a few curious stares. The stranger cut the engine and vaulted athletically to the dock, grabbed the rope at the bow of the boat, and fastened it to the post next to the scale. He was hatless, his dark curly hair, wet from hours of rain, framing a strong, handsome face.

"Am I under the deadline?" The question was addressed to no one in particular.

"Indeed you are. 12:54—that's what I call cutting it close. Don't believe we've met. I'm Charley Mikkelson—you might say I'm in charge here. At least I weigh the trout. Any luck?"

"Good to meet you. I'm John Britingham," he said as he took Mikkelson's outstretched hand. "The answer is yes; I have a trout or two for you to weigh."

Britingham stepped back into his boat and, like a magician performing before a mesmerized audience, whipped an oilskin cover off a chest in the bow of the boat and, reaching in, hoisted a large lake trout out of the chest by its gills. There were appreciative murmurs from the crowd on the dock, but Charley was quite sure that this was not a prize-winning fish. There had been several as big or bigger that morning.

"Let's weigh it." Britingham passed the fish up onto the dock. Mikkelson squinted at the scale.

"You ready, Jimmy? Okay, it'll be nine pounds seven ounces." He turned back to Britingham. "That's a very impressive trout. One of the biggest we've seen today. Where'd you catch it?"

John Britingham smiled and shook his head.

"No, no. We fishermen don't give away our favorite fishing spots. But tell me, is it going to put me in the money—win, place or show?"

"Well, now, I'm not absolutely sure. I'd have to go through the log here. But we've had a few bigger. Best so far is just about twelve pounds. You don't need to feel bad, though. This is a good one." Mikkelson's praise was genuine. "Not often a newcomer catches one this big. Congratulations."

Britingham, still in the boat, nodded his acknowledgement of the compliment and then, wiping the water from his face, broke into a broad grin. He turned again to the chest and brought out a second and even more beautiful specimen of the trout for which Crooked Lake is famous, its silver gray back and white belly glistening in the midday rain. The gasp from the crowd on the dock told the story: this was indeed a prize-winning catch, and for many of the veteran fishermen present, the largest they had seen in these waters.

"Better than twelve pounds, wouldn't you say?"

Holding his prize aloft, Britingham climbed triumphantly out of the boat.

"Incredible. I think you've got it, no question," Charley said as he hooked up the fish. Jimmy captured the reaction of the crowd with one word—"Humongous!"—as he entered the weight in the log. Thirteen pounds, eleven ounces.

Another fisherman was trying to dock, but everyone's attention was riveted on the man no one seemed to know, the man who had pulled into the town dock six minutes before the competition deadline, the man who had lifted out of his boat in dramatic fashion a trout for which some of those present would have traded a few earthly possessions.

One of the men on the dock pushed his way through the crowd.

"Hi. I'm Freddie Jonathan, and I want to congratulate you in person. That's about as fine a looking trout as I've seen, and I've been fishing this lake since I was a kid."

"Jonathan? A pleasure. You have any luck today?"

"Sure, but not your kind of luck. I didn't look to repeat, probably wouldn't have anyway, but this one's in another league."

"Freddie took the Cup last year." Mikkelson spoke up from his seat by the scale. "Won it twice, in fact. You guys should get to know one another."

"Good idea," Britingham agreed. "Sorry to break your monopoly, Jonathan. Anyway, now you've got another fish story."

The prize money wasn't to be given out until the ceremony that evening at the Cup picnic, which by the look of things would probably be moved indoors at the high school. But there was no longer any doubt about it. John Britingham would take first prize, fifty percent of the take from registration fees. Charley confirmed for those gathered around the scale what he already knew: Mike Snyder had earned second prize with a catch that weighed twelve pounds three ounces. A shame in a way. Snyder had looked like the winner until those last few minutes.

It seemed as if everyone on the dock was trying to move in for a closer look at the prize-winning fish and the man who had caught it. There were questions, fisherman's questions. No one appeared to mind the rain, which was now falling steadily.

"What'd you use?" somebody asked.

Britingham was obviously enjoying the attention, not at all anxious to be on his way.

"Fish finder. Top of the line Lowrance," he replied, pointing in the direction of his boat.

"No, I mean what kind of spoon," the questioner persisted.

"Oh, just an old standby of mine—here, I'll show you." He was in and out of the boat quickly, holding up the spoon.

The voice came from somewhere in the knot of people.

"A fish finder? You used a fish finder?"

The buzz of excitement, which had provided background for the impromptu question and answer session, died quickly away, so Britingham's reply was clearly heard by all on the dock.

"Of course I did. That's the way to find the buggers. Why? Didn't you?"

The owner of the voice, which had asked about the fish finder, walked up through the crowd and stopped at the edge of the dock. He leaned over Britingham's boat, pulling the oilskin cover aside.

"Yeah. That's a Lowrance, all right. But it isn't legal. Didn't anyone tell you?"

"Legal? Are you kidding? Of course it's legal. They sell them over the counter all over the country. These sonar devices have revolutionized fishing. I thought everyone used them these days."

"Yes, I know," the other man went on in a quiet voice. He was similar to Britingham in build and color, if perhaps a few years younger. But there was something in his voice that suggested that the two men inhabited different worlds. "I use one, too, a Garmin. But not for the Cup. It's against the rules."

Mikkelson spoke up.

"Snyder's right. Fish finders aren't used in the competition. I'd have said something, I suppose, if you'd come in yesterday. Didn't think to mention it to your secretary, and besides..."

"Now wait a minute," Britingham interrupted. "Where does it say they're against the rules? Where? My secretary told me there are three rules and three rules only. She's a very observant lady—said they were posted on a refrigerator in your store. Nothing at all about fish finders."

"Well, yes, those are some of the rules—the basic ones, you might say. But there are some others, you know, more like tradition."

"Like my having to come in person to register?"

"Oh, your secretary told you about that?" Charley sounded apologetic.

"She did. But she didn't say anything about sonar being outlawed. And I can't for the life of me see how it should be."

Mike Snyder, who had raised the issue, tried to provide an explanation.

"When they first came on the market, not everyone could afford to buy 'em. It seemed more fair to fish without 'em. It's been that way ever since—like Charley says, a tradition. And it's more sporting in a way, just us against the fish."

Britingham examined Snyder as if he were some kind of unfamiliar species.

"Now that's a quaint attitude, isn't it? Why not use a bamboo pole and a safety pin? That would be really sporting. What's the matter with you people? Good lord, we're not living in the horse and buggy age, or haven't you noticed?"

Charley Mikkelson was beginning to realize that Britingham was not going to accept graciously the news of his disqualification. And he was an important man. Charley was worried.

The debate over the use of fish finders had been joined by several other fishermen on the dock when Britingham suddenly held up his hand.

"Just a minute." He turned toward Snyder and walked up to within a foot of him. "What did our impresario here call you? What's your name?"

"Snyder. Mike Snyder." He felt very uncomfortable with this stranger crowding him, but he was at the edge of the dock, and there were people directly behind him, so he couldn't easily move further away.

"Snyder. Yes, that's it. Didn't our friend here tell us who the runner up in this competition was? And wasn't his name Snyder? Is that you?"

"Yes, I guess so. Why?" The man was almost literally in his face, and Mike found himself involuntarily bending backward.

"I'll tell you why, Mr. Snyder. If you could get them to disallow mine"—he gestured toward his fish, still on the scale—"if you could get these people to buy this bullshit about sonar, then you'd take the prize, wouldn't you? Wouldn't you?"

Britingham repeated his accusation, jabbing his finger at Snyder.

Charley was trying desperately to think of some way to put a halt to the unpleasantness, but Britingham gave him no opening. Brushing aside Snyder's protest, he continued his attack.

"What is it? The money? You need the cash? Well, damn it, take some risks. That's the trouble with everybody around here. No ambition, no imagination. Following the old rules, the old stupid rules. There was nothing to keep you from using your Garmin or whatever you've got. But you haven't got the balls—and you lost!"

Mike had never been talked to like this before in his life, not even by his estranged wife during one of their frequent quarrels. Britingham had just indicted most of the people on the dock and in the town of Southport, but all Snyder could think of was the attack on his own manhood and, most of all, the implication that he had wanted to disqualify the man so he could collect a few hundred bucks.

He had to put down a powerful urge to wade into Britingham, to punch him. Instead he said, "Keep your goddam prize! I wouldn't touch the money."

"Mike, please, we'll sort this out." Charley tried to play peacemaker, but it was Freddie Jonathan who ended the confrontation by wrapping an arm around Mike's shoulder and walking him firmly down the dock toward Water Street. Those fishermen who had remained and witnessed this unanticipated conclusion to the contest began to drift off, more in shock than anger. A few stayed to help Charley clean up and to express their sympathy. They knew that this was his day, and that it had ended badly.

Britingham reclaimed his fish and sought to have the last word before pushing off.

"I didn't mean for it to get nasty, but I really don't think you can run a competition like this with old-fashioned rules. Especially when you don't tell us what the rules are."

Charley was folding the umbrella.

"I'll see about publishing a full set of rules, Mr. Britingham," he said. He knew that Britingham had a point, but there was no excusing his behavior. He wished he had stuck by his guns when Miss Weber had come in the previous afternoon.

"See you tonight at the ceremony," Britingham hollered back as he pulled away from the dock.

Yes, thought Charley as he wheeled down the dock toward town, but it will be a mighty small turnout. He was, of course, right. The sun made a belated appearance, and the picnic was held outside at Woodside Acres, but kegs of beer went untapped and many, many hamburgers were not cooked. Twenty-three people showed up, and Mike Snyder was not among them.

CHAPTER 14

The museum. That's what Kevin called George and Edna Morgan's cottage, and they took it as a compliment. They hadn't intended to create a museum, and of course they hadn't, not in any conventional sense of the term. But guests invariably had a strange sensation of stepping back in time when they entered the Morgan living room. It spoke unmistakably of another era.

It was the walls that first caught the eye. They were filled, quite literally, with photographs taken many years before with more primitive cameras and framed in a consciously antique style. All were in black and white or the sepia tones popular at the turn of the 20th century, which gave the room a subdued, even somber look. But what was most distinctive was the subject matter of the photography. The Morgans' living room was, in the main, a gallery of ships. Most were the steamships of various designs that had plied Crooked Lake in the 19th and early 20th century. They were pictured at dock and on the lake, boarding passengers, under steam, being christened, and, in one case, listing badly, apparently after a fire which had blackened the hull. Most bore labels, painstakingly printed by hand, presumably by Edna or George. These labels identified the steamers by such names as *Vineyard Queen*, *The Commodore*, *West Wind*, *Captain Andy*, and *The Gull*. The most prominent of these was *The Commodore*, which appeared in no fewer than seven of the photographs and obviously had been granted a place of honor in the Morgans' gallery.

The steamships dominated the room, but there were other reminders of that bygone era as well. A ship's wheel from the pilothouse of one of the steamers stood in a corner, mounted handsomely on a platform of oak. The table lamps had been fashioned from ship's lanterns. Sharing one wall with the steamships was a large contour map of the lake region, with the depth of various parts of the lake clearly marked. Someone had used a pen to place several Xs on the map, and closer scrutiny showed a name inscribed in ink beside each one. Most of the Xs were on the shoreline, and were concentrated at the village of Southport, but three were further from shore. The chart had been lacquered and was displayed in a frame of simulated ship's halyards.

The Morgans had continued the nautical motif throughout the first floor with mixed results. Kevin may have likened it to a museum, but Dan Milburn insisted that the decor reminded him of dozens of seafood restaurants he had visited. On one thing Kevin and Dan and nearly everyone agreed: George and Edna had an obsession with Crooked Lake history that virtually guaranteed that conversation at any social occasion at which they were present would turn to lake lore, and usually sooner rather than later.

On the afternoon of Memorial Day in late May, the Morgans were hosting a party. Not surprisingly, most of their guests were talking about Crooked Lake as it had been in the days of the steamships. For some of the guests, both the cottage and the conversation were familiar. For others, like John Britingham, this was a first-time introduction to local history.

The new owner of the Silver Leaf Winery found the subject fascinating. He had arrived relatively early and for the first five or six minutes his host had taken him around the room, introducing him to the people who were to become his neighbors on Blue Water Point. George had somehow missed Emily Hoffman in his round of introductions, but she stood out as the most attractive woman in the room, and at the first convenient moment Britingham had remedied that oversight himself. He had made a mental note to cultivate a relationship with this woman, and then had sought out his host to inquire about the lake steamers.

George Morgan was engaged in a conversation with the Milburns when Britingham appeared at his side.

"Mr. Britingham! How are we doing? Getting acquainted, I hope. I can't remember; did you meet Dan and Rachel Milburn? They live down…"

"Yes, thanks. Met them when I came in. I don't want to interrupt, but I've been wanting to ask about these ships."

Dan took advantage of the opportunity.

"Go ahead, George. Fill him in. I need to freshen my drink anyway. Coming, Rachel?" He was relieved to escape another retelling of *The Commodore* disaster. George Morgan was a decent man, Dan mused, but he did wish his conversational repertoire were a bit more varied.

"I'm sure you get tired of people asking about the ships," John Britingham was saying. He brushed aside Morgan's demurrer. "But I've always been interested in ships. About the water, really—about oceans, lakes, marine life, shipwrecks, you name it. I used to be a Jacques Cousteau freak. Sometimes I wonder if I wasn't born in the wrong century. I mean, wouldn't it have been something to have sailed with Drake?"

George was accustomed to holding forth on his favorite subject. His guests were typically cast in the role of listeners, while he played raconteur. But Britingham was giving his host little opportunity to display his knowledge of Crooked Lake.

"I take it that the lake once had some commercial traffic," he went on. "Who'd have guessed it? What are the figures—only about twenty, twenty-one miles long, and it can't be more than two miles across at its widest point."

Britingham was genuinely animated. He was full of the discovery that this lake, which had first attracted him because of the surrounding vineyards, not only had some good fishing but an intriguing past as well. He had assumed that there were Indians in birch bark canoes well before settlers entered the region; he hadn't imagined ships of the size of those displayed in the Morgans' living room. Some of them looked to be more than 100 feet in length, although he found it hard to believe that many people actually rode on them back in the 19th century when this region must have been even more sparsely populated than it was now.

When Britingham took a sip of his scotch, George stepped quickly into the conversation.

"Well, Mr. Britingham—may I call you John?—you'd have made good use of some of those ships if you'd been in the wine business in this country a hundred or so years ago. They were needed to move grapes and wine up the lake and through the canal to Parkerville. They got transferred there to barges for the trip down the river to the city. You probably haven't seen what's left of the canal. They used to dredge the inlet at the end of the lake to keep the channel open, but now it's pretty much filled up. If you drive east on the old Braxton Road, you'll see the ruins of some of the locks. And the cellars around here were something, too. They were great for storage—thick stone walls and plenty deep; kept the grapes cool until the steamers picked them up. Of course, there aren't many of the original houses left, but when they burned down people just rebuilt on the same foundations. That's what happened to this place, must have been eighty years ago."

"I'd love to see your cellar, George," Britingham interrupted, "but first, what about those ships?"

"Weren't they something?" Morgan steered his guest closer to several of the pictures of the shipbuilder's art. "I happen to like the sidewheelers best. They weren't the fastest, but there's something about their lines you have to like. The *West Wind* though, she held the record for the run from Southport up to Yates Center. Did it in one hour and 27 minutes. She was one of the big ones, 148 feet long and 25 feet in the beam. She drew six feet of water, and that was a lot back then."

Britingham had yielded the floor to his host, who was now well launched on his favorite subject.

"Here she is." George ran a finger lovingly along the frame of a picture of a steamer pulling out from a dock, dark smoke rising from a stovepipe funnel, while passengers on deck waved to a knot of people on the shore.

"They built her in a yard up at West Branch. It used to be a bustling place, you know. But the cars came along, and roads got built, and the shipbuilding business kind of died out. I don't know where they build the boats you see on the water nowadays. Not here, that's for sure. They're all fiber glass."

His voice made clear his disdain for such material. For George Morgan, the only good boat was one made of wood.

"What about this one?" Britingham asked, pointing to a photograph of *The Commodore*. "You've got six pictures of it. Was it something special?"

"Seven," George corrected him. "There's these four of her at dock, and two over there under steam. And over by the couch I've got a good one of her under construction. That makes seven. You could say she was special. Didn't do much while she was in service, just hauled passengers and grapes up and down the lake. But she made her reputation when she went down."

"She sank?" Britingham asked in genuine surprise.

"Yes, she did. Several of these boats sank. See the crosses on the chart over there? Well, each one marks a place where one of those steamers sank. Most of them capsized at their docks, so they didn't exactly sink. They weren't loaded properly, I suppose, or they got pounded into the dock in a storm or something. Three of them burned. Here, do you see this one?" Morgan pointed to the photograph of a badly charred boat, listing precariously beside a dock lined with people who had come to see the disaster. "That was the *Waverly*, named for its owner. Some of them could be salvaged, but not her."

"But what happened to *The Commodore*?"

"That's quite a story." George leaned down and knocked the cold ashes from his pipe into a large ashtray. He pulled a tobacco pouch from his jacket pocket and began to refill his pipe. It was clear that the story of *The Commodore* could not be told until he had dispensed with the preliminaries. George was in his element.

He took a couple of puffs on his freshly lit pipe and then started in on the tale of *The Commodore*'s fatal final trip. So often his listeners were merely polite, but John Britingham seemed genuinely interested. There would be no need today to embellish the story a bit to make it more entertaining.

"It was the summer of 1913. People didn't know it then, but it wouldn't be many years before the steamers would be gone, all of them. But there was still a lot of excursion business then. Crowds would come over by train from Cumberland and Parkerville— some from even further away—just to take the circle trip on the lake. There was local business, too—people going from Yates Center or West Branch to Southport to shop or to Woodside Acres for picnics. That was a favorite spot, especially on Sundays. It wasn't spoiled like it is now with those garish concessions.

"But we were talking about *The Commodore*. She was a workhorse, one of the point-to-point ships. Used to pick up and drop people off all along the lake. Sort of a milk run, you might say. Anyway, there came this day in July of 1913, and she was making her usual run when a bad storm came up. You've seen our storms, I suppose. I don't mean your average thunderstorm. I'm talking about one of the real big ones. They don't come often, but when they do, this lake's a different place. And they can come up fast. The water gets gray and mean, with those big whitecaps, and it's not smart to be out there in any kind of boat, no matter how good a sailor you are.

"Well, *The Commodore* was making its way from Southport to Granger Point in the late afternoon at about the same time the *Cumberland* was coming down the lake from West Branch. They were both out in open water when the storm came up. Within minutes it was a real gale. Reports had the wind up to 75 miles an hour. *The Commodore* was having trouble making headway and staying on course because of the wind. The waves were coming right over the prow, and water was getting into the fire hold. I guess she might have made dock okay, though, if it hadn't been for the *Cumberland*. She was a bigger ship—that's her over there, near the lamp.

"I'm not sure who had the right of way. There's always been disagreement about that, even after the inquest. But the *Cumberland* was bearing down on *The Commodore*, the wind pushing her at a pretty good clip, when something happened to her propulsion mechanism. The wind must have knocked a beam loose. All of a sudden, she wasn't responding to the pilot's efforts to steer her. You can imagine the rest."

"It must have been one helluva collision," Britingham said.

"That it was. The amazing thing was that the *Cumberland* didn't sustain more serious damage. She was back in service in a couple months' time. But *The Commodore* wasn't so lucky. She got ripped up pretty badly and somehow a fire got started—can you imagine that in a driving rain? Well, they got the passengers into life jackets and off the boat. She drifted back toward Southport, must have been close to two miles, before she sank. They say that..."

Edna's voice stopped her husband in mid-sentence.

"George, you mustn't forget your duties here. Some of our guests have to leave." Edna was standing near the door with the Snyders. Reluctantly, George excused himself and went over to say good-bye to them.

Preoccupied as he was with his retelling of the story of *The Commodore*, he still noticed that Gloria Snyder looked very tense, and he wondered why the Snyders, whose separation and probable divorce were common knowledge on the point, had chosen to come to the party together. He wasn't quite sure what the appropriate words were in the circumstances; the usual pleasantries seemed out of place.

"Sorry, I didn't get to talk to you folks. You know me, I get all wound up and sort of forget myself. Anyway, thanks for coming. I hope Edna took good care of you, even if I didn't."

The Snyders' problems had a lot to do with Mike's drinking, and if taking care of the guests meant keeping their glasses filled, Edna had done the Snyders no favor.

"She took care of me fine, George," Mike said. "Found me a ginger ale. I'm really off the sauce."

Gloria rolled her eyes at this, and Edna, trying to help avoid a potentially awkward moment, took her arm and steered her out the door.

The Morgans surveyed the room and saw that the party was breaking up. The first departures had prompted others to look at their watches. The etiquette of the situation seemed to call for a general exodus. It looked as if George would not have the opportunity to finish his story. He found himself apologizing to John Britingham.

"I didn't mean to leave you in suspense, Mr. Britingham."

"John. I wish you'd call me John. And don't worry; I like the suspense. It guarantees that we'll be getting together for another chat, doesn't it?"

"That would suit me just fine. Of course Edna tells me I go on too much, that I bore people."

"No, no," Britingham protested. "You don't bore me at all. This place has a fascinating history, and you're the keeper of that history. People should be grateful."

The flattery was obvious, but George Morgan loved it. Britingham promised to give his host a call, and made his departure. Within a few minutes the last of the guests were gone, and the Morgans were contemplating the task of putting their house back in order.

The Milburns and John Britingham stood outside the cottage, exchanging small talk before going their separate ways.

"What did you think of *The Commodore* story? Did you get the deluxe version?" Dan asked with the knowing smile of one who had heard the deluxe version several times.

"It's a good yarn," Britingham replied. "What I heard of it anyway. I don't think he finished—people started to leave, and we didn't get around to the part about the inquest or raising the ship."

"You'll have to get George to tell you about the inquest, but I know they didn't raise *The Commodore*. She's still down there. George claims she lies in 140 feet of water. It's a pretty deep lake for its size. There used to be talk of diving down and taking a look for her, but I don't think anyone ever proposed trying to raise her. And the Morgans are dead set against anyone even going down and mucking about. It's become a sort of crusade of theirs."

"Seems a bit odd. I'd have thought they'd be intrigued with the prospect of recovering things from her, maybe finding something to add to their collection of memorabilia."

"You really didn't get the whole story, did you? It's Edna's aunt. He must have mentioned her."

Britingham had no idea what Dan Milburn was talking about and said so.

"This woman—barely more than a girl, I'd say—she drowned when *The Commodore* sank. There was one other fatality. They never recovered either of the bodies. Edna and George have a thing about desecrating her grave by disturbing *The Commodore*. It's like those people who've protested efforts to remove things from the *Titanic*. I guess something like that can raise some pretty powerful emotions."

"An aunt, you say. No wonder they're so wrapped up in lake history. I'll be damned." John Britingham regretted that he hadn't suggested staying for another drink and the rest of the story. He lived on adventure. It was life-sustaining oxygen for him. And the more he heard about it, the more *The Commodore* disaster seemed like an adventure. It was too bad the Morgans were opposed to exploring the wreck. It might be fun to look at it. Nobody else had done so, apparently. He could be the first. Britingham decided to pursue the matter with the Morgans at the earliest opportunity.

When the Milburns had gone and he was climbing into his car for the drive back to his house, John Britingham was feeling very good about the day. There had been that strikingly attractive woman he would have to get to know better, and now the possibility of doing some diving in Crooked Lake. Within the span of two hours, he had discovered Emily Hoffman and *The Commodore*.

———

It was generally agreed that Edna's side of the family was the more interesting. Both her people and George's had grown up in rural upstate New York, but George's grandparents and parents had never strayed far from the land that had nurtured them. At least one Fielder had been a different story. Edna's paternal grandfather, Henry, had grown up in the same region during the frantic decades after the Civil War, but he had caught the gold fever while in his thirties and had gone west, first to the Klondike and later to Nome when gold was discovered there, taking his wife and children with him as far as California. The Klondike had been a bust for Henry, but in 1899 he had become one of the most successful of those who sought gold in the Nome rush.

Henry Fielder was not, however, a practical man. He had never been quite sure what to do with his gold. His tastes were simple, and he hadn't gone to Alaska to make a fortune as much as to have an adventure. The months he spent there turned out to be the high point of his life; from that time onward his luck turned as he encountered one disappointment after another. The worst occurred in 1903 when his wife died at the end of an ill-advised pregnancy. Three years later, Henry himself was dead at the early age of 39.

John, the oldest of the two surviving children at 17, might have been able to make his way in California, but he had to assume responsibility for his younger sister, Elizabeth. The only family members in a position to lend a helping hand were back in New York, so John packed up their limited belongings, and they made the trip across country by train to the region in which the family had had its roots. John turned his hand to farming and in due course married, the marriage producing two children, a son, Amos—a charming, precocious but sickly child—and then, quite a few years later and to the surprise of all, a daughter, Edna.

But neither Amos nor Edna ever knew their aunt. Elizabeth had graduated from normal school and moved to Southport in 1912 to take up a position as an elementary school teacher there. Within a year of her arrival in Southport, Elizabeth was dead, a victim of the collision that sent *The Commodore* to the bottom of Crooked Lake.

It was not until a great many years later that Edna Fielder Morgan and her recently retired husband, George, decided to take up residence on that same lake. They were familiar with the area, having visited from time to time to see her brother, Amos, in a nursing home in Cumberland. When a suitable property became available on Blue Water Point, they had bought it. Edna felt an obligation to be near Amos, who was now an elderly man and who had no family of his own, and they had both fallen in love with the lake and its ever-changing moods. The decision was sealed when George, who needed a hobby to take up the slack of retirement, had discovered an old book in the Cumberland public library on one of their visits to see Amos. The book, which had been published in the late '20s and hadn't been checked out in several years, bore the unpromising title, *A History of the Crooked Lake Navigation Company*. George opened it and was almost immediately hooked.

———

When the last glass had been put away, the Morgans collapsed into overstuffed chairs in the room which George's hobby had created.

"I thought it was a success, didn't you?" Edna asked.

"Definitely, if you don't count the Snyders."

"I know. It's so sad. But otherwise, it's a pretty nice group. How's Mr. Britingham? You certainly spent a lot of time with him."

"Seems like a regular fellow to me," George responded. Edna had been sure her husband would approve of the man; after all, he'd listened attentively to George for the better part of half an hour.

George started to elaborate on his impression of John Britingham when the phone rang. He answered it on the kitchen extension.

"Mr. Britingham! We were just talking about you. Only good things, of course." Then he listened for twenty seconds or so.

"I don't see why not. Let me check with Edna." He cupped his hand over the phone and turned to his wife.

"It's John Britingham. Wants to know if he can come over for a few minutes. Says he forgot to give us a bottle of wine he'd brought along as a house gift this afternoon. I think he's eager to hear more about the lake, too. I promise not to keep him long. Are you tired?"

George was trying to be solicitous of Edna, but he was obviously anxious to regale Britingham with the rest of the story of *The Commodore*. Edna allowed herself a small sigh of resignation and said, "No, I am not tired," and, "Yes, he should come on over."

And so a little over two hours after he had left their party, John Britingham was once more sipping scotch in the Morgans' living room.

"I really shouldn't intrude like this. I'll bet you'd like a little peace and quiet." But their guest had made himself comfortable and gave no indication that this would be a one-drink visit.

"No intrusion at all," George assured him. "No one bearing a bottle of your good wine could ever be called an intruder."

Britingham, having made his polite if indirect offer to be on his way, got right to the subject uppermost in his mind.

"You left me in suspense, you know. But I think I just happened to learn something about that ship disaster from one of your guests as I was leaving. It was a personal tragedy for you, wasn't it, Mrs. Morgan? You lost a family member—an aunt, am I right? I had no idea. What a terrible thing."

"Didn't George tell you?" Edna seemed surprised. "Well, yes, it was my aunt, Elizabeth Fielder. George tells me that only four people were lost in all the years of steamship navigation on this lake, two in that accident, and one of them my father's sister. Of course I wasn't even born yet. I'm not sure I even remember it being discussed at home. Of course I later heard all about it, mostly from my brother—he sort of became the keeper of our family history. Anyway, it's funny how today I feel I know my aunt very well, even if she died fifteen, sixteen years before I was born."

Edna was now doing most of the talking. *The Commodore* was George's story; Elizabeth was hers.

"The poor girl was going to be married, you know. She was teaching in Southport. She hadn't been here very long, and she'd met this nice young man, a dairy farmer from around here. There was a school outing, and she'd taken her class on a picnic at Woodside Acres. I don't remember why he was there, but I guess they hit it off real good, and he began to come down to see her. Amos tells me it was a wonderful match. Amos—that's my brother—he knows a lot more about Elizabeth and that Conklin boy than we do. He has a whole box of Elizabeth's letters, all the ones that Gerald wrote to her while they were courting and all the ones she wrote to our father while she was in normal school and after she came here to Crooked Lake. Poor Amos. It's so sad. He can't talk since his stroke. Sometimes I think it's his memories of Elizabeth that keep him going. Imagine, memories of someone he only knows from letters. He's read her letters so many times they're all dog-eared. Especially her last one to Father, the one about going to see her beau and give him the gold."

"Gold?"

"Oh, I'm sorry, Mr. Britingham. I'm just rambling on about people you've got no reason to care about."

"No, no. This is fascinating. I'm sorry to hear about your brother's illness, but those letters—what was it you were saying about gold?"

"Elizabeth's last letter talked about her plans to take a steamer up to West Branch to meet Gerald and give him the jewelry so he could have it assessed. It was all she had, and it was like her hope chest."

George picked up the narrative.

"Edna's grandfather struck it rich in Alaska during the gold boom of the '90s." George figured he could stretch the facts a bit here. Britingham might be impressed. And rich, he rationalized, is a relative term. "Most of his gold he had made into jewelry for Elizabeth. And there were some other things she inherited. We understand she kept it in a little strong box. She didn't have much need for it, but when it came time to get married, she must have decided to use it to help them get started. Anyway, it appears she had it with her at the time of the accident."

Britingham found this news more than a little interesting. There didn't seem to be any hard information about the value of the items in the strong box, although George had spoken of a fortune. But there was apparently a letter that offered proof that she was planning to take the strong box with her on her fatal journey, and perhaps that letter offered a clue to the gold's value. Even if she had the box with her, there was at best a slim chance that it could still be found after nearly a hundred years at the bottom of Crooked Lake. But Britingham's appetite for diving, already whetted by Morgan's story of *The Commodore*, was further sharpened by this interesting new twist to that story. He would need a lot more information, of course, and equipment would have to be procured, but he could already feel the familiar tremor of excitement. John Britingham needed to be in action, even if it was on a relatively small scale.

"I have a proposition for you." Britingham had decided to approach the matter positively. Perhaps Milburn had overstated the case. "I don't want to appear immodest, but I have a pretty fair reputation as a diver. You may have seen the piece in the *National Geographic* on the *Salamanca* expedition, or maybe those stories on the Confederate frigate we found off the Carolina coast. I'd like to dive to *The Commodore* and see what can be recovered. There may not be much, but on the other hand there might be some interesting artifacts. You can have them; add them to your collection. The adventure would be reward enough for me. And we just might put Crooked Lake on the map again."

He had expected some resistance, but had not counted on the vehemence of the Morgans' reaction. He could see it coming. At the mere mention of diving, Edna had gripped the arm of her chair, her knuckles suddenly white. George's face reddened. If her reaction was one of fear, his was close to anger. It was George who spoke first.

"Mr. Britingham, I know you mean well. But we don't want that ship disturbed. There's nothing down there we want. Nothing!"

"It's Elizabeth's grave in a way," Edna explained. But her husband was less interested in explaining their position than he was in telling Britingham that diving to *The Commodore* was out of the question.

"We can't have it. We don't want anyone diving down there. We had a scare a few years ago when people at the state historical society began talking about exploring the lake wrecks, but it turned out to be just a lot of talk. We can't go through it all again. So, please, just let's forget it."

"I think you misunderstand," Britingham persevered. "I'd just locate the ship, take a look around, maybe get a few pictures. There are some very sophisticated cameras for underwater photography, you know. And I would think you'd love to have some tangible memento of *The Commodore*."

George Morgan was struggling to maintain his composure.

"I can't speak it any plainer, Mr. Britingham. We don't want anything from that ship, not even a picture. We want it left alone."

"What if you found Elizabeth? I don't think I could stand that," Edna said, her voice betraying the nightmare vision in her head.

"You needn't worry. Elizabeth won't be there, not after all these years. I won't be finding any bodies." He was going to explain why, but thought better of it.

"No, you're quite right." George was on his feet. "You won't find Elizabeth. You won't find her because you won't be going down to that ship. Go dive for the *Mercury* if you like. She's in shallower water anyway. But not *The Commodore*. I think it's plain how we feel about her."

Britingham had made no irrevocable decision to dive. There were records to check and logistics to consider, and before he got around to it, his interest might be engaged elsewhere. But he resented the proprietary attitude of the Morgans. The fact that they were telling him that he couldn't dive to *The Commodore* increased his resolve to do so.

"Maybe I've missed something," he said, "but wouldn't I be correct in assuming that no one has a legal claim to that ship anymore? I'll check it, of course, but I've had some experience in these matters, and I'm pretty sure I'm entitled to bring up whatever I please from her. I know I have a right to dive. And I'm sure she doesn't belong to you, so I don't understand how you can tell me I can't do this. What you mean is you'd rather I not explore the wreck. I'll certainly give your views some thought. But the decision is mine."

Edna started to say something, but George silenced her with a peremptory wave of his hand.

"I can see that I misjudged you, Mr. Britingham. If I had known you'd be so unreasonable, so disrespectful of our wishes in this matter, I'd never have told you about it. We're not young anymore. We don't need much or want much. We don't make demands of people. All we ask is that you—everyone—stay away from *The Commodore*. She's not important to you. You didn't even know about her until today. But she's very important to us. She's part of our lives, our family history. So leave her alone, for God's sake."

Britingham rose to take his leave. The tension of the moment could have been eased by a conciliatory word, even by a promise to sleep on it. But the two men were stubborn by nature, and John Britingham also had a cruel streak. He managed to have the last word.

"I've been trying to figure out why you would go to the trouble of creating all of this, this evocation of the steamship era, and then reject my offer to add a new chapter to the story. What are you afraid of? Do you think maybe I'll find there's nothing down there but some rotted planks, buried in the mud? That if people know too much, all the mystery and romance will go out of your Crooked Lake tales? Is that it?"

George did not dignify this speech with a reply as Britingham walked to the door.

"Thank you for the wine," he managed, his voice stiff and hard.

"And thanks for the scotch," came John Britingham's rejoinder.

CHAPTER 15

The first customer at Jack's Tavern on a sunny Saturday afternoon in June was tall and sunburned and walked with the slightly awkward gait of a man favoring a knee which had been torn up on high school football fields years before. He took off his billed cap and ran his fingers through the few strands of hair that could no longer conceal a nearly bald head.

"Afternoon, Hank." The man who was polishing glasses back of the bar smiled broadly as he greeted his customer. "Isn't this some day? No good for business, of course. Most folks don't want to sit around inside on such a nice weekend. No game today, huh?"

"Yeah, we're playing. The Moose Lodge, but not until four. Thought I'd take in a few innings of whatever game's on TV. Somebody said the Yankees were playing."

"Right. Yankees and Royals. Should be starting in about ten minutes."

The man identified as Hank pulled out one of the barstools and sat down. His big, muscular arms, like his face, were reddened from exposure to the sun and covered with freckles of the kind that would become so numerous over the course of the summer that they would merge in many places. It was clear that he was a regular in the tavern, and that he and the proprietor went back a long time. Jack drew a beer from the tap and set it beside his customer's cap.

Hank took a sip of the beer and shook his head.

"Glad it's the Yankees. Can't get very excited about the Royals, but it should be better than last week. What was it, Pirates and Brewers? Don't know why they do those lousy matchups."

"I guess they have to give 'em all a little TV coverage." Jack knew that Hank, a die-hard Yankee fan, wasn't going to leave in protest over the fact that the Kansas City Royals were the day's opposition. He looked at his watch, and then flicked on the TV set above the seldom-used cordials and brandies and turned it to the channel where an announcer was giving the starting lineups for the afternoon.

104

The tavern door opened and the man who entered paused and looked around. He was obviously unfamiliar with the place.

"Where's the cigarette machine?" he asked.

"Don't have one, but we've got cigarettes behind the bar. What do you need?"

"Make it Camels, if you would, please." The man fished in his pants pocket for his wallet. Both Jack and Hank thought he looked too well dressed for a Saturday afternoon in Southport. It was a very informal village, except on Sunday morning, and anyone dressed with the casual elegance of this man was sure to pique the curiosity of the locals.

"You must be from out of town." Hank spoke up, doing his best to be friendly. "Welcome to Southport. I'm Hank Bauer. And you're...?"

He put his hand out to the stranger, who took it in a firm grip.

"Pleased to meet you. I'm Johnny Bench."

Bauer's face displayed his puzzlement. He knew baseball, and he knew who Johnny Bench was. Who wouldn't? This man wasn't that Johnny Bench, Cincinnati's great Hall of Fame catcher. Probably just a coincidence.

"Johnny Bench? Like the guy who caught for the Reds?"

"Sure, Johnny Bench. Just like you're Hank Bauer." The stranger had a broad smile on his face, and he hadn't released Bauer's hand.

Hank blushed, his face an even darker red. Was this man making fun of him? The proprietor of the tavern produced a pack of cigarettes and tried to help his friend.

"Hank, here, is a real baseball fan, has been for years. He knows more about baseball than anybody. His name's Bauer—just like that guy who used to play with the Yankees back in Mantle and Berra's day. That's why everyone calls him Hank."

Jack looked proud, as if his friend were a celebrity.

"Oh, I see," the stranger responded. "You're not really Hank Bauer, is that it?"

"My real name's Norman, but we all pick up nicknames, I guess, and mine's been Hank for a long time." His eyes remained on his beer as he said it.

"So, okay, Norm, Hank. Whatever. And I'm not Johnny Bench. I'm John Britingham. And I'm not a stranger here, either. I live here. In fact, I own the Silver Leaf Winery. But I couldn't resist a bit of fun. I'm a baseball fan, too."

Norman Bauer was trying to cope with this information. Like everyone else in Southport, he'd heard of Britingham. More importantly, he even worked for him. How could he never have seen him around the winery? Probably just hadn't paid enough attention. Or maybe Britingham was one of those absentee owners who let his plant manager run things.

"I'm sorry, Mr. Britingham. I should have recognized you. I work at the winery—at your winery."

"No need to be sorry. I haven't been here long, and I've been pretty busy. Haven't been around the production areas. Guess I'd better get out of the office and meet the men. What do you do, by the way?"

"I just drive a truck," he said, and immediately regretted the apologetic tone he had used. "You know, that and odd jobs."

"Well, it's obvious I've got to get around more." He picked up his cigarettes and change from the bar. "By the way, what do you think of Bauer as a player?"

"Why, pretty darn good, I'd say." Norman, or Hank, was relieved to be given an opportunity to talk baseball, especially when it concerned his favorite team and his namesake who had played for it. "Didn't get the press that Mantle or Whitey Ford or Yogi or some of the other guys got, but he was a big part of those great Yankee teams back in the fifties."

Britingham shrugged.

"Maybe. Of course I don't know whether you ever saw him play. But the record book tells a different story. Did you know he had only about ten years with the Yankees, then kind of bounced around with a few other clubs before he hung up the spikes? Lifetime average nowhere near .300. Some power, I suppose, but nothing special. He wasn't bad, mind you. Just a capable journeyman ballplayer, I'd say."

Britingham walked through a patch of sunlight that fell across the tavern floor and over to the front door.

"Nice to have met you, Hank, and you, too—is it Jack? Your game's on. Enjoy it. I'll have to come back one of these days and join you for a few beers. We can watch the Yankees play. Thanks for the cigarettes."

After the door had closed, neither of them said anything. Jack fiddled with the TV set, seeking a sharper picture. Bauer drained his beer and stared at the empty glass. It was Jack who finally broke the silence.

"I wouldn't give it another thought if I were you, Hank. So what does he know? It's probably not true. About Hank Bauer, I mean. Hell, he's younger than you, so what can he know about those old-timers? You saw Bauer play, after all."

Jack had read somewhere a piece about bartenders as psychologists, providing therapy for their customers. He couldn't remember any of the details, but he saw himself as a therapist of sorts, tending to the needs of the guys who sat on his barstools. And Norman Bauer—Hank to his friends—was now in need.

The announcer was just reporting that the Royals had a man on base with one out, and Norman 'Hank' Bauer tried to focus on the game. It was better than dwelling on the unpleasant conversation with the owner of the winery. A couple of regulars had just entered the tavern, and Hank began to offer an impromptu color commentary on the game. Jack allowed himself a sigh of relief and started to fill glasses from the tap.

———

Norman Bauer was something of an institution in Southport. He enjoyed a reputation as the finest athlete the local high school had ever produced. In the mid 1950s he had lettered in three sports, quarterbacking the football team, playing first base on the baseball team, and somehow finding time between fall and spring seasons to lead the basketball team in scoring. His best sport had been baseball, but a knee injury sustained and aggravated in football had destroyed any possibility of what he and a loyal local following had hoped would be a big league career. The Philadelphia Phillies had been interested in him, and for a couple of years he had toiled for one of their farm teams. But the promise he had displayed in terrorizing pitchers from area high schools was never realized, and before he turned 23 he was back in Southport, working for the winery and playing semi-pro ball with pickup teams that went barnstorming through the upstate area on weekends when work schedules permitted.

In 1955 Norm had gone with some friends to New York, the trip a graduation present from fond parents who were pleased that their son, a fine athlete but a poor student, had finished school. They had financed the trip even if they could ill afford it. On that trip he had seen his first major league baseball game and, as luck would have it, the Yankees' Hank Bauer had enjoyed one of his finest days at the plate. Norm Bauer of Southport developed an instant and enduring affection for Hank Bauer from New York, and in time became, in his own mind and by the indulgence of his many hometown friends, Hank, too.

He read the box scores avidly, and scoured the record books for information about his hero, who became even more important to him as his own prospects dimmed. His interest in Hank Bauer's statistics gradually evolved into a fascination with baseball records in general, and in time Norm became the resident authority on the game. He could quote batting averages and a host of other figures, and he had strong opinions about such matters as who belonged in the Hall of Fame and who were the game's most overrated and underrated players. A good-natured man who had never complained about the great disappointment in his own life, Norm—or Hank—was well liked around the lake and always paid the compliment of a respectful hearing when he talked about baseball.

The conversation with John Britingham at Jack's Tavern had been very unsettling for Hank. People had always accepted him on his own terms. He was Hank, had always been Hank, or so it seemed, and even those who knew his real given name never kidded him about it. He was accustomed to enlightening others about the feats of this or that player. He was the trivia expert—it was his role, and a more important one by far than being a truck driver for Silver Leaf Wine Company. Maybe Britingham had not meant to belittle Hank Bauer the player. Jack had tried to smooth it over, but Hank felt humiliated in front of his friend nonetheless. He had eventually become engrossed in the game, and they had not talked about it again. But the afternoon had not been very enjoyable. He couldn't quite get Britingham's remarks out of his mind, and in the days that followed, he found himself brooding about them.

It is doubtful that John Britingham gave a further thought to the matter of Hank Bauer's statistics after leaving the tavern. Baseball was an interest of his, but it was only one of many interests, and other matters occupied his mind in the days following his meeting with Bauer. On the other hand, Britingham's knowledge was encyclopedic, and whether by conscious design or not, he tended to file information away in his head for future use. And so it was that the business of Bauer's hero-worship of his namesake was on file, easily recalled, like data on a great many baseball players, when Britingham next ran into Bauer.

It happened in late June, on a day when Britingham was practicing management by walking around. He had told Bauer he would be making an effort to get to know his employees at Silver Leaf, and it was on a hot Friday morning that he finally got around to the loading bay where Hank was working. It was much too early in the season to bring in the grapes, and on this particular day no bottles were being shipped; so the trucks were idle and the drivers were engaged in relatively routine maintenance. It was a slow day.

The black Mercedes passed under the gleaming metal tubes that carried the wine from the hill plant down to the bottling facility. It turned right and crossed the parking lot, past a row of forklifts, and pulled up alongside a low cinder block building that housed Silver Leaf's small fleet of trucks. One of the men was rotating tires on one of the trucks, and another was hosing the dust off another. The company insisted that its blue vehicles with their silver leaf logo on the door panels be kept clean and polished, a never-ending task due to the dusty roads that crisscrossed the vineyards. The rest of the men were gathered in front of the building, most of them seated on a long bench. John Britingham had arrived during a coffee break.

Everyone knew who their visitor was. Many of the men had never seen Britingham, but all Silver Leaf employees knew that the black Mercedes with the vanity plates belonged to the company's new owner. There was some momentary confusion. It was not possible to conceal the coffee mugs or simulate work, and the little group looked decidedly ill at ease as Britingham approached.

"Good morning, men." Britingham stuck out his hand and started a round of introductions. "I'm John Britingham, I guess you know. I should have been down here before this. No, no, don't put your coffee down—in fact, there wouldn't be a cup for me by any chance, would there?"

One of the men said he thought there would be and stepped into the building, where he quickly rinsed out a recently used mug and filled it from a pot on the coffee-making machine under the assignment board.

"Cream and sugar, Mr. Britingham?"

"No, thanks. Just as it comes from the pot." The owner was pumping the hand of a man who had been identified by his colleagues as a new father.

"Sorry, but I don't have a cigar in my pocket. Congratulations, anyway."

Britingham moved on to the next man in what now looked something like a receiving line. Recognition was instant.

"Mr. Bauer, it's good to see you again. I told you I'd drop by, and here I am. I'll bet you didn't expect to see me again so soon."

Britingham was right. Hank had not expected to see him again so soon, or here. He had doubted that the owner of the winery was really interested in meeting his employees. And he was not happy to be reminded of the unpleasantness in Jack's Tavern.

"Hello, Mr. Britingham. This is a nice surprise."

"Well, I don't know about nice. I'd be kidding myself if I thought you men enjoyed surprise visits from the boss. But I'm not checking up on anybody—just wanted to meet the troops. Is there anything I can do for you?"

Hank saw it as a dangerous question. There were things that most of the men would have liked the company to do for them, policies they would like changed. And there was, of course, the question of wages, which were never adequate. But they didn't know this man, and a candid reply to his question might get them into trouble.

"Not that I can think of. You might ask the other men, but I can't think of anything."

One of the other men, Fred Clarkson, spoke up, at first hesitantly, but then more confidently as the conviction grew that his suggestion was not going to be controversial.

"There is maybe one thing, Mr. Britingham. Our team in the Crooked Lake Softball League could use some new equipment. We're pretty good, you know, but our uniforms are kind of shabby. You ought to see the ones the Vernon Lumberyard team wears."

"Or the Moose Lodge," someone else added.

"Have you been over to our field?" Clarkson continued. "It's seen better days. It doesn't drain good after a rain, and the backstop's not solid anymore. I thought maybe we could fix it up and have ourselves a field and a team we could be proud of."

The men were watching Britingham's face for signs of his reaction to this safest of all requests that might have been made. He didn't disappoint them.

"No, I haven't seen the field, but I don't want anybody to say that Silver Leaf doesn't go first class. I'll get somebody on it right away. And the same goes for the uniforms. What about the rest of your gear? How many bats do we have? Bauer, why don't you make me a list of all the stuff the team needs. You're the baseball authority around here; you take care of it."

Hank felt a wave of uneasiness, but he nodded.

"That's great, Mr. Britingham. You ought to come to a game." Clarkson was enormously relieved, and obviously proud, that his proposal had been positively received.

"I'll do that, you can count on it. Who's the big stick in your lineup? Bauer here, I'll bet—but no, that's not likely, you're getting a bit long in the tooth for that, aren't you?"

"Hank can still hit with the best of 'em," a young man named Chadwick volunteered.

"Better than the real Hank Bauer, I should hope," Britingham responded.

"But Hank Bauer was a great ballplayer, Mr. Britingham," Chadwick protested. "He just never got the credit he deserved because of Mantle and Berra and all those big name players."

"Really? Where did you get that information?"

"From Hank here. He really knows all there is to know about baseball, and he says that Bauer was one of the best."

John Britingham took his cigarettes from his pocket and lit one, exhaling the smoke in a deliberate fashion. When he spoke, his remarks were addressed to the group, but his eyes were on Bauer.

"What makes you think our friend, Mr. Bauer, knows all there is to know about baseball? Nobody knows all there is to know, isn't that right, Bauer?"

"Well, of course, Mr. Britingham. I never said I knew everything." Hank was uncomfortable, and his friends, with the best of intentions, weren't making it any easier for him.

"Oh, come on, Hank, don't be modest." Fred Clarkson gave his companion a friendly poke in the ribs. "It's amazing what he knows, Mr. Britingham, really amazing."

"Yes, I'm sure it is." Britingham set his empty coffee cup on the end of the bench and turned back to Bauer. "Your Bauer's Yankees got into the World Series quite a few times in the fifties, didn't they? I'm sure you remember the year Larson pitched his perfect game."

"Hard to forget something like that, Mr. Britingham. It would have been 1956, against the Dodgers." Hank's friends beamed at this demonstration of his knowledge of the sport. Britingham would have to concede that he really was good. But Hank didn't like the situation. He knew what they didn't: that Britingham, in their first meeting in Jack's Tavern, had produced spur of the moment information on the real Hank Bauer's career that not one person in a thousand would know. This man knew a helluva lot about baseball.

"Yeah, I guess every baseball fan knows that," Britingham said. And then, casually, "I'm sure you know the Yankees won that series. Know who pitched the clincher for New York?"

"I think it was Johnny Kucks. Am I right?"

"Nice going. Amazing, isn't it, that those two pitchers really had ordinary careers—both lost more games than they won, neither got a hundred wins in the bigs." But in spite of Hank's knowledge of Larson and Kucks' performance in the '56 series, Britingham suspected that he was stronger on the Yankees than other teams, and that he probably knew more about batting than pitching stats. And he was right.

"Okay, so Larson and Kucks tossed shutouts in that series. But we know they didn't do it often. Know who holds the record for shutouts in a season? Let's be fair, and just talk about the modern era. Forget Cy Young."

Hank's hands began to sweat. He had no idea who owned that record.

"I don't remember," he said quietly, having decided that it was better not to guess and make a fool of himself.

"Bob Gibson, Cards, 1968. Now, I'm sure you remember the last pitcher to win thirty games in a season."

Hank thought he knew, but Britingham cut him off before he could respond.

"Denny McLain, back in the late sixties. But that's an easy one. How about the last pitcher to do it before McLain?"

Britingham was now bearing down, confident of his advantage. When Hank hesitated, he supplied the answer to his own question. "You must remember Lefty Grove—did it in 1931. But, hell, only real baseball experts would know that—right, Bauer?"

Clarkson, embarrassed for his friend, interrupted in an effort to shift Britingham's attention.

"Why do you suppose pitchers don't get so many wins any-more, Mr. Britingham? Are the hitters better today?"

"I wouldn't think so. Look at those great Yankee teams of the late twenties. Hell, everyone hit .300. Even guys you never heard of. They don't do that anymore. No, it's the relief pitchers mostly. Managers don't leave the starters in long enough to rack up thirty wins."

In a matter of moments a lively if somewhat awkward discussion was underway, with Britingham at the center of it. The men seemed to realize that he had put Hank down, but they found his ideas interesting, and they rather liked the novelty of engaging in so informal a discussion with their employer. Once or twice someone tried to involve Hank, but those efforts failed and after a bit he drifted away from the group and into the washroom in the corner of the garage.

He turned on the cold water in the sink and cupped his hands under the faucet and brought them to his face, repeating the process several times. He looked at himself in the mirror; he didn't look different, but he was sure he would never be the same again. He felt totally humiliated, miserable, sick inside. It was a feeling unlike any he had ever known. And it had all happened so quickly. Half an hour before he had been a contented man, loafing through an easy workday, chatting with his fellow workers, looking forward to the evening's softball game against old and good friends from the Moose Lodge. He could not see how he could possibly play in that game now. Everyone would know; everyone would be feeling sorry for him. They would try to cheer him up, and he couldn't stand that, or they would walk on by and say nothing, and that would be worse. He didn't see how he could ever talk baseball with these people again. He began to hyperventilate.

Later, after he had slipped away from the plant, Hank got into his car and drove for half an hour or more, up West Lake Road, then onto the road toward Cumberland, and finally down an old and rarely used dirt track that passed a couple of abandoned farms and ended beside a barn that had collapsed years ago but was still home to swallows and field mice.

He sat there in his car for a long, long time, until finally the sun was very low on the horizon. When he finally started the engine and turned the car around, he had largely overcome the despair that had gripped him earlier in the day. In its place he felt the first stirrings of a new sensation. Hank Bauer, normally a very kind and patient man, was angry.

CHAPTER 16

Grace Hess liked to think of herself as a tough old bird. No one who knew her would have wished to quarrel with that self-image. At 75 she was in better shape than most of her neighbors on Blue Water Point, including quite a few who were barely half her age. Seated in her spacious living room with a cup of tea in her hands, Grace was not a young-appearing woman. She had never had a facelift or dyed her hair. She wore her age like a badge of honor. But when she rose from her chair to perform some errand, the years seemed to fall away. When she walked, there was a spring in her step and she moved quickly. She was lean and firm, a woman accustomed to exercise, including gardening, swimming, and jogging, the latter a daily ritual, regardless of the weather.

But Grace Hess was tough in other respects as well. She was a hardheaded, unsentimental woman who had survived the death of her husband and then the loss of her only daughter and her family in a tragic car accident, all within the short space of three months some six years ago. She had occupied herself in the difficult period that followed with an extensive renovation of the Blue Water Point cottage, and turned to the stock market with a single-minded determination to convert her substantial inheritance into a fortune. None of her neighbors knew her financial worth; she didn't flaunt her money. But there was little doubt that she had been successful in the market, or for that matter that she would be successful in whatever she undertook to do. Once she had been a very sociable neighbor. Since her husband's death, however, she had become withdrawn—not unfriendly, but simply less disposed to become a part of the community on the point. Whereas most people in her situation would have welcomed and sought the support of friends to help them overcome grief and escape from loneliness, Grace seemed to find strength in solitude.

Her only companion was a golden retriever. Before Victor Hess's death, when they had divided their time between the city and the lake, a dog had been out of the question. The city was no place to keep a dog, and certainly not a retriever. But after Grace had sold their apartment and taken up year-round residence on

Crooked Lake, a dog had become possible and she had bought Jeff. She wasn't sure that the desire to own a dog had not been a decisive factor in the decision to move to the cottage. In any event, Jeff enjoyed the lake environment as much as she did, burning energy at a prodigious rate as he romped about through the woods and fields near the lake, chasing squirrels and otherwise behaving very much like a healthy specimen of his breed.

Grace led a relatively simple existence. She had trouble going to sleep, with the result that she often turned night into day. She frequently spent the late evening and early morning hours watching old movies. Her fondness for films from Hollywood's golden years provided her with an alternative to sleeping pills, which she refused to take. Whether she fell asleep at a conventional hour or at two in the morning, she was usually up and about no later than seven, at which hour she could be seen jogging along the gravel road behind the cottages on Blue Water Point. On especially nice days she often extended her run onto West Lake Road, frequently going as far as the roadside stand from which Scarborough Farms sold fresh corn and tomatoes in the late summer and apples in the fall. Grace Hess in her blue sweat suit was a familiar sight to neighbors like Mike Snyder and Larry Sanderson when they set off to work in the morning. More than once the men had been heard to vow that if Grace could stay in shape at her age by jogging, they should be getting more exercise as well. Her regimen was a goad to the conscience of quite a few of her neighbors.

She was also arguably the best gardener on the point. She had coaxed a variety of vegetables and flowers out of the inhospitable soil in the small plot near the boundary between her property and the adjacent lot, which John Britingham had recently purchased. There was too much shale for a truly impressive garden, but Grace persevered and, in addition to the pleasure she derived from getting things to grow, she was able to keep cucumbers and squash on her table and cut flowers in vases around the house.

Dinner was typically a private affair. She seldom cooked out; after all, people didn't build a charcoal fire to cook a single hamburger. Instead, Grace Hess stayed in her kitchen and whipped up omelettes or experimented with a wok she had purchased on a whim. Once in a while she accepted an invitation to dine with neighbors, but she had declined so often that invitations had become rare.

Grace remembered the last time she had been out for dinner. It was a day in June, and Rachel Milburn had surprised her one morning while she was weeding in her garden. She had found it harder to make an excuse in a face-to-face conversation than over the phone, and the Milburns, she knew, were intelligent and thoughtful people; so she had accepted their invitation. It was from Dan Milburn that evening that she had first heard of John Britingham's real plans for the development of his lakefront property. Her life had not been the same since.

Whenever she weeded and watered her garden or pinched deadheads from her dahlias, she could not help but see the shack which Britingham had put up beyond her garden plot in a small clearing on his property. Initially it had been an inevitable first step in his announced plan to build a small cabin so that he could have better access to the lake for fishing. The big home which Britingham had bought when he moved into the area was not on the lake, and she had understood his need for a place to put a boat into the water and had appreciated it that he had had the courtesy to speak to her and tell her of his plans. He had acknowledged that the shack was a bit of an eyesore, but insisted that it was only temporary, a place to store some equipment and, as he put it, to serve as a command post during construction of his cabin. He had described the cabin he planned with great enthusiasm—a single one-bedroom affair with combination living room and kitchen, designed to blend into the woods.

"You won't know it's there," he had said.

That conversation had taken place in early May and had done much to ease the anxiety she had felt when Britingham had purchased the undeveloped forty acres just south of her property. That land had been vacant for so long that everyone had taken it for granted that it would stay that way. Unlike the rest of the point, it had no natural beach. The beach, such as it was, extended in the shape of a wedge for perhaps thirty feet beyond the property line, but was crowded by an increasingly steep rocky bank and then disappeared altogether. For the next quarter of a mile or so the land dropped sharply into the water, often at an angle of nearly ninety degrees. This change in the topography of the shoreline had given Grace a natural barrier to the encroachment of the outside world, and she had come to think of this unspoiled, wooded area as her own.

Once Britingham had put her worst fears about development of the area to rest, she had seen his plan for the lot as a godsend. Soon there would be a small, unobtrusive cabin tucked away in the woods about fifty or more yards from her home. Its owner would come by occasionally to fish, but would rarely stay over and certainly wouldn't be entertaining there when he had a big, elegant home only a little more than two miles away. This was so much better than uncertainty about the future of one of the last undeveloped areas on this side of Crooked Lake.

But her peace of mind had been shattered that evening by the Milburns, who hadn't realized that Grace knew nothing of Britingham's more ambitious plans. Grace had first assumed that the Milburns had been misinformed, but Dan's informant had been Britingham himself, not some bit player in the Crooked Lake rumor mill, and the information was less than 48 hours old. It quickly became apparent that her new neighbor had either changed his mind or had been deliberately misleading her about his intentions. Either way, she was faced with a situation which seemed to her to be little short of a calamity: John Britingham planned not just to build a small cabin, but to develop the entire plot of land adjacent to hers, constructing as many as five new cottages on Mallard Cove.

She had tried to dissemble the rest of the evening, but it was impossible to give her full attention to any other subject, and she had politely declined the Milburns' offer of an after-dinner drink so that she could get away and think about what she was going to do.

———

As it turned out, Grace Hess did not confront John Britingham with the Milburns' information as a part of any plan which she had worked out. It was a spur of the moment decision that brought them together a week later. It was a pleasant, cloudless morning, and Grace had taken a longer route along West Lake Road than usual when she went jogging.

She had been thinking about her problem, as she had been almost continuously since the evening at the Milburns, when she remembered that the dirt road which branched off of West Lake Road near Scarborough's stand led to the old Keighly estate and John Britingham's home. She hadn't been up that road in years, although she recalled clearly the day that she and Victor had gone up there and, like a couple of kids on an illicit adventure, had prowled around the once lovely, but then empty and decaying, house. It would only be another tenth of a mile or so to the house, she thought, and she was confident that her wind and legs could easily manage it. And so she turned up the dirt road, partly out of curiosity about what Britingham had done in restoring the place, but largely out of a vague notion, just then taking shape in her mind, that she might meet the owner and confront him with the matter of his plans for his lake property.

The dirt road curved sharply for much of its short length, and the gradient was moderately steep. It was impossible to see the house until one was almost upon it. When Grace rounded the last bend, the mansion—and it was a mansion—came into view. It looked for all the world like a transplanted antebellum Southern home, complete with portico and two-story pillars, a fresh coat of paint gleaming in the early morning sun. It was immediately obvious that a lot of work had been done here; instead of a dilapidated structure ravaged by years of neglect and vandals, the house which Grace Hess beheld was a testament to what could be done if money were no obstacle. Work was not complete, as evidenced by a pile of lumber on the lawn, a power saw on the north veranda, and several windows where new frames had not yet been installed. There was a lot of landscaping to be done, and it was quite possible that interior restoration was still underway. But the Keighly estate, as it had been called for decades even though no Keighly had owned it since the 1930s, was obviously experiencing a rebirth.

Grace had only a moment to take in this transformation because John Britingham was standing not fifty feet away beside his car, a black Mercedes covered with a layer of dust from the road and the work area around the house. He was talking with another man, presumably a carpenter, and it was apparent that he was about to leave for work. Grace was suddenly much less sure that she wanted to talk with him than she had thought she would be, at least at this time and in this place. He said something to the other man and walked down the sloping lawn toward where she was standing, catching her breath and mopping the sweat from her brow with the sleeve of her jogging suit.

"Mrs. Hess," he called out. "What a pleasant surprise. Have you come all this way on foot? That's really remarkable."

"Good morning," she responded, not thinking her morning exercise had been especially remarkable.

"What brings you here?"

Grace decided that if she did not come right to the point, they would soon be engaged in an aimless exchange of false pleasantries. Moreover, she would look very foolish.

"Mr. Britingham, I'm glad I caught you before you left for work. Something's been bothering me and perhaps you can clear it up. When we spoke a while back about your plans for the property you bought down on the lake, you told me you were going to build a small cabin so you could have water access and fish when you wanted to. Now I've..."

"That's right. I am going to build myself a cabin. I hope to start as soon as this is finished." He gestured toward the house behind him.

"But now I've heard," Grace continued, "that you're going to subdivide and build a lot of cottages and sell them—that you're going to develop the whole south end of the point."

John Britingham frowned and made a point of looking at his watch.

"Who told you that?"

"I don't think it's important who told me. The question is whether that information is correct. I'd like to think I've been misinformed, that somebody has started a baseless rumor." Grace was trying to be firm without sounding unpleasant.

"I really can't imagine who—but, no, you're right, it doesn't matter. You want assurances that the point will not be—how shall I say it?—junked up. Tacky cottages, cheap places that will lure undesirable types. Well, Mrs. Hess, I can promise you that it won't happen—you have my word."

"That isn't my question." Grace could see where this conversation was going; the Milburns had been right. "Are you planning to develop the property or just build a cabin for yourself?"

"My dear Mrs. Hess, I'm sure you can appreciate that we are talking about a very valuable piece of land. It cost me a great deal of money. I'm a businessman as well as a man who enjoys fishing. I propose to put a cabin on that property. As I told you, it will be a small place that I can use from time to time, and it will give me a place to dock my boat. The rest of the property can't just sit idle. There's room for at least four or five cottages, as you can see. And they will be tastefully designed. Look at this place. It was a ruin, and it will soon be one of the finest homes in this region. Do you think I would build anything but quality cottages?"

Grace felt hotter than she had while jogging.

"You made it very clear to me that you didn't buy to develop and sell off lots. You know I don't want that to happen, and you gave me your word."

"Oh, come now. We had an informal talk about things, I suppose. But I made no commitment not to develop that land. I don't recall exactly what I said, but you obviously read more into it than you should have. I can't help that."

Suppressing her rising anger, Grace made one more effort to state her case.

"Mr. Britingham, my home on the lake means everything to me. A great part of the pleasure I get out of life comes from the tranquility of the setting there. It's so unspoiled. Your cabin is one thing, but full-scale development is something else. You'd have to take down a lot of the trees, carve up the shoreline, build artificial beaches with bulkheads—you'd turn a beautiful spot into a messy construction site for two years, and when you're done, it would all be crowded and ugly. It won't be an eyesore for you because you'll be up here in this beautiful home. But my home is there. I won't be able to get away from it."

But John Britingham had said all he had to say.

"I'm sorry, Mrs. Hess. As I said, I'm a businessman. I cannot afford to be sentimental. The results will not be as bad as you imagine. You're really making a mountain out of the proverbial molehill. Why don't you wait and see the results? I'm sure you'll be pleasantly surprised. Now, I have to go to work, so if you'll excuse me..." He threw her a mock salute and turned and headed for his car.

As he opened the door of the Mercedes, he called back to her.

"You'll be interested to know that we're moving forward. I've filed for a variance. We shall be starting work after Labor Day. Oh, I'd offer you a lift, except that I know that you joggers have a thing about accepting rides. Besides, I'm going the other way. Bye."

Britingham started the car and was pulling away when Grace called after him, "I'll fight you on the variance."

And then she was left in the dust as the Mercedes swung onto the dirt road and disappeared around the bend.

It had taken her a long time to cool down. She had been grateful for the fact that she had had to jog home; it had given her a chance to think about what she could possibly do to avert this impending disaster. She had threatened to fight Britingham on the variance, but she had done so as a way of having the last word, of not appearing to concede defeat. She was very doubtful that she could block him.

On the other hand, she couldn't see any other option. He owned the land. There was, unfortunately, no zoning or other barrier to his breaking that property up into as many lots as he wished. People wanted lake properties; a developer could market at hefty prices small lots with only a very modest strip of lake frontage—perhaps as little as fifty feet, enough for a dock and a boat hoist, just 'a piece of the lake,' as one of the more aggressive real estate agencies said in its ad.

And so Grace Hess was left with the issue of a variance. The county had an ordinance that forbade the construction of dwelling places on lakeside lots unless there was twenty feet of beach between the high water line and the bank. The purpose of this provision had been to preserve the natural shoreline of the lake insofar as possible and, even more importantly, to prevent construction which could create health or safety problems because of difficulties with septic tank placement, the routing of utility lines, and erosion. But the record showed that the county's board of supervisors had been very generous in granting requests for a variance, with the result that the ordinance had not been much of a barrier to development. Some contended that the ease with which prospective builders could obtain a variance was due to the dominant position of developers and their friends on the board. Others, less inclined to view local politics as an exercise in cynical manipulation and mutual back scratching, argued that the original rationale for the ordinance had lost much of its persuasiveness due to improvements in construction techniques.

Grace was well aware of this particular aspect of Crooked Lake's recent history, and she was inclined to the view that it was a developers' board. Nonetheless, she decided to try to block Britingham and went over to Cumberland a few days later to take the necessary first steps. She discovered that her new neighbor had indeed asked for a variance for the whole of his lakeshore property, and that it was intended to cover the construction of not five but nine cabins. Even in the process of admitting his duplicity, the man had tried to mislead her. She completed the papers that placed her objection on the public record and was told that she would be notified when a hearing was scheduled, but that it would probably not be held until after Labor Day. She checked the names of the members of the board of supervisors to see if there might be a potential ally among them, but found to her regret, if not to her surprise, that she knew none of them. Victor, she thought ruefully, would have had more contacts and probably would have had a better prospect of success in denying Britingham's request.

In the days and weeks that followed, Grace tried to stay busy and avoid worrying about the hearing. She polished the remarks she would make, and she believed that she had a good case, at least for people who treasured the natural beauty of the lake. She feared, however, that the board would not be disposed to see it her way in the best of circumstances, and that they would be particularly loath to deny the request of so powerful a member of the community as the owner of the Silver Leaf Wine Company. She considered canvassing her neighbors in a bid for support, but she was reluctant to involve them in her fight. The only neighbors whose view would be altered by Britingham's plans were the Sandersons, and he worked for Silver Leaf and could hardly be expected to take on the boss. The Milburns might go along as a matter of principle, and she was still debating whether to ask them when John Britingham paid her a surprise visit one evening in July.

Grace was sitting in an old leather chair, worn to a pleasant comfortability over its many years of service, reading a novel which she hoped would engage her interest but which so far had been disappointing. The lamp by her side provided ample light to read by, but in one of the few concessions she made to loneliness, she had turned on most of the lights in the living room and den, so that when Britingham approached the house he at first thought she must be having company. He had parked at the back of the driveway and walked cautiously around to where he could get a good look into the living room. He was relieved to see that Mrs. Hess was alone, and proceeded, now more boldly, to the back door where he knocked loudly.

Grace was unaccustomed to visitors at any hour, and especially at nine o'clock in the evening. Even so, John Britingham was the last person she might have expected. It was the first time she had seen him since their unpleasant confrontation in front of his mansion on the hill, and Grace was momentarily uncertain whether to ask him in or not. Common courtesy prevailed.

"Well. Now it's my turn to be surprised. Won't you come in?"

"Indeed I will," he replied, closing the door behind him. "I can see that we both have the same appreciation of quality workmanship. You have a very lovely home here."

"Thank you." Grace decided that if Britingham was going to be pleasant, she should try to dissemble. "We had it build about twelve years ago. I had some changes made after Victor's death when I decided to live here the year around. The kitchen has been remodeled, and I opened it up a bit with those picture windows."

"I'm impressed; I really am. I'm sure it's the best cottage on Blue Water Point. Do you have any idea what it would bring if you put it up for sale?"

Grace's face flushed. Was this man going to compound his offense by trying to buy her property?

"No, I don't, and I've never inquired because I like it here. I plan to stay."

Britingham walked about the living room, peering into corners, studying the large Persian rug, running his hand along the gracefully turned railing of the stairs to the loft.

"I can't say I blame you, Mrs. Hess. This house is—what shall I say?—a monument to good taste. And these lovely touches, clearly the best that money can buy."

He was looking at an obviously very old and very valuable stone lantern beside the fireplace hearth, but the remark had been intended to cover many of the room's furnishings, including an intricately carved sandalwood chest, a pair of museum quality oriental vases, and a variety of objets d'art and wall hangings, which gave the room a decidedly Eastern cast.

Grace Hess was proud of her home and agreed with Britingham's assessment, but there was something about his manner that she found disturbing. Why this carefully studied appraisal of the house, this self-conscious inventory of the contents of the graciously furnished living room? Why did he seem to be attaching a price tag to everything?

"Do you mind if I sit?" Britingham had taken a seat near the fireplace. She debated offering him coffee or something from the liquor cabinet, but decided to defer this gesture of hospitality until he had stated the purpose of his visit.

"No, of course not. Perhaps you could tell me, Mr. Britingham, why you have come. I appreciate your compliments, but surely you did not come here tonight to admire my home."

"You're quite right. I must come to the point. I wouldn't want to keep you up while I ramble on about your home. Although I must say, I am impressed." He leaned forward in his chair, as if to add emphasis to what he had to say. "Mrs. Hess, I am going to develop the property adjacent to yours, as you know. Those lots don't have a beach, so I have to build out and put in bulkheads; that requires the permission of the board of supervisors. I am informed that you are going to oppose my request, and I have come here tonight to ask you to reconsider your position."

Grace had half suspected this.

"I'm sure you realize that what you ask is impossible. We have already discussed this, and I think you know how I feel about the development of that land. You have complimented me on my home tonight. Can't you see how your plan would depreciate its value? And I'm referring to its aesthetic value. I have no doubt that its market value would be affected as well."

"I am asking you to withdraw your opposition to my request for a variance." Britingham spoke in a calm, controlled voice.

"Don't you hear me? I have said that I won't do it." Grace started to rise from her chair.

"Please sit down." Something in his tone of voice induced her to do as he asked. "Mrs. Hess, a lot of money went into this house. Where did that money come from?"

"Why, from my husband's business ventures. He was a very successful businessman. We always lived very comfortably, and he left me well cared for when he died. But what does this have to do with your property?"

"Perhaps nothing. But I think you should hear me out." Britingham had begun a rhythmic drumming with his fingers on the arm of his chair. "What were those business ventures of your husband's, Mrs. Hess? How did he make his money?"

"I don't see the point of this. Victor had a variety of business interests. I suppose he was most active in shipping."

"Yes, shipping. Would I be correct in assuming that he was a high ranking official with Conroyd?"

Grace answered in the affirmative, and nothing in her outward demeanor conveyed any sense of inner distress. But John
Britingham, she now realized, was a very dangerous man. He
would not have mentioned Victor's Conroyd association unless he
knew something about that company's difficulties and perhaps
even her husband's involvement.

"Let me see if I understand," Britingham continued, as if trying to demonstrate his command of an especially complex lesson.
"The Conroyd firm, your husband's company—I'm sorry, your
late husband's company—operates both liners on regularly
scheduled cargo routes and tramps that take on cargo wherever it
is available. Sometime about 1994 it is discovered that a Conroyd
freighter is carrying a very large cache of heroin. The circumstances suggest possible collusion between the traffickers and
company personnel, so the government starts paying close
attention to other Conroyd carriers, including liners that regularly
visit the Asian port where the tramp's cargo originated. And voilà,
within a matter of months, more drugs are found in Conroyd
cargoes. Do you know anything about this, Mrs. Hess?"

"What are you driving at?" Grace hoped her face did not be-
tray her feelings.

"I wondered if you knew that the investigation into Conroyd
was going to produce an indictment of your husband? Of course
his death pretty much closed the case. They got some small fry,
but the main man was gone, beyond the reach of the authorities.
You did know this, didn't you?"

"Mr. Britingham, the events you are describing, if they happened at all, are at least—what?—eight years old or more. I am
sure that my husband was not involved in any way in drug
smuggling, and I resent the implication that he was."

Her visitor got up from his chair and crossed over to the
nearer of the large oriental vases.

"Let me tell you something. For quite a few years I imported
goods like this from the Orient. I was pretty successful, too. And I
knew people. You don't get to the top in that game without getting
to know all kinds of people—in Bangkok, in Jakarta, in Hong
Kong. And of course in Japan. If I were in the business today, I'm
sure I'd have good contacts in Shanghai and elsewhere in China. I
don't need to go into detail with you, Mrs. Hess. Suffice it to say
that I have it on good authority from a man I've known for many

years that your husband had been a key figure in moving heroin out of Asia for some years before his death."

Grace Hess stared impassively at this man who was going to despoil the beauty of Blue Water Point and who was now exhuming a part of her life she had thought buried and forgotten.

"What I'm telling you is that all of this...," he tapped on the vase with one hand and took in the rest of the room with a sweep of the other, "...all of this was bought with money earned from smuggling heroin into the United States. What's it worth, Mrs. Hess? Can you put a price on it—on this art, on this house? Does it bother you that your happiness was bought at the expense of someone else's misery?"

"I think you had better leave, Mr. Britingham. You are a cruel man. My husband was never indicted, much less convicted of any crime. You have come here to insult his memory and to bully me. I've had quite enough. Now get out." Grace did not rise from her chair; she merely gestured toward the door.

But Britingham was not quite finished.

"You have done quite well as custodian of your husband's memory, especially with your story of his fatal heart attack. Don't you think that if we probed a bit we'd find that Victor Hess committed suicide—that he took his own life rather than face the scandal that would have ruined him—and you—had he lived? It's not a pretty picture, is it?"

By now, Grace's strength had ebbed out of her entirely. She looked every one of her 75 years.

"I'll be going. You needn't get up; I can show myself out." He paused for the effect it would create, and then, in a matter-of-fact voice, added, "I think it would be a very good idea if you withdrew your opposition to the variance."

The door closed quietly behind him, leaving Grace Hess alone and afraid in her beautiful home.

CHAPTER 17

Dan Milburn stepped back to survey his handiwork. It was a warm, cloudless June morning, and he was nearly half finished with the task of replacing the screens on his front porch.

Time for a break, he thought, and as he headed for the door he saw his next-door neighbor approaching across the lawn.

"Morning, Larry. Beautiful day, isn't it?"

Larry Sanderson returned the greeting and complimented Dan on the screens.

"Although to be honest," he added, "the old ones looked pretty good to me."

"Oh, they weren't bad, but you know how it is. Time on my hands up here; got to keep busy. Besides, I like to stay ahead of the rust."

"Do you have a minute?" Sanderson asked.

"Sure. All morning for that matter. You taking some of your vacation?"

Dan waved his neighbor to a beach chair and sat down in one himself. Sanderson was, as Dan knew, a foreman at the Silver Leaf Winery, and might normally be presumed to be working on a weekday.

"Just a day," Larry answered. "I needed to take care of some things. Look, I won't take much of your time. It's just that I've got a problem and thought maybe you'd be able to give me some advice."

"Glad to help if I can."

Dan waited, conscious that Larry both looked and sounded uncomfortable. The Sandersons and the Milburns were good neighbors, but were not particularly close. Whatever was on Larry's mind, Dan figured that he was probably reluctant to talk about it.

"You may have heard that the new owner of Silver Leaf has terminated contracts with some of the growers," Sanderson began, apparently having decided to plunge ahead.

Dan nodded, acknowledging that he knew of this development.

"Well, I'm one of those growers. My job is down at the winery, but I own about ten acres of vineyards up on the hill. Anyway, it's some of the viniferas they're cutting back on, and that's what I've planted—mostly Chardonnays. They're also shipping stuff in by bulk from Mr. Britingham's California winery. If the growers here want to sell their grapes, they're going to have to take a pretty bad price. It's way down from a couple of years ago. Some of 'em are talking about leaving the business."

"Sounds bad," Dan sympathized.

"I know Mr. Britingham has a right to make his profit. Hell, they get more grapes per acre out there in that California climate than we do here. I don't know, maybe even a ton or more. He's not going to pay us more than he has to. And if he wants to suppress competition from our viniferas, I guess he's entitled to do it, although it's a lousy deal after we've been encouraged over the last few years to switch over from hybrid reds to viniferas, especially Chardonnay and Riesling."

"I'm sorry, Larry, but am I missing the point? The situation is bad for our growers, but like you say, it's a business decision. How can I help?"

"I guess I'm having a hard time getting it out. Look, I'll have to make a decision about my vineyards. They won't be a total loss this year, so I'll give it a year or two and see what happens. But I'm going to lose money. The problem is that the growers have decided to make a collective appeal to Mr. Britingham to rescind the termination of contracts, or at least phase in a new deal between the growers and Silver Leaf. And I'm this year's president of the CLGA—you know, the growers' association—so I'm expected to make our case."

"Sounds like a reasonable strategy," Dan said. "You probably won't get exactly what you want, but it's worth a try."

"Yes, I know, but I'm in a bad position. From what I hear about him, Mr. Britingham doesn't like to be challenged. I work for him as well as sell to him. What if he sacks me, you know, uses my role in the growers' association as an excuse to get rid of me? My wife and I don't have a lot of money, Mr. Milburn. We've got a pretty big mortgage—big for us anyway, not to mention taxes on the property. I'm hurting if I can't sell my grapes, but I'm really in trouble if I lose my job, too. I just can't see how we could keep up payments on the house. And it means everything to us,

Chris especially. You live here, you know how attached you get to a place on the lake. It really is our life."

Sanderson paused briefly, then put his question to Dan.

"Could he fire me like that? Do I have any legal rights?"

Now it was Dan's turn to feel uncomfortable.

"Larry, the truth of the matter is I don't know much about matters like this. I'm no lawyer. In fact, it strikes me less like a legal matter than one of diplomacy. I assume you aren't union at Silver Leaf, that right?"

Dan knew the answer to the question, which Sanderson confirmed.

"My hunch is that you need to rely on Silver Leaf's sense of fairness, not on the law," Dan continued. "I can't imagine they'd fire you for making a plea on behalf of people whose livelihood is at stake. You aren't talking about threatening the company, after all."

"I know that. But like I said, Mr. Britingham doesn't take kindly to being criticized. At least that's what I hear. And we'd be criticizing his decision if we proposed he change it. They've already laid off more than ten per cent of the personnel without any notice at all. They'll claim it was for business reasons, not out of spite, but you're gone just the same, either way."

"Why don't you let someone else speak for the growers, if you think he'd resent you doing it?"

"It wouldn't work. He knows who I am. Even came by at the plant the other day and kidded me about my role in the association. Only I don't think he was kidding. I think he was telling me to back off."

From where they were sitting, the hills across the lake presented a lush, quiet picture at variance with the turbulence Larry Sanderson had been describing. Trouble in paradise? Dan had counseled patience and plain talk and had tried to sound optimistic, but he sensed that Larry had good reason to be anxious.

When Sanderson left, he thanked Dan for hearing him out, but he was no less worried than before about his job security. He and Chris agonized for days about the most effective and least dangerous strategy for approaching the company regarding contracts with the growers. It was ironic that Larry had become president of the CLGA. Many of the growers had thought it desirable for their spokesman to be someone who also held a position with the company, someone whose credibility would be enhanced by his status as an insider. Larry was a foreman in plant number three, where the riddling process occurred that removed sediment from the bottles of champagne, one of Silver Leaf's biggest sellers. He had been flattered to be chosen, especially in view of the fact that his acreage was relatively small when compared with that of many of the other growers.

But with the passage of time, that logic had seemed increasingly dubious, and Chris had finally persuaded her husband to follow Dan Milburn's advice and try to get one of the other growers to represent the association in bargaining with Britingham. It had been a dicey meeting, but his colleagues had reluctantly bought Larry's argument and named a three-man team to present their proposals to the company.

———

One day in late June, and before the CLGA had its meeting with company officials, Larry Sanderson received a note stating that John Britingham would like to speak with him. Although the note did not specify a time, Larry assumed that it was a matter of some urgency. He had never been invited to meet with the top brass in the winery, either under this or the previous ownership, and in spite of the cool temperature which was always maintained in this part of the plant, he found himself breaking into a sweat. There were only two reasons he could think of for Britingham to seek a meeting with him. One had to do with his job at the winery and the other with his role in the growers' association. He feared that Britingham would want to talk about both, and he doubted very much that he was going to be offered a raise or a promotion.

Larry went back to his cubicle of an office and called the owner's office. The voice that answered reminded him of the woman's which informed you that the number you were dialing was not in service.

"Mr. Britingham's office. May I have your name, please?"

"Yes, this is Mr. Sanderson in plant three. I have a note that Mr. Britingham would like to see me. May I make an appointment?"

"Mr. Sanderson, Mr. Britingham is waiting for you now. I'll tell him that you are on your way. Thank you."

Not even time to think about what to say, Larry thought as he put the receiver down. He ducked into the washroom. The face that greeted him was pale, much paler than that of most of his colleagues. He was light complected and burned easily, so he tried to avoid the sun, but today the pallor was also a product of the fear that gripped him, settling into his stomach and causing him to take hold of the sink for support. He took a deep breath and then ran a comb through his hair.

The main offices were located in an old building with thick ivy-covered walls that stood on a hillside above the rest of the winery. To get to it, Larry had to walk down a long concrete floor past rack after rack of champagne bottles, all inverted so that sediment would collect against the temporary stoppers that plugged their necks. Then he had to go through a covered walkway to plant one, pass through rows of fermenting vats, and eventually cross a parking lot to the main building. Larry walked at a brisk pace, trying to anticipate questions and plan answers.

The main building was a tribute to the fine art of public relations. All of the other buildings were triumphs of functional design; this one existed to impress the visitor who would be drinking the end product. It included a testing room, complete with magnificent bar, a small auditorium where visitors could see a film on wines and winemaking, and, inevitably, a shop where the public could buy Silver Leaf wines and assorted wine paraphernalia. As Larry went up the stairs and along the interior balcony that provided access to the offices and gave their occupants a view of the visitor center below, he made a mental note of the fact that recent layoffs seemed not to have affected the staff of public relations people who had absolutely nothing to do with the making of Silver Leaf's wines.

When he entered Britingham's outer office, he was greeted by a young, smartly dressed woman whose voice told him that she was the person he had spoken to only a few minutes earlier. He found it depressing that one so young should already have cultivated such a formal, humorless manner.

"Mr. Britingham will see you now," she said, even before he had introduced himself. How could she be so sure who he was, he wondered?

The inner sanctum, as Silver Leaf employees were wont to call it, was intimidating. The desk behind which John Britingham sat was immense; it made the room seem smaller than it actually was. Two corners of the room contained trophy cases, and they were full of gleaming silver and gold figures mounted on matching pedestals, a three-dimensional résumé of Britingham's exploits as a sportsman. One wall was lined with bookcases and seemed to contain an impressive personal library on enology. Had Larry had the luxury of time to study the titles, he would have found, in addition to many books on wine, a surprisingly large collection of books devoted to the history, folklore and geology of the region. The most bothersome thing about the office was the light coming through the wide curtainless window behind Britingham. It was so bright that it was difficult for Larry to see clearly the features on the face of the man across from him, and he sensed that the effect was the one Britingham desired.

"Mr. Sanderson, how nice of you to come and see me!" Britingham made it seem as if the meeting had been at Larry's initiative. "Please take a seat. May I offer you a sherry? It's some of the best, right out of our own cellars."

Larry Sanderson was not interested in a glass of sherry at this hour of the afternoon, but didn't want to offend his boss.

"If you're having one, sir, I'd be happy to join you."

Britingham pressed a button, and the formal young woman with the deep voice and precise enunciation entered the room mere seconds later, carrying a tray with two glasses and a cut-glass decanter of sherry.

"Cheers!" Britingham raised his glass, took a sip, and then, dispensing with further preliminaries, turned to the agenda for the meeting.

"This is a difficult business, Sanderson. As a businessman, I don't like to do all the things I have to do. Now if it were a hobby, it'd be something else. But it isn't. I'm in no position to be setting up unnecessary competition between some of the viniferas from around here and those we produce out in the Napa Valley. It would be a big investment and a chancy one. So what's the percentage? And frankly, we're overcommitted on some of the hybrids, too, especially the reds. People just aren't drinking the stuff."

He paused and leaned forward, elbows planted on the big desk.

"Do you follow me, Sanderson? Oh, by the way, please have some more sherry."

"Yes, sir. I still have some, thanks."

"Well, we all drink at our own pace, don't we? Now I think you see my situation. The growers are going to ask me to strike a deal with them. New contracts, give them time to shift to other varieties. You know about that, you're one of them. Frankly, I don't think it looks very good for one of my employees to be standing up with the growers against my policies. If Jamieson Farms and Fitch and the rest want to spit into the wind, why I guess that's their own business. But not one of my own foremen. I want you to disassociate yourself from the others when this big confrontation takes place."

"Mr. Britingham," Larry spoke up, weighing his words carefully, "I don't think of it as a confrontation. The group just wanted to present you with their problems, let you know how they're being affected. We thought maybe..."

"No, Sanderson." Britingham cut him off sharply, if softly. "I don't need the lecture. I know you've got problems. So have I. But what I'm trying to tell you is that my employees can't be on both sides of the fence. I expect you to support me."

Larry didn't know what he should—or could—say. Britingham was, in effect, exacting an oath of loyalty. And he was in the process of making his position even more dramatically clear.

"Let me tell you something about business, Sanderson. A lot of farmers around here raise grapes, sell some to Silver Leaf, and then open up those crazy little boutique wineries that are popping up all over. You know, those guys who set up equipment in their barns and bottle a hundred cases or so that they market with their cute little designer labels. Well, as the man said, I'm through being mister nice guy. I don't need to subsidize other businesses. It costs less per acre to raise grapes in California than it does in this climate. I'm not going to bore you with the figures, but I can do very nicely without some of these local vineyards. Very nicely."

Britingham got up from behind his desk and walked around to Sanderson's chair and leaned on the back of it so Larry had to twist around in his seat to maintain eye contact. He slapped his foreman on the shoulder, his tone suddenly avuncular.

"So you see how it is. There's no money in what you're doing up on the hills. Why don't you just concentrate on being a damn good foreman here at Silver Leaf?"

As if on cue, Britingham was summoned to his desk by a call from his secretary. Their conversation was brief.

"I'm sorry, Sanderson. I'd like to talk more, but I have a long distance call. Sounds important. You keep my advice in mind, okay? I'll appreciate that."

Britingham hovered over the phone until Larry had let himself out. The formal secretary never lifted her eyes from the desk as the foreman from plant three crossed the outer office and disappeared out onto the balcony above the Silver Leaf visitor center.

CHAPTER 18

Emily Hoffman's companion reached for the pack of cigarettes on the bedside table, went through the ritual of lighting one, and settled back on the pillows, pulling the lavender sheet up to his chest in an act of mock modesty. She had never particularly liked this habit of a post-coitus cigarette. Perhaps he saw it as a mark of virility or even sophistication; for her, it was merely a mundane conclusion to their moment of passion.

He turned to look at her and with his free hand traced lazy circles around the nipple of an exposed breast. It was an idle gesture, neither expressing affection nor seeking to stimulate her. Emily tolerated his wandering fingers for a few moments and then, gently brushing them aside, swung her legs over the side of the bed and sat up. She ran her fingers through her hair, now slightly damp from their exertions, and with her toes tried to locate her slippers.

"How about some coffee?"

"Sure. And maybe some cognac?"

"In your coffee?" Emily knew that was how he liked it, but the question was asked because he expected to be asked, and she wanted to please.

"Of course." And then, as if offering her a gift, "Take your time."

She stood up and bent over to extract the slippers from under the bed. She was conscious of her body and the effect her nakedness had on the man in her bed. The light from the lamp in the hall beyond the open bedroom door was flattering, she knew, and she made the act of retrieving her peignoir and putting it on a leisurely one.

Emily managed a wry smile as she moved to the kitchen.

We really are a pair, she thought. Herself a narcissist, she recognized another, and John Britingham was in a class by himself. If he gave pleasure, it was incidental. The act of making love was an occasion for him to show off his lean, hard body and for a woman to admire it, to feel gratitude that she should be allowed such intimacy.

My God, Emily thought, he even takes pride in his own erection, as if I had nothing to do with it.

She flipped on the light in the kitchen and mechanically went about the business of making coffee. She didn't really understand their affair. In the six plus weeks since they had first gone to bed, their only relationship had been sexual, a series of clandestine meetings when her husband was in the city. Even the sex had been disappointing, she had to admit. Only rarely had she reached her climax, and John gave no evidence that this troubled him, that he had somehow failed her. The excitement of their early lovemaking had given way to casual routine.

They didn't talk much. Occasionally he would launch into a story about some trip he had taken or a hunting or fishing exploit, but these monologues usually petered out when it became apparent to him that she didn't share his interests. She hardly ever mentioned her interests, which included interior decorating and ballet. She knew without asking that he would be indifferent and conspicuously bored. He was, very simply, not a good listener. In fact, she acknowledged reluctantly, they really were not compatible. Only sex sustained the relationship, and even that had begun to seem artificial, more like a glossy commercial for perfume or wine than the coming together of real people.

Emily found herself remembering the circumstances in which her affair with John Britingham had begun. It had been at an open house at the Morgans late in the spring. She had almost declined the invitation. The Hoffmans did not socialize, and in any event Alan had been in the city on business. She wasn't sure why Edna Morgan had invited her, but assumed it had something to do with the fact that they were neighbors, and that a failure to ask her would have looked like bad manners. Emily had decided to drop by for only a few minutes, and then excuse herself.

It hadn't gone as she had expected. The guests were not her friends, and most were not even people she knew. She had accepted a glass of sherry from her host and moved to a corner away from the buffet where she could survey the room and best avoid the awkwardness of idle conversation with strangers. It was there that John Britingham had spotted her.

He had maneuvered around a cluster of people to join her in her corner. She remembered that she had felt pinned there, her escape blocked by this handsome stranger whose sudden presence had seemed both threatening and intriguing. It had been his manner more than what he had said that had unnerved her, made her heart race even as she considered how to extricate herself from her disadvantageous position.

He had drawn nearer to her than the crush of people in the room made absolutely necessary, taking hold of her arm as if to protect her from the jostling crowd. It was some time before he released her arm, and by then he had introduced himself, learned her name, and complimented her on her dress and a finely cut topaz pendant she was wearing. She had been shocked, but pleasurably so, when he took the pendant in his hand to examine it more closely; the light touch of the back of his hand on her cleavage had been deliberate, she had been sure. She had recognized a practiced philanderer, and she should have excused herself and walked away. But she hadn't. She had enjoyed the frisson of excitement in their meeting.

Emily had no clear recollection of what either of them said at the party. Words had been exchanged, but they had been but a thin veneer of convention. Beneath the polite conversation there had grown a suspicion, and then a conviction, that she would have sex with this man. When the time came to leave, she had looked into his eyes as if to fix the moment, and then when she had turned to go he had let his hand trail across her bottom, a gesture so casual that it would have been taken as an unintended contact by anyone who happened to see it. She had understood the invitation.

———

No one could have been more surprised by what happened than Emily. She had led a monogamous life. Her marriage to Alan Hoffman had been comfortable—not exciting, but certainly satisfactory. It had never occurred to her to be unfaithful. There were no children, and although they rarely talked about it, they seemed to have reached a tacit agreement that there would be none. Some people are self-sufficient in the sense that their life has an inward focus; they are wrapped up in themselves and don't need lots of attention. Emily was such a person. She preferred to attend the ballet alone. She could lose herself in the mesmerizing mood that the music and the movement of the dancers created and not have to engage in intellectual discussions with a companion about whether the choreography in one production was better than in another. She enjoyed poring over magazines like *Architectural*

Digest and *Southern Living*, a solitary activity. And while not a trained artist, she had a flair for design and took pleasure in planning and sketching changes in their lake home's decor, some of which she had turned into reality, although few people other than Emily and Alan ever saw the results.

Her wardrobe was extensive, and shopping for it probably her greatest pleasure. The lake country didn't begin to provide the range of shops that the city did, but a few places had been opened in the area that were sustained by people who pretended to enjoy the rough informality of the country but really preferred to bring their carapace of luxury with them on vacation. And from time to time she accompanied Alan to the city, both to attend the ballet and to go on a clothes-buying spree.

When they purchased the lake property, it had been their plan to use it as a second home, a place for summer vacations and long weekends. But they had both become more attached to it than they had anticipated, and before many months it had become clear that their home was on Crooked Lake and that the city apartment would be Alan's pied-à-terre. At first he had had trouble adjusting to the separation, but it wasn't long before they had settled into a routine which neither of them minded. Although they may not have said so to each other, both Emily and Alan actually came to like the new arrangement. It gave them a freedom they hadn't experienced before, and both realized that they enjoyed it.

Alan Hoffman typically left Crooked Lake for the city late on Sunday afternoon and returned Friday evening. Once every month or so, the press of business would keep him away for two weeks at a time. He made it a practice to phone Emily from their city apartment each evening; he always called at or near 10:30 so that he could watch the eleven o'clock news. It had been Alan's adherence to a predictable schedule that made it possible for Emily and John Britingham to hold their assignations on weeknights after midnight without fear of interruption. Indeed, the Hoffmans were very much committed to a lifestyle that suited Britingham's purposes admirably.

The last weekend in June had been particularly gray and damp, the kind that sends people with short vacations into fits of depression as they watch the days slip by without a chance to improve their tans. No such worries troubled Emily and Alan. They did not cultivate tans. Emily was as pale in July as in January; she pampered her skin, which had a luminous porcelain-like quality and was, she believed, her best feature. Alan's lack of interest in the sun had nothing to do with concern for his complexion or the danger of skin cancer. He simply did not care for outdoor activities, preferring to spend his weekends reading, working on jigsaw puzzles, and practicing his considerable culinary skills.

On this rainy Saturday morning, Alan had indulged himself, staying in bed to finish a novel he had been working on for two weeks. While he could have taken it to the city with him and finished it in an evening or two, that would have been contrary to routine. Novels were for lake reading. His city reading consisted of whatever files and papers were in his briefcase, and it was always full. He had made himself a promise never to bring his work to the lake, and the price he paid to keep that promise was many a long, hard evening between Monday and Thursday.

Emily had made corn muffins, and they had eaten in bed, an uncommon treat. She had cleared the dishes and, leaving him to his book, had retired to the large and elegant bath-cum-dressing room which had become her private retreat.

Later, the book finished, Alan debated whether to shower and shave first or put a few pieces in the giant puzzle, which covered the table in the den. He was not compulsive. Puzzles of this size, with upwards of 2000 pieces, took a long time to complete, but he did not like to pass the table without fitting at least two or three pieces into the emerging picture, in this case a reproduction of a Monet painting. Pleased with the prospect of a lazy day, Alan climbed out of bed, shaking a piece of the corn bread that had become trapped in the bedding onto the carpet as he did so. When he stooped to pick it up, he spotted a book of matches under the dust ruffle of the bed near the nightstand, and he picked it up along with the corn bread.

The matchbook was one of those with embossed lettering; his fingers told him that before he saw it. Once, as a boy, he had collected matchbooks, and he had particularly prized the special ones with fancy artwork and embossing. He felt a moment's twinge of nostalgia for those simple pleasures, and realized that he couldn't remember what had happened to that collection—or, for that matter, to his stamp albums. Probably his mother had found them in a box in the attic after he had gone away to college and, knowing that he had outgrown those interests, had tossed them out in one of her thorough spring cleanings.

Alan turned the matchbook over and learned that it had come from a restaurant called The Silver Peacock, identified as San Francisco's finest. It was a classy piece of graphic design, silver on silver, with a peacock, tail spread in display, behind the lettering. Quite a few of the matches were gone, and the book looked as if it had been sat on or crushed in a pocket or purse.

Just then, Emily came into the room, still in her dressing gown and with her hair wrapped in a towel, turban style. Alan waved the book of matches in her direction.

"Where do you suppose these came from?" There was no suggestion of suspicion in his voice; it was a matter-of-fact question.

But there was nothing matter-of-fact about Emily's reaction. She couldn't see the lettering on it, but she could see that it was a matchbook in her husband's hand, and she knew immediately that she was in danger. She struggled to maintain her composure, to conceal the alarm that she felt and to find words that would deflect his curiosity. Emily knew, and she knew that Alan knew, that usually there were no matches in the Hoffman cottage other than the long ones in the cylindrical pot on the hearth in front of the fireplace. She used a cigarette lighter; Alan didn't smoke. Of course either one of them might have picked up a book of matches at a restaurant or bank or someplace, but the scene in front of her—Alan standing by the bed, a matchbook in his hand—suggested one thing only: John had left his matches, she had not noticed them when she had made up the room, and Alan had discovered them.

"I've no idea. What do they say?" She walked over and took the matchbook from her husband and studied it. The San Francisco address confirmed her worst fears. It might have been possible to explain the presence by their bed of matches from a local establishment; they would have left some room for creative fabrication. But San Francisco was a different matter. John Britingham traveled back and forth to the Bay area regularly. Emily had never been there. If Alan were to view this as a puzzle to be solved—and he did like to unravel mysteries, such as the identity of the sender of an unsigned Christmas card, or the source of a familiar but elusive quotation he had heard somewhere—if Alan decided he must get to the bottom of the mystery of the San Francisco matches, she had no doubt he would discover her affair with John Britingham. It wasn't that Alan was by nature suspicious or untrusting. But he was logical, and he was patient, and he would find her out.

"I can't imagine where they came from. Maybe they were in an old jacket pocket and fell out when I was reorganizing the closet last week. I had the stuff all over the bed." She hoped that she sounded appropriately matter-of-fact; she had tried to finesse the San Francisco origin of the matchbook by ignoring it.

Emily dropped them into the wastebasket. She knew that Alan could fish them out later, if he wanted to, but she thought that casually tossing them out would be less likely to arouse Alan's suspicions than pocketing them. Then she changed the subject.

"You know, I came in here for something..." She let the sentence trail off inconclusively while she made a point of searching the top of the dresser. "Oh, here it is. I'll be out in just a few more minutes."

Emily picked up a hand mirror from the dresser and returned to her dressing room sanctuary.

Alan stood pensively where he had been since his wife entered the bedroom. Something wasn't quite right. One thing that wasn't right was the mirror. The bedroom dresser held a few of her things, but they were mostly his. She had a much larger dressing table in the adjoining room, and on it was everything a well-groomed woman would ever need or want. He knew that she had a lovely tortoise shell mirror in her own dressing room. He didn't remember her ever using the one she had just taken from his dresser, and he couldn't understand why she had wanted it now. There had been something in Emily's manner, too. Nothing pronounced, just a hint of—what was it?—a tenseness?

He turned this vague feeling over several times in his mind. It made no sense. Was it the matchbook? But why would Emily be uncomfortable talking about something so small and insignificant as a book of matches? Maybe there had been something else on her mind that had distracted her. That had to be the explanation. He wanted to know what was bothering her, but he knew he wouldn't ask. Both of them had long since made a tacit bargain: none of those "what's wrong?" and "nothing's wrong, why do you ask?" exchanges that invariably ended unpleasantly. He tried to reassure himself with the thought that if the problem had been at all important, she would have shared it with him. But he didn't find the thought terribly reassuring. He realized that there were probably many things that Emily didn't share with him. She had cultivated a private life, and he had respected it. The result, he had to admit, was that after nearly thirteen years of marriage, they were in many ways still strangers to each other.

Alan went to the wastebasket and picked the book of matches out from the nest of used Kleenexes and looked at it again. The Silver Peacock. San Francisco. San Francisco. The Silver Peacock. He stared at the small crushed piece of cardboard, uncomprehendingly, then dropped it back into the wastebasket and went into the den to work on Monet's *Le Jardin de Giverny*.

PART III

INVESTIGATION: ONE STEP FORWARD, TWO STEPS BACK

CHAPTER 19

The responsibility for performing autopsies and officially pronouncing the cause of death in Cumberland County belonged to Dr. Henry Crawford, a somewhat rotund man who might have been described as a teddy bear except for the fact that he was completely bald. He was invariably cheerful, a quality that some were known to find a bit much, especially when they did not share his mood. On the morning of the day following the discovery of John Britingham's body on the Whitman dock, Crawford stuck his head through the door of Sheriff Kelleher's office and put on a mock stern expression.

"What are you doing, Sheriff? Gathering wool? Don't you have something to do, like solve a crime?"

"Dr. Crawford!" Carol was out of her seat and across the room, hand extended to the man who had long been a friend of her father's. "I was just about to call you."

"Please, I've always been Henry to the Kellehers. Although, come to remember it now, your mother, bless her soul, used to call me Doc. How're you liking law enforcement?"

"So far, so good, but I'm kind of uneasy about this Britingham business."

"Well, I thought I'd give you my professional opinion on that one in person. Worked on it most of yesterday and half the night—figured you'd be wanting a quick report. Write-up isn't complete, but I can tell you what it'll say. Interested?"

"What do you think? I've been on pins and needles for more than 24 hours." The sheriff hadn't expected him to pay her a personal visit, but she wasn't exactly surprised. He would be as fascinated by this case as anyone else, and would welcome the chance to see how Carol reacted to what he had to tell her, not to mention the opportunity to get a firsthand report on the progress of the investigation.

"I wish I could tell you it had been a shark attack," he said with an exaggerated guffaw. "Something exotic. But you'd just tell me there aren't any sharks in Crooked Lake. No sense of humor, Carol. That's what you need, a sense of the ridiculous—like your dad."

In spite of the banter, this was a big moment for Henry Crawford. Like Sheriff Kelleher, he was a small-town official who was faced with a case which could attract a lot of attention, and both of them were most anxious not to mishandle it.

The doctor perched on the edge of the sheriff's desk and polished his glasses with a tissue. His position was a part-time one. He was a pathologist who had moved upstate many years before to escape the pace of the city, which he had found intolerable. His specialty was in limited demand in the quiet, mostly rural area around Cumberland, however, so he had gradually retooled and become a general practitioner. He now divided his time between sustaining life and explaining the cause of death. The Britingham case posed a problem or two, but fortunately it was relatively straightforward.

"What do you want to know first—when or how?"

"It's your report, Henry. It's all important."

"Okay. Let's start with the easy part. I'll tell you what didn't happen. The guy didn't drown. He was already dead when he went for a swim. Condition of the lungs tells us that. In fact, he was hardly in the water at all. That's just a red herring. What did him in was a one-two knockout punch—the knife in the gut and the crack on the head."

Carol's eyes widened with this news.

"He got hit on the head, too? Damn, I missed that. What with?"

"Don't know. And don't feel too bad about it. He had a lot of hair. And the gut was such a mess, there probably didn't seem to be any reason to look any further. Anyway, he took a blow on the left side of the skull just below the suture between the parietal and occipital bones. Whatever hit him—or he hit—was very hard and very sharp, and it was no tap."

Crawford had been willing to excuse her for failing to see the head injury, but Carol was upset with herself for missing it. The doctor might chalk it up to her inexperience, but Carol knew it was just plain carelessness, and that she could not afford.

"So what are you telling me—that somebody whacked him on the head?"

"Can't be sure. But it's highly unlikely. It's the occipital that took the force of the blow, and it's too low. You hit somebody over the head with enough force to do that kind of damage, you'd have to come down on the skull from above. So I'd say the trauma was probably the result of a fall. Probably, mind you.

"Now, about the abdomen, his gut looked like he'd taken shrapnel on the battlefield. Or maybe tried to commit hara-kiri. And it almost certainly was a knife, and a fairly long one at that. It looks like it was plunged in with a lot of force, and then either the guy with the knife jerked it hard to one side or Britingham fell sideways with the knife still in his gut. It didn't bleed as much as you might think, but it sure tore up his innards."

"So what killed him?"

"No way of being absolutely sure," Crawford answered, aware that his uncertainty would be disappointing to the sheriff. "Either one could have done it. The knife wound might not have finished him if he'd gotten medical attention immediately, but it's pretty likely that the crack on the noggin would have left him unconscious, so he wouldn't have been in any shape to get the medical help he needed, at least not on his own. I'm assuming the two wounds were incurred at the same time. Can't prove that either, but the evidence says that they were both very recent. You want me to tell you what I think? I'd bet he got knifed, and then fell and cracked his head."

"Could he have done it himself, I mean stabbed himself?"

"I suppose so, but if he did, it was almost surely an accident. People just don't commit suicide that way. We aren't into hara-kiri."

"You don't think it was an accident, though, do you?"

"Well, no, but there's something else you ought to know." Crawford was going to further complicate Sheriff Kelleher's investigation. "Britingham had a helluva lot of alcohol in him. I mean enough to be rip-roaring drunk. So he could have been unsteady enough to have had an accident."

"Then why do you believe somebody stabbed him? You make it sound as if an accident would have been just as likely."

"Because if he stabbed himself with enough force to do that kind of damage, he'd almost certainly have done it by falling on the knife. And that would mean falling forward. Yet it's the back of the head he landed on. But if someone stabbed him, the force of the blow could have pushed him off balance, so he'd fall on the back of his head."

Carol looked skeptical.

"We're speculating now, aren't we?"

"Right. Sorry, but it's not an exact science, you know."

"You can't be sure, then, can you, whether he was able to move around after he was stabbed?"

"Can't be sure, but I'd bet he didn't go anywhere. The shock to the system from a wound like that would probably have put him out of commission, even if he wasn't unconscious from the blow to the head. And it's hard to believe he wouldn't have been—unconscious, I mean."

Carol shifted the subject from one area of uncertainty to another.

"When did this happen?"

"You want more guesswork? Well, one thing I know is that Britingham had been dead for a while before that man found his body. Not long, but a few hours. Rigor had begun to set in, but wasn't complete. Gamble's report on the temperature of the body helped, too. I'd say he died somewhere between eleven p.m. and three a.m. That good enough for you?"

The sheriff was doing some quick mental arithmetic.

"What that means is Britingham was already dead when Whitman—he's the one who found him on his dock—when he went swimming. And if I'm to believe him, the body wasn't on the dock then, but was there a good half hour or more later. Which means the killer—or somebody—went to the trouble to put a man who'd been dead for at least a couple of hours on Whitman's dock while he was taking his early morning swim. Now, why in hell would he do that? And where was the body all that time?"

"I'm glad that's your worry, not mine," Crawford said. "Anyway, I'll get a written report to you right away. It'll contain all the usual medical mumbo jumbo, so you can sound appropriately erudite."

The doctor waited, obviously hoping Carol would have something to say about her fledgling investigation. But she already seemed absorbed in contemplation of the information she had been given, turning it over in her mind, trying to decide where it might lead. One thing for sure: it hadn't clarified matters nearly as much as she had hoped it would.

Kevin had finished putting away the breakfast dishes and found himself contemplating the kitchen bulletin board where he posted shopping reminders. His eyes rested on a list of phone numbers. The morning before he had called 911, but he had since looked up the sheriff's number and had added it to his list. He hoped it wouldn't be a number he would need to call frequently, but at the moment he felt an urge to talk with the sheriff. His motives, largely unexamined, were, he realized, mixed.

There was, of course, the matter of simple curiosity. What, if anything, had the sheriff learned since their conversation of the previous day? Other people would be curious as well, and the sheriff could hardly be expected to give every caller a report on her investigation. But Kevin saw himself as a special case, the man whose report of the discovery of Britingham's body gave him a compelling reason for wanting to know what the sheriff was doing and thinking. Self-interested curiosity, yes. But he was fascinated by the puzzle of the body on his dock, and the idea that he might solve that puzzle, or at least share in finding a solution, had taken root in his mind. And then there was Carol Kelleher. She had never mentioned her given name, but Kevin had made a mental note of it when he looked up the sheriff's phone number. Sheriff Kelleher and Carol Kelleher were one and the same person, but he found himself, almost unconsciously, separating the two. Who was she? Aside from being sheriff of Cumberland County, that is?

It was nearly ten o'clock when he put the call through. By that time the sun was well up in the morning sky, the Brocks' grandchildren were at play in the lake, and Kevin's house was in order. He was lucky. The sheriff was in, and her secretary connected him immediately, thinking, no doubt, that the sheriff would want to listen to whatever this key figure in the Britingham case might have to say.

"Morning, Mr. Whitman. Been swimming yet today?"

"No, but I've been thinking about yesterday morning and that man being on my dock. We agreed, I think, that it was unlikely he could have climbed out of the water at the end of the dock where I found him. Well, I thought it would help if I could come up with a precise figure of the depth of the lake there. So I measured it myself this morning. It's six feet four inches. I even tried to pull myself out of the water, but with no ladder there, I couldn't do it."

"You called to tell me that?" The sheriff sounded unimpressed with Whitman's information. "I thought it was pretty obvious when I looked at it yesterday. And by the way, the way we work, my department does the research—we don't rely on the public to do it for us, especially people who are technically under suspicion themselves."

Kevin hadn't believed that the measurement was very important, but it had given him an excuse for his call to the sheriff. Now he felt like a fool.

"Well, I guess it was obvious," he said lamely. "I just thought, you know, that..."

The sheriff interrupted.

"Look, I didn't mean to be rude. But the depth of the lake at the end of your dock is moot. Do you want to know why? Facts. You've got a theory about how Mr. Britingham got onto your dock, or rather how he didn't get there. But I've got the facts. Britingham was almost certainly dead by at least three a.m. Very drunk and very dead by three a.m. I just got the autopsy report. So unless we've got a reenactment of *Night of the Living Dead*, he didn't climb onto the dock or wander out to the end. Somebody put him there."

The sheriff paused.

"Unless, of course, it didn't happen the way you say it did—like maybe you didn't find him there after your swim, you put him there. How's that for a theory?"

"You don't really believe that, do you?" Kevin protested.

"I suppose I could, but no, I don't. Anyway, you see how solving one problem doesn't clear up the whole mystery. So officially, I still suspect you. I suspect everybody. But thanks for the call. Oh, and by the way, I'm going to insist that you not tell any of your neighbors what I've told you about the time of death. Don't tell anyone, do you hear me? I want to be the one to do that."

Kevin cradled the phone and gnawed at a fingernail. What was he to make of that? He didn't think he had made any headway in his quest for a better relationship with Carol Kelleher. She was still wearing her sheriff's hat, and she had not been impressed with his stated reason for calling. On the other hand, she had shared important information with him, which strongly suggested that she had crossed him off her list of suspects, even if that didn't constitute an invitation to help her in the quest for Britingham's killer.

His mind turned to what now appeared to be the big question: where was John Britingham's body between three and five o'clock on the fateful morning?

————

Later that morning, Kevin decided to take a quick dip before lunch. There was too much boat traffic on the lake for serious swimming, but the water would be refreshing. A number of his neighbors were paddling about in the area, including Billy and Darrell Keyser, who were busy trying to dislodge each other from their floats. Billy, being the larger, was having the most success, but Darrell seemed not to mind the occasional ducking.

Kevin was simply floating comfortably on his back when one of the boys bumped into him.

"Sorry, Mr. Whitman, we didn't see you." It was Darrell, clinging to what looked very much like an inflated shark.

"I saw him, dumb-o. I told you to look out." Billy wanted there to be no doubt about responsibility for the collision. It wasn't his alligator that had done it.

"Hey, I'm okay," Kevin laughed. "Those are great floats."

"Yeah," Darrell was quick to agree. "This one's Jaws."

"They're okay—for kids, really." Billy sounded as if he was ready to graduate from sharks and alligators.

"You boys got to see some pretty heavy stuff yesterday, didn't you? It was awful, but I'll bet your friends back home will be impressed when you tell them."

"Do you think they'll believe us? I mean about seeing this dead guy—you know, seeing him alive and then—bam!—seeing him dead?" Billy was sitting on his alligator, earnestly seeking an opinion from the neighbor on whose dock the body had been found.

Kevin had been ready to swim back to shore and towel off for lunch, but Billy's question made lunch suddenly less urgent.

"You saw that man before he was killed? I mean before you saw him on the dock?"

"Sure. Like I told the sheriff, we saw him walking around out back."

"You did? That's great! Maybe you can help solve the crime. When did you see him?"

"Oh, maybe five o'clock. Sun wasn't up yet, but it was beginning to get light. Light enough to see him."

Kevin had had no experience in getting the whole truth and nothing but the truth from children, but he knew he couldn't simply leave the matter at that.

"It's lucky you saw Mr. Britingham—that's the man's name. But we may have a problem. From what I hear, he was killed some time in the middle of the night." He paused, uneasy about what might be construed as a violation of the sheriff's injunction not to talk about the time of death. "Does it bother you to talk about this?"

Both boys seemed quite eager to discuss the murder, so Kevin set his misgivings aside and went ahead, spurred on by curiosity to find out what, if anything, they had in fact seen.

"Like I said, it looks like he was killed in the middle of the night. But you saw a man. Maybe it was someone else, or maybe it was Mr. Britingham, but at some other time. What do you think?"

Billy upended his alligator and swam over to the shark for a few whispered words with Darrell. The conversation over, he paddled back to where Kevin was treading water.

"If I tell you a secret, will you promise not to tell Grandma?" Billy inquired.

"Of course. You can tell me anything." Kevin wasn't sure how he would deal with his conscience, but he wasn't going to lose the opportunity to hear Billy's secret if he could help it.

"We didn't really see that man in the morning—I mean before he was dead. That's what I told the sheriff because Grandma would have a fit if she knew we were still awake when we saw him. It was the middle of the night—I don't know just when, but it was dark and real late. We could see him because of the bug light they keep on out behind old lady Pierce's."

"And it was Mr. Britingham, the same man you saw on the dock yesterday morning? You're sure of that?"

"Sure. Why would I lie to you?"

Kevin didn't have an answer to that question. He tackled the subject indirectly.

"What did Mr. Britingham have on when you saw him sometime in the night?"

"The same things he had on out on the dock, except by then they were all wet. No, wait—he went by the tent twice, and he had a sweater on the second time he went by, but not the first."

In due course, Kevin got the story very much as Billy had presented it to Sheriff Kelleher, with the major difference that the sighting of Britingham was alleged to have occurred sometime in the middle of the night instead of at dawn. He was about to head in for lunch when another question came to mind.

"I understand why you told me you saw Mr. Britingham sometime around five o'clock. And I won't say anything to your grandmother. But were you awake then—I mean when it was just beginning to get light? Did you see anybody else?"

"Just that dumb Jeff," Billy answered.

"Jeff?"

"Mrs. Hess's dog. He came around the tent and woke us up, real early. He just comes right into the tent and starts licking your face."

Kevin decided not to press his luck any further. The boys were beginning to lose their interest. Darrell was rocking his shark and paying little attention to Kevin, and Billy was looking anxiously at his alligator, which had floated some distance away. Kevin complimented them again on their floats and swam off toward shore and lunch, thinking about the points he might score with the sheriff when he presented her with the revised version of Billy Keyser's story.

CHAPTER 20

By the time she had finally crawled into bed, some eighteen hours after Officer Barrett's call reporting the discovery of John Britingham's body, Sheriff Carol Kelleher had talked with the occupants of every cottage on the point except the Sandersons. Having been foiled both in the morning and in the evening in her efforts to question them, she had finally called and arranged to stop by after Sanderson returned home from his job at the winery the following day. And so, for the third time in two days and with the implications of Doc Crawford's report uppermost in her mind, the sheriff set off for Crooked Lake after a late lunch.

As she made the drive, she found herself thinking about Whitman. He was very much the odd man out on Blue Water Point. All of the other cottagers were year-round residents who worked in the area, retirees, or vacationers enjoying a short stay away from jobs and the bustle of the city. But Whitman fell into none of these categories. He was much too young to be retired, and, by his own admission, had a job in the city. Yet he seemed to have settled in on Crooked Lake for the entire summer. Did people in the academic profession really have so little to do? Carol remembered the only member of that profession she had known at all well. He had been her instructor in torts, and they had had a brief relationship during the summer prior to her final year at law school. She had worried about the propriety of an instructor dating one of his students, but had decided that if it didn't bother him, she shouldn't let it bother her. Of greater interest had been the fact that he seemed to have an infinitely flexible schedule; his summer, like Whitman's, had appeared to her to be without professional responsibilities. Carol knew, of course, that her law professor had probably spent more time than she realized cranking out notes for law reviews. What did Whitman do with his time? His phone call earlier in the day suggested that he might want to involve himself in her investigation of Britingham's death. Why? Because he had time on his hands? Or because he had something to hide, and had decided to deflect suspicion by pretending to help her with the case?

The sheriff turned her attention back to the purpose of her trip. It was too early for Sanderson to have returned from work, but there would be time to take a closer look at Britingham's construction shack before their meeting. The Sanderson cottage was less than a hundred yards from the boundary of the property John Britingham had recently purchased and on which he had planned to build, so the sheriff parked there and walked. Beyond the Hess cabin and through the trees, she could see the shack that Britingham had put up as a base of operations for the construction work he was undertaking.

The area was still heavily wooded. Only a relatively few small trees had been cleared out for the small frame building, which was set toward the back of the property, away from the lake and fairly close to the Hess place. The boundary was unmistakable. There was no fence, but on one side of the imaginary line were grass and a well-tended garden, on the other dense brush. The shack itself was undistinguished: a small twelve- by eighteen-foot structure perched on large cinder blocks, with another cinder block serving as a step to the door at the end of the shack facing the gravel road. Although no work of art, the building seemed sturdy enough and the tarpaper roofing looked as if it would keep the interior dry. A wire strung from the main line along the road to the shack by way of an insulator fastened to a large oak tree indicated that electricity was available. The sheriff wondered who had granted approval for this jury-rigged power supply.

An official notice from the sheriff's department forbidding entry to the shack had been affixed to the door, and a board had been nailed across the entrance to deter anyone who might not take the notice seriously. The padlock hung uselessly to one side, just as it had when Bridges first visited the shack on the morning of Britingham's death. Carol had no particular trouble removing the board, and she made a mental note to chastise Bridges for not having done a better job of securing the shack. But she was also upset with herself. She hadn't given enough thought to the shack and to the fact that the padlock had been pried loose, when and by whom she didn't know. It was possible that Britingham's killer had used the shack; even that he—or she—might still have some need to get back into it. And she had just demonstrated how easy that would be. On the other hand, it was conceivable that the shack might only have attracted the attention of local kids. But that thought did not make the sheriff feel any better.

The sheriff pushed the door open and stepped carefully into the room. It looked much as Bridges had described it. At the back, opposite the door, a couple of shelves had been nailed between the two-by-fours. They contained a box of nails, a claw hammer, and little else. Under the shelves, in the corner, were two rolls of tarpaper and next to them, standing in a pail, a bunch of metal stakes. To the right of the door was a long built-in draftsman's desk that ran two-thirds of the length of that wall; its large surface was clear except for a note pad, a retractable yardstick, and an empty beer can. Against the third wall, the one with the shack's only window, was a cot, which had been slept in and left unmade. Next to it stood a small table with a Formica top. It held a lamp; its base was made of an undistinguished piece of driftwood, and its white shade was scorched from contact with a hot light bulb. At the foot of the bed were a butcher-block table and an old refrigerator. A hot plate, a coffee pot, a jar of instant coffee, a sugar bowl, a dirty cup, and a spoon cluttered the table's surface. A jungle of wires from the several appliances were linked by an extension cord to the outlet near the lamp. It looked as if an attempt had been made to run the cord through hooks along the ceiling, but the distance had apparently been too great and the cord now snaked unprotected across the floor.

No toilet, no sink, no running water. Where did he get water for coffee, Carol wondered. Probably the lake. But why does he—did he—use the place at all? Why the bed, the primitive cooking facilities? There was little evidence that the shack was serving its purpose as an office for the construction project. There were no blueprints, no supplies or tools that would indicate that work was about to begin on the cottage that Britingham was alleged to be building. The place had no character at all; it was just there, a bare-bones room without any obvious purpose.

Carol went over and opened the refrigerator door. It was a pre-frostless model, and there was a substantial buildup of ice inside. Two cans of beer, a carton of milk, and a package of processed cheese stood on otherwise empty shelves. She sniffed the milk; it had gone sour.

The condition of the bed matched Bridges' description. Scattered across the tangled bedclothes were two girlie magazines. She glanced at one of the magazines, which lay open on the bed. It featured a young woman of impressive endowments and promised even more revealing poses on subsequent pages. Carol was mildly curious as to how far the editors had dared to go, but she left the magazine alone. And hoped Sam had done the same. They'd need to look for evidence as to the identity of the shack's most recent occupant, and Carol figured that the magazines as well as the beer can and coffee cup would be prime sources for good fingerprints.

Now even more concerned about the failure to secure the shack, the sheriff headed back to her car, from which she called and left word for Bridges to get over to Blue Water Point and do the job right. Then she moved her car down to the pull-off near the shack, figuring that the sight of an official vehicle would deter snoopers and whoever had been using it. There was still at least a quarter of an hour before Sanderson would be home from the winery, so Carol set off to look around the plot of land which Britingham had so recently purchased.

At the south end of Blue Water Point there had been no cottages to serve beyond the Hess place, and the local town fathers, mindful of the old adage that the shortest distance between two points is a straight line, had decided that the gravel road should simply extend in a straight line from West Lake Road to the big bend in the shoreline near the Milburn cottage, rather than follow the contour of Mallard Cove. As a result, Carol found herself further and further from the road as she walked over Britingham's property. After a few minutes of trudging through the woods, she could no longer see the construction shack. A steep bank lay between her and the water, so although she could occasionally see the lake through the trees, she could not see the shoreline. There wouldn't be much of a beach, she thought. Building here would be no picnic.

In view of the need to meet the Sandersons, the sheriff decided against continuing all the way to the far end of the property. She also felt the call of nature and looked about for a place to relieve herself, thinking as she did so that Britingham, without running water, must have had to do the same thing if he had ever made much use of the place. Of course it would have been easier for him than for her; Carol had never regretted her gender, but she had to acknowledge that guys did have some advantages. In any event, John Britingham would have no more occasions to take a pee in these woods. Why, she wondered, would he ever have felt the need to stay in that primitive shack when he lived so close, barely more than two miles away? Of course Britingham's home, according to Sam, was still unfinished, but at least it was spacious, had running water, a relatively well-stocked pantry, and a much more comfortable bed.

Although she was surely well out of sight of everyone, the sheriff was drawn to the even greater privacy of a dense thicket of sumac and scrub pine. Pushing through it with urgent purposefulness, Carol was suddenly brought up short in her tracks. Ahead of her, well concealed by the trees and bushes, was an automobile. And it wasn't an abandoned car either, but a recent model black Mercedes, which, in spite of a layer of dust, looked well cared for.

"Britingham's!" She said it out loud. The sheriff had puzzled over the dead man's missing car ever since the previous morning when they had been unable to locate it on the point, at Britingham's home, or at the winery. Sam had been sure it was in a shop for maintenance, but Sam had been wrong. Carol went around behind the car and looked at the license plate. A vanity number, JB-WINE, removed all doubt. The front door was unlocked, and through the closed window she could see that the keys were still in the ignition.

Using a handkerchief, the sheriff carefully opened the door and slid in behind the wheel. She hoped that there were prints on the door handle and steering wheel other than Britingham's, but a search of the car's interior and trunk turned up nothing else of interest. It appeared that Britingham had had a fetish about the neatness of his car.

It was clear how the car had gotten there. No road entered this section of the woods, but there was a natural passage, provided one had cased the area first and negotiated a few turns through the trees. The sheriff pocketed the car keys and followed the narrow path out of the sumac grove. She realized that no one entering Blue Water Point would ever suspect that a car was parked less than two hundred yards from the road. Unless you were looking for it.

One mystery solved, Carol thought. But she was now faced with the mystery of Britingham's car being parked, and obviously hidden, among the trees on his own property. Either Britingham himself had hidden the car because he had not wanted people to know he was on the point, or someone familiar with Britingham's property had done so. Suddenly, remembering the mission that had sent her into the sumac grove in the first place, Sheriff Kelleher hurried back into the woods and out of sight from the road.

CHAPTER 21

The screen door which opened into the Sandersons' kitchen was not hooked, and the sheriff's knock was answered by a woman's voice telling her to come in. Mrs. Sanderson met her in the kitchen, put a glass of iced coffee in her hand, and escorted her onto the screened porch overlooking the lake. Her tour of Britingham's woods, together with the unexpected discovery of the missing car, had taken longer than she had anticipated; Larry Sanderson had not only arrived home from work, but had also changed clothes and was relaxing on the porch, along with the owners of Ciao, one of the dogs she had met the previous day. They were seated around a large table that looked as if it were used for meals, card games, and small household projects. Two dogs were stretched out on the floor, one of them Ciao. It ignored her. The other rose to its feet and came over to inspect the newcomer. Its pedigree was doubtful, but it was large enough to be a contender, along with Grace Hess's retriever, for the role of Whitman's mystery dog.

The two men presented a striking contrast. Sanderson was fair and pale; Carlino, dark and swarthy. The women came from the same stock as their husbands, refuting the notion that opposites attract. One could have been forgiven for thinking that the wives were their husbands' siblings.

"Missed you last evening when I was making the rounds on the point," the sheriff commented after the preliminary courtesies had been exchanged. "You had a ball game, I understand."

"Right. We play for the winery. I didn't know you were coming by."

"No matter, today's fine." Carol tried to set an informal tone. "Did you win the game?"

"I'm afraid not. It was a blowout. We don't seem to win many these days, not without Bauer."

The sheriff wasn't really interested in the ball game or the trials and tribulations of the Silver Leaf entry in the Crooked Lake softball league, but she was willing to indulge the men for a few minutes if they wanted to share a misfortune more modest than murder. But it was Mrs. Sanderson who spoke up, her voice tinged with sadness.

"I don't suppose you know about Hank, probably don't even know who he is. But it's such a shame. He's always been such a spark. He won't come anymore. We tried—everybody's tried—but he won't play. He says the fun's gone. For us, too, I guess."

"I'm sorry to hear it." Carol tried to give the impression that she empathized with their loss of pleasure in the sport, but she found it more interesting that they preferred to talk about a man they would know she didn't know or care about than about the man who had been killed and in whom she was very much interested.

"Sheriff, do you need to talk with Larry and Chris alone? We can shove along." It was Bernie Carlino who changed the subject. But the sheriff, on impulse, decided that she wouldn't mind having both couples present. The Carlinos had been reticent to talk about Britingham; maybe they and the Sandersons would be more forthcoming with each other's moral support.

"No, no. Please stay. But I do have something I need to ask Mr. Sanderson first."

She reached down and began scratching the head of the Sandersons' dog, which had flopped at her feet, apparently convinced that she was a friend.

"Do you ever walk your dog early in the morning, say around five o'clock, either you or your wife?"

"Bernie said someone had seen a man and a dog on the beach yesterday morning around the time they found Mr. Britingham. It sure wasn't me. Or Chris. Sandy doesn't need to be walked. She goes out on her own."

As if to prove her master right, Sandy got up and went to the door that opened onto the beach and pawed at it. Mrs. Sanderson let her out and resumed her seat.

"Might she have been outside yesterday morning and tagged along with someone else? We don't know that the dog belonged to the man she was seen with." Or, she thought, that there had even been a man and a dog on the beach. There was only Whitman's word for that.

"It's possible, Sheriff, but I'm pretty sure not. I can't remember whether she was in or out last night. Sometimes she sleeps on the back steps. But she's lazy, almost as lazy as Ciao here. I doubt that she was following someone along the beach at that hour."

"And you, when did you get up?" The question was obviously intended for both of the Sandersons. Mrs. Sanderson replied. "Somewhere around seven. With the kids at scout camp, I'd normally have made breakfast for Larry and then gone back to bed. But I wanted to go to that new outlet store over in Cumberland, and I wanted to be there when it opened."

"That's about right," Larry said. "We were out of here a little after eight, I'd say. Chris dropped me at the winery. I didn't hear about Britingham until later in the day at the plant. I still can't believe it. Do you have any theories?"

"That's what I wanted to ask you. Let's assume he was killed, that it wasn't an accident. Why would anyone want to kill him? Who might have wanted to?"

These were the questions the sheriff might have been expected to ask, the questions the Sandersons should have been prepared to answer. Yet the answer was slow in coming. Carol had the distinct impression that Larry Sanderson was pretending to think now about something he had already given a lot of thought to.

"I don't think anybody really liked him. Well, I probably shouldn't say that—I don't know all the people who knew him. Maybe somewhere there was someone who thought he was a great guy. The fellows over at Silver Leaf didn't think so. I didn't. Bernie wasn't a fan, or heaven knows, neither was Hank Bauer. Not to mention Mike Snyder—and I'm only thinking of my friends. But we're talking about murder, aren't we? No, I can't imagine why anyone would want to kill him. You don't kill someone just because you don't like him."

Sheriff Kelleher sighed. She'd heard almost exactly the same words from several people the day before.

"What was your relationship with Britingham?"

"I'm a foreman in one of his plants. And I sell him grapes from a few acres I own up on the hill."

This wasn't quite what the sheriff meant, and she said so.

"I mean personal relationship. What caused you to dislike the man? Did he demote you? Kick you out of his office when you asked for a raise? I don't understand all the animosity—what did the man do to you?"

Sanderson and Carlino looked at each other. Chris Sanderson looked at the floor. Finally, Larry broke the awkward silence.

"I guess we all feared for our jobs. They've been laying people off. Stopped buying our grapes. My contract was terminated, along with a lot of others, but the grapes keep growing and still need care. A lot of us feel sort of like we've been hung out to dry. It's hard to like an employer who does that to you, even if he's basically a nice guy."

"Which he isn't," Carlino added.

"What do you mean?" The sheriff turned to the shorter and darker of the men, pressing for details.

Bernie looked as if he regretted what he had said and the tone in which he had said it. He fumbled for the appropriate explanation.

"Well, it's just the way he treats people."

"No, Mr. Carlino, that's not good enough. You meant something much more specific. I want to know what this man has done, other than lay people off and cancel contracts with grape growers. Come on, what is it?"

"Okay," he said with a shrug. "It's like what he did to our friend, Hank Bauer. Tore him down in front of the guys, embarrassed him. He really ruined Hank's self-confidence. He won't even come out to the ballpark now. That's what I mean about him not being a nice man."

"What about you—any of you? Did Britingham ever treat you like he treated this Bauer fellow?"

"No, nothing like that," Larry answered, his face a blank which told the sheriff nothing.

"Where were you the night before last, say between ten p.m. and three a.m.?" Carol hoped the sudden change of subject would catch them off guard. The question was directed at Larry Sanderson, but the sheriff's eyes swept over the four of them, looking for reactions, for any of the little signs that they might be experiencing anxiety. She had no reason to suspect any of them of murder, but she knew more or less when Britingham had died, and she would now have to question people on the point about where they had been during those critical hours.

"Where was I on Monday night?"

"Yes, Monday. All of you, for that matter. What were you doing during the late evening and early morning hours?"

Chris Sanderson answered for them all.

"I assume you mean that Mr. Britingham died sometime during those hours, is that it? Well, I can tell you that all four of us were right here—in these very chairs—along with Mike Snyder and Hank Bauer, from around 9:30 until midnight or a little after. We were playing cards, talking, just socializing."

The others were nodding. They looked as if they were pleased to have each other to vouch for their whereabouts.

"So the party broke up between twelve and one, you say. Then what?" The sheriff persevered.

"People just went home," Mrs. Sanderson said, the implication being that that was what people always did when a party was over.

Larry Sanderson spelled it out.

"Mike and Hank and Bernie and Rose went on home. Chris and I cleaned up. You know, tossed out beer cans, loaded the dishwasher. I put the snacks away."

The sheriff wasn't especially interested in the division of labor in the Sanderson household.

"Did you see John Britingham during the evening?"

"No, of course not. Why would he..."

"Just asking, Mr. Sanderson. You didn't see him, any of you, after the party broke up?"

"No, I'm sure no one did," Larry said. "Should we have?"

"That's what I was asking you."

"I can't imagine why he'd have been anywhere near here— oh, but of course, he was found dead on the point in the morning."

"Exactly. Now, when did you finish the kitchen?"

"I'd say around one or close to it." Mrs. Sanderson anticipated the sheriff's next question. "And we went straight to bed, both of us. That's what you were going to ask, right?"

"I suppose so," she acknowledged. Turning to the Carlinos, she asked, "And what about you two? What did you do when you left here?"

"Like Larry said, we went right home." It was Mrs. Carlino who answered. "It was real late, and I was exhausted. I was out like a light in ten minutes."

"Mr. Carlino? Were you out like a light, too? I remember you didn't go to work yesterday. Maybe you stayed up awhile after your wife went to bed."

"Well, yes I did. Made myself a sandwich and had a glass of milk."

Carol, observing Carlino's paunch, could readily believe that the man had drunk beer and snacked through an evening of cards and then gone home and had another meal after midnight.

"Did you go out again?"

"Oh, no, just ate my sandwich and looked at a magazine."

"Hear anything?"

"No. Well, we've got a noisy water pump. I've gotta fix it. But except for that, it was pretty quiet."

"Are you sure Snyder and Bauer went right home after the party, too?"

"I'm sure of it," Sanderson assured the sheriff, obviously pleased to be able to speak on behalf of his friends. "Like Rose said, it was awfully late, too late really for a weeknight."

"They'd had quite a few beers," Mrs. Sanderson added, "and they were really bushed."

Sheriff Kelleher decided the time had come to bring this discussion to an end. She needed to reflect on what, if anything, of importance she had learned from these night owls who stayed up playing cards and drinking beer until the wee hours on a work night. It was a lifestyle she did not understand. But more importantly, could she trust their claims that they had not seen Britingham? Or that Snyder and that other man—what was his name, Bauer?—had indeed gone straight home? How would they know?

"I'll probably want to talk to you again, but right now I'd better be moving. By the way, what were you playing? Poker?"

"Not Monday," Larry Sanderson said. "That night it was just a nickel-a-hand game we play sometimes. Called Screw Your Neighbor."

CHAPTER 22

Sheriff Kelleher was beginning to realize what a potentially large and open-ended investigation she had undertaken. It had begun on Blue Water Point with her questioning of that man who had so improbably been swimming before sunrise. And after Whitman, there had been the other people who lived near the place where John Britingham's body had been found. With the news that Britingham had purchased property there, she had felt it necessary to question all of the victim's 'neighbors' on the point. Those who had known Britingham—well, known of him would probably be more accurate—had more or less agreed that he was not a very nice human being, and they had made it clear that their opinion was shared by others. A man named Bauer was one of the others, and he had been on the point the night Britingham had been killed. But if the deceased had had so many detractors, where would it end? Would she need to work her way through the ranks of Silver Leaf employees, questioning them all? Would she need to seek out all the grape growers in the area? All of the people with whom Britingham had had business dealings? Carol Kelleher felt a headache coming on.

Bauer would, at least, be a beginning. The sheriff was not far from Southport when she left the Sandersons, and they had told her that Bauer lived in a cabin just beyond the village on the other side of the lake. So she had driven over to that address instead of doing what she really wanted to do, which was to head home for a hot shower and a decent meal.

Although the winery had been closed for the day for nearly two hours when the sheriff arrived at Bauer's cabin, no one was at home. She had no idea whether the man had stopped off for a few beers on the way home or had gone out for the evening. She made a guess that the first explanation for the empty cabin was the more probable, and decided to give Bauer another fifteen or twenty minutes before calling it a day.

Blue Water Point was indeed prime real estate when compared with this particular stretch of the lakeshore. There was no beach here, but so eager were people for a place on the water that they had constructed small cabins flush up against the bank, accessible from the road only by long flights of steps. There was little room for anything fancy and barely enough for necessities. The standard layout consisted of a combination kitchen-living room, one bedroom, and a tiny bathroom with a shower stall on the upper floor, and a storage room for a boat and fishing gear beneath it, with direct access by boat ramp to the lake.

The sheriff had taken a preliminary look around to assure herself that no one was at home. It was, she decided, the typical fishing cabin. It needed a coat of paint, and the only hint of landscaping was a couple of hollyhocks at the edge of the pull-off next to Bauer's mailbox. A variety of locally successful weeds had pushed their way up between the wooden steps, and a dangerous looking bed of poison ivy was encroaching on those steps where they made a ninety-degree turn to go down to the boat ramp. A sixteen-foot aluminum boat was tied up to a stub of a dock at the end of the ramp. It was in better shape than the house, and sported both a heavy duty gasoline-powered engine and a much smaller auxiliary electric motor, as well as a pair of oars, a life jacket, a tackle box, and two fishing poles. Bauer, like most lake residents, seemed not to be worried about theft.

The sheriff was unable to see into the cabin. There would be windows across the front, of course, facing the lake, but the only window facing the steps was the one in the door, and it appeared that Bauer had placed a large calendar or something over it. Satisfied that no one was at home, Carol had climbed back to her car to wait.

As it turned out, she had guessed correctly that Bauer would be back soon. She was sitting in her car in the small gravel pull-off about thirty steep steps above the small cottage when Bauer drove up. The old Ford that squeezed into the pull-off beside the sheriff's car was no more than basic transportation. Bauer obviously treasured his boat more than his car. It was a large, slightly stooped man who stepped out of the Ford, an athlete gone to seed, and Sheriff Kelleher recognized him as someone she had seen around the county. She was willing to bet that in his youth he'd been called Red.

Bauer came around the car, studying the visitor. But it was Carol who spoke first.

"You'd be Mr. Bauer, that right?" she asked as she climbed out of the car.

The answer was yes, but it was a surprisingly weak reply.

"Good to meet you," the sheriff said, seizing the big freckled hand which Bauer seemed reluctant to put forward. "I've seen you around, but I've never had the pleasure. My name's Kelleher, and I'm the sheriff here in Cumberland County, as you might have guessed from the car and the uniform."

"Yes, ma'am. You want to see me?"

"I do. It won't take but a few minutes. Can we go inside?"

"Sure. What's the problem?" Bauer led the way down, looking over his shoulder every few steps as if concerned that the sheriff might not be able to negotiate the steep descent. She chose not to answer the question until they were inside, and Bauer did not press for an explanation.

The first thing that struck Carol when they entered the cabin was the absence of what is typically called a woman's touch. She was almost immediately certain that the man wasn't married. Nowhere in the drab and unimaginatively furnished room into which she was ushered was there a touch of color or personality, if one discounted one of those embarrassingly bad paintings on black velvet over the couch. The place had a musty smell as well as the faint odor of stale bacon grease. The dishes from several meals were stacked in the sink or hadn't yet been cleared from the small wooden table, which was used both for dining and as a means of separating kitchen and living areas. Through the open door ahead, Carol could see an unmade bed. It would not have been uncharitable to say that the cabin was a mess. She began to feel depressed even before she started talking with Bauer.

"I'm sorry to barge in like this," the sheriff said as she took a seat on a couch whose springs were well past their prime. Bauer looked as if he were going to remain standing, but thought better of it and pulled a chair out from the table and sat on it. Carol wondered at his choice of the straight-backed wooden chair over the upholstered one in the opposite corner; perhaps its springs were as bad as those on the couch. More likely, she thought, Bauer simply didn't want to make himself too comfortable. It might encourage a longer visit, and he didn't look as if he relished a lengthy conversation.

The sheriff finally explained her business.

"You must know about John Britingham. I guess everybody does. Did you know that his body was found over on Blue Water Point?"

"I'd heard that, yes."

"Well, I've been talking with people over there, trying to find out if anyone can shed any light on his death. I mean, why would he turn up dead on that point? I wondered if anybody might have seen him around there on the night he was killed."

The sheriff paused, giving Bauer an opportunity to say something. He didn't.

"I understand you were playing cards with some friends on the point that night, am I right?"

"I was, yes, along with the Sandersons and the Carlinos and Mike Snyder. They're all friends. We play quite often."

"So I hear. Well, good. So, any chance that you saw Britingham that night?"

"No, I'm afraid not. Why would I?"

"I take it then that you'd know him if you saw him." It was a statement rather than a question.

"Yeah. I work for him, you know. But I didn't see anyone, anyway. Except Larry and—you know, the people who were at the Sandersons."

"At any time? When you arrived? When you left?"

"I'd like to help you, but no, I didn't see anyone else."

Bauer reminded the sheriff of a big basset hound. It was a sad face.

"Do you remember when you left?"

"Not really. When the game broke up, whenever that was. Larry could probably tell you. It was later than it should have been, I know that."

"Oh, why's that?"

"We had to be at work the next day, you know. It wasn't too smart staying up so late. But Mike—that's Mike Snyder—he was kinda down because his wife had left him, and we just got to talking. I think Larry and Chris had us over to help Mike."

"And did you?"

"Hard to tell. It wasn't a fun evening. We really should have called it a night way before we did."

This line of questioning isn't going anywhere, the sheriff decided.

"I got the impression from someone that Mr. Britingham wasn't well liked. Know anything about that?"

Bauer's sad countenance seemed even more pronounced as he considered the question.

"You're probably right. I think his employees were afraid of him."

"Were you?"

"Afraid? No, not really. Not afraid. That's not the right word."

"What word would you use, Mr. Bauer?"

"Why don't you call me Norm? Mr. Bauer sounds, I don't know, too—heck, I'm not Mr. Bauer, if you know what I mean."

Hadn't the Sandersons and the Carlinos spoken of Hank? Sheriff Kelleher found this request puzzling, but she'd try to remember to use Norm.

"Sure, whatever you say. But you were going to tell me your feelings about Mr. Britingham, I think."

"What's there to say? I just wasn't close to him."

"Well, no, I wouldn't think so. He ran the company, and you—what is your job at Silver Leaf?"

"I drive a truck," Bauer answered quietly. Or was it defensively?

The sheriff wanted to get away from this man with his sorrowful expression and his gloomy house. Bauer should have a dog—or even a cat, she was thinking. It seemed highly unlikely that she'd learn more by prolonging this sterile dialogue, but there had apparently been some sort of tension between this man and Britingham, and she had to pursue the matter.

"Your friends seemed to think that Mr. Britingham embarrassed you somehow. Is there any truth in that?"

For the first time since she had met Bauer, Sheriff Kelleher thought she detected a hint of animation in the man.

"I wish they'd leave it alone. It's nothing. Really, it's nothing. Just a misunderstanding one day at the plant. You know how friends are, they want to stick up for you, even if they don't have to." Bauer looked as if he was going to say more, but seemed to decide against it.

Carol tried another angle.

"Your friends tell me they miss you on their softball team. I got the impression they want you back." She assumed that people like to hear that they are appreciated and needed, and there had seemed to be some connection between Bauer's quitting the team and the contretemps with Britingham.

"I don't want to talk about it," was Bauer's only response. Whatever had persuaded the man to put his ball-playing days behind him, it was obvious that it still caused him distress.

"I'm sorry. I didn't realize it was such a sore subject," she said, trying to sustain a flickering hope that Bauer might explain why it was a sore subject.

"Didn't mean to be rude, Sheriff." His apology sounded sincere enough. "But I just don't want to get into it, okay? I'd just..."

He stopped in mid thought and got up abruptly from his chair.

"It don't matter. I've got more important things to do." His meaning was clear: there were more important things to do than play softball, although by the look of the cabin, Bauer wasn't doing them. But Sheriff Kelleher chose to interpret it as an invitation to leave, her curiosity piqued but unsatisfied for the time being.

"Look, Norm. I've got to be getting back to Cumberland, and you're going to want to get yourself some supper. Give me a call if you think of anything that might help me get to the bottom of this Britingham business."

She thanked Bauer for his cooperation and made her way back up to her car, thinking how lucky she was that she didn't have to climb all these steps, twice a day, day after day, season in and season out. It had been another in a series of unsatisfactory interviews since Britingham's death, but none had been more dispiriting. What had she learned? That talking about his role on the Silver Leaf softball team got Bauer worked up about Britingham? Where did that lead her?

Sheriff Kelleher was shaking her head as she got into her car. She was discouraged, not only about the case, but also about the human condition as well.

CHAPTER 23

The library in West Branch, like Jack's Tavern down in Southport, was a social center for lake residents, although it attracted a somewhat different clientele. The book selection in the small two-room building was limited; the titles ran mostly to lightweight summer reading. Only occasionally was it used for study, and then typically by school students who did not have Internet access in their homes. In fact, there were only half a dozen seats in the library other than the one behind the desk occupied by Mary Payne, the cheerful and garrulous librarian. Her job, which she shared with two other women, was a part-time one, and the library was only open four days out of the week, and then only on a limited schedule.

Thursday was one of those days, and at ten o'clock in the morning of the second day after the discovery of John Britingham's body on Blue Water Point, Mrs. Payne was attending to the needs of four people. One of them, a young woman carrying an infant on her back, was browsing through shelves marked 'Gothics.' The other three were gathered around the librarian's cluttered desk. A short man who was perspiring freely had assembled a rather large stack of books and was in the process of checking them out. He was obviously either a fast reader, or he was making selections for a whole family of readers. The other two customers, patiently waiting their turns, were Edna Morgan and Kevin Whitman, and the librarian was engaged in animated conversation with them even as she stamped the books for her other patron.

"It's such a shame about that Mr. Britingham," Mrs. Payne said, shaking her head. "Do you suppose they'll ever find out what happened to him, or will this be another one of those unsolved mysteries?"

It sounded to Kevin as if Mary Payne did a lot of reading herself, because he doubted if in real life the woman had encountered that many unsolved mysteries.

"Oh, I imagine that the police will apprehend whoever killed him in time," he said.

"I hope so. Do you know, he was in here less than two weeks ago. He doesn't read the sort of stuff most people do..."

She caught her breath, as if aware that this might be an implied criticism of the reading habits of her customers of the moment.

"You know what I mean. He wasn't into mysteries or spy stories or that sort of thing. At least I don't think he was. Anyhow, this last time he wanted to know if we had books on the history of steamships on Crooked Lake. Can you imagine, a history buff? Well, of course, I said we didn't have many. We don't get much call for such things. I suggested he try Cumberland—they're much bigger than we are, got a better selection. But he'll never do any reading on that subject now, will he? Poor man."

Mary Payne paused to say good-bye to the perspiring man. Edna, Kevin noticed, looked pale. She was leaning on the librarian's desk for support.

"Are you all right, Edna?"

"Yes, just a little dizzy." But she didn't look all right, and Kevin was suddenly worried for his neighbor. Mrs. Payne didn't seem to notice.

"As I was saying, people certainly do have different tastes in books. Now I don't read much non-fiction, I have to confess. But I admire people who want to improve their minds, learn about the past. That was Mr. Britingham. Always studying up on things. He said he was interested in steamship accidents. Don't I remember that your husband is interested in that sort of thing, too, Mrs. Morgan?"

Kevin was now thoroughly convinced that Edna Morgan wasn't well.

"Mrs. Payne, I think my friend is sick. Could you get us some water?"

"Oh, I'm sorry, I didn't realize—just a second." The woman disappeared into the small bathroom at the back of the library and returned with a glass of water and an air of solicitude.

"Please, don't make a fuss over me. I'm fine."

"I don't think so, Edna. Let me get you home." Kevin expedited their departure by leaving the books he had planned to check out. Apologizing to Mary Payne for the hasty exit and promising to return later for the books, he steered Edna Morgan out the door and into the car.

Once under way on the drive back to Blue Water Point, Kevin turned to his companion.

"Now what was that all about?"

"What do you mean?" Edna asked, eyes fixed on the road ahead.

"Edna, we've known each other for several years, and I've never seen you like that. You were upset by that Payne woman's chatter, weren't you?"

"Why should I be? No, like I said, I just felt a bit dizzy. Maybe it's the heat."

"Dizzy? Maybe. But Mrs. Payne starts talking about John Britingham, and you turn to jelly. Why? Everyone's been talking about Britingham, including you and George. So that's not the problem. But she told us that Britingham wanted books on lake steamers. And who do we know that makes a hobby of lake steamer memorabilia? You and George, Edna. I wasn't born yesterday. You were really shaken by the news that Britingham was seeking information about those boats. Let me guess. It has something to do with that accident that cost your aunt her life? Right?"

Kevin had spoken in a friendly but firm voice, and Edna Morgan reached over and patted his arm.

"I'm sorry, Kevin. I didn't mean to drag you into this. It's really not a big thing, you know. We've been afraid that Britingham would try to explore the wreck of that ship. It was a shock to hear Mary bring it up—after he's dead, I mean. It hurts to be reminded of something like that."

Kevin maneuvered the car around a big curve in the road.

"I understand your feelings about the boat—what was it called, *The Commodore*? And I hadn't known that Britingham had been thinking about exploring the wreck. But, Edna, Britingham is dead. He won't be doing it now. Aren't you overreacting?"

Edna Morgan was silent for a moment. She rummaged in her purse for a mirror and examined her face as if looking for an answer to Kevin's question.

"I suppose so. It just hit me that that man's death may have spared us the indignity of..."

Edna stopped in mid-thought and busied herself exchanging the mirror for a tissue, with which she dabbed at her face.

"I'm fine now," she announced. "Let's not talk about it. What did you find to read?"

"I didn't check anything out. You went all funny on me before I'd gotten around to it. Maybe I'll go back this afternoon. You didn't get any books either, did you?"

"No, I guess not." She said it quietly, but she was now angry with herself for having allowed the Payne woman's conversation to make her so visibly upset.

When they got back to Blue Water Point, they found George on the Morgan porch. And he looked upset, too.

"Edna, where in God's name have you been? You mustn't do things like this. I've been calling people, walking up and down the point. You really had me worried." He tried to look stern, but he was clearly relieved that his wife had returned home.

"Oh, George, it was just a spur-of-the-minute thing. Kevin saw me and said he was going to the library and did I want to come along. You must have wandered off someplace yourself. Anyhow, I figured we wouldn't be gone long." There, she thought, now we're even.

"We've been talking about Britingham again," said Kevin. He decided to sit, invited or not.

"George, I told Kevin that Britingham wanted to go searching for *The Commodore*. It came up at the library—that Payne woman was talking about him, that he'd come looking for books on the subject. I'm sorry, dear." She turned to Kevin. "We thought it was our worry and didn't want to bother other people."

If George Morgan was upset by his wife's apparent indiscretion, he didn't show it.

"What's done is done," he said, and then suggested that Edna get them some ice tea.

When the three of them had settled down with their glasses of tea, George returned to the subject of Britingham's interest in the lake steamers.

"I don't really know whether Britingham would have tried to find *The Commodore*. He talked about it with us once, and he didn't really understand our position. We don't like the idea of somebody poking around down there. I guess you knew that. But I suppose he saw it as an adventure. Anyhow, we hadn't given it much thought lately, but his death sort of reminded us. It doesn't matter now."

"Does Sheriff Kelleher know about this?"

"Why would she need to? Like I said, it doesn't matter anymore."

"I was just thinking that she'll probably hear about it. My guess is that it would be better if she heard it from you."

"Hell, Kevin, she's got to be looking for reasons why someone would have a reason to kill Britingham. I don't want her to start thinking about me." George considered his drink. "You're not going to say anything, are you?"

"I'm not going to bring it up, if that's what you mean. But I can't pretend I don't know anything if she asks." Kevin set his glass down and leaned toward the Morgans. "Look, you know as well as I do that unless they get lucky and somebody confesses he killed Britingham or they find a weapon with somebody's prints on it—something like that—we're going to have the sheriff over here day and night, asking questions and more questions. It seems to me that it's better if we tell her what we know, rather than have her drag it out of us. So while you're thinking about what to tell the sheriff, there's another thing we ought to talk about. Do you want to let me know why you didn't level with me about when you got up the morning I found Britingham on my dock?"

"What do you mean?" George looked decidedly uncomfortable, a tall, lanky man shrinking down in his seat.

"I'm worried, George. I don't pretend to know what's going on, but you told me that morning that you didn't get up until around six, that the police car was already there. If you told me, I'd guess you told the sheriff the same thing. Why'd you say that? I'm sure you were up earlier."

"But Kevin, I..."

"George, it won't wash," Kevin interrupted. "When I was swimming back from the end of the point, there was smoke coming out of your chimney. That was before 5:30. And it wasn't from a fire you'd had the night before, because there wasn't any smoke when I came out to swim. So you—or Edna—had to have built a fire sometime around five o'clock Tuesday morning. I don't care when you have fires in your fireplace, George, or when you get up. Good lord, we all live on our own schedules up here. But it could look like you were trying to cover up something. When the sheriff's investigation gets serious, there'll be questions, lots of them, and she's going to wonder why you didn't tell her the truth."

"You don't think I had anything to do with Britingham's death, do you?"

"No, but that's not the point, is it?"

George Morgan finished his ice tea, set it down, and reached over to take his wife's hand.

"No, I guess not. You're right. I did burn some trash in the fireplace. It's a strange time to be doing it, I suppose, but I was up early and was just puttering around, doing those silly things you do when you're not really wide-awake. I don't know why I told the sheriff it was six o'clock. There's nothing to hide, but I can see how it might look bad, my fudging the time I got up. It's so stupid—I didn't really think about it. I just didn't want to get involved, I guess."

He stretched his long legs and pushed himself out of his chair.

"I'd appreciate it if you didn't say anything to the sheriff, Kevin. I'll do it myself. I don't know why Britingham's death has turned us all into a bunch of nervous Nellies. Stupid. Downright stupid."

Kevin had gotten the message—better to be moving along, let the Morgans talk things over by themselves. As he walked back to his own cottage, he thought about George's choice of words. Nervous Nellies. He hadn't heard that expression in years. And Britingham's death, he reflected, had not turned us all into nervous Nellies. George Morgan should speak for himself.

CHAPTER 24

Dolores Weber closed the door behind her and kicked first one and then the other of her shoes across the room. One landed on the couch; its mate barely missed the glass lamp on the end table, bouncing off the wall and back onto the table, where it sat like some mod decorator's whimsical touch beside the lamp. She crossed to the kitchen and opened the cupboard beneath the sink. There, next to the liquid soap and the scouring pads, was what passed for her liquor cabinet. She extracted a bottle of vodka, poured a generous portion into one of the glasses in the crowded drain rack, and went back to the living room.

From the couch, Dolores surveyed her efficiency apartment. She didn't like what she saw. Five months ago she had arrived in Cumberland, excited at the prospect of renewing an affair with John Britingham. The apartment was serviceable at best, but she had considered herself lucky to find a place in this area of single-family homes, so unlike the Bay area. She had at first been fearful that she would have to rent a room with kitchen privileges in one of the old homes on Sycamore Street, but a clerk in the pharmacy had alerted her to a possible vacancy in what was apparently one of only three sets of apartments in town. When she saw it, she had immediately revised her expectations downward. A tiny, dingy apartment was the price she would have to pay for privacy, and she had paid it gladly.

For a time Dolores had entertained the hope that John might invite her to move in with him, but while he was willing to live with some speculation and gossip about his private life, he had apparently drawn the line at a live-in secretary, whether because of a concern for appearances in a small community or a need to preserve his own privacy she did not know. In any event, the apartment had been tolerable because there had been the nights at John's, sometimes as often as three times per week and rarely, except for the times when he had been away on business, less than once a week. Now all that was over. There would be no more nights with John Britingham—in his home or anywhere else.

And this apartment, this miserably cramped place that she had called home for five months—she would put it, too, behind her as soon as she could get someone else to assume responsibility for the balance of the year's lease. Then she'd go back to California. She had no illusions about keeping her job at Silver Leaf. It would take them—whoever they were—some time to sort things out and make the necessary decisions about the winery. But she realized that she was expendable, that sooner or later, and in all probability sooner, she would be released. They would, of course, be polite about it. They would regret the need to let her go. She was already fed up with the patently phony solicitousness of people at the winery. John had not been well liked, that she knew, and she was his person, sharing his unpopularity, even earning some of it for herself by the manner in which she had dealt with his employees. No, she would be gone soon. She gave herself a month at most.

But she knew she would have left anyway after the discovery of his drawer full of mementos. Dolores saw herself as monogamous. Well, at least serially monogamous. And she expected her men to share that philosophy. She had been furious with John that morning, and even the news of his death—and the knowledge that he was already dead when she found the jewelry and the pillbox and, yes, the panties—had not wholly assuaged her anger.

There had been so much to do in the first 48 hours following his death that she had not had time to nurse that anger or decide what, if anything, to do about it. The deputy sheriff had badgered her for information, and she had become so irritated with him on the occasion of his second visit that she had been tempted to feed him a few small lies, even though she knew nothing about Britingham's death. And there had been the local paper, and a dozen or so plant officials, all of them shocked, some of them curious, and none of them devastated by the news of the untimely and violent death of the owner of the winery. The phone had rung incessantly.

And so it was not until Thursday afternoon, more than two days after the murder—for Dolores Weber was convinced that John had been murdered, that she began to think seriously again, not about the death of her boss and lover, but about the life he had led. She freshened her drink, adding a couple of ice cubes to the glass this time, and left it on the dresser while she stepped out of her dress and slip. She always changed to slacks and a blouse after work, but today she paced around the room in her underwear, observing herself in the mirror on the inside of the closet door and wondering why John had found it necessary to take up with another woman.

"Damn him!" There was no one to hear her, but Dolores felt better for giving voice to her frustration. She felt no sorrow, no sense of loss, only pain at John's betrayal. It was too late to punish him. She tried to clear her mind of fragments of imaginary conversation she would have with John, conversations in which she would heap abuse on him—conversations she would never have. She tried to focus on what she would do, for she had to do something. Perhaps she would punish the other woman.

Dolores didn't know who the other woman was. For all she knew, there might have been several other women. What she had were some personal belongings, one of which, the pillbox, bore the initials EHH, and several phone numbers. She drank some of the vodka and began to go through her purse, looking for the Rolodex page with the numbers on it. Anyone walking down Dunbar Street past the Village Garden Apartments would have been treated to the sight of a physically attractive, well-tanned, young woman, dressed only in her underwear, examining the contents of a large shoulder bag. But Dolores was oblivious to everything except the woman with whom John had been unfaithful. She was convinced that one of the numbers on the Rolodex page belonged to EHH, and that she would pursue the matter until she knew who EHH was, until she had met her, until she had confronted her with the evidence in John's desk.

And then for the first time something occurred to her that made the search for the woman even more urgent. Had John been with this woman the night he had been killed? Might she be implicated in his death? The authorities would be interested in the relationship, even if it turned out that EHH had had nothing to do with John's death. Dolores Weber felt the adrenalin flowing. She had a mission.

There were four numbers on the card in front of her, one of them the number of her own former California phone. She knew she would have to try all three of the other numbers, if only to satisfy her curiosity. But it was the local number that interested her most. For ten minutes or so she carried on a silent conversation with herself, trying to settle on a plan—what to do if a man or a child answered, or for that matter how to raise the subject if it was a woman. She hadn't resolved all of the questions on her mind when she finally dialed the number. But she knew she had the advantage of surprise, and she had confidence that her voice and manner would put the other woman on the defensive. Dolores listened to the phone ringing, hoping that it rang at the home of John Britingham's other woman.

"Hello, this is Emily Hoffman." The voice, coming after the phone had rung four times, was pleasant but rather flat. Dolores could hardly believe her good luck. One call. A woman on the line. And one of those rare, polite people who identify themselves to callers. Emily Hoffman. EHH. She wanted to ask what the other H stood for.

Suddenly the conversation she had planned became moot. There would be no need to make up an explanation for the call or take refuge in indirection. It was going to be easy. Dolores stretched the extension cord to its full length and sat on the couch, putting her feet up on the coffee table in front of her.

"Yes, Ms. Hoffman. I'm so glad to have found you in." She didn't know whether Emily Hoffman was single or married. Personally, she hated Ms., but it was useful in this situation. "I'm calling about the late John Britingham. You know about that tragedy, don't you?"

There was a momentary silence. Dolores could picture the woman, shifting gears mentally, realizing that this was not a routine call from a neighbor or friend.

"I'm sorry, who did you say was calling?"

This was the one question Dolores did not intend to answer.

"I didn't, and it's really not important. We're taking care of Mr. Britingham's effects, and have come across some things that belong to you." She had decided not to hedge; she would act as if she knew that the items she had found in John's desk belonged to this woman. "I thought you might want them back."

The voice on the other end of the line was steady.

"I don't know what you're talking about. Perhaps you have a wrong number."

"No, I don't think so. These things are rather personal, and we thought they should be returned to their owner."

"Really, I don't know this John Britingham. There has to be a mistake."

Dolores was prepared for this.

"Well, it is possible, I suppose. That's okay; we probably have an obligation to turn them over to the police anyway. It's just that I thought—well, you know, that it might be better if personal things like this were just quietly returned to their owners. These investigations are so messy."

Once again there was silence. She thought it lasted a bit longer this time.

"I suppose they are. What are these things you're talking about? The ones whose owner you're looking for?"

Dolores sipped her vodka and smiled.

"Let's see. There's some jewelry, quite elegant and distinctive—oh, yes, and some underwear." She described the earrings and the brooch very carefully, but made no mention of the pillbox.

"What made you think they might be mine? It sounds as if they could be anyone's."

"It was the phone number, Ms. Hoffman. It seemed reasonable to assume that these things would belong to the person whose phone number was found with them."

Silence again. It lasted so long that Dolores began to wonder if Emily Hoffman had gone away from the phone.

"I can't imagine why this Britingham person would have my phone number. And I'm certain those things aren't mine. Maybe I should see them, then we'd know for sure they aren't."

For the first time since she had opened John Britingham's desk drawer on the morning of the murder, Dolores Weber was having fun.

"Yes, I think that's an excellent idea. And if it turns out they aren't yours, then we can give them to the police. They'll know what to do. Why don't you give me directions? And I'll come out to your place."

"Oh, no, that won't be necessary." There had been just a trace of panic in the woman's voice. "Where are you?"

"I wasn't thinking of getting together right now. There's no great hurry. If you'd rather not meet at your house, let me suggest Leppart's in Southport. Why don't we do it Monday—is Monday okay with you? Say ten o'clock for coffee?"

Leppart's was the coffee shop and ice cream parlor in Southport, convenient to the winery. But Emily Hoffman was not happy with that suggestion either.

"Could we meet in Cumberland?"

"Well, of course, if you live in Cumberland."

"No, I don't..." The Hoffman woman stopped in mid-sentence, then resumed. "I mean it just seemed to be a good idea. Can you suggest a place?"

So, Dolores thought. The woman is not from Cumberland. She's probably from around Southport and doesn't want to be seen having this meeting in her own village.

"Of course. Why don't we meet at that tearoom on State Street, the Flower Basket? I'm sure you know it. Is ten on Monday all right?"

"Yes, of course. Ten. This is really a wild goose chase, you know, but you'll feel better if I can assure you that those—those things—aren't mine. By the way, how will I recognize you?"

"I don't think there'll be a problem. The breakfast crowd will be gone, and it's too soon for lunch. We'll spot each other, I'm sure. And thank you, Ms. Hoffman. It'll be such a relief to have this taken care of."

Dolores cradled the phone and danced around the room. She had found the perfect therapy for her anger. Once more she consulted the Rolodex page of phone numbers. She hadn't recognized the area code for the fourth number, but a quick scan of the directory told her that it was downstate in or near the city. She didn't expect to learn anything of interest from the call, and was surprised when a male voice on an answering machine provided the following message.

"Hello. This is Alan Hoffman. Neither Emily nor I can come to the phone at the moment. Please leave a message, and one of us will get back to you as soon as possible."

Good, thought Dolores. A married woman. A married woman with two homes. A married woman who probably has opportunities to fool around while her husband is out of town. Feeling for all the world like a detective who has just cracked a tough case, Dolores freshened her drink one more time.

––––

Later, after getting properly dressed and warming and eating a weight-watcher's dinner, Dolores was once again in the mood to use the phone. There was only one number still to be explained, and it had interested her less because it was a California number and therefore more likely to be only of historical interest. On the other hand, she now began to wonder if perhaps John had been seeing someone else on his occasional business trips to the coast, or if he had been having another affair even while he was sleeping with her back in California. The more she thought about it, the more she knew she had to track down the fourth and final number on the Rolodex page.

By this time it was past seven o'clock, which meant four-something on the west coast. She'd try now, she decided, and if nothing happened she'd wait a couple of hours and try again.

It was a rough, uncultured voice that answered the phone, and the owner of the voice did not identify himself.

"Yes?" The man managed to give that one word an inflection that made it clear that he did not welcome the interruption of whatever he was doing.

"Oh, perhaps I have a wrong number. I was calling about John Britingham—does that name ring a bell?" It wasn't what she had planned to say, and she silently berated herself for failing to plan the conversation more carefully. Why had she called? With whom had she expected to speak?

"Britingham? What about him?"

Dolores sat up straight on the couch, willing herself to be the self-assured person who had managed Britingham's affairs and had twisted Emily Hoffman around her little finger less than two hours earlier. The man in California, it would seem, did know Britingham. She didn't know who the man in California was, and she guessed that she would be expected to. She didn't ask his name.

"Mr. Britingham passed away earlier this week. I'm calling people—we didn't know who might have heard the news."

"Yeah, I read the obits. Who are you? You can't be family. You work for him?"

"Well, yes, in a manner of speaking."

"Personally? Are you his secretary? I mean his personal secretary?"

Dolores was puzzled. She was supposed to be asking the questions, but she was losing control of a conversation that no longer seemed to have a goal. The man on the other end of the line gave her no opportunity to reply.

"Look, Miss. I'm glad you called. You say you work for Britingham. What do you do for him? Personal stuff? Money? Do you handle his finances?"

There was no longer any hint of irritation in the man's voice. But it wasn't clear why he should be so interested in her role in Britingham's life. Dolores was now very much on her guard.

"It was a professional relationship," she offered ambiguously.

"But did you keep his records? Do his banking?" The man in California had shifted to the past tense. And he was tenacious.

"I'm afraid I don't know what you want. I worked for Mr. Britingham, and I've been making phone calls to people I thought would want to know about his death. I figured I'd reach either you or your wife."

It was a long shot, and it failed.

"I don't have a wife. But let's talk about your boss's finances. This is all off the record, but I'll put it to you straight. Maybe you can help. Britingham owes me money. There won't be any record of it, you see—it was a personal matter. And I'm sure there won't be anything for me in his will. So how do I collect? And we're talking about a pretty nice pile of cash. I thought maybe you could take something and send it to me—you know, from his safe or wherever he keeps the stuff. Maybe you could even get into his bank account, you know, use some excuse or other—there's gotta be a way."

Whatever Dolores Weber had expected, it wasn't this. She was trying to get some information about another woman in Britingham's life; the last thing she needed was to get mixed up in some illegal effort to skim funds from his estate before probate.

"I didn't handle Mr. Britingham's money, except petty cash. I don't see how I can help you. Why don't you talk to his daughter? I assume she'll be the executor, and she'll probably want to see justice done."

"Are you kidding? What am I going to tell her? That her father had this deal that never got put into a contract, and some guy in Frisco wants what's coming to him?"

"Yes, that's just what I'd tell her. I'm sure she'd want to see her father's wishes carried out."

"Lady, you don't know nothin'. No offense, but Britingham would have been only too happy to welch on this one. And when he died, he did. What happened to him? Old lady Hess put rat poison in his highball?"

Dolores may have lost control of the conversation, but she hadn't lost interest. It looked as if Britingham had been involved in some shady scheme with the man she was talking to. But there were too many missing pieces for her to make sense of it. She didn't know the man's name. She had no clue whatsoever as to the nature of the deal. And who was old lady Hess? Suddenly Dolores wanted very much to keep this man on the line, to coax more information out of him.

"I'm sorry—about you not being paid, I mean. Maybe I could make some discreet inquiries"—she stressed discreet—"and see if there's some angle we could use to make some money available. Can you tell me how much he owed you? Or anything about the nature of the debt?"

Dolores held her breath while the man in California considered her offer and her questions.

"Like I said, Miss, it wasn't peanuts." There was now an unmistakable note of caution in his voice. "I'd settle for three grand. I suppose they don't have that kind of money lying around in petty cash, not even where Britingham is concerned. And I don't think you need to know—I don't think you want to know—what it's for. It doesn't matter. A debt is a debt. Let's just say I got what he wanted on the Hess case, and he owes me three. Then we're square. He can rest in peace, and I can put a new stereo in my boat."

"Okay. I'll do my best. I'm not optimistic, you understand, but I'll look into it." Then casually, as if it were an afterthought, she broached the matter of his name.

"By the way, I've been working off a list here, and I'm not sure I have your name right. Can you help me?"

She knew at once she shouldn't have asked.

"My name? Why surely you have it. You called my number, didn't you? Maybe you should tell me yours." When she hesitated, he added, "I see. Well, then, if you're going to remain Britingham's anonymous secretary, I'll remain his anonymous partner."

Dolores stared at the phone for some seconds after he hung up, trying to make sense of the conversation and its abrupt end. No matter, she finally said to herself, and went to the kitchen to pour herself one more shot of vodka. She hadn't drunk this much in years, but then she hadn't experienced such an exhilarating day in years. Sex was exciting, but intrigue was off the chart.

On any other evening, if she were at home and not in John's bed, she would have watched television or read one of her pop psychology magazines or a novel. But this evening there was too much to think about. She had made three phone calls and was pretty sure she had discovered that John had been sleeping with a woman named Hoffman while her husband was off in the city and that he had been involved in some under the table deal with a disreputable character on the coast, which had to do with someone named Hess. What could she do with this information?

She had already decided to meet the Hoffman woman and return her things, all except the most revealing. The poor woman might fuss and dissemble, but she would accept the jewelry. But Dolores would keep the pillbox, and her possession of it would give her a hold over Emily Hoffman. The prospect pleased her.

The California connection was more complicated. She had no intention of helping that man, whoever he was, recover his $3,000. He could probably find her out by calling the winery; if he did so soon enough, she might even be the one to answer the phone. But she had said nothing that could compromise her; he, on the other hand, had mentioned a name, Hess, and she had his phone number. She wondered how easy it might be to match a number with a name. Anyone could do it with the time to work through the San Francisco directory. Maybe there was a shortcut.

And then there was Hess. Old lady Hess. The Hess case. She tried to remember conversations with John. Had that name ever come up? John had shared very little, she realized. Very little that mattered. Winery business, an occasional binge of nostalgia for the greater sophistication of the Bay area, lots of small talk about TV shows and the 49ers and the Giants. Once in awhile some talk, always vague and nonspecific, about the two of them taking a trip to some exotic place some day.

But she didn't want to think about that. It was more fun contemplating her meeting with Emily Hoffman. She wasn't sure what she was going to do with the rest of her life, but she was really looking forward to the next few days.

CHAPTER 25

Carol Kelleher didn't drink a lot, and she rarely did her drinking in bars. But on this particular evening, three days after John Britingham's death, she was parked on a barstool in Jack's Tavern, contemplating a beer and a crime. The beer was welcome after a tiring and frustrating day, but it wasn't the beer that had brought the sheriff to Jack's. She had decided to drop in to find out what people were saying about the summer's most dramatic news story. While the sheriff was unknown to the residents of Blue Water Point, Jack Varner had been a friend of her father's, and his tavern seemed like a good place to hear scuttlebutt about the demise of the community's most famous citizen.

"So tell me, Jack, what do you think? About the late Mr. Britingham, I mean."

"About the man or the murder?"

"Is that what people are saying, that it was murder? It hasn't been proved, you know. But yes, I guess I was thinking about how he got killed. And about him, too, if you know anything. Ever meet him?"

"A few times. He wasn't a regular. I can't somehow picture him in here having one with the boys."

"Any favorite candidate for the killer? If, of course, it was murder." Carol was careful to provide the usual disclaimer, but Jack ignored it.

"Most people figure it was someone connected to Silver Leaf. A lot of those fellows come in here—bring their wives, too. They didn't much like him. He'd had 'em all sweating about job security. No way to make yourself popular."

Carol was absent-mindedly moving her glass around, making a pattern of rings on the bar top.

"Don't any of your customers think it's a bit odd that someone would kill the boss over the possibility of a job layoff?"

"I know it sounds far-fetched. But you asked what the talk is, and that's the number one theory. Of course I like the idea of a stranger, someone who's not from around here, someone with an old grudge. Like that guy who was looking for Britingham just the other day."

The sheriff came halfway out of her seat.

"Someone in here looking for Britingham? Someone who's not from the area?" Her voice betrayed her excitement. "What day was this?"

The owner-bartender filled an order for his waitress while he tried to recall the day the stranger had come into the tavern.

"I'm not real sure. Probably Sunday. Yeah, I'm sure it was Sunday. He wanted a place to stay, and I remember telling him it was the weekend and the motels would most likely be filled up."

Sunday. Britingham had been killed sometime Monday night. A stranger coming into town and asking for Britingham less than two days before he gets killed just a few miles up the lake. The sheriff was very glad she'd dropped in for a beer.

"Well now, I'd say that's interesting." It was surely the understatement of the day. "Tell me about him. Did he give you his name?"

"No, no name. It wasn't much of a conversation. He just said he was new in the area, wanted to look up John Britingham, and did I know where he lived. Said he'd got an address but didn't know how to find it."

"You told him?"

Varner nodded.

"What'd the guy look like?"

"Young. In his mid-twenties, I'd guess. Well past high school for sure, but young. Good-looking guy, though. Hair a little shaggy. He was wearing jeans and a shirt with the name of some rock group on it."

"You said maybe Britingham got bumped off by some stranger with a grudge, and then remembered this guy. Did he seem to have a grudge against Britingham?"

"He didn't talk about Britingham. Just wanted to know where he lived. I didn't mean the guy had a grudge, just that maybe the killer was someone from someplace else who was carrying a grudge. After all, Britingham hadn't been around these parts long. If he treated people out in California like I hear he treated 'em around here, there could be a line waiting for a crack at him. Oh, and by the way, this guy stopped in again, next day—that'd be Monday. Wearing the same duds, as far as I could tell. Said he just wanted to let me know he appreciated the directions—told me he'd found the place with no trouble. I thought that was pretty decent of him. It wasn't a big thing, but most people don't give you any thanks."

"You didn't happen to ask where he was staying, did you?"

"He mentioned that he'd found a motel, but I didn't ask which one and he didn't say."

"No matter. If it turns out to be important, I'm sure we can locate him."

There was no question in Sheriff Kelleher's mind that it was important. She was trying to keep her excitement in perspective After all, there might be some perfectly innocent explanation for this coincidence. But here was a man, according to the reliable Jack Varner, who was not from the Crooked Lake area, who had come into town and inquired about how to find John Britingham's house less than two days before his death and who had still been in the area less than 24 hours before Britingham's body had been found on Whitman's dock.

Carol thanked Varner for the beer and the information and made a quick trip back to the patrol car to call Bridges. As luck would have it, the deputy sheriff was out of touch with his radio. She was about to try to contact Officer Barrett, when it occurred to her that she was just across the town square from the office of the village police. Southport's chief of police Joe Donegan had been one of her father's good friends and among those who had prevailed upon her to run for the position his death had left vacant. Donegan would be glad to help.

To her great relief, Chief Donegan was still at his desk, engaged in what appeared to be a leisurely chat with one of his patrolmen.

"Hello, Joe. Hi, Bob." The sheriff was slightly out of breath from her sprint across the square. "I don't know what you're doing here at this hour, but I'm damned glad you are."

"You look as if you've cracked your case, Carol. What happened, somebody confess?" The chief of police presented a surprisingly scholarly appearance behind steel-rimmed glasses and under a head of gray hair and a permanently wrinkled brow.

"Hardly, but I've learned something of interest, and I wonder if you can help me."

"Well, sure, if it doesn't call for manpower I can't spare. Always glad to give our underfunded friends in the county a hand."

The sheriff filled in her colleague from Southport on the stranger who'd been looking for John Britingham.

"Now we need to look for him. What I hope you can do for me is check the motels, ask around to see who might have talked with this guy, find out who he is, where he's from, what he was doing here. And whether he's still in the area, of course. Sorry to be asking, but we ought to be on this right away, and I thought, you know, your men being right here and all..."

Chief Donegan waved off the apology.

"Always glad to help. Town's real quiet right now, and besides we might just get to enjoy a little of the glory when you nab the killer. Shouldn't be too hard. Bob, here, can start right away. I'll bet we have something for you by morning."

"I'll start out at the Pioneer Motel," Officer Stevens volunteered. "If they didn't see him, I'll head out 23A. I'll check the bed and breakfasts, too."

"Good. I really appreciate your help. And I'll get one of my men onto it first thing in the morning. Maybe there's nothing in it, but I don't believe in coincidences."

They went their several ways: the sheriff back to Cumberland to go through the day's reports, Donegan to his home for an evening with family, and Bob Stevens, on duty for several more hours, to the motels on the outskirts of Southport where, with any luck, he would learn the identity of the stranger.

———

Much as she regretted the need to do so, Sheriff Kelleher stopped off at the office before taking her tired feet and empty stomach home. Most of the papers on her desk pertained to matters other than the Britingham case, reminding her of how mundane her work normally was. Only the Britingham file engaged her interest, and it was discouragingly thin. But there was one new item in it, the report she had requested on Britingham's clothing. She had continued to be bothered by the sweater, at once seedier than the rest of the outfit he had been wearing and quite obviously not his size.

The report was the result of some rummaging through Britingham's closet at 'the mansion,' as people were now calling it, plus some preliminary inquiries of the San Francisco tailor whose name appeared on many of the labels in Britingham's wardrobe and on a business card they had found in his wallet. Sarah Washburn had reluctantly accompanied Deputy Sheriff Bridges when he went through the dead man's closet and dresser, but she had refused to be drawn into a discussion of his sartorial style except to say that she had never seen him wearing a cardigan sweater.

It appeared from the report that the man's wardrobe, or at least that part of it he had brought east with him, was almost entirely custom tailored and relatively new. Even those clothes that were presumably used for fishing were, in a manner of speaking, high fashion. There was no variety in size; the jackets and sweaters were all size 44. The San Francisco tailor claimed to have made all of Britingham's suits, jackets, and slacks for twelve years, in which time there had been no need to alter sizes. He said he had never had a client who was so conscientious about his weight and physical condition. No one could account for the cardigan Britingham had been wearing when his body was discovered. The tailor had been very doubtful that he owned one. "Too much like an old man's sweater," was how he had put it. The label was missing, and there was no indication of size. Bridges had asked the owner of Harvey's Men's Shop on State Street to give his best estimate of the sweater's size, and after much fussing around in the back room, Mr. Harvey had cautiously settled on a 40.

There was no concrete proof of it, but the clear implication of the report in front of her was that Britingham did not own a cardigan sweater. Carol considered the problem. He had borrowed the sweater. But why? And from whom? It had been put on him by his killer. But why? And, no, that couldn't be. The lab report had confirmed what her eyes had told her: Britingham had been wearing the sweater when he was stabbed. More likely he had borrowed it. The bad fit suggested he'd done so on the spur of the moment—it had simply been available. And why would someone borrow a sweater? Because it was cold? As she remembered it, that had been a somewhat chilly evening for August. She'd have to check the record for the temperature the night Britingham had been killed.

Great, Carol thought, shaking her head. Have I got to go looking for someone who wears old cardigans and is now missing one because it's locked up as evidence over here in Cumberland?

She jumped when the phone rang, interrupting her speculation about the sweater.

"Sheriff Kelleher."

"Sheriff, this is Officer Stevens over in Southport. I think I've
got something for you."

"Already?" She wheeled around in her chair, the adrenalin
flowing again. "That's great. Let's have it."

"Well, I started out, like I told you I would, at the Pioneer
Motel. They're just a couple of blocks..."

"Bob, please, I don't need a step by step account of what you
did. What did you find?"

"Oh, sorry. Well, the girl at Pioneer remembered him. They
get mostly older people, couples, families. They were all booked
up, but she called Sebring Courts out on 23A, and they had a
room."

"Is he still there?" The sheriff was having trouble containing
her excitement. Stevens promptly deflated her expectations.

"No. He checked in Sunday and checked out Tuesday."

"Gone? On Tuesday? Did he move to another motel?"

"I don't know. But there's something funny. According to the
man at Sebring he never slept there on Monday night, the night
before he checked out. Do you want me to check other motels?"

"I sure do, at least until I can put Barrett or one of my other
men on it. What's this man's name?"

"I'm not sure. He signed the register at Sebring as John
Laughlin, but the man there isn't sure that's his real name. Said he
looked kind of nervous and confused when he was asked to sign
the register, as if he was reluctant to give his name. He paid cash,
by the way—no credit card."

"What about his car?"

"The Sebring man said he noticed the car, thought it might be
a rental. It had in-state plates."

"Luggage?"

"The man said he brought in a duffel bag, one of those all-
purpose things young people carry their stuff in. The man at the
motel was pretty observant. Either he's naturally nosy, or he was
suspicious about the guy faking his name. Anyway, he sort of kept
an eye on him. He tells me he slept in on Monday, but was gone
the rest of the day. Not sure when he got back, but he did check
out on Tuesday. Never had any phone calls—the manager says he
didn't make any either. They'd have shown up on the bill."

"That's funny. You'd have thought if he wanted to see Brit-ingham he'd have called him, either at home or at the winery. I suppose he could have used a pay phone somewhere."

"I'll keep on it if you want me to, try to find out where he spent Tuesday night—you know, see if he checked into another motel when he left Sebring."

"Yes, you do that, please," Carol responded, remembering that the Southport police were doing her a favor. "And one other thing. We need to get the car license number from the Sebring Courts register and find out who owns it. If it's a rental, they'll have a record of who had it over the past weekend and whether it's been turned in. Just get the number. I'll have one of my men trace it in the morning. And stay in touch. And thanks, Bob—I really mean it."

Sheriff Kelleher stared at the phone as if there were more in-formation still to come over the now broken connection. The old clock on the wall said 9:52. Time to go home. The thought depressed her. Here she was, confronted with what might be the first break in the Britingham case, needing to talk with someone who would understand her exhilaration, someone who would listen and throw out ideas and argue—and appreciate what all this meant to her. Nobody like that was waiting in Cumberland. Bridges, if she could reach him, would simply be deferential. He might well disagree with her, but he would keep his own counsel. In any event, he didn't have a creative mind. And he certainly wouldn't have any idea what it was like to be Carol Kelleher. She found herself thinking about Kevin Whitman. It had been obvious that he wanted to involve himself in her investigation of the case. His motive was suspect. Or was it? The man who had found Britingham's body was an enigma. She really should talk with him again; try to get him to open up, to abandon the nervous defen-siveness he seemed to feel when she questioned him. Maybe if she didn't mention his strange swimming habits or imply that he was a suspect, maybe then they could have a fruitful discussion of the week's events. It surprised her to realize that she wished she might have that discussion that very evening.

Okay, Carol thought, time for a reality check. She put the Britingham file away in the file cabinet, turned off the light, locked the door, and headed home.

After a boring dinner of leftovers, Carol took a long shower and crawled into bed, hoping to unwind with a novel. But she was unable to put the Britingham affair out of her mind. One by one she revisited the conversations with the people on Blue Water Point. Who might have been shading the truth, hiding something that was relevant to the matter at hand? She examined her suspicions about Whitman's neighbors—and Britingham's. But how reliable were suspicions, mere gut feelings, especially at this early stage? She recalled one of her first cases as sheriff. A young fellow named Haskell had been accused of vandalizing the high school. Nervous as a cat, he made up a cock and bull story that nobody believed. And then it turned out he didn't have a thing to do with it. She would have to proceed cautiously.

The stranger was another matter. She hoped they would find him (why hadn't she asked Jack Varner the name of the rock band on the guy's T-shirt?). It would certainly be better if it turned out that an old California connection had murdered Britingham, rather than someone from the Crooked Lake area. But she was having difficulty thinking about the man Jack Varner had described as someone who would have reason to kill Britingham. He sounded too young to have had time to develop a grudge against a man probably twice his age. Why, the stranger was young enough to be Britingham's son.

Britingham's son! Of course. The fugitive thought prompted Carol to sit up straighter in bed, knocking her book onto the floor. Why hadn't that possibility occurred to her? Britingham's son. He had one. What was the name the stranger had used? Laughlin. She ran the name through her memory bank, but came up empty.

Then Carol came out of the bed in a hurry and began a search of the house for the week's *Gazette*. She had to see the Britingham obituary.

Fortunately, she had not tossed the papers, and there it was: Britingham's second wife, the former Sandra Laughlin, had died in a boating accident in 1988; and one of his survivors was a son by that marriage, John Britingham, Jr., of San Francisco. Unfortunately, there was no reference to the date of the Britingham-Laughlin marriage, but it must have been in the late '70s or early '80s. She quickly did the math in her head. The son could well be in his mid-twenties, very much the age of the young man Jack Varner had described.

I'll bet the house, she mused, that the kid who came into town last weekend looking for Britingham was his own son. That did not, of course, rule him out as the killer. One step at a time. She didn't know anything about the boy or his relationship with his father. But if the stranger were indeed young Britingham, Carol might—just might—have a very different case on her hands. And perhaps an explanation for the ill-fitting cardigan sweater.

CHAPTER 26

On the day following Sheriff Kelleher's discovery that a stranger in town had been looking for John Britingham just days before his death, Kevin Whitman embarked on a series of casual conversations with his neighbors. The urge to do so was born of his chat with the young Keyser boys and his own impromptu lecture to George Morgan on the value of speaking truth to the sheriff. By Friday afternoon, he had abandoned all pretense of working on the article he had been writing on Puccini's treatment of his operatic heroines. The Britingham case had become priority number one.

Kevin approached Grace Hess with trepidation, but he was determined to be direct about the dog. If she was surprised to see him at the door, she didn't show it.

"Mr. Whitman, I presume. The man who found our murder victim. Please come in."

He was ushered into the log cabin he had admired so often from afar, most recently on Tuesday morning, roughly half an hour before his discovery of Britingham's body on his dock. They spent a minute or two in the obligatory dialogue about the elegant furnishings, but Grace soon brought him back to the more immediate reason for his visit.

"Has the sheriff been camped on your doorstep ever since you discovered the deceased? She probably wonders why you were swimming at such an hour."

"We've talked quite a bit, yes. Is my swim really that notorious?"

"Oh, yes." She emphasized the point and waved him to a chair on which he was reluctant to sit. It was like sitting on a Hepplewhite in one of the great English country houses, and it made him nervous.

If Grace Hess was conscious of his discomfort, she didn't show it.

"You should be enjoying your instant celebrity, Mr. Whitman. It won't last. Did you know the man?"

"No, I didn't. Did you?"

"Too well. One shouldn't speak ill of the dead, but it's hard to muster any sympathy, isn't it?"

Kevin marveled at her strong face and strong voice. Had he been wrong about the woman's age?

"My feelings were mostly shock, disbelief," he said. "Who would ever expect to find a dead man in circumstances like that? Do you have any idea who might have done it?"

"None at all. I'm not sure I want to know."

"What puzzles me is how he got onto my dock. He sure wasn't there when I went swimming; yet there he was when I got back. And he'd obviously been dead for hours."

Grace Hess looked mildly surprised, and then broke into a smile, which rearranged the lines in her face in an altogether pleasing way.

"Is that so? How did you know? Or maybe I should ask where you heard that?"

Sheriff Kelleher had not wanted Kevin to spread the news of the results of the autopsy, so he tried to find a formula that would permit him to pursue his conversation with Mrs. Hess without violating the letter of the sheriff's injunction.

"I'm no medical doctor, but it was clear even to me that Britingham had been dead for some time." In fact, no such thing had been clear to Kevin at the time of his discovery of the body, and he felt obliged to qualify the lie a little. "And that seems to be the word from those in the know as well."

Grace seemed to accept this oblique explanation. She rose from her chair and walked to one of the large picture windows that provided a splendid view of the lake. She stood there for a moment, and then turned to face Kevin. Small of stature and framed by the panorama of nature behind her, she nonetheless looked quite formidable.

"I'm going to tell you something I didn't tell the sheriff. It would be difficult for me to say this to her, at least for now. You see, I didn't tell her the truth when she asked what I was doing Tuesday morning. I believe that you saw somebody with a dog when you went swimming. The sheriff didn't say it was you, but I think it was. If it wasn't, it doesn't really matter. Well, I was the person on the beach with a dog, with my dog, Jeff. I didn't see you, didn't see anybody in fact. My eyes aren't as keen as they once were, and besides, I wasn't looking for anyone. I had nothing to hide."

Grace Hess crossed the room and resumed her seat. Kevin was mesmerized by her story, the very thing he had come to ask about and had not even mentioned.

"Jeff had brought me a present. He's a retriever, you know, and it's bred into them, although he's trained not to bring things into the house. He persisted until I got up and slipped into a robe and went outside with him. Jeff likes to play, so he grabbed up his present and ran off with it. I followed him, and we ended up down the beach in front of the Sullivan cottage. Jeff gave up his present there. It was just an old tennis shoe, long past wearing. I could have taken it back and dropped it in the garbage can, but I didn't. On impulse I heaved it out into the lake. It's pretty deep there, and I figured no one would mind. Then I went home."

Kevin looked at Grace Hess and wondered aloud, "Why are you telling me this?"

"Conscience, I guess. And someone ought to know, just in case people think I was up to no good. But if Mr. Britingham had been dead for several hours by the time Jeff and I were seen on the beach, there's no harm in my being frank, is there, even if I didn't like the man?"

"Were you afraid you might be suspected?" The thought seemed slightly ridiculous to Kevin.

"Of course. I didn't like Britingham at all, and that was a well-known fact. Somebody was bound to get the idea that an old woman might not have much to lose by killing a man like that, a man who was going to ruin her most precious possession, her privacy. Of course I thought I would be suspected. So I lied to the sheriff. But then I began to worry about the dog you'd seen—it was you, wasn't it? I could hardly pretend it wasn't Jeff. Have you seen the other dogs around here? And if people knew it was Jeff, then why not me? Wasn't I the logical one? Then you tell me Britingham was killed earlier. So there's no longer any reason not to own up, is there? I couldn't have been out there killing him at five, or whenever it was."

They had talked on for another ten minutes or so, but even before he left Kevin realized that something was bothering him. He found it hard to credit the woman's anxiety that she would have been suspected on the basis of so mundane a motive. According to Dan Milburn, she had taken legal steps to meet Britingham's challenge. Wouldn't she be expected to let the process run its course? And no matter what shape she was in,

Britingham was much bigger, much younger, and himself in excellent shape. It seemed highly unlikely that she could have stabbed him to death, much less have gotten his body onto the dock.

And why had she told two stories about her morning activities, one to the sheriff and one to him? Jeff was apparently friendly to everyone, and there had been no identification, as far as he knew, of the person seen with the dog. Certainly he had been unable to make such an identification or even to give a helpful general description. Why had she felt it necessary to contradict her earlier story? She hadn't even waited for him to ask questions. Indeed, she couldn't have known he had wanted to discuss what he had seen on the beach.

Everything Mrs. Hess had said was plausible. But Kevin didn't know whether one of the mysteries of the Britingham affair had been solved or whether he was only being used by this remarkable woman for some reason of her own.

––––

Later in the day, when he figured Mike would be home from work, Kevin wandered down to the Snyder cottage with a piece of mail which had been delivered to his place by mistake. It was only junk mail, and the name had even been misspelled, but it provided Kevin with a convenient pretext for talking to Mike.

"Your mail," he said, handing over the envelope to his neighbor, whom he found in the kitchen, studying the cooking instructions on a box of noodles.

"Thanks. Looks like Gloria's kind of stuff. There's no end to the junk coming through the mail, is there?" Mike dropped the envelope, unopened, into a sack of dry garbage, which would go into the fireplace later.

Kevin pulled out a kitchen chair and sat down.

"What's the news with Gloria? Are you going to be able to work it out?"

"Wish I could tell you. I'd like to, but it's tough. These things get out of hand. It was just little things at first, but then they became big things."

Snyder paused, looking momentarily choked up.

"Do you think I drink too much?" he asked.

"We probably all drink more than we should. I don't know what's too much—it's probably different for different people. Gloria thinks you're an alcoholic, doesn't she?"

"Yeah. Do you think I am?" Mike Snyder was obviously living under stress.

"There's no way I could tell you, Mike. Are you beginning to believe it?"

"Sometimes. I don't think I am, but then some days I just can't stop. Like Monday night, when we were playing cards over at the Sandersons. I'll bet I had five, maybe six beers, easy. Chris hovered like a mother hen, worried all night about me. Now why do I do that?"

"Look, you're asking me something I don't know anything about. See a doctor. See a shrink."

Kevin Whitman and Mike Snyder weren't close friends, but they'd seen a lot of each other over several summers, and Kevin felt a genuine sympathy. He picked up on the invitation Mike had indirectly given him to shift the subject to the night of Britingham's death.

"You had a bad night Monday?"

"Not too good. But I made it. Haven't had a drink since." Mike acted as if he'd rather not discuss it. "Hey, enough about that. What do you hear about this Britingham business?"

Kevin preferred to be asking the questions, not serving as a conduit of information from the sheriff to the residents of Blue Water Point. He suggested they go sit on the porch, so the two men went out onto a screened porch which obviously missed Gloria Snyder's hand. Magazines were scattered about, and a potted plant, blown over by a breeze, hadn't been put back on its stand or the spilled dirt swept up. Mike pushed some of the magazines off a chair and sat where he could put his feet up on a railing. Kevin followed suit.

"I've been able to piece this much together," Kevin began. "Britingham was dead before he ended up on my dock. So somebody had to have put him there. You see the problem. You and I were up—we admit it; besides, we saw each other. Now I know I didn't have anything to do with this, and I can't imagine that you did. But put yourself in the sheriff's shoes. She's going to wonder about us, what we were doing. So let's try to think it through.

"I went for a swim. Went in a little ahead of five. You came out to your boat about the same time. But I didn't see you take off because I was in the water, swimming the other way. So when did you leave? I mean, how soon after you came down to your dock?"

"What is this, the third degree? You sound like the sheriff." Mike looked restless. "Hell, I can't really say. But it wasn't long. Had all my gear together, the engine worked fine. I'd say two or three minutes, no more than three."

"Now don't get annoyed with me, Mike," Kevin said, sure that Mike would in fact be annoyed, "but that just won't do. Maybe you forgot something and had to go look for it. But I didn't hear your motor start up until I was all the way around past the Milburn cottage. It must have been a good eighteen, twenty minutes."

"Damn it, Kevin, what's this all about? What are you trying to tell me?" Mike was now quite obviously agitated. He started to reach for a drink that wasn't there. Kevin was sure that he would have gotten one had he been alone.

"I'm trying to tell you what the situation is. It may seem unfair that we have to account for every minute, but I think it may come to that. There seem to be two critical periods we'll all have to account for as best we can—the middle of the night, let's say up to about three a.m., and then between 4:45 and around 5:15 or a little after. I told the sheriff that I thought your boat started up after I'd made the turn into Mallard Cove. And it took me something like twenty minutes or so to swim that far. Now you tell me you took off well before that. Is that what you told the sheriff?"

"I think so," Mike replied dully, looking as if he very much wanted a drink.

"One of these days the sheriff's going to remember that our stories don't jibe. She's probably noticed it already and just hasn't gotten back to you. And me, of course." Kevin hoped that the sheriff would be more inclined to doubt Mike's timetable than his own. "So I think you're going to have to account for those extra minutes."

"Look, I didn't know it was so long. I said I took off right away because I didn't want the sheriff to think I'd done anything. To Britingham, I mean. I didn't, you know. I was as surprised to hear he was dead on your dock as you must have been when you found him. But you see how it looks, me right there."

"I know. That's the problem. What did you do?" Kevin didn't particularly like prodding his neighbor like this, but it was now too late to drop the subject.

"I had to go to the bathroom, for Christ's sake. And I decided to put some coffee in a thermos. But who's gonna believe that?"

"Why not? You should have said so. It's the best explanation in the world."

"Maybe, but I can't prove it. You've talked with the sheriff more than I have. What do you think? Is she smart? Do you think she'd be suspicious of me?"

"Oh, she's smart all right. But why would she suspect you? Why on earth would you have anything to do with Britingham's death? I'm sure she'll be looking for someone with a good reason to want him dead."

"Even if I'd said some pretty nasty things about him?"

"From what I can figure out, everyone around here said nasty things about him. You know that as well as I do." He was remembering some of the nasty things Grace Hess had said only a few hours before.

"Yeah, I suppose so." Mike still didn't look convinced. "You said Britingham got killed earlier, some time in the night. Is that true? Can they really tell about things like that?"

"It seems they can. And I'm sure the sheriff will be around again, asking questions about where everyone was, not only at dawn, but also at midnight and one and two in the morning. And I'd be willing to bet that most everyone will say they were in bed, sound asleep."

"Great. How do I prove it? No Gloria. No kids. Who's gonna say I was in the sack at two or in the john at five?"

"Were you?"

"Sure. We'd been playing cards. Like I said, I'd had a few. We should have packed it in way before we did. Chris was hinting it was time to call it a night, and she was right. I probably left around 12:30. You'd think I'd have crashed and slept like a baby. Damn bladder wouldn't let me—all that beer, you know. Anyway, I tried to get some sleep, finally gave it up and went fishing."

Kevin finally left Mike to his bachelor cooking efforts, his worries about his wife, his drinking problem, and his explanation of his movements Monday night and Tuesday morning. The lake had taken on its characteristic early evening calm, although there was something of an overcast. The hills, deprived of the rays of the setting sun by the gathering clouds, were a darker green than usual. Kevin walked briskly toward his cottage, anxious to get away from the clouds that hovered over Mike Snyder's life.

CHAPTER 27

The idea had first been planted the night before and had germinated in her sleep. When she awoke on Friday morning, Dolores Weber knew she had to call the sheriff's office and drop the hint that the late John Britingham had been having an affair with a married woman named Emily Hoffman. She wouldn't have to draw the implications of this information for them. Whatever their level of competence, and she suspected that it wasn't very high, they would grasp at once its relevance to their investigation of John's death. It might come to nothing, but it would keep them busy for a while. The thought gave her a perverse pleasure. Even more importantly, it would cause trouble for Emily Hoffman, and that pleased her even more.

Dolores had no other plans for the morning, so she puttered around the kitchen, enjoying a more substantial breakfast than usual and killing time until she thought someone would be on the job at the county sheriff's office. She guessed that with the Britingham case on their agenda, the police would be putting in a seven-day week and long hours, so she tried the sheriff shortly before 8:30.

The woman who answered the phone sounded as if she had already put in several hours. Dolores got right to the point.

"Good morning. Is the sheriff in? I think I might have some information about John Britingham that he might want to hear."

"No, I'm sorry, she's not here at the moment." Miss Maltbie corrected her caller's pronoun. "Let me put Deputy Sheriff Bridges on the line."

The news that the sheriff was a woman did not account for the scowl that crossed Dolores's face. She remembered her experience with Bridges. He had irritated her, both because of the persistence with which he had pursued his not very imaginative line of questions and because he had come off as a particularly annoying kind of male chauvinist. At least John had had charm.

She waited impatiently for Bridges to come to the phone. It took him only a little more than fifteen seconds.

"Hello, who's calling, please?"

"I've been following the Britingham case," she said, ignoring his question. "Fascinating, isn't it? I thought you ought to know that just prior to his death he was having an affair with a woman named Emily Hoffman."

"Hoffman?"

"Yes, that's right, Hoffman. She's married to a man named Alan Hoffman. They live around here. I believe Mr. Britingham was seeing her while her husband was down in the city on business. It occurred to me that this might have something to do with Mr. Britingham's death. With his murder."

"I don't have your name, ma'am. We need to know who's giving us this information."

"I think you ought to make inquiries, don't you?" Dolores asked, and gently hung up the phone. She cleared her throat. Thank God, she thought, my voice isn't really like that.

She was pleased with herself. Exceedingly pleased. But there was still other unfinished business to attend to. She had been motivated by anger and—yes, she had to admit it—by jealousy to pursue the matter of John's relationship with another woman. She hadn't given much thought to the matter of his violent death. Now, sitting on the couch with her coffee and contemplating the rest of her day, she had to concede that her priorities were really a bit perverse. She had been more concerned about his cheating on her than about his murder. She had told the deputy sheriff that Britingham's affair with the Hoffman woman might be connected in some way with his death. Her implication had been that a jealous husband had killed him. It was a real possibility, but she had no idea whether that's what had happened.

There were other possibilities. After all, her former employer and lover had not been a terribly popular man. She had seen plenty of evidence of his unpopularity at the office. And then there was the note, the note that had been tucked away in the drawer of his office desk, the note that had said, quite cryptically, that he'd pay for it.

Pay for what? For his affair with Emily Hoffman? That had been her first assumption, and it would mean in all likelihood that Alan Hoffman had discovered his wife's infidelity and threatened John. But Dolores realized that she hadn't really given the note much thought. It had been less important to her than the woman's things she had found in his study and the phone numbers on the Rolodex card.

Now that she had learned to whom the jewelry and the pill-box and the panties belonged, and had set in motion her scheme to squeeze a bit of money out of the Hoffman woman and alert the sheriff to John's liaison with her—now that she had done what she had to do to satisfy her own emotional needs, she found herself thinking about his death. And this meant thinking about the note. The more she thought about it, the more puzzled she became.

Was it the kind of note a man would send to his wife's lover? Dolores found it hard to put herself in the man's shoes. She would not have sent such a note to Emily Hoffman; yet, she was determined that Emily should "pay for this." But there was something about the note she had found in John's desk that bothered her. Surely the note could not be that of the man whose voice she had heard on the Hoffman's answering machine, a voice that spoke of education and refinement, quite at odds with the tone of the note she held in her hand. The note was more like one that might have been written by the coarse man in California she had spoken with the night before.

It was while she was speculating about these things that it first struck her. That handwriting. She had been thinking about the message, the crude threat to Britingham, not the hand in which it had been written. And as she looked at it more closely, she suddenly remembered that she had seen something very much like it. But where?

Dolores concentrated very hard. She had always had a good memory; in fact, her ability to memorize had produced good grades in high school and later in college, even when she hadn't really understood the material. And her memory for names and faces was an important factor in her success as a secretary. This time, however, she was having difficulty recalling where she had seen handwriting similar to that on the threatening note. She was about to give it up—had indeed gotten up from the couch and headed for the bedroom to get ready to take a shower—when it came to her. Halfway to the bedroom door, she paused, squeezed her eyes tightly shut, and focused her mind.

Yes, she decided, that's it. It must be. I'll go down to the office as soon as I get dressed. Then I'll know. Then I'll make another phone call.

"I shall not take but a few minutes of your time, Sheriff."

The young woman who sat across Sheriff Kelleher's desk at 9:15 on Saturday morning did not look as if she would take much of her time at all. She sat close to the front edge of her chair, both feet on the floor. Her pearl-gray suit was well tailored, if somewhat wrinkled from travel. She wore her dark hair in an attractive mannish cut, displaying her angular but striking features to good advantage. Had the sheriff not known it for a fact from Miss Maltbie's message, she would have guessed that this was John Britingham's daughter.

"No, please, Mrs. Carson, I'm glad you're here. That probably sounds unkind. I'm sorry about your father, very sorry, but I welcome the chance to talk with you. Can I have Miss Maltbie make you some coffee?"

"No, thank you. I don't drink coffee. Sheriff, I'm not going to pretend to be in mourning. I'm here because arrangements have to be made, and I have to make them. I would have been here earlier, but I was told that there would be an autopsy and that the weekend would do. It's a long trip, as you must know, what with the connection from Sacramento, and then the long flight east and the car trip at the end. I got in last night, but didn't have a very good sleep. I'm sorry if I look a little the worse for wear. Your secretary said there would be a few things, official things, that I'm expected to do. I want to know what they are, and then get on with it."

Did no one like this man, the sheriff asked herself? Not even the family?

"Of course, Mrs. Carson. I know that this is difficult. More difficult because it wasn't a natural death. But would you mind terribly if I asked a couple of questions? I gather that you and your father weren't close, but whatever the family situation, we have to find out how he met his death. Maybe you can help us."

"I doubt that very much," she said, but she did adjust her position so that she looked less perched on the chair. "There is nothing I can tell you about what happened. I don't know any of my father's acquaintances here, either business or personal. He hasn't called or written since he came east, and neither have I. I think he may have tried to contact me on a California trip earlier this summer, but we didn't get together. I last saw him last autumn."

"So you have no idea as to who could have killed your father—or might have wanted to?"

"None." The sheriff may have expected some elaboration, but she left it at that.

"I know it sounds like an impertinent question, Mrs. Carson, but this is a murder investigation. What accounts for your estrangement from your father?"

Britingham's daughter gave the sheriff just the smallest suggestion of a smile.

"There is no great mystery. He left my mother when he saw a business opportunity that lay through another woman. Excuse the double entendre. If it hadn't been her, it would have been someone else. I didn't realize it when I was small, but it became very clear very soon that my father was not interested in anybody but himself. He treated Mother shabbily. I'm sure he treated his second wife shabbily as well, although she's not with us to testify to his character. At least he finally seems to have had the good sense to stop marrying the women he charms and then misuses. If you want to learn something about the real John Britingham, find one of his recent conquests and question her. Don't ask my mother, though. She went through hell once. She won't be put through it again."

Carol thought she had never watched or listened to such a demonstration of carefully controlled bitterness.

"Why are you here? You have a halfbrother, I believe. Couldn't he have handled this?"

"I doubt very much that he could. I don't know John very well. I do know that he disliked his father as much as I did. It is my understanding, though he never said so to me, that he thinks that his father was responsible for his mother's death. I really can't picture him coming out here to pick up the pieces. Besides, when I called him after I got the news about father, I couldn't reach him. He's a bit of a nomad, I think. It's quite likely he still hasn't heard about his father's death."

"Would it surprise you if I told you that your halfbrother has probably been right here in the Crooked Lake area in the last week? Maybe even on the day of your father's death?"

This news obviously did surprise Linda Carson.

"Are you sure? I can't imagine John coming to see his father, alive or dead. And I'm sure he didn't kill him, if that's what you're thinking."

"But you said he thinks his father had something to do with his mother's death. That would be likely to stir up some pretty strong feelings, wouldn't it? What did he think happened?"

"Sheriff Kelleher, I don't know what goes on in John's mind. You'll have to ask him. I've never discussed it with him. Let's just say that he blames his father for his mother's drowning. But John wouldn't—no, he couldn't—kill anybody. Anybody! He's a vegetarian. And a pacifist. For a while he was into Buddhism, worried about hurting any living thing. He'd be torn up inside about his father, but he wouldn't kill him."

"Why was he here then?"

"Was he? I really don't know." She brushed a piece of lint off her skirt and picked up her purse. "May I go now? Your secretary said she had some papers for me to sign, and she hinted that there are some other things I must do. I'd like to leave."

"Yes, of course. Miss Maltbie will take care of you, I'm sure." Carol stood and offered her hand. "There is one other question, the inevitable question, I suppose. Your father had a considerable fortune, I assume. What disposition does he make of it in his will?"

"I really have no idea," Mrs. Carson said, color rising in her face. "He may never have made a will. People who think they are immortal rarely do, I'm told. We'll find out soon enough. If I inherit, I'm not going to be so foolish as to refuse the money. If I don't, I shall be equally happy. My husband and I do quite well."

This was not, Carol suspected, the typical speech of a prospective heiress. Nor was she satisfied.

"Mrs. Carson, I'm sure you can appreciate that money is often a motive for murder. You may not care whether you inherit from your father or how much, but I have to concern myself with whether he made a will or changed a will, and whom he left his money to. We know that his legal affairs are handled by a San Francisco firm, Courteney, Weiss and Newton, and we have contacted them. I hope, for your sake, that there are no surprises in the will. And yes, he did make one."

"You will do what you have to do, I'm sure, Sheriff. The will is not uppermost in my mind."

There seemed to be no need to escort her to the door.

"Thank you for coming by. We may need to be in touch with you again, you know. And let me know if there is anything I can do."

"Thank you." And John Britingham's daughter was gone, leaving Sheriff Kelleher to ponder this latest contribution to the mounting tide of evidence that the late owner of the Silver Leaf Wine Company had been thoroughly and widely disliked.

CHAPTER 28

"You know this means a trip down to the city, don't you?" Sheriff Kelleher looked across the desk at her deputy and found herself wondering whether Sam would see it as an adventure or an imposition, especially on a weekend.

John Britingham's daughter had left, and the sheriff had finally had time to discuss with Bridges the telephone tip that Britingham had been having an affair with Emily Hoffman. Carol had met the Hoffman woman and could imagine that she would appeal to someone like Britingham. Her husband lived and worked in the city, creating an opportunity for lakeside hanky-panky. And if the anonymous tip was accurate and the husband had learned of the affair, was it not entirely possible that the murder might turn out to be a crime of passion, the act of a cuckolded spouse?

It was obvious that they would have to know Alan Hoffman's whereabouts on the night Britingham met his death. And while she might obtain that information by phone, Carol believed that there was always more to be gained through a face-to-face dialogue. So she had decided to send Bridges down to the city to talk to people at the Hoffmans' apartment building. Sam's tenacity would, she hoped, compensate for his lack of tact.

"When do I go?" Deputy Sheriff Bridges had expected this, but he didn't look happy. The problem, Carol realized, was not that Sam didn't like long drives and unfamiliar places, but that he would see it as a high-risk assignment. What if he came back empty-handed? The prospect of a 300-mile wild goose chase was what was worrying him.

"No point putting it off. Let's get on down there. Just don't let them give you the runaround. They'll have a record of who was on duty. If he's not there, get his address and go see him. Hell, it'll be a little spice in their life. Make them feel important, getting asked questions about a murder suspect."

"I thought we weren't going to call him a suspect."

"No, of course not. We're just conducting a routine investigation. But you know as well as I do what the staff in the apartment building will be thinking. You'll make their day, just discussing Hoffman's nighttime habits."

As it happened, the man on duty at the Hoffmans' apartment building was a tougher nut to crack than the sheriff had anticipated, but in the end the results were all that she and Bridges could have hoped for.

Getting to the place had been Sam's first problem. On the map, the grid-like street layout made it look easy, but one-way traffic patterns and a major avenue that defied the grid, cutting across it and channeling traffic in a direction other than the one Sam wanted to take, conspired to bring him to the Clarion Arms just ahead of two o'clock, almost half an hour later than he had anticipated. The delay nearly cost him an opportunity to talk with Salvatore Martinez, who, although Sam didn't know it, was the very man he wanted to see.

The two men behind the reception desk broke off their conversation and watched Bridges cross the lobby toward them. Both looked to be Hispanic, both were identically attired in dark blue suits, and both responded to Bridges' presence in a manner at once polite and vigilant.

"Yes, Sir, what can I do for you?" the younger and thinner of the two asked.

"I need to talk with you about one of your residents," Sam replied. He quickly surveyed the lobby and noted a lot of mirrors, half a dozen large and unfamiliar plants in ornate tubs, and a few pieces of fancy furniture that looked more decorative than functional.

"Go ahead, Sal. I'll take care of it," the thin man said to his partner. Then turning to Bridges, he resumed his inquiry into the stranger's business. "Who is it you'd like to see? I'll ring and see if they're here."

"No, I don't want to see anyone. I want to ask you about a man who lives here. Name's Hoffman."

Sam pulled out his identification and held it up for the deskman to study. The other man, the one referred to as Sal, had been on his way to the door marked 'Employees Only' at the end of the aisle behind the reception desk. Sam's request was apparently unusual enough that Sal stopped to hear more.

"Police?" The thin man's eyebrows rose with his voice. "But what is this—this Cumberland County? I don't understand."

Sam rested his elbows on the counter and gave the man the speech he had rehearsed in the car on the way to the city.

"Like it says, my name's Bridges, and I'm with the sheriff's department upstate in Cumberland. I'm investigating the death of one of our citizens, and need to account for some people who are neighbors of the deceased. I understand that one of those neighbors has an apartment in this building, a man named Alan Hoffman. We need to know where he was last Monday night. Can you check your records and tell me who was on duty that night?"

"Well now, Mr. Bridges—or Sheriff Bridges, I don't know. We're not supposed to give out information about our guests. Mr. Haggerty's very strict about that. Privacy, he says. Never talk about anyone. They say a guy got fired two, three years ago for talking about a couple up in the penthouse."

Sam took a deep breath.

"Look, I understand this privacy thing, Mr.—I don't believe I have your name."

"Torres, Juan Torres. And this is Salvatore Martinez," the thin man said, motioning toward his stockier and older colleague, who had decided he could wait a few minutes before going off duty and had returned to the counter.

"Okay, Mr. Torres. I don't want to get you into any trouble with the manager, but this is police business. Like I said, I'm investigating"—Sam decided he had better use the word—"what may be a case of homicide. Nobody's accused Mr. Hoffman of anything. I've been checking on a lot of other people, too. So you see, it's just a matter of getting information."

Torres remained skeptical. He looked to his colleague for support.

"You tell him, Sal."

"I'd suggest calling Haggerty," was Martinez's contribution to the settlement of the impasse. "He's on his summer vacation, but he's supposed to be back in another week."

"A week?" Deputy Sheriff Bridges was losing his cool. "Now look, this investigation can't wait a week. You guys wouldn't be giving me this routine if I was from police headquarters downtown or wherever it is here. Somebody comes up our way and asks for cooperation, we cooperate. People believe in law and order."

"Oh, so do we," Torres hastened to assure the lawman from upstate.

"Let me handle this, Juan." The older man leaned across the counter and addressed Bridges. "You said last Monday, didn't you?"

Whether Martinez feared the manager less or believed in law and order more was not clear. Perhaps he was just naturally more curious. In any event, he seemed ready at least to discuss the terms of cooperation with the representative of Cumberland County law enforcement.

"I did. Monday." Sam tried not to show his eagerness. Play it straight, he thought. Remember, he's not doing you a favor. "All I need to know is whether Alan Hoffman was here in the Clarion Arms that night. Do you remember who was on duty?"

"Sheriff, do you have a card on you? I'd like to show it to Mr. Haggerty—if he asks, that is—so he can call you, and you can tell him what you've told me."

Sam produced the card, suppressing an urge to grumble over the request.

"Now about Mr. Hoffman. You were going to tell me who was on duty last Monday night." At least he hoped that was what Martinez would tell him.

"I was," came the surprising reply. "Not only Monday night. All week, through Friday. We rotate the shifts, and I had the graveyard last week, 10 to 6. Unless you want the early evening. Belcher had that one."

"Good. I don't know whether I'll need to see this Belcher or not. Depends. Can you remember Monday night—late Monday night?" Sam was afraid the nights would all look pretty much alike. He'd found that people's memories weren't very good when it came to dates.

"Of course." Martinez seemed offended that his ability to re-call something as recent as last week should be questioned. "Not many of our people are going out at those hours on weeknights. You remember the ones who do. Mr. Hoffman did. I mean he left the building just ahead of 11:30. When Juan came on at six, he still hadn't come back."

Martinez looked at Torres, as if expecting his partner to pick up the narrative. Torres, obviously uncomfortable with the conversation, didn't respond on cue.

"You say 11:30. How do you know that's when he left?" Sam was afraid that Martinez's precision about the day and hour would vanish under questioning, but he was excited nonetheless.

"It's my job, Sheriff. Besides, you can't miss people coming in and going out. There's only this one door, except the fire door around to the side, and nobody uses that. Don't see many people going out that late. They come in late, of course, like from the theater or parties or wherever they go. But I remember Mr. Hoffman going out that night, and I looked at the clock here because it seemed pretty late, even for him." Martinez nodded his head toward the clock on the wall behind the reception desk. "It was almost 11:30, maybe 28 or 29 after. He even waved to me when he left."

Torres had retreated to a corner, where he leaned against the wall, nibbling at a fingernail and looking worried. Martinez, having decided to talk about Alan Hoffman, was warming to the task.

"You're going to ask me whether I could have missed him coming back, aren't you?" For all he knew, the implications of what he had to say might be serious for Mr. Hoffman, but Salvatore Martinez could not suppress the hint of a smug smile. "Well, I didn't. I never left the desk. Strong bladder, you know. Cut out coffee a couple of years back, and since then I hardly ever miss a minute of my shift. And I'm telling you, Mr. Hoffman—he left at 11:30 and wasn't back by six the next morning. Juan didn't see him on his shift either. We talked about it, Mr. Hoffman staying out all night—he's done it three, four times lately."

Bridges marveled at the Martinez bladder and the man's pride in his ability to work an eight-hour shift without a trip to the john. But mostly Sam was congratulating himself on this avalanche of information. Whatever Hoffman had been up to on the night of Britingham's death, his nocturnal habits sounded suspicious, and Sheriff Kelleher would be pleased with the report she'd be getting when Sam returned to Cumberland.

"You say last Monday wasn't the first time Hoffman was gone all night. Let's have some more detail."

"Well, I didn't write it down or anything—couldn't know somebody'd be asking questions. But we're pretty sure it was twice the week before last. Of course he stays out on weekends, you know, Friday and Saturday, sometimes Sunday. He's got a place out in the country somewhere—him and his wife. I guess that'd be around where you're from, where this crime took place. Can't see why she's there and he's here; I wouldn't leave my woman alone like that. And she's a beautiful lady, let me tell you. We don't see much of her anymore, though."

Martinez made it sound as if Emily Hoffman's decision to live most of the time at the lake had taken some of the sunshine out of his life.

"Do you ever talk to Mr. Hoffman? Any idea what he does when he stays out at night?"

Martinez shook his head.

"None of my business," he replied, as if Haggerty had appeared at his side. "Anyway, he doesn't say much. You know, 'good morning,' 'nice weather.' Sometimes he asks about the missus, but he doesn't stand around and talk like Mr. Ferris or the Cohns."

Bridges didn't know Ferris or the Cohns and said so, and it soon became apparent that he had learned about all he was likely to learn from Martinez.

"Just one more question. Did the other deskman you mentioned—what's his name, Weller?—did he happen to mention whether Mr. Hoffman came home at the usual time on Tuesday or whether there was anything strange about him that day?"

"Belcher," Martinez corrected. "Not to me. I don't think Juan asked. Jim—that's Belcher—he doesn't mix. We don't talk much. Do you want to see him? This is his week on the graveyard. He'll come on after Juan."

Sam didn't answer this question because another had occurred to him.

"Where would Mr. Hoffman keep his car?"

"We've got our own garage, but there's no one on duty. The tenants have their own keys."

Martinez had anticipated Bridges' next question. Bright man. And very observant. And pretty well spoken, too. Salvatore Martinez had not only provided the Cumberland County deputy sheriff with some useful information. But he had also modified Bridges' perception of Hispanic Americans, of whom there weren't more than a tiny handful in the upstate area around Crooked Lake.

———

Sam's report did not tell Sheriff Kelleher where Hoffman had been or what he had been doing on the night of Britingham's death. But it did suggest that he hadn't been where he might have been expected to be, in his own apartment, doing what he might have been expected to be doing, sleeping. The sheriff wished she knew what several people had been doing that night, and where. She was determined to find out.

PART IV

A FATEFUL NIGHT
IN AUGUST

CHAPTER 29

The third Monday in August had been a typical summer day. Perhaps a bit cool, but there were those who welcomed a break in the heat and the humidity. For many of the residents on Crooked Lake the only problem was the message on the calendar: Labor Day was just two weeks away, and with it, the end of vacation time and escape from life's responsibilities.

Of course there were those who had other things to worry about. Foremost among those worries for some was the owner of the Silver Leaf Wine Company, for John Britingham had threatened the livelihood of grape growers, set in motion an offensive development scheme, publicly humiliated more than one well-liked local figure, ignored the wishes of people haunted by an old lake tragedy, and bedded another man's wife

Yet when the sun set on that Monday evening, no one—not even those who had reason to hate the man—could have imagined that John Britingham would be dead by violence before sunrise the following morning. But on that night, fate had conspired to bring Britingham and several of those he had wronged together on normally tranquil Blue Water Point. The result was that some who may have had a motive for killing the man now had an opportunity to do so.

Murder, when not premeditated, is frequently a consequence of an unanticipated encounter, of words spoken in anger, of a situation escalating out of control. In the dark hours of that Monday night in August, any and all of these things were possible.

CHAPTER 30

George and Edna Morgan had agreed back during the winter that they would visit her brother, Amos, at least twice a week. It had long been their habit to drive over to the nursing home in Cumberland once a week, and almost always on Sunday. But the old man had obviously been failing, and over breakfast one morning Edna had expressed the thought on both their minds.

"How would we feel if they called and said he'd passed away, and we hadn't been over to see him for a whole week? We'd never forgive ourselves."

They had debated whether they should make even more frequent visits, but George had argued that they weren't that young themselves and shouldn't wear themselves out running over to Cumberland all the time. After all, Amos couldn't talk to them, so conversations were invariably one-sided, with Edna going on about the jam she was putting up or the new curtains she had made for the bedroom, or about old times and family matters. Edna usually conducted these monologues while busying herself around Amos's room, rearranging the cut flowers, plumping up the pillows, straightening the handful of old pictures, even dusting off the surfaces which she was convinced the nursing home staff regularly overlooked. There had even been occasions when Amos didn't seem to recognize them, and they would end up sitting quietly in his room, George doing a crossword puzzle and Edna reading or knitting until they sensed that they had done their duty and could leave with a good conscience. So they had decided that two visits a week was about right.

It was after supper on a Monday night in August, while she was clearing the table, that Edna raised the subject.

"Are you up to going over to see Amos tonight?"

"I guess so," George responded, his tone of voice suggesting resignation rather than enthusiasm.

"Well, then, let me finish up here. Do you suppose he'd like some of the cake?"

"I don't get the feeling anything tastes very good to him, but he'd appreciate the thought. If he's lucid, that is."

"I hate that word."

"I know, but what are we going to call it? It's not the word that bothers you; it's the idea that we're losing him—that his mind is going."

Edna sat down at the table and took up her half-empty cup of lukewarm coffee. She was near tears. George gave her a reassuring pat.

"Let's not get maudlin. Amos has done pretty well, considering."

But Amos hadn't done well at all, as they both knew all too well. He had lived a long life, but he had spent too many years of that life in hospitals and then in a nursing home, a mere shell of the brother Edna had known when she was a little girl. And it had now been many months since he'd even been able to go for a ride in their car.

The dishes had been put away, but neither Edna nor George hurried. No clock regulated Amos's waking and sleeping hours, and the nursing home personnel were content to let him keep whatever hours he wished. He was as likely to be awake at two in the morning as at two in the afternoon, the television set droning on. And the Morgans were so well known at the home that they had the privilege of coming at any time of day or night. They actually preferred to see Amos at night, because they could more easily bring the visit to an end by saying it was their bedtime. In spite of his erratic sleeping habits, he seemed to accept this better than the excuses they made to leave during the day.

When the clock on the mantel struck nine, George put down the paper and carefully knocked the ashes from his pipe and announced that they had better be on their way.

"Good. I'll get the cake." Edna was on her feet and making preparations before George had finished his little ritual with the pipe. It was 9:13 when they pulled out of the driveway and headed for Cumberland.

They chatted about inconsequential things on the way over to the nursing home, and at one point lapsed into companionable silence for several minutes. It was Edna who finally broke that silence.

"Do you realize that this is the first time in weeks we haven't spent most of the drive over here talking about that man Britingham?"

George nodded.

"So why bring it up now?"

"Oh, I just thought it was interesting," Edna replied. "It's been such a worry, and here we are talking about something else for a change."

As a matter-of-fact, they hadn't been conversing at all for several miles.

"Do you suppose it's over?" Edna wondered. "I mean, he hasn't done anything, or bothered us again. Maybe he's just one of those people that likes to stir things up. Mostly talk."

"I wouldn't make excuses for him. He's a downright unpleasant man, and I wouldn't bet he's given up on *The Commodore.* Anyway, let's not borrow trouble."

Trying not to borrow trouble, the Morgans drove the last mile and a half through the town of Cumberland to the nursing home on its northern outskirts. It wasn't really in the suburbs because Cumberland wasn't large enough to have proper suburbs. But it was far enough from the downtown area that the streetlights were few and far between. It looked dark and foreboding, an old weathered pile of stone set well back from the road and easily missed by a driver who didn't know of its existence.

Only a few pale rectangles of light defined the shape of the building when George turned into the nearly empty parking lot. His headlights swept past a van with faded lettering on the side panel and a few cars, all parked close together near the main entrance to the building. The taillights of one of the cars flashed red, and the car backed out of its space and turned to leave as George drove by. He headed for the far end of the lot from force of habit, pulling into a corner close to the side entrance that they habitually used because it was closest to Amos's second-floor room.

"Ready?" George shut off the ignition and reached over to take Edna's hand. He sounded tired, less from the day than from the weeks and months and years of such visits.

The north entrance opened directly onto a dimly lit corridor, with a stairwell immediately to their right. The elevator was further down the hall. The Morgans rarely took the stairs, but tonight there was something about the sound of raised women's voices from the floor above that propelled them through the open door and up the stairs. The words were not distinct, but there was a note of urgency in at least one of the voices, and what they were hearing was more nearly shouting than conversation, a marked change from the usual tomb-like silence of the nursing home in late evening.

Both of them had the same thought: Amos is having an attack. A nurse could have spilled a tray of medications, or a toilet could be overflowing. But both Edna and George were always expecting the worst, and the voices were coming from the general direction of Amos's room.

A nurse they knew saw them emerge from the stairwell and hurried down the hall in their direction.

"Oh, Mr. and Mrs. Morgan, thank goodness you're here. We need you to calm him down." She turned and called back down the corridor to an invisible colleague. "Helen, the Morgans are here. Do you hear me, Helen? Never mind the call. They're here."

Edna moved faster than George, past the nurse and into her brother's room. She was greeted by a scene of confusion in slow motion. Nurse Campbell appeared to be wrestling with the patient. His scrawny arms were flailing about, pummeling the nurse ineffectually, while he struggled through contorted features to make the words that wouldn't come.

"Here, let me." Edna tried to take over and received a surprisingly sharp blow to the side of her head for her efforts. Between the two of them, they managed to get him back into a reclining position, each pinning an arm. The room quickly filled up as George, the nurse who had met them in the hall, and the nurse named Helen crowded in.

"I'm going to sedate him," Helen announced. She moved efficiently to the bedside and administered the shot that soon calmed Amos Fielder and restored order to the room, which for too long a time had been his home.

"He'll be all right now. You can go on back, Dottie." Helen Parsons gave her colleagues instructions, and the room emptied almost as fast as it had filled up, leaving only the Morgans and the head nurse.

"What happened?" Edna asked for at least the third time.

"I'm not sure," Nurse Parsons said. "Why don't you sit, and I'll tell you what I think."

The Morgans settled into the two chairs in the room as they had on so many other occasions. The nurse leaned against the wall beside the door, where she could observe the now empty corridor.

"I've seen him upset, but nothing like this," Edna said. "I thought he was having a seizure of some kind; didn't you, George?"

George shook his head sadly. It had seemed to him more like a tantrum, a reminder that with old age sometimes comes reversion to childhood.

"If it helps, I can assure you he wasn't having another stroke. I'm certain nothing happened to him medically. Dr. Sloan will be here in the morning, and I'll have him examine your brother. I'd call him or Dr. Nardini now if I thought there was any reason to be concerned."

Helen Parsons was a seasoned, no-nonsense nurse who would never be called friendly, but who nonetheless inspired confidence. The Morgans were reassured but still puzzled.

"What *do* you think?" George wanted to know.

"What I think is that the man who was visiting Mr. Fielder upset him."

"What man? Somebody was here tonight?" The inflection in Edna's voice said it very clearly: she could not imagine that Amos had had a visitor other than George and herself. Theirs had been a lonely vigil. Gloria Snyder used to drop by occasionally before her marital problems had consumed her, and the Brocks had been over once or twice. But these were exceptions, and rare ones. Edna could think of no one who might have been to see her brother that evening, much less someone who would have caused the scene that had greeted them on their arrival.

"This man came about an hour ago. I don't remember ever seeing him before. He asked for your brother's room, and then we didn't pay any more attention. One time when I went past the room I saw him sitting there where you're sitting, Edna, but everything seemed to be all right. They were just talking—well, you know what I mean, the man was talking, and your brother was listening."

"What did this man look like?" Edna wanted to know.

"I'm sorry, but I really didn't give it much thought." It was about as close as Nurse Parsons would come to an apology. "But he had dark hair, and he was dressed casual. I'd guess he was in his 50s, but I'm not really sure about that."

"Is that all?" Edna was disappointed. "Was he tall or short? Good-looking or, you know, ordinary?"

"I didn't see him when he came in, and when someone's sitting like that it's hard to tell how tall he is. Fairly tall, I'd say. I don't know about handsome. Matter of taste. Yes, I guess you'd say so."

George leaned forward in his chair, a scowl on his face.

"So what do you think happened? You make it sound like a nice, quiet conversation, and then this explosion. When did the ruckus start? When did the man leave?"

"Oh, he must have left just before you got here. I didn't see him go, but when Mr. Fielder began to carry on, Dottie and I hurried down to his room, and the man was gone. It all happened just a few minutes before you arrived. I'd just gone down the hall to call you."

A phone rang somewhere in the building. The nurse stuck her head out into the corridor and, apparently sure everything was under control, took up her position against the wall again.

"What makes you think it was the stranger who upset Amos?" George asked.

"Well, doesn't it figure? This man comes; Mr. Fielder gets hysterical; the man leaves."

"Of course," George nodded. "But was there anything else? Anything to give you an idea why Amos went off like that?"

"He couldn't tell me," Nurse Parsons began, stating the obvious, "but he seemed to be trying, like he was pointing at the door. The man was gone, and I figured he wanted to tell me that the man had caused the trouble."

"Did any of the other staff talk to this man as far as you know?"

"It's possible that Dottie did. I don't know. You can ask her."

"I think I will," George said, and, leaving Edna and Nurse Parsons with Amos, headed off in search of the nurse who might be able to provide more information about the stranger whose identity he was beginning to think he could guess. Dottie Campbell was not hard to find, but her only contribution to George's picture of the man was that he was about six feet in height and had a nice speaking voice. Additional questions did little, however, to clarify what Dottie meant by nice.

When he got back to Amos's room, Nurse Parsons had gone, having assured Edna that her brother would sleep through the night.

"Edna, I'm as sure as anything that Amos's visitor was Britingham. Description's kind of vague, but it sounds like him. And who else could say something that would set Amos off like that? I'll bet Britingham came by to get more information out of him and told him what he planned to do. Damn his hide! Wouldn't that upset Amos and then some?"

"But how could he get any information out of Amos?"

Suddenly George's face darkened. He walked quickly to the table on the far side of the bed and yanked open the drawer and began rummaging through it. He fished out an old cardboard folder and carefully extracted its contents. The inventory was a familiar one, sad mementos of a sad life. But George's sudden burst of intuition was proven correct. The treasured letter from Edna and Amos's aunt, Elizabeth, was missing. He busied himself at once, pulling the bed covers aside, looking on the floor under the bed, hoping he would find the old, now tattered letter. It was a vain search.

"He's got Elizabeth's letter, Edna. That's what got Amos so worked up. When he realized Amos couldn't speak, he probably sweet-talked him into showing him the letter and then just took it and left. I'll bet that was him leaving the parking lot when we drove up. Damn!"

"But if it was Britingham, why would he want to hurt Amos by taking the letter? You'd already told him about it, and if he was still curious, he could have read it here. I don't see why he'd take it. That's just plain cruel."

"He is cruel. He must still be planning to go after *The Commodore*, and here we were saying just tonight how maybe he'd given it up. If he'd do that after we begged him to leave it alone, he wouldn't give a hoot about Amos's feelings, now would he?"

Neither Edna nor George had much to say during the drive back to the lake. Edna was experiencing a sense of helplessness that had the effect of dulling the desire even to talk about it. George was seething inside. He kept turning over in his mind the things he would say and do to John Britingham. He doubted he would get to say them or do them, but rehearsing them provided an outlet for his anger.

Nor did the Morgans feel like sleeping when they got home. Edna made a pot of strong coffee, an admission that a normal night's sleep would be difficult in any event. They talked about it some, but came to no decision as to what they would or could do. Eventually both of them ran out of steam, and in spite of the coffee, retired to a restless sleep.

CHAPTER 31

Chris Sanderson was surprised by her husband's midday call. It wasn't his habit to phone home.

"Is everything all right?"

"Sure. I just wondered if you'd mind if we played cards with the gang for a while tonight?"

"Tonight? This is Monday. What's up?" The Sandersons and some of their friends often got together for a game of cards, but almost never on weeknights.

"It's Mike," Larry replied. "He dropped by on his lunch hour, and he's really down. I think he's finally decided that Gloria's not coming back."

"Well, he's probably right, unless he decides to get help. She's told him she won't bring the kids up in that situation any longer. So what are we supposed to be doing, taking his mind off his problem?"

"Something like that. I don't think it'll do much good, but I figured it was worth a try. I already asked him. And Hank. Can you call Rose and see if she and Bernie can join us? I'm sure they'll be free."

It wasn't the way Chris would have preferred to spend the evening, but it did not occur to her to say no. She knew that while her husband was thinking of Mike Snyder, he was also doing it for himself. The ultimatum from the owner of the winery had shaken them both, but it was Larry who had to go to work every day, never sure when John Britingham would summon him to his office and raise the level of tension. Or even personally hand him his walking papers. Larry, too, was in need of the therapy a card game with friends might provide.

"Okay, we play. What time do I tell Rose?"

"I'd make it nine. No need to rush dinner." Larry figured he was already pushing his wife; he didn't want to overdo it.

"Are we going to work on Mike?" Chris wondered aloud.

"Oh, lord, no!" He was emphatic. "You know how he gets when people start lecturing him. He'll quit when he's ready. I just want to get his mind on something besides Gloria. Let's just agree not to talk about her or his drinking."

"Come on, Larry. All he'll talk about is Gloria. And that'll lead to their quarrel about whether he's an alcoholic. And all the while he'll be drinking our beer because if we tell him to lay off we'll be siding with Gloria."

Chris was very fond of Mike, as was Larry. They liked Gloria, but she was a friend because of Mike, not the other way around. But they also knew that Gloria was right about his drinking. She may have gone about it the wrong way—no, she *had* gone about it the wrong way—nagging, hollering, ridiculing—but he was an alcoholic, and they all realized that something had to be done. The trouble was that no one knew what. They were embarrassed by their role as enablers. That's what Gloria had called them, and it was true. They hadn't had the courage to refuse Mike a drink when he came to their house, and they had taken refuge in the belief that only Mike could help Mike. Besides, he was an old friend of the shirt-off-the-back school, and they couldn't bring themselves to drive him away.

And so it was that shortly after nine on a Monday evening in August, Chris and Larry Sanderson, Rose and Bernie Carlino, and Mike Snyder were sitting on the Sandersons' screened porch, enjoying their first beer of the evening.

The five of them were part of a larger group of no fixed membership. For several years the Sandersons and the Snyders had been its core. Sometimes the Carlinos joined them. There were also three bachelors as well. One, Hank Bauer, had long been divorced; another had never married; and the third lad lost his wife to cancer some years ago. Their participation provided evidence that the group had had its origins in a poker game among the men. At one time or another there had been an empty chair at the table, and one of the wives had joined the game. Gradually it had become a mixed group, but the bachelors were always welcome and continued to come on occasion. On this particular evening, the Snyders were no longer a couple, two of the bachelors were otherwise engaged, and the third, Hank Bauer, was late.

Larry spotted the light at some distance, but didn't give it a thought until it became apparent that the boat was coming into their dock. Its approach was nearly silent, and it wasn't until Larry stood up to get a better look and they stopped talking that the purr of the electric motor became audible.

"Hello?" He opened the screen door and stepped down onto the path that led to the dock.

"Hi! It's me—Hank. Be right up." The occupant of the boat, now identified as the missing member of their card party, had climbed onto the dock and was securing the boat.

"What's this all about?" Larry asked. "Where've you been?" They hadn't expected Hank to arrive by boat.

"Just a little fishing." The boat secured, Bauer took off his life jacket, dropped it back into the boat, and came up the path, waving at the people on the porch. "Thought I might catch myself a couple of bass, so I came over early to try my luck in your cove. Damned if I didn't get a nice one around thirty, forty minutes ago, and you know how it is—catch one and you figure there's gotta be another in the same place. So I kept at it until I told myself if I didn't get over here you'd have drunk up all the beer. Only got one more, but look at 'em."

He held up two nice small mouth black bass for the approbation of his friends.

"Not bad, huh?"

They agreed the fish weren't bad, but they were more interested in getting a game started. Especially Chris. Mike had lived up to her prophecy. Ever since he had arrived, there had been nothing but a litany of his grievances against Gloria, and Hank's arrival held out the promise of a change of subject.

"Can I borrow your kitchen for a minute, Chris? I need to clean these fish." Bauer headed for the kitchen with the comfortable assurance of an old friend who knew his way around the house. "Got a newspaper I can spread out on the counter?"

"There should be a pile of papers over there by the back door," Chris called out. "Need anything else?"

"Just some foil to wrap 'em."

Reluctantly Mrs. Sanderson got up and followed Bauer to the kitchen. It was easier than trying to explain which cupboard contained the foil.

Hank Bauer had lost count years before of the number of fish he had caught and cleaned and eaten. Unlike Mike Snyder, whose taste for fishing greatly exceeded his taste for fish, Bauer lived on fish and reduced his food bills significantly by catching his own. He extracted the knife from its case on his belt and with practiced hand began the task of preparing the two fish on the counter. Chris didn't want to watch the performance. She had never relished this aspect of lake life, and was privately pleased that her husband was little interested in fishing because she was fairly sure that had he been, the job of cleaning the fish would have fallen to her.

Minutes later, the fish neatly cleaned, wrapped in foil and tucked away in the Sandersons' refrigerator, Bauer reappeared from the kitchen.

"So what're we playing tonight?"

Hank was quite sure he knew the answer to that question without asking, but he was willing to be surprised. The women didn't like pinochle, and the men, other than Mike, who'd play any card game, didn't care for gin rummy. If it weren't for the Carlinos, they'd have settled down for an evening of poker, but Rose had a thing about poker, so it, too, was out.

"How about Screw Your Neighbor?" It was Rose's suggestion, but it might as well have been a statement of fact, for this was almost always the game of choice for this particular group. A mindless way to spend an evening, its principal objective was to avoid being stuck with low-count cards and was played by passing them to the player on one's left, acting as if you had nothing but a face card when you'd just been handed a deuce. Larry always referred to it as Old Maid for adults, but the truth was that they all enjoyed it.

"Okay, Screw Your Neighbor. What do we play for, nickels?" Larry reached into his pants pockets for change, and finding mostly dimes, changed the stakes. "Let's make it dimes."

"Speaking of Screw Your Neighbor," Mike interrupted, "have I told you that Gloria thinks that son of a bitch Britingham is screwing our next-door neighbor?"

"What else is new?" Bauer wanted to know. "He's screwing you and me and Larry, too, and who knows how many others."

"No, I mean it. Gloria's sure he's really screwing the woman—you know, in bed, or wherever they do it. Sorry, Chris."

"Oh, come off it, Mike." Chris Sanderson didn't want to be cast in the role of prude.

"I guess she saw him one night leaving the Hoffmans' house. You know, that stucco place next to ours. We'd had a fight, and she'd stepped out to have a smoke and cool off. It was like two a.m. or something, and he just pops out the door and gives the Hoffman babe a big kiss and leaves. And she was sure it was Britingham—she'd met him at the Morgans' party just a few weeks before."

"Is your neighbor single, or is Britingham beating somebody's time?"

"She's married. Good-looking woman, too. Anyway, her husband's gone most of the time. So Gloria figures the woman's bored, and then along comes God's gift to women and, well, they get it on."

"I don't know the woman," Bauer interjected, shaking his head. "Don't really understand women, for that matter. But I can't figure how she'd want to be in the same room with him, much less the same bed."

"I wouldn't underestimate him," Larry said. "He seems to get what he wants."

"Wouldn't it be nice if hubby came home and found Britingham in the sack with his wife? I'd love to see that one." Bauer's face lit up with the perverse pleasure of the thought.

Chris was trying to get them to the card table.

"Come on, aren't we tired of that man? It's all I hear. Let's play—and change the subject."

Changing the subject, however, proved difficult to do. Although they had all been friends for some years and had sat around the same table on the same porch on many an occasion before John Britingham moved into the area, and into their lives, and although they had never lacked for things to talk about, in recent weeks Britingham had become an obsession, dominating their conversation as surely as if he had been there with them.

There is no element of stress in Screw Your Neighbor. But the players at the Sandersons' table were under considerable stress. Although most of them were drinking, including at least one, Mike Snyder, who should not have been, two of them were medicating their stress with many more drinks than either prudential concern for their health or a proper respect for the limits of their host's beer supply warranted. One of them was Snyder. The other was Hank Bauer.

The two men reacted to the alcohol in their systems in different ways. Snyder became increasingly belligerent, which was quite the opposite of what Larry Sanderson had had in mind when he suggested cards to get Mike's mind off his marital problems. Bauer, on the other hand, became morose and introspective. And it was John Britingham who was the common denominator. All efforts to shift the subject of their discussion failed. It was as if every topic led inexorably back to the owner of the Silver Leaf Wine Company.

"Did you hear that we got some new softball equipment at the plant last Friday?" It was around 11:15 when Bernie Carlino addressed the question to Bauer. "It's really first-class stuff. Balls, bats, even some snazzy warm-up jackets, if you can believe that. First time the company's sprung for new stuff since I've been here."

Carlino's motive for bringing up the subject of the softball equipment was transparent. They all knew that Hank had quit playing for the winery team, and they missed his presence on the field and worried about his state of mind. Perhaps the news about the new equipment would be the tonic needed to snap him out of it and bring him back to the game he had always loved and still played well for a man his age.

"He really got it, did he?" Bauer's question was not meant to be answered. "I figured it was a lot of talk."

"You knew about it?" Larry asked, mildly surprised.

"Hell, yes. Mr. Big I Am was making like a friend of the employees that day in the motor pool. Asked me to come up with a list of things we needed, and like a fool, I gave him his list."

They had, of course, known of Hank's humiliation by the owner of the winery, but neither Sanderson nor Carlino worked in the motor pool, and they had not known that their friend had made a list of the winery team's softball needs for Britingham.

"Anyway, it ought to make the game more fun. Why don't you come back and give it a try?" Bernie pursued his original objective, trying to pretend he hadn't noticed the edge in Hank's voice.

"I was a damn fool to do it. I should never have cooperated with him." Bauer was clearly not planning on resuming his place on the softball team. "It's like I sold out. The man dumps on me, and I didn't have the guts to tell him to stuff it."

"Hey, Hank, no way you could have done that," Chris said, trying to make him feel better but thinking about her husband's problem as well. "You have to put bread on the table."

Snyder, who didn't work at the winery, had been listening to this exchange and getting angrier by the minute.

"It seems to me we've all put up with too much crap from that man," Mike said, his voice hard, as he shoved a three of clubs toward Rose Carlino. "Isn't it time someone told him where to get off?"

"Sure, Mike, and get fired. Where'd that leave us?" Chris spoke up for the Silver Leaf contingent. "You might get away with it, but we can't."

"If enough of his employees did it, what could he do? Fire everybody?" Mike polished off his fifth beer and examined the glass, as if puzzled to find it empty.

"Be sensible, Mike," Larry argued. "It doesn't work that way. He's got all the high cards. You can't expect people to risk their jobs because some of their buddies have gotten a raw deal from the boss."

The game continued in a mechanical way, cards moving from right to left. Bernie Carlino and Chris Sanderson had the largest piles of dimes remaining, but the usual joking about high stakes winners and losers was missing. Mike was still pressing his point.

"I don't care what you say—something's got to be done."

"Maybe the guy whose wife is getting laid by Britingham will do it for us," Bauer said quietly.

"Do what?" the women asked, nearly in unison.

"I don't know," he replied, "get rid of him."

"Kill him?" Rose asked, her voice rising an octave. She couldn't believe what she was hearing.

"Maybe." Snyder was thinking about it. "There must be a dozen guys out there who'd like to do him in, and a helluva lot more who'd like to give the guy that did it a medal."

The conversation was making some of the players uncomfortable, but for Mike Snyder it was taking on the character of a game.

"Mike, you don't mean that," Rose protested.

"Why not?" Mike demanded. He got up and went into the kitchen to the refrigerator for another beer, raising his voice as he went back through the cottage. "Name me one person who'd shed a tear for the bastard."

"That's not what you meant, Hank. Tell him," Rose urged Bauer.

"Sure it is," Mike told her as he came back to the porch. "The only difference is that Britingham hasn't stuck it to you and Bernie personally."

Bauer didn't take issue with Snyder. His big frame simply sank lower in his chair while he stared at the cards. Larry Sanderson was silently cursing himself. They'd gotten Mike's mind off his wife, all right, but at what a price. He'd drunk more than usual and was rapidly turning a civil conversation into one they'd all regret. The women were visibly embarrassed.

"Come on now. How'd *you* do it?" Mike poked a finger in Sanderson's direction. Then in Bauer's.

It was Chris who brought the situation under control.

"Look, you guys can plot ways to do away with our friend Britingham if you like, but I think right now we're keeping the neighbors awake. And it's getting chilly out here. Let's move inside. I'm for a cup of coffee. Anyone want to join me?"

She didn't wait for a show of hands, but swept up her dimes, got to her feet, and went into the living room, switching off the porch light as she went. Rose Carlino joined her, as Chris knew she would, and Bernie and Larry took the cue and followed. The card game was over, and the coffee hour was about to begin.

It took awhile for the conversation, if it could be called that, to shift to other subjects. But the move into the living room had the effect of making it easier for those who wished to ignore Mike to do so, which the women did by making coffee and straightening up the kitchen. Bernie did it by turning on the television, ostensibly to catch the baseball scores. He knew it was too late for the sports news, but he killed some time by changing channels in what he knew would be a futile search.

"Damn it, Bernie, shut that thing off," Bauer barked at him after he had located two talk shows and a grainy black and white film that sounded as bad as it looked. "You're not going to get any scores at this hour."

As it turned out, this was the last unpleasant remark of the evening. A combination of coffee, Chris's persistent cheerfulness, and the fatigue that was catching up with all of them produced a gradual winding down of emotions. Both of the Sandersons were ready to shove people out the door well before midnight, but they also wanted to put more coffee into both Mike and Hank, so it wasn't until shortly after twelve that Chris, with a pointed nudge, prevailed upon Rose to discover the hour and announce that they had to be leaving.

Mike was far from sober, but he had brought himself under control enough to apologize for his behavior.

"Hey, I'm sorry about my big mouth. It's just the beer talking, you know."

Larry brushed the apology aside.

"Forget it. What are friends for if we can't sound off to each other? We're all uptight about things.

"I know, I know." Mike draped an arm around Larry's shoulder. "You've got it tougher than me."

No, Larry thought, I don't. I've got a good marriage. He didn't say it, however, but gave his friend a gentle slap on the back as he went out the kitchen door and set off unsteadily down the point toward his cottage. Larry turned on the rear floodlight to help Mike find his way.

Rose lingered a few minutes to help clear the remaining coffee cups, and then she and Bernie said their good-nights and made their exit.

Hank Bauer was the last to leave. He had put his cap on, but remained glued to his chair until he finished his coffee.

"What would you do if you were in my shoes?" he asked his host.

"I don't know what you mean. About what?"

"About my job. It's hard to look the guys in the motor pool in the eye. I've thought about asking for a transfer to another part of the plant, but everyone knows. Do you ever feel trapped? Really trapped. I mean, no way out."

The big ex-athlete had had too many drinks and heard too much talk about the man who had made his life so miserable. He wiped a sun- and work-toughened hand across his face. Larry thought he was trying to conceal the fact that his eyes were moist.

"I don't know what to do. I don't know anything else." He was close to tears, and neither Larry nor Chris knew what to say. 'Come back and play softball' just wouldn't do. Larry looked at Hank and felt anger toward Britingham more powerful than any he had felt on his own behalf.

"You'll make it," he said, his voice full of false conviction.

It wasn't until fifteen minutes later, when Chris was getting ready to set the sacks of beer cans out back with the garbage, that she remembered Bauer's fish in the refrigerator. She realized that they had not even thought to turn the porch light on for him when he left. Too late now. The night had been difficult for all of them. So had the whole summer.

She took off her apron and gave her husband an impulsive hug.

"We'll make it," she said quietly.

CHAPTER 32

He had missed the turn. The man in Southport had said that if he passed a small red barn with a hex sign on it, he'd have gone too far. And there it was, coming up on his left. There was a moment's idle speculation as to why a barn should be there when he could see no farmhouse anywhere in the vicinity, but there were more important things to think about. Such as the need to take the next right turn, which he had been told would bring him back to the entrance he now realized he had passed on the drive up the lake. He hoped the next turn would be better marked than the first one, and it was.

Trees had been cleared here, and the access road to the point was visible from some fifty yards away. The blue Ford made the turn, and then slowed to a leisurely 15 miles per hour as it followed the road toward the lakeshore and the cottages ahead. He decided that 15 was a good speed, not so slow as to call attention to the car but slow enough to enable him to get a good look at the houses and spot the one he was searching for. He wasn't sure when under state law he was supposed to turn on headlights, but he could see well enough, and without lights the car was less conspicuous. The lights remained off.

There was little to see. A few lights had come on in some of the cottages. A dog was nosing around a small green tent, which had been set up behind one of the cottages, but there were very few people in evidence along the point, which pleased the driver of the Ford. They were probably inside finishing dinner, or perhaps on front porches, enjoying the last light of day.

At the lower end of the point the road bent fairly sharply to the right. He realized he was now heading back toward the main lake road, and he slowed to a crawl. Had he missed the building? He concentrated very hard on the remaining cottages—a small white ranch-style place, a larger log cabin—and then he spotted it. The low, crude structure in the wooded area was the only building he had seen on the point that looked at all like a temporary construction shack.

His informant had provided directions to a house, and then, very much as an afterthought, had mentioned the shack. His decision to try the shack first had been prompted by lingering ambivalence about his mission. He was, in effect, buying time while he sorted out his thoughts, while he decided just what it was he would do.

Now he faced a dilemma he hadn't considered. Where should he park? If he pulled onto the dirt track that went up to the shack, his car could be easily seen by anyone driving along the Blue Water Point road, and it would certainly be seen by anyone coming to the shack. But there didn't seem to be any other place to park the car where it wouldn't be on someone's property or in plain sight. As he thought about it, however, he decided that it wouldn't matter if the car were in plain sight as long as it wasn't close to the shack or the other houses. He reached the entrance to the point, which he had missed on the drive north from Southport and turned onto West Lake Road once again. As he had remembered, there was a pull-off just over a tenth of a mile down the road, within sight of the barn. If the car were seen there, no one would think much of it.

Seven minutes later, the Ford had been parked well off to the side of the road and John Britingham, Jr. had walked back to his father's shack on Blue Water Point, a nearly invisible figure in the rapidly fading twilight. He had suspected that the building would be locked, and he knew that it might be impossible to get in, in which case the evening might be wasted. But his plans were still evolving. There was no hurry. He wasn't even sure what he would do if he got into the shack. In fact, he wasn't sure why he was being so cautious, so indirect. Would it have been better to drive boldly up to the old man's house, pound on the door, and confront him there? Or march into the winery, brush past his secretary, and barge into his office? Maybe. In the end he might do just that. But he needed to feel his way, to get closer, but not too close, until he had regained the confidence he had felt when he left California.

The shack was a challenge, but not an insurmountable one. The single door was fastened with a simple padlock. He didn't doubt that he could break it if he had a hammer or some other weapon with which to pound on it; he had no reservations about doing so. After all, if he was going to accuse his father of murder, mere breaking and entering would be no problem. However, he didn't want to call the neighbors' attention to himself, so he would need to devise some other means of entering the shack. And then he saw how he could do it. There was a tire iron in the trunk of the car, he remembered, right next to the spare. He would use the tapered end, the one for prying off hubcaps. It could be wedged down behind the hasp, and using the doorframe as a fulcrum, he could simply pry the lock loose. It would mean a trip back to the car, but he had plenty of time, and problem solving, even at this modest level, was a confidence builder.

Fifteen minutes later it was completely dark and John Britingham, Jr. was inside the shack, getting his bearings. The place smelled of new wood. It had the warm and stuffy feel of a room that had been closed for some time. He pushed the door further open to let the night air circulate. John cursed as he banged his shin against something in the dark, angry with himself for not having the foresight to bring a flashlight. A nonsmoker, he didn't carry a lighter or matches either.

For the first time since he had left San Francisco, John was berating himself for his failure to plan his mission. It had all been improvisation—all except the final encounter with his father, which he had rehearsed many times in his mind. Even that began and ended vaguely and inconclusively. He didn't know how or where he wanted to meet the old man, nor did he have any clear idea of what would happen, or even what he wanted to happen, after he had brought his indictment. Suddenly, standing there in the dark in a rough construction shack on Crooked Lake, John saw all too clearly the folly of what he was doing, or rather in the way he was doing it. So he had gained entrance to his father's property. So what? It was as if he were engaged in combat and had captured an enemy outpost, only to discover that it had been abandoned and had no military significance. The analogy to warfare was distasteful. John couldn't imagine why it had occurred to him. He scowled and spit on the floor, as if to cleanse himself of the thought.

For a moment he considered going back to the car and then to the motel. This was a waste of time. But whether because of curiosity or simply a reluctance to retrace his steps to the car for the second time, John decided to make the most of his situation and check out the shack. Even in the dark he could make out shapes. He worked his way along the edge of the object against which he had struck his shin, groping with his hand to get some sense of its contours. To his surprise it felt like wool or some other material, and it was flat. A bed. For God's sake, he thought, this is a blanket, and there's a bed here.

It was while he was digesting this information that he felt something hit his face. Instinctively his hand came up to brush it away, and he touched a wire. He followed it toward the bed and found a lamp, which he almost knocked over. He fumbled for a moment, trying to find a button or switch. And then he did, and the shack was bathed in a dull light from a low wattage bulb.

Quickly John pulled the door shut. Anyone observing the shack would still see the light through the one small window, but he didn't feel as vulnerable with the door closed. John sat on the edge of the bed—really a narrow cot with a single blanket and pillow—and contemplated his surroundings. His initial impulse was to take a quick inventory and then flick the light off, minimizing the chances of being discovered. But as he looked about him, a plan began to take shape in his mind. Why should he worry about a light being seen in the shack? If there was a bed, it must mean that the old man, for reasons of his own, slept there occasionally. If he did, then no one would think it strange if a light were on in the shack; people would assume it was his father. But what if his father were to come to the shack? Well, didn't he want to confront him? And wouldn't it surprise him to find the wayward, unloved son there waiting for him?

In the meantime, John could stay in the shack, as long as he was prudent about his comings and goings. There was a bed and a refrigerator and even a hot plate. No water, apparently, but there was a lake nearby and plenty of woods when nature called. And he could always duck into a restroom at a gas station in Southport when he needed to freshen up a bit. It would save motel money, and he would be right there, waiting, when his father showed up.

John had no idea, of course, when his father would show up. It might be tonight, or later in the week, or, for that matter, not for a long time. But he was too pleased with his new situation to worry about that now. One step at a time, he thought. He would use the shack in the meanwhile, and with luck the old man would come by—perhaps on the weekend. John had learned about the plans for developing the lake property, and given his father's responsibilities at the winery, it was logical that he would turn his attention to the development project on weekends. Too bad he hadn't heard about the lake property sooner; he could just as well have sacked out there as at the motel the day he'd arrived in Southport.

Having made up his mind about his sleeping arrangements, John turned his attention to the shack itself. He was used to spartan quarters, and this was spartan in the extreme. Why on earth would his father, who loved luxury, want to sleep here? Ever? That was one of the many things that had led to estrangement—his father's chronic and unconcealed annoyance with his lifestyle, his carelessness about clothes and living environment, his indifference to creature comforts. He could still recall vividly the scene that ensued the one time his father had visited him in his flat in Berkeley. There had been a scalding lecture, focused first on the condition of the room, and then on the person who could live in such a place. It had been followed by a shouting match. They hadn't seen each other since. No, the shack was not the kind of place in which he could imagine his father sleeping, even for one night. But John was equally certain that there could be no other explanation. In any event, he would see.

It took no time at all to survey the contents of the shack. There was little to suggest that any construction work was about to begin. The refrigerator was the most interesting item in the room. Its contents were disappointing, however, although the cans of beer were a welcome sight, as well as proof that the place had a visitor from time to time. The jar of instant coffee on the table had been opened but was nearly full. John tested the hot plate, found that it worked, and decided that a cup of coffee would taste even better than a beer. He looked about for a container to carry water in, but in the end had to settle for a long-handled pot.

John had seen the lake through the trees when he first arrived. He figured it was only a few dozen yards from the shack, and there was just enough light so that he could make the trip without running into a tree. As it turned out, he had underestimated the difficulty of reaching the lake, if not the distance. The ground was very uneven and, while he managed to avoid the trees, he became entangled in low bushes along the way, and then tripped over a root and fell down the bank near the water's edge. From where he lay sprawled on the tiny beach he could see that the ground dropped off quite sharply. The light from the shack was now hidden by the bank, which must be six or more feet high. He picked himself up, his hand scraped and probably bleeding from the effort to cushion his fall, but otherwise not hurt. He knelt on the shale and reached out into the dark water with the pot, filling it.

The return trip was easier, once he had gotten to the top of the bank. This time he was more aware of the lights in the log cabin off to his right. He was unable to see into the cabin, but it was obvious that someone was home in this nearest house to the shack. If anybody was aware of his presence, it would most likely be these people, whoever they were. He wondered if they were friends of his father's. Unlikely, he thought. How could anyone make friends with that man?

John made himself a cup of coffee. It seemed to confirm his claim on the shack. He now had a room, and he could make himself at home. He sat cross-legged on the bed and once more revisited the conversation he would have with his father, a conversation that now seemed much nearer than it had at any time since his arrival from California. Sometimes he tried to fill in his father's answers—his denials, his excuses—and sometimes it was simply a monologue.

"I know you did it, you know," was the way he would begin. And then he would wait.

His father's response, he was sure, would be, "What are you talking about?" Or perhaps, "Did what?"

In either case, John did not intend to provide the answer immediately. Instead he would be watching the face, looking for signs of guilt as his old man tried to postpone the moment of truth, first with questions, then with evasions. But John wouldn't let him off the hook.

"You know what I mean. There's no point in pretending." He would enjoy this verbal torture. It was possible, of course, that his father would persist in a charade of incomprehension. John was ready for that. After an interval of testing, he would come out with it, not in the form of a question but as a straightforward accusation.

"You killed my mother. You left her to drown. You know it, and I know it," he would say, and then would throw down the gauntlet.

"I don't intend to let you get away with it!"

It was at this point that the scenario became fuzzy, and it became fuzzy because John was not sure himself what he would do. Sometimes he would simply turn and walk away, leaving John Britingham, Sr. to the torment of uncertainty as to what his son would do. At other times he would stand his ground and demolish his father's protestations of innocence, one by one, reducing him to the pathetic creature John had decided he really was. There was always the possibility that Britingham would lash out physically, seeking to win by force what he could not win by argument. This was the most troubling outcome, and John would always push it to the back of his mind and move on to other things. But one way or another, justice would be done. Something would be said, some small word—or maybe, just maybe, an arrogant admission—that would lead to criminal charges and eventually a conviction.

John lay back on the bed, hands clasped behind his head. It had been a good day. He felt vindicated in his decision to come east. Tomorrow he would check out of the motel and later, after dark, bring his bag back to the shack. Then he'd settle down to wait for his father. But for the moment he only wanted to savor the day's accomplishment. Within minutes John Britingham, Jr. had fallen asleep.

CHAPTER 33

When Emily Hoffman heard the knock on the back door, she nearly jumped out of her seat. She was sitting on the couch in the living room, legs tucked beneath her, deeply engrossed in a book. The last thing she had expected to hear was someone at the door. She looked at her watch; it told her that the hour was five minutes of eleven.

In the city, Emily would not have answered the door at this hour of the evening, or at any other time of day for that matter, without being absolutely certain who her visitor was. At the lake, things were different. Doors were rarely locked. People were trusting, and few could remember an episode that might call that trust into question. Emily's slow response was the result of surprise, not anxiety.

The knock came again as she got up and started for the kitchen, but her visitor pushed the door open and came on in before she reached it.

"Emily?" John Britingham called out her name, then almost collided with her as she entered the kitchen.

"John. What are you doing here?" She was genuinely surprised and obviously distressed to see him.

"Drink?" He headed for the liquor cabinet, took out a bottle of scotch, and poured himself a generous glass. "Come on, you too. We're going to celebrate."

"No, I'd rather not," she said, waving aside the glass of scotch Britingham was already pouring for her. "What are you doing here? You know we have rules about this."

John marched past her to the refrigerator in search of ice cubes. His eyes were bright, and there was a feverish excitement in his manner.

"Rules." He gave the word a derisive twist. "This is no night to worry about rules. I've got some good news. We're going diving."

"You shouldn't be here—someone could see you. There'll be people still up, maybe next door. I don't understand what you're doing." Emily was not in a state of panic, but she was alarmed. It was one thing to carry on an affair which had an element of risk, but it was quite another to court discovery by imprudently coming and going at hours when neighbors might notice.

"For heaven's sake, Emily, relax. There's nobody out there. These are old folks; you said so yourself. They'll be in bed early. You're not listening to me. We're going diving—at least I am. I really think I'm onto something."

Emily Hoffman wanted to say that the Morgans might be old folks, but the Snyders weren't. And neither she nor John knew much about the habits of her neighbors on the point. In his strangely euphoric mood he probably wasn't even much concerned about being seen entering or leaving the Hoffman house. She suddenly had the disturbing thought that he may never have shared her worries about being caught, that he had gone along with her 'rules' only to placate her. While he wouldn't necessarily want their affair to be discovered, he was an adventurer, a risk taker by nature, and he might find some perverse pleasure in having it known that Emily Hoffman was one of his conquests, that he was actually bedding this beautiful woman in her own home. Emily shuddered involuntarily.

John downed his drink quickly and poured another from the bottle of scotch he had set on the sideboard.

"This is one of the good nights. And it's going to get better. You're going to help me celebrate."

The confident, aggressive way in which he approached her reminded her of the time they had met at the Morgans' party. He put an arm around her and drew her to him, kissing her roughly on the mouth. Then he stepped back and took a sip of scotch while with his free hand he pulled loose the sash of her robe. It fell open.

"No, John, we can't do this," she said, backing away and pulling her robe together.

"Can't? Why not?"

"I don't know what this celebration is all about, but we can't have it here—or now."

"Okay, so I didn't call. And you're nervous about the neighbors. But I've got to tell you about the ship and the gold. It'll be a first on Crooked Lake—nobody's ever gone down there. You can't blame me for being excited. Or for wanting to celebrate."

John had set his glass down. This time he had decided to use both hands to take off her robe. Emily twisted out of his grasp and went to get the untouched glass he had poured for her.

Color was rising in Britingham's cheeks. He was unaccustomed to rejection.

"What is this? Why the modesty act? The blinds are all drawn. I'm the only audience, and you won't find a better one. So what's the problem?"

Emily had to face the fact that John would not be put off by her protestations about his unannounced visit at an hour considerably earlier than they had agreed upon many weeks before. She tried another tack.

"I don't know what your news is, John. I'd like to hear about it; I really would. And I mean soon. But I just can't be romantic tonight. I was almost asleep on the couch when you came to the door. If it's really big news, we should celebrate when I'm not exhausted. But I am. I'm glad for you that it's your night. It just isn't mine."

She thought she had been convincing. Even if John didn't believe her, she thought he was enough of a gentleman to give her the benefit of the doubt and desist. She was wrong.

"If you're tired, I know how to wake you up." He scooped her up in his arms and carried her through the house and into the master bedroom, ignoring her objections and depositing her on the bed.

"Don't argue. It'll be fine; you'll see."

As he knelt in front of her on the bed, she brought her knees up and tried to push him away. But he was stronger and, placing one hand on each of her knees, he forced her legs apart.

I can't believe this, she thought. This man I've been sleeping with for two months is going to rape me.

But whether Britingham had considered forcing her to have sex with him or not, in the end he didn't. Cursing under his breath, he climbed off the bed and went back to the living room to get his drink. When Emily had straightened her clothing and composed herself, she, too, returned to the living room, where she found him sitting, glass in hand, looking sullen. It was an awkward moment, and she wasn't sure what, if anything, she should say.

In the end, it was Britingham who broke the silence.

"Do you want to hear about it?" His tone was petulant, suggesting that she probably did not want to hear what he had to say.

"Of course, if you want to talk about it." Emily was not at all eager to have him stay. On the other hand, she didn't want him to be seen leaving the house, and she decided it would be better if he stayed at least until midnight, provided the conversation remained civil.

Britingham finished the scotch in his glass and went to the sideboard for more. Emily looked at the level of liquor in the bottle and realized that John was drinking heavily. This was his third scotch in less than twenty minutes, and all had been stiff ones. He was no longer diluting his drinks with ice or water. She had never seen him drunk, but if he continued at this rate, that would soon change. She wanted to say something to persuade him to stop drinking, but she was afraid of him at the moment and didn't want to push him.

"If you'll wait a minute, I'll make some coffee. Would you like something to eat?" She wasn't sure what there might be to snack on, but thought she could find something.

"No, I don't want coffee. Or food. I'm not drunk, so don't patronize me. Just sit down somewhere and let me tell you about the ship. And the diving. I felt pretty good when I got here. Maybe I'll get it back."

Emily picked a straight-backed chair she almost never sat in. She didn't want to sit on the couch next to John, and the other comfortable chairs were across the room, and he would assume she was deliberately sitting as far away from him as possible.

"Maybe you remember—or maybe you don't," he began, "but there are a few ships at the bottom of this lake. I think I may have mentioned it. And I don't mean little fishing boats or things like that. I'm talking about big steamers like the ones that ran on the lake a hundred years ago. That's how people got around back then. Well, there were a few accidents, and ships went down. Not many. I know of three. And one of them is really interesting. I'm going to dive down and take a look at it."

"Like the ones in the pictures over at the Morgans?" Emily was trying to sound interested, although she didn't think that those pictures did anything for the Morgans' cottage, which she remembered as rather drab.

"Yes, and the one I'm interested in is the star of their gallery. Called *The Commodore*. Anyway, Mrs. Morgan's aunt was on that ship when it sank. She went down with it."

"How dreadful." Emily suddenly found the Morgans' taste in interior decoration even less appealing than she had previously.

"It was a long time ago. That girl who was lost in the accident had a strong box full of gold jewelry with her at the time. I've been thinking about going down and seeing what's left of that ship, just for fun. I haven't been diving lately, and I understand that nobody—can you believe that, no one—has ever dived down to any of the lake wrecks. Well, now there's an even better reason to dive—there just may be some gold down there."

Britingham became more animated as he talked. If he hadn't forgotten his anger over Emily's lack of responsiveness, he had at least gotten out of his funk.

"But would you really dive just to look for some girl's jewelry? I mean..."

He brushed aside Emily's negative reaction.

"Of course it wouldn't be much. But from what I hear from the Morgans, it's interesting stuff. Her father—the girl's father—joined one of those Alaska gold rushes, and unlike some of those poor fools, he found a lot of gold. Some of it got made into jewelry."

"How can you be sure you'll find it? Won't it be buried in the mud? It seems like an awful lot of trouble with no assurance you'll even recover anything."

"Damn it, Emily, what's eating you? I come in here full of fire, and you won't go to bed with me. Now you can't find anything positive to say about that ship and the gold. You're a real downer. I'm not asking you to get into a diving suit. Lord knows, I wouldn't want you to mess up your pretty hair. But I'd think you could get a little vicarious pleasure out of my going down and exploring the bottom of this lake—and just maybe coming up with a piece of an old mystery. Jesus!"

Emily knew she should dissemble. But her interest in John's adventure was nil. She was, once again, aware of how little they had in common. She was supposed to wax ecstatic over his plans for trying to recover a dead girl's jewelry from the muck at the bottom of Crooked Lake minutes after he had nearly raped her and less than an hour after he had violated their rules about his coming to the Hoffman cottage. And the wreck didn't even have any of the romance of the other diving adventures he had told her about. It was only a little coal burning boat on a small inland lake, and it wasn't even old enough to have any real historical interest.

She had been trying for several weeks to rationalize this increasingly sterile affair, to convince herself against persistent and rising doubts that John Britingham had a place in her life. Tonight she found her arguments for the relationship collapsing one after another. It was a rout. Emily knew, with a clarity of conviction that surprised her, that she wouldn't be seeing John again.

He was going on, saying something about a nursing home and a letter he'd gotten that evening from some old man. Emily was no longer listening. She was rehearsing in her mind how she would dismiss him, looking for the words that would be least painful for them both. She had no illusions about John's reaction. He would find it incomprehensible that a woman could reject him; he would deny what she was telling him, protecting his ego from the truth for as long as he could. She didn't know whether his denial would take the form of an angry outburst. He might as easily try to change her mind by turning on the charm, which would be even harder to deal with.

Britingham's monologue came to an end, and he helped himself to another scotch.

"Okay, so I was wrong. I thought you'd get a kick out of it. Well, maybe when it's all over the papers, you'll see it differently. Or when I spread the jewelry out right here on your coffee table."

In her mind's eye Emily could picture mud-caked rings and bracelets fouling her immaculately kept living room. She moved forward in her chair and tackled the difficult subject.

"John, I think..." she began, went silent for a moment, then started over. "Look, we've had some very good weeks, and I won't pretend that I don't find you attractive. But this can't go on. There's no easy way for me to say it, but I can't see you again." She had been going to say that she didn't want to see him again, but she hoped 'can't' would hurt less, and besides, it was nearer the truth.

She had expected words of one kind or another, but what followed was silence. He stared briefly at his glass of scotch, then drained it. When he had finished refilling his glass, the bottle was almost empty. He crossed to the south window, facing the Morgans' cottage, and pulled the drape aside. She experienced a momentary knotting in her stomach. What if her neighbors were still awake and could see John, outlined against the lights of her living room? Was this some not-so-subtle form of blackmail, a hint in pantomime that unless she let him back into her life he would let the world know about their affair? Emily felt an overpowering need to break the awful silence. And to get him away from the window.

"Please, John, come back and sit down. We can talk about this like mature adults." She didn't really want to talk about it. There was nothing to be said. She certainly didn't want John to start berating her, but she found his silence unnerving.

Eventually he left the window and came back to where she was sitting. The effort to maintain his self-control was palpable. His face was grim, and he was clenching the glass so tightly that Emily feared it would break in his hand. When he spoke, his words were measured, deliberate, and—did she imagine this?—threatening.

"I'm leaving now. This is no time to talk. I'll only regret what I'd say. But I'll be back, because it isn't over between us. Count on it."

He walked through the kitchen and let himself out the back door, still holding the empty glass. Emily sat rooted to her chair, her hand twisting the sash of her robe. She had the room to herself for all of a minute when the back door opened. John was back.

"Don't worry," he called out to her. "I'm not coming back to argue. This glass belongs to you. Oh, and I'll bring a bottle of scotch the next time. I need a jacket or something. It's chilly, and I've got to walk all the way down to my cabin."

Emily felt a wave of relief when she realized he hadn't changed his mind. It was now around midnight, and if he'd just be quiet about it, no one should notice his leaving.

"I'll see if I can find something. Alan must have some old coat or sweater he won't miss." She wasn't sure about this, but she would deal with that later. Right now she had to get John out of the house. She had to be alone.

"Emily, my dear, it's only for tonight. I'll get it back to you right away so your precious Alan won't have to wonder what happened to it."

John Britingham was not only sarcastic. He was also drunk. He had held his liquor reasonably well, considering how much he had put away in such a short span of time. But his mood was no longer buoyant enough to sustain a semblance of sobriety. It was as if he had simply let go, had, in effect, decided to be drunk.

Emily was having trouble finding something suitable for John to borrow. Unlike herself, Alan did not have a large wardrobe, and most of his clothes were in the city. She had to be careful to select something that he was unlikely to wear on weekends. As she rummaged through his closet, it occurred to her that John's request for something warm to wear was only a ruse, that he was creating an excuse to come back to see her. She experienced a terrible sense of frustration, a quiet, helpless rage. She didn't want to see John Britingham again; yet, she would have to get Alan's jacket back, and quickly. Emily found herself biting her lip to hold back the tears.

Alan's closet yielded nothing that she dared give to John. Fighting to maintain control, she went to the hall and started in on the items hanging from the hooks in the closet there. Near the back, under a raincoat, she found an old cardigan sweater. It had been a couple of years, she thought, since she had seen Alan wearing it. He probably didn't even remember it. With a tremendous sense of relief, she took it from its hook and brought it into the living room.

"Here, take this." She thrust the sweater at John as if it were too hot to hold.

"Thanks, and please thank Alan for me."

Emily did not think she could possibly endure another minute of this. She closed her eyes briefly and tried to will him to leave. John took his time putting on the sweater.

"It'll do," he observed in the same sarcastic tone. "You can go to bed now. I won't be back tonight."

Before he left he reached out and, in a crude parody of his parting gesture the day they had met at the Morgans, patted her firmly on the bottom. This time Emily locked the back door, and then went through the living room and into the hall and locked the front door as well.

It was nearly 12:30 when she threw herself on the bed and had her first real cry since high school.

CHAPTER 34

Dusk was rapidly descending on Blue Water Point. The sun had disappeared behind the hill that cradled the lake on the west, and several bats had taken wing in their nightly hunt for insects along the shore. It was a peaceful moment, but Grace Hess was not at peace.

She stood on the beach in front of her home, toweling off after an evening swim, which had been physically invigorating but had done nothing to wash away the worry preying upon her mind. Quite the contrary. The tranquility of the time and place only served to remind her of what she stood to lose if John Britingham were to go through with his development plan. And she was sure that he would go through with it. She had racked her brain for weeks, searching for a strategy that would thwart Britingham without reopening the painful issue of her late husband's activities. But no such strategy had occurred to her, and she was feeling increasingly desperate.

And tired. Grace had not been a good sleeper for years, but now she was truly an insomniac. Her nights had become a time of ongoing struggle, of fitful sleep alternating with an abandonment of any pretense of sleep, at which time she would read or watch films. On some days she was able to nap after lunch, but those naps were too few and too brief to compensate for so many bad nights.

You can't go on like this, she said to herself, as she pulled on her beach robe. He's killing you just as surely as he's destroying your property.

Grace was not one to feel sorry for herself. Practical minded and by nature a problem solver, she would have to do something soon. Even take sleeping pills, something she had promised herself she would never do. Thank God for the movies, she thought. An inveterate film buff, Grace had watched far more than her share of old films at all hours of the day and night on television—good ones, bad ones, truly awful ones—westerns, comedies, romances. She liked to think that she had discriminating taste, however, and her preference was for Hollywood films of the so-called golden age of the 1930s and '40s. But her addiction was such that she would sit through almost anything.

Her old VCR had let her exercise more control of her film fare. The rental outlet in Cumberland had a limited selection, with the result that Grace had inquired about video mail order houses, received some catalogs, and gradually built up quite an impressive personal library of films. Her collection of vintage movies had sustained her through the Britingham crisis, giving her something to occupy her mind during the long nights when sleep would not come and when her neighbor's threats took on an even more frightening aspect than they did during the day.

Grace gathered up her towel and walked back toward the house by way of the garden plot that ran along the property line. There was no visible hint of the trouble that had developed between Grace and John Britingham. The wooded area beyond her garden was nearly dark now, but it was a quiet, inviting darkness, punctuated by the occasional firefly. Only when she reached the end of the garden at the back of the house did the shack come into view, huddled among the trees in the near distance, a shadowy box of a building, its unpainted walls not much lighter than the surrounding woods. She tried to tell herself that there was nothing sinister about the shack, but her heartbeat quickened perceptibly. That modest, unimposing building was, by its very presence, a constant reminder that her new neighbor was a man of ill will. Soon, she feared, it would become the nerve center for a construction project that would mark the end of the peace she had found since Victor's death.

There was nothing she wanted from the garden this evening. Grace had taken that path because it always drew her, like a magnet, to the place behind her home where the shack could be seen most clearly. It was as if she had to torture herself, needed to keep her worries at a boil. Once in the house, Grace started the water for tea and then retreated to her bedroom where she would brush out her hair, put on her nightgown and robe, and otherwise complete her ritual preparations for the night.

Jeff accompanied her to the bedroom and flopped down near the door, from which vantage point he watched his mistress's every move. His presence was comforting, even if he was too friendly to be an effective watchdog. But he was a large dog and the exuberance with which he launched himself at every visitor, known and unknown, had given her a feeling of security during the days following Britingham's blackmail visit.

Grace Hess had experienced a number of dreadful nights in which she had fully expected her neighbor to come back and ratchet up the war of nerves he had initiated and in which he already held the upper hand. The first wave of panic had passed, and she had now settled into a state of chronic anxiety that deprived her of sleep but no longer produced the cold sweat of fear. The gun she had oiled and loaded and placed in her bedside table was still there, but she did not now feel the need to check the drawer each night to reassure herself of its presence. Grace was still angry and frustrated and deeply worried, but she had largely banished the terror. If only she could get some sleep.

It was nearly ten o'clock when Grace turned her attention to the selection of the movie of the evening. The top shelf in one of the bookcases in the study and nearly half of the shelf beneath it were lined with her films, and she ran her finger along their spines, checking for a promising title. Her collection suggested a fondness for Bill Powell and Myrna Loy, as well as for Colbert and Davis. Even the Marx Brothers had a niche, and she paused briefly over *A Night at the Opera* before moving on and pulling *Maytime* from the shelf. Sentimental schmaltz, she thought, but it seemed, for reasons she didn't examine, to suit her mood.

Grace puttered around for another fifteen minutes, engaging in tasks that had become part of her nighttime ritual. She let Jeff out briefly and then lured him back with his nightly treat of a large milk bone. She went from room to room, closing the drapes and turning off the lights except for the few she preferred to leave on for safety's sake. When everything had been made ready, Grace finally settled down to watch the film. *Maytime*, she had to acknowledge, was not a particularly good movie. Nelson Eddy was a wooden actor, and the plot simply could not be taken seriously. But she was very fond of Jeanette MacDonald, and the film's ending always brought a lump to her throat. Tonight Grace found herself focusing on John Barrymore's character—and detesting him. He was the villain, the man who stood between MacDonald and happiness. Barrymore, Britingham. She was transferring her feelings about her duplicitous neighbor to the screen. There was no real similarity between her situation and that of the movie's beautiful opera star, nor between Britingham's behavior and that of the jealous husband of the film. But preoccupation with her problem acted like a powerful solvent, washing out the differences between the fiction on the screen and reality of her troubled life. She was remembering the saga of the real-life John Barrymore, an alcoholic at this stage of his career, unable to remember his lines, an unpleasant man, a shadow of the star he had been. And the Svengali-like impresario, played by Barrymore, who had put the MacDonald character on the road to stardom and then tied her to a loveless marriage and eventually killed the real love of her life. And, of course, Britingham. Barrymore. Britingham. They merged and separated and merged again. The old movie took on a surreal quality in Grace's mind, the plot following paths the director had never intended. Only at the end, when MacDonald and Eddy, united in death, sang the title song, did Grace pull herself together and shed the tears which the movie so shamelessly coaxed from its audience.

"I've really got to get a hold of myself," Grace muttered under her breath, the meanwhile drying her eyes on the sleeve of her dressing gown. She knew she was turning her problem into melodrama, and that was not like her. She pushed the rewind button and began to consider what she would do next. It was after midnight. Sleep seemed as remote as it had been when the movie started. How she wished she were like Victor, who used to fall asleep in front of their television set with predictable regularity. Another film was a possibility, but she didn't think she was any longer in the mood. There was nothing she particularly wanted to read.

Grace was feeling irritable. Angry at Britingham for causing her this distress. Angry at herself for allowing him to do it. There was no excuse for the cycle of sleepless nights in which she was trapped. She looked at Jeff, sleeping like the proverbial log, and envied him his innocence.

Had she been a drinker, Grace would have turned to the bottle. But she wasn't, and she didn't. Coffee or more tea would only make things worse. With no clear objective in mind, she put her slippers on and went to the kitchen anyway.

As she reached for the light switch, she noticed a small patch of light in the distance through the kitchen window. The window faced Britingham's property, and the light, she decided, must be coming from his shack. Grace's hand moved away from the switch, leaving the kitchen in darkness. She crossed the room and, leaning on the sink, peered out the window. A breeze was moving the branches of trees between her house and the shack, so that the light appeared to break up and reform as she studied it. She was unable to see into the building, but the light seemed to suggest that Britingham was using his shack.

Why?—she wondered. What would the man be doing in that wretched little box in the woods at this ungodly hour? Working? On what? Grace knew that no water hookup had been affected. It didn't occur to her that anyone might be spending the night there. She couldn't remember seeing a light in the shack before, and the fact that one was now on aroused her curiosity and, quite irrationally, she had to admit, her anxiety. Surely nothing was going on over there—not at this hour, anyway—that signaled the start of construction work. But why would Britingham be visiting his property in the middle of the night? Had he left something there that he needed? But whatever it was, why would he need it now? She wished she could get a better look at the shack.

Driven by her fixation with Britingham, Grace Hess decided that she had to investigate. She wouldn't go over to the shack, of course. That would be foolhardy in the extreme. But she would go out back of the house, where she would have a better chance of seeing what was going on. And she was convinced that something was going on, and that it bode ill for her.

She went to the closet and took out a long dark raincoat. No point running around outside in a white bathrobe. She exchanged her slippers for a pair of old, flat shoes. She briefly considered waking Jeff and taking him with her, but decided that he would go crashing about in the woods and that might call Britingham's attention to her as well as the dog.

It came as something of a surprise to Grace when she stepped out of the door to find that her other neighbors, the Sandersons, had left the light on over their back door. It was bright enough— and near enough—that anyone watching her cabin would have been able to see Grace as she came out into the yard. There were lights on in the Sanderson cottage as well. She hadn't noticed them before; her study and bedroom and kitchen all faced the other way, and she had assumed that she was the only person in the neighborhood who was still awake, except perhaps for Britingham.

But Grace was not curious about Larry and Chris Sanderson. They were decent, quiet, mind-their-own business neighbors, and if they wanted to watch television or entertain friends until after midnight, that was their own business. No cars were behind their cottage other than their own pickup truck and Chevy, though. Probably just the two of them, watching a late show. Must have forgotten the outside light, which was now attracting several moths.

Grace hesitated, but only momentarily. She was quite certain that Britingham wouldn't see her, not at this distance through the trees. Not unless he was spying on her. But if he was doing that, he wouldn't have the light on in the shack. She would still need to hurry, however, to get away from the Sandersons' light and into the shadows on the other side of the house, near her garden.

To her disappointment, Grace saw no one in the shack. She followed the boundary line out to the gravel road, but nowhere between the road and the garden was she able to gain a wholly unobstructed view. When she found what she thought was the best vantage point, she lingered, hoping to see movement within the shack. But she didn't wait long. What if she did see him? It would probably be impossible to tell what he was up to, so she would be left as puzzled as before. All she was accomplishing, she decided, was to work herself up—that and to kill some time until she was finally so tired that she could fall asleep.

Acknowledging the futility of her mission, Grace began to make her way through the small vegetable plot at the end of the garden and back toward the house. She had just gained the grassy lawn beyond her cucumber patch when she saw him. He was on foot, and he was coming down the gravel road from the north end of the point, heading her way. He was at the far edge of the area illuminated by the Sandersons' light, still an indistinct figure. It was impossible to tell for sure at such a distance who it was, but Grace was instantly certain that it was Britingham. She had assumed that this man who had haunted her for weeks was in his shack, but here he was, walking toward her from the opposite direction.

By now she was on open ground, the sheltering bushes several yards behind her and the back door of her cottage quite a bit further away. To reach it she would have to move toward the approaching man. What was he doing? Did it have anything to do with her? Did he see her? How could he not see her? Should she walk? Run?

In the two or three seconds while these thoughts flashed through Grace Hess's brain, the man suddenly paused, took another step, and then stopped. He has seen me, Grace thought, her mind racing. Why hadn't she taken the gun? As she watched, momentarily frozen by indecision, Britingham—if indeed it was Britingham—turned off the road and began to move away from the light and around to the lake side of the Sanderson cottage. Stealthily, she thought. She was now gripped with the overpowering conviction that Britingham had seen her, but didn't know that she had seen him. That he was going to circle the cottages, away from the Sandersons' back porch light, and surprise her.

Grace's indecision vanished. She sprinted, if that term can be applied to the quick action of a woman in her 70s, toward the door of her cabin.

CHAPTER 35

Alan Hoffman said goodnight to his wife, hoping he had sounded more affectionate than usual, and gently replaced the phone. He debated pouring himself a drink, but he knew he shouldn't drink and drive, and inasmuch as he planned to drive more than 150 miles in the next several hours, he chose to forego the highball.

Alan had at first been angry with himself for even imagining that Emily was having an affair at the lake while he was at work in the city. But he had been unable to lay the doubt to rest. It had tugged at the edge of his consciousness, sometimes so gently that he almost forgot it was there, and then more insistently, more urgently. It had been three weeks earlier that he had finally given in and made the decision to discover the truth.

Some men in similar circumstances would have confronted their spouses. Confrontation was not Alan Hoffman's style. He lived by indirection. The matter was serious, but Alan approached it almost as a game, one in which by stealth he would gather information and build his case, day by day, indiscretion by indiscretion.

He had surreptitiously looked through Emily's desk for an unfamiliar phone number or a note, but had found nothing. He had even gone through the stubs of bills from credit card companies and stores where they had charge accounts. Emily had always been the keeper of their accounts, the one to write the monthly checks, and it was conceivable that she had made some purchase that would give her away, confident that he never concerned himself with such matters. As a result he learned things about Emily's shopping habits which he hadn't known, but discovered nothing which suggested that there might be another man in her life. From time to time he had explored the carpet around the head of the bed where the vacuum cleaner could not reach, thinking that he might find a hair that was neither his nor hers. These, too, had proved to be futile searches.

Gradually his interest in what he found himself thinking of as the matchbook affair had waned in the absence of anything that might pass for evidence, be it tangible or circumstantial. But just when he was beginning to lose interest in the hunt, the upstate area had experienced a nasty and unseasonably cold weekend. Summer or not, Alan had decided to lay a fire. He'd brought in a couple of logs from what was left of the winter's cord at the back of the cottage and found a short stack of copies of the weekly *Cumberland Gazette* in the basket next to the fireplace. As he was crumpling one of these papers to start the fire, his eye caught a modest headline on a page devoted to the comings and goings of the local populace. It read, simply, "Silver Leaf Owner Returns from San Francisco."

Emily had reasoned that a subscription to the *Gazette* would help her to understand the area and its people. Whether it did or not, Alan neither knew nor cared. As for himself, he never read the *Gazette*. He remembered growing up in a small town in Wisconsin and hating the fact that his mother was always calling the local paper to feed it stories about his progress through high school and college. He could still picture some of the headlines: "Local Youth Wins County Speaking Contest," "Alan Hoffman to Attend Princeton," "Hoffman on Dean's List," "European Trip Caps College Career for Hoffmans' Son." His mother, of course, had been proud of him, but he found the publicity embarrassing, and he came to realize quite early that this was an important difference between small towns and big cities. In the former, life was lived in a goldfish bowl. Everyone knew everyone else, and the local paper's principal function was not to print the news, of which there was precious little, but to keep the community informed about the mundane and modest accomplishments of its residents. In the city, on the other hand, it was the real news that sustained circulation. Alan and thousands like him could remain anonymous.

The headline in the *Cumberland Gazette* had caught his attention, however. It was just the sort of nonstory he remembered from his youth, no more than two and a half column inches of copy reporting a nonevent. What had prompted him to pull the paper back from the fireplace and smooth it out so that he could take a better look was the reference to San Francisco. Alan had given so much thought to the matchbook and its origins in San Francisco that the headline had triggered a reflex response. For the first time since they had purchased the lake property, Alan Hoffman had read a story in the local paper.

"John Britingham, the owner of the Silver Leaf Wine Company in Southport, returned Saturday from an eight-day trip to San Francisco and the Napa Valley area of California, where he still owns one of that state's largest wine companies. Mr. Britingham bought Silver Leaf in November of last year, and brought with him to Cumberland County many years of experience in the wine business and a reputation as one of the country's foremost vintners. The world-renowned sportsman now lives on West Lake Road on the west side of Crooked Lake. His far-flung business interests take him to California frequently, but he is proud to claim our county as his new home."

A nonarticle, indeed, Alan thought, but a prospectively important one if you are looking for an explanation for the presence of a book of matches from a San Francisco restaurant under your bed. Alan had crumpled the paper again and put it in the grate, but he was thinking about a man named Britingham. How old was he? What did he look like? Was he the kind of man Emily might find attractive? What kind of man *would* Emily find attractive?

But this was silly. He was jumping to conclusions, and it was a very large leap. A local man named John Britingham visits San Francisco; a book of matches from a San Francisco restaurant is found under Emily and Alan Hoffman's bed. Ergo, John Britingham is sleeping with Emily Hoffman. There had to be more likely explanations for the matchbook. On the other hand, the matchbook came from the Silver Peacock restaurant and Britingham owned the Silver Leaf Winery. Alan had considered this a coincidence and dismissed it. Or tried to.

Over the next two weeks, Alan found time to do quite a bit of extracurricular sleuthing. He found nothing to link his wife to John Britingham. But he did find a picture of Britingham in the heretofore-ignored *Cumberland Gazette*, and he was struck by the man's appearance. Assuming that the photograph was a fairly recent one, he had to concede that Britingham was handsome in a rugged, not a pretty boy way. And while he knew, rationally, that this did not establish the link, Alan managed to convince himself that the owner of Silver Leaf was very probably frequenting both the Silver Peacock in San Francisco and the Hoffmans' conjugal bed on Crooked Lake.

Acting on impulse, he had driven back to the lake the previous Wednesday night. He had known that the odds of his finding Emily in a compromising situation were poor to nil. But he had been seized by the need to do something, and he had made the trip because 'he had to.' He had neither learned anything concrete, nor had he expected to. However, he had made a discovery, innocent enough in itself, that had turned his suspicion into a fixation. That discovery was nothing more dramatic than a light in the master bedroom of their cottage at two in the morning. It had been extinguished only a little more than ten minutes later, but he had seen it, and he knew that Emily regularly took a sleeping pill and that she invariably slept through the night. So why had a light been on at such an hour? There were several explanations, and Alan Hoffman had considered them one by one. Two lodged in his brain and grew to a point where other more innocent explanations for the light all but disappeared. The one was that another man had been there and had left shortly before Alan's arrival. The other was that the man was still there, lying next to Emily in the large bed in the dark.

After completing his nightly call to his wife, Alan packed his briefcase so that he could go directly to the office when he got back to the city in the morning. It was 11:25 when he left the apartment, and five minutes later when he pulled out of the Clarion Arms' underground garage and headed west through light traffic.

The roads between the city and Crooked Lake are not identified as scenic on any map or in the guidebooks to the region, with the exception of the final 45 miles. For much of the distance, the highway is four lanes wide and divided, and the state continues to talk of widening it to six lanes to ease congestion into and out of the city. After that, the most direct route involves secondary roads, none of them divided, which take the driver through attractive pastoral countryside. Alan liked to think of this stretch, with its pleasant vistas and a quaint small town or two, as a reward for having endured the wearying exodus from the city on Friday afternoons. On this particular night and at this hour, however, there was nothing to see except the taillights of cars ahead of him and an occasional pair of headlights as cars in the opposite lane approached and passed. Even the towns were dark. Probably took up the sidewalks in mid-evening, Alan thought, just as they were alleged to do in the Wisconsin of his youth. But as he drove the last leg of the trip to Crooked Lake, he was thinking mostly about a man he'd never met and a woman he didn't know as well as he'd thought he did.

The drive gave Alan plenty of time to decide what he would do when he reached the lake. For one thing, he would not leave until dawn. He had berated himself for having left so early the first time he had driven back to the lake in the middle of the night. It was conceivable that Britingham did not leave the cottage immediately after satisfying himself with Emily. Perhaps he spent the night, leaving in the morning, although he would of course have to be up and out early to avoid being seen. Alan tried to imagine what he would do in a similar situation, but gave it up as useless speculation. It was even possible that these assignations were at Britingham's place, at least some of the time. Alan decided this was unlikely. He had found the matchbook from San Francisco in their cottage under their bed, and he was all too well aware that his own indiscretions always took place at the woman's apartment, not his own. Nonetheless, he would have to check out Britingham's house.

Fast moving clouds intermittently hid the moon when Alan Hoffman made the turn off state road 23A onto West Lake Road. He had carefully scouted out the location of Britingham's place, and knew to the tenth of a mile when he would come to the turnoff to the big house on the hill. Even in the dark it would be no problem. The digital clock on the dashboard changed from 1:38 to 1:39 as he cut his headlights and pulled into Britingham's driveway. He downshifted to second gear and eased the car to the side of the driveway about fifty feet off the highway and well before the big bend that brought the house into view. He cut the engine and slipped out of the car, closing the door quietly behind him. He walked on the grassy shoulder to avoid kicking loose gravel, but quickly decided that these precautions were unnecessary. The house was completely dark. The only sound was the wind in the trees flanking the porch. No car was in sight, and it took only a minute to ascertain that the garage was also empty. Britingham was obviously not at home. As he had expected, he wouldn't be finding his quarry here. Britingham's absence only served to increase Alan's conviction that the owner of Silver Leaf was at that very moment at the Hoffman cottage barely two miles away.

The moon reappeared when Alan turned off West Lake Road onto the Blue Water Point road. He would have negotiated the drive along the point without the car lights in any event, but the moon made it easy. As he crept by their cottage he could see

Emily's car in its customary place. There was no sign of Britingham's car, but he hadn't expected it to be there. The man would not be fool enough to advertise the affair by parking at the Hoffmans' door. His car would be somewhere nearby, close enough for convenience but far enough away so as not to arouse suspicion. There were numerous places to pull off the drive, and plenty of trees to provide a semblance of cover. Alan had found just such a place to park his own car, and he headed for it now. There had been the possibility that Britingham would be using this same pull-off, but he wasn't, so Alan parked and set out along the Blue Water Point drive in the direction of the cottage. He would have liked to poke around along the point to see if he could find Britingham's car, but he was even more anxious to set up a vigil at his own house.

The Hoffman cottage was as dark as Britingham's had been, and the moon had again taken cover behind clouds, making it even darker. Alan made a careful and quiet circle of his own property, checking at every window for hints of light and life. He saw neither. Then came the hard part. He would have to hunker down somewhere nearby where he could observe both front and back doors for several hours. This, too, he had anticipated, and had decided that the best place from which to watch the cottage would be the spirea bushes beside the Morgan cottage. It was fortunate, Alan thought, that Mr. Morgan had let his bushes grow. They were badly in need of heavy pruning, and provided excellent cover. He didn't really want to hide so close to someone else's cottage, but he was sure that the old couple would be sound asleep at this hour.

He wished his watch had a luminous dial, but it didn't much matter. It couldn't be much later than 2:10, if that, and he'd be leaving at dawn. Alan first settled into a crouch, but soon abandoned it for a more comfortable seat on the bare ground, his back against the cement foundation wall of the cottage and several feet away from the nearest window. The back door of his own cottage was almost directly across from where he sat and some thirty yards away. The front porch was further away, most of it out of his line of vision, but the screen door by which Britingham would have to leave faced the Morgans, so there was no way the man could leave undetected. Unless, of course, Alan were to fall asleep, which he was determined not to do, or Britingham simply wasn't there, about which he could do nothing. But he had convinced himself that the handsome owner of wineries on both coasts was there. Alan Hoffman waited patiently.

He had no clue as to how much time had passed since he had taken up his position under the spirea bushes. It seemed like an eternity. He heard a bird, and wondered if its song anticipated the morning. Was the sky slightly less black, or was he imagining it? Alan guessed that it was after four o'clock, but he doubted that it was yet close to five.

It was while he was trying to find a more comfortable position in which to wait out the rest of the night that he experienced a scare that sapped his confidence in what he was doing. It was a simple thing, but it brought him back into a crouch, temporarily more concerned about being discovered than about John Britingham. A light went on in the Morgan house only a few feet to the left of his hiding place. In spite of the bushes, the area between the Morgan and Hoffman cottages seemed bathed in light. Alan held his breath, listening for some sound that might indicate that the Morgans had noticed his presence. The silence that had been his ally only moments before now seemed ominous, a prelude to trouble. But after a few minutes the light went off, and Alan began to breathe more easily. In all probability someone had simply taken a trip to the bathroom, but it had shaken him and raised doubts about the wisdom of creeping around in the middle of the night, spying on his own wife, when he should be many miles away, sound asleep in his bed in the city. It was several minutes before his heartbeat settled back to normal.

The light had changed nothing, but somehow it had changed everything. He had not, of course, been caught, and he had almost certainly not been in any real danger. But he no longer felt secure in his role as hunter. What if someone were to see him, skulking around his own house? What if someone were to find his car, not very well hidden behind someone else's property? It would be he, not John Britingham, who would have some explaining to do. And what would he say? The game was losing its appeal.

And dawn was approaching. It was still dark, but to someone who had been staring into the night for several hours it was definitely less dark. If Britingham were indeed in the cottage, he'd have to leave sometime within the next hour, maybe even the next half hour, or risk being seen by some early riser. But Alan was now more concerned about himself than he was about Britingham. He knew he had to leave, and leave quickly.

Just as he was beginning to crawl out from under the bushes, he heard a sound, not loud but distinct in the quiet of the predawn hour. It sounded like metal striking metal, followed by a slow grating noise, and it sent Alan quickly back to the security of the Morgans' bushes, all of his senses alert. The light in the Morgan cottage had startled him, causing him to rethink the wisdom of what he was doing. But the aural evidence that someone was up and about, and not very far from his hiding place, brought him to the edge of panic. The sound had come from somewhere ahead of him. He momentarily entertained the idea that it had come from his own cottage. Britingham preparing to leave? But no, it had obviously originated from some place closer to the lake and somewhat further away. Someone moving about down by the water, someone who had dropped something, someone—then it came to him. Someone was loading gear into a boat. He waited, breath drawn in, for the sound to resume. It didn't.

Slowly, quietly, Alan Hoffman slipped out from beneath the spirea bushes and began moving low to the ground toward the lake, just a few dozen feet down the sloping lawn between the cottage and the beach. He needed to dash some cold lake water on his face, and then he'd hurry back to the car and be well on his way to the city before sunrise. He heard a splash and pictured a fish breaking the water to catch some insect, flying too close to the lake's surface. A large fish, too, by the sound. There was still almost no light, and so, in spite of his vigilance, Alan's failure to see anyone else along the beach on Blue Water Point that morning was quite understandable.

PART V

INVESTIGATION:
TWO STEPS FORWARD,
ONE STEP BACK

CHAPTER 36

It was Sheriff Kelleher's habit on Sunday morning to sleep in as late as she could and enjoy a second cup of coffee with the sports section of the *Upstate Herald*. Once in a while she experienced a twinge of conscience that prompted her to forego the usual leisurely morning and instead attend ten o'clock mass at St. Mary's. But this particular Sunday was different. Bridges' report on his conversation with the observant deskman at the Hoffmans' apartment building had altered her priorities. She would drive over to Blue Water Point for a few words with Alan Hoffman.

Carol decided to take her own car. To drive up in the official car would only fuel gossip needlessly. If she got there around 9:00, she reasoned, Hoffman would almost certainly still be at home. Maybe he wouldn't be dressed, but the hour would not be so early as to produce undue alarm. There was, of course, the problem of speaking with Hoffman alone, rather than in the company of his wife. The sheriff had considered avoiding that problem by using the phone, but she wanted to meet the man and observe his reaction when asked where he had been the night of Britingham's murder. Carol decided that she could manage Emily Hoffman.

The man who opened the back door of the Hoffman cottage had what she thought of as a bookish appearance, probably due to the horn-rimmed glasses and the worry lines that creased the forehead of an otherwise smooth and youthful face. Alan Hoffman was shorter than the sheriff had pictured him after first meeting his wife, who was tall for a woman. He was wearing a maroon dressing gown over a pair of casual slacks and a blue polo shirt, and he had to shift his coffee cup to his left hand in order to acknowledge the sheriff's greeting.

"Sheriff Kelleher, Cumberland County. You're Alan Hoffman, am I right?" Hoffman nodded in the affirmative as they shook hands. "I'm sorry to interrupt your Sunday morning. But I expect you know about the tragedy we had here this past week, and I haven't had a chance to talk to you about it yet. You've been down in the city, I understand. Missed all the excitement."

"So I gather. Please don't worry about us—you aren't interrupting anything very important. Just a lazy day. Won't you come in?" Hoffman's voice also surprised Carol. It was unusually deep, and it didn't seem to go with the glasses and the lines on the forehead.

"We could just sit here," the sheriff said, pointing at the wooden benches that flanked the back entrance to the house. "No need to bother your wife."

As if on cue, Emily Hoffman appeared at the door.

"Sheriff Kelleher!" She seemed genuinely surprised. "Is there some problem?"

"Same problem, Mrs. Hoffman. I'm still trying to figure out why John Britingham got himself killed last week. I've talked to just about everyone around here except your husband, and I thought I'd come over and remedy that oversight."

"Oh, I thought maybe you were going to—oh, never mind, please come in."

"Going to what, Mrs. Hoffman?" The sheriff's tone was conversational.

"Nothing—really nothing. It's just been such a week. Anyway, do come in."

"Thanks, but I think your husband and I will just sit here. I'll only be a few minutes. Why don't you go ahead, do whatever you were doing."

But Emily Hoffman showed no inclination to leave, so the sheriff had to explain police procedure, a procedure which was nowhere codified and which she herself had frequently ignored, even several times since Britingham's death.

"I think it's best if I talk with your husband alone, like I did with you. We find that people say things just a little bit differently with someone else around. I'm not entirely sure why, but it happens—an unconscious thing, I guess. Like I said, it'll only take a few minutes. I have to get back to Cumberland for church." There, she thought, knowing that the church bit was a lie, that should make it all seem mundane and routine.

Emily's disappointment showed, but she retreated into the cottage after offering the sheriff a cup of coffee, which she declined. Hoffman and the sheriff sat on the benches—the one struggling to disguise his anxiety, the other her expectations.

"Just a couple of questions, Mr. Hoffman. Did you know Mr. Britingham?"

"No, not at all."

"Know anything about him? Any idea what kind of person he was? I'm trying to get a fix on who might have wanted to kill him." Carol had decided not to bother with the usual disclaimer; she no longer believed that his death might have been an accident.

"I'm sorry I can't help you. I don't know anything about the man. My job is in the city, as I suppose Emily told you, and I'm down there most of the time. I really know very little about local matters. Hardly know my next-door neighbors, I'm afraid." Alan Hoffman gestured toward the Morgan cottage as if to identify the neighbors he hardly knew.

"Okay. Question number two. Where were you last Monday night?"

This was a different kind of question, and the difference wasn't lost on Hoffman. The lines on his forehead deepened.

"In my apartment in the city, of course. Why do you ask?"

"Were you at home all night?"

"I think I ate out that night, but I was home early. Almost always am. There's no social life when your spouse is a hundred and fifty miles away. I'm pretty sure I called Emily mid-evening, well, probably later—between 10 and 11. I worked on some files I'd brought home, and went to bed I'd guess somewhere around midnight. It was a typical night—they're all pretty much the same."

"Mr. Hoffman," the sheriff said, "what if I told you that I have it on good authority that you left your apartment building at 11:30 p.m. and didn't come back at all that night?"

"But that's crazy. Who told you that?" Hoffman was genuinely agitated by this turn in the questioning.

"I don't think the person who told us this is crazy. And he certainly wasn't trying to put you in an embarrassing position. The man who was on the desk at your apartment building is the one who told us you went out and didn't come back. He was just doing his job. Seems to be a bright and observant fellow. He wouldn't lie to us, now would he?"

Hoffman closed his eyes and sighed. It was a small sigh, but it said as clearly as words that he was retracting his statement about Monday night.

"So," the sheriff asked, pursuing her advantage, "where did you go?"

"Look, Sheriff," Hoffman said, his voice now much quieter, "I'd like to talk about this, but not here. Emily, she's likely to wonder what's going on and come back out. I don't want her to hear about this. Can I come over to your office—later, I mean? I can make it this afternoon."

"I think we'll do it this morning. I can miss church. Meet me at the county office building in Cumberland in an hour."

A fleeting look of something short of panic but more than normal anxiety crossed Hoffman's face.

"But that's too soon. If I leave right away, after you go, Emily's bound to think something's wrong. Let me read some of the paper, putter around here for a little while first. Can we make it noon?"

"Let's say eleven. The building will be locked, but I'll meet you at the front entrance at eleven. Say good-bye to your wife for me, will you?"

———

Well, well! Carol thought to herself on the way back to Cumberland. The wife is allegedly having an affair with Britingham. The husband sneaks out of his apartment the night Britingham is murdered and doesn't reappear until sometime the following day. And he lies about leaving the apartment. She wondered what kind of story Hoffman would have concocted by eleven o'clock. It was probably a mistake not to have pursued the matter then and there on the back porch of the cottage.

According to Sam, the deskman had been adamant about the time of Hoffman's departure from the Clarion Arms. If he had exceeded the speed limit while driving to the lake, he could have arrived as early as 1:45. If he'd observed the speed limit, he could still have made it around 2:00. Either way, he would have arrived well within the period of time when Doc Crawford said Britingham had met his death. Of course he might not have driven to the lake at all. Anyway, the sheriff would hear Hoffman's version of what he'd done that night soon enough, and she was also willing to bet that it would be another lie.

When Alan Hoffman arrived, the two of them climbed the stairs to the sheriff's office, which was uncomfortably stuffy. Carol considered the air conditioner, but opted for opening the window instead. A low-pressure system had come in overnight. It had produced a gray morning, and a light rain was now beginning to fall. In a matter of minutes the windowsill was damp.

"I'm sorry I didn't level with you, Sheriff," Hoffman began. "I'm sure you'll understand why. It's Emily—I don't want her to know. We've got a good marriage—well, a funny one, I suppose, her living up here most of the time and me down in the city. Most people would think it's unusual. But I can't—hell, let's get it over with. I spent Monday night with another woman, at her apartment."

If Alan Hoffman expected the sheriff to be shocked, he was mistaken. Carol couldn't quite understand why so many men took their wedding vows so lightly, but she knew personally of cases in which they did, and it was certainly a staple of many a TV show she'd watched and book she'd read.

"Well, then, you have an alibi, I guess," she said in a matter if fact tone.

"An alibi? What do you mean?" Hoffman sounded as if he'd never heard the word.

"I suppose it does sound a bit melodramatic," the sheriff said. "But John Britingham was apparently killed on this point last Monday night. His body was found only two cottages away from yours. I'm trying to find out who might—and please note that, Mr. Hoffman, *might*—have killed him. Or who couldn't have. If you were with some woman in the city, then you couldn't have, right?"

"But like I told you, I didn't even know the man. Why on earth would you even think I need an alibi?"

"Mr. Hoffman, everyone I've talked to says the same thing. No one really knew him, or so it seems. But he's dead just the same, and he didn't die of natural causes. I can't take people's word for things, now can I, not when a crime's involved. So I'd like you to give me the name of this woman and tell me how I can find her."

Alan Hoffman was now genuinely agitated.

"I can't drag her into this. For God's sake, can't you see what would happen?"

"All that's going to happen is that I'll verify your account of last Monday night. Period. No one else needs to know. I'm not interested in your marital situation," Carol added somewhat disingenuously. "All I want to do is get to the bottom of this business with Britingham. Now, of course, if you don't tell me, I can figure that maybe you're not telling me the truth about that night. After all, you've already lied to me once about where you were."

"Look, it's even worse than you might think." Hoffman got out of his seat and went to the open window. He stared down at the street and ran his hand back and forth along the wet window sill for a moment or two before turning back to face the sheriff. When he spoke again, the deep voice sounded hoarse and strained.

"She's a prostitute."

Carol couldn't imagine why this was worse than the alternative. She herself found the idea of prostitution abhorrent. But she thought it likely that Emily Hoffman would be quicker to forgive her husband a prostitute, however disgusting she might find such a relationship, than the proverbial other woman, who would be infinitely more threatening. Or would she? The sheriff didn't really know her. Her first impression of her had almost certainly been wrong.

"Doesn't change things, Mr. Hoffman," the sheriff said. "I'll still need the name and an address where I can reach her."

"I'd never forgive myself if I got her busted." Hoffman's concern had shifted from his wife to the still unnamed lady of the evening.

"She won't get busted. I'm interested in murder, not the minor vices. Besides, I don't have jurisdiction down there. I don't plan to say anything to the city police. Why should I? Even if I did, I imagine they've got more important things to worry about than hassling whores. I think we've gone around the mulberry bush long enough for one day, don't you? Or do you want to call your lawyer?"

Hoffman sat back down and tore a page out of the back of his pocket calendar and wrote down the information the sheriff wanted. His protective instincts were now focused on himself rather than the women in his life.

"Crystal Starr?" the sheriff asked as she read Hoffman's note. "That her real name?"

"I don't really know. Probably not. It doesn't matter, does it?"

"Not as long as I can find her. May I infer that Monday wasn't your first visit to Miss Starr?" Carol was interested in the fact that Hoffman had produced the woman's address and phone number from memory.

"Yes, I've seen her several times," Hoffman admitted.

CHAPTER 37

Sunday had turned into an unpleasant day. It was warm enough, but the sky had been overcast all morning and by early afternoon it had started to rain, a steady downpour that promised to last all afternoon. The far shore of Crooked Lake across from Blue Water Point was nearly obscured by a curtain of rain, and the slate-colored waters of the lake were stippled by it. There were no boats or swimmers in sight. Next door to Kevin's cottage, the horseshoe pits in front of the Brocks were beginning to fill with water. It was a good day to be indoors, and that's where Kevin was. He had nearly finished with the Sunday edition of the city paper, the umbilical connecting him to the real world beyond the lake.

He was mentally taking issue with one of the paper's editorials when the phone rang. Much to his surprise, the caller was Sheriff Kelleher, saying she'd like to drop by for a few minutes. Kevin experienced both a surge of uneasiness and a distinct sense of pleasure. Uneasiness because he worried that the sheriff might still have problems with his account of events the morning of the murder, pleasure because he realized that he wanted to see her again. He assured her that he was doing nothing but sitting around on a rainy afternoon, and that it would be fine if she came over. In the time before her arrival he neatened the living room, made a pitcher of ice tea, and speculated as to what the sheriff wanted to talk with him about.

After her arrival on Blue Water Point for the second time that day, the sheriff wasted no time in telling him what was on her mind.

"What do you think you're doing, Mr. Whitman?" she asked while accepting a glass of the tea and making herself comfortable. "Here I am, conducting a serious investigation into the death of one of our area's best known citizens, and I find out that you're going around doing the same thing. Don't you think it would be better if we had just one investigation, the official one?"

Kevin hadn't been sure what had triggered the sheriff's visit, but now he could guess. This was obviously no social call, but he was relieved that she didn't seem interested in revisiting the subject of his early morning swimming habits and his faulty memory.

"I'm not sure what you mean," he answered in an innocent voice.

"It appears that you have been questioning your neighbors about the Britingham affair and urging them to tell all to their friendly neighborhood sheriff. That's very nice. Everybody should cooperate with the law. But I like people to talk when they feel they need to do so. If they don't talk, or if they conceal things, they have a reason. Their silence may be as revealing as what they have to say."

Kevin was waiting for the bill of particulars. He was also thinking that the sheriff looked less formidable—and rather more attractive—in a blouse and jeans than she did in her uniform.

"Your neighbor, Morgan, called me. Told me he ought to straighten out any misimpression he may have given me about when he got up on the morning of Britingham's death. Now he says he was up way before one of our officers arrived—that's not what he told me when I first questioned him. Had to go to the john, he now says, and just stayed up, did some chores. Put away the dishes, burned some trash. Didn't see a thing, of course. Nobody did. But he admits he was up during the time we know Britingham's body ended up on your dock. And why did he tell me this? Because you told him to. That's what he says."

"But..." Kevin began.

"There's more. Our fisherman friend, Mr. Snyder, dropped by to see me yesterday. And what do you suppose was on his mind? 'Whitman and I were talking,' he says, 'and it seems I'd gotten the times mixed up on Tuesday morning. Whitman says I ought to correct my story.' So he tells me he fiddled around for a good ten minutes or so after you saw him, before he went fishing."

The sheriff began tapping rhythmically on her knee.

"That's two of your neighbors coming to me to change their stories in less than two days. And I'm supposed to give you credit for making honest men of them. Why are you being so helpful?"

Kevin wasn't sure the sheriff would appreciate—could appreciate—the extent to which Britingham's violent death had fascinated him and almost wholly preempted his professional writing project for the summer. But he very much wanted her to understand.

"I didn't think how it would look to you, I guess. But I'm really interested in the—what are you calling it? The murder? The Britingham case? I can't deny it. It isn't every day someone shows up dead on your dock. Anyway, I think you'd have heard from Morgan and Snyder even if I hadn't said something. Did they tell you anything else?"

"Should they have? You seem to be the one with the answers. But no, that's all of it." Carol looked thoughtfully at Kevin, trying once again to size up this man who had discovered the body, this unusual specimen of lake dweller who lived alone, didn't appear to fish, didn't own a powerboat, and taught and wrote about opera. Oh, yes, and went swimming before sunup. And apparently fancied himself as some sort of private investigator. She crossed her legs and took a sip of her ice tea.

"There's one other thing." The sheriff's voice was matter-of-fact, but she had made no effort to conceal the look of irritation on her face. "It would appear that the mystery of the dog on the beach has been solved. Seems the dog belongs to Grace Hess, that woman down at the other end of the point. She now admits to being out with it the morning you found Britingham on your dock. Like just about everyone else, she decided to change her story. That your doing, too?"

Kevin was relieved that he could honestly say that, no, he hadn't urged Mrs. Hess to tell the sheriff about Jeff. He'd figured that if she was ready to share that information with him, she'd have no problem talking with the sheriff about it. But Carol was not about to let him off the hook.

"Whether you urged her to change her story or not, I'm willing to bet she changed it because she knew Britingham was already dead when she went walking with her dog. Now, how did she know that? I hadn't told her. But I had told you. You wouldn't have mentioned it to her by any chance, would you?"

It didn't really matter. Since receiving the autopsy report, the sheriff had been asking people to account for their whereabouts in the hours before 3 a.m. Whether she had said so or not, the implication had been clear: that was when Britingham had met his death. Any one of several people could have passed this information on to Grace Hess. But Carol had specifically instructed Whitman not to tell others what she had told him about the time of death, and she was annoyed with him for interfering with her investigation. So why not make him sweat a bit?

But she didn't wait for an answer.

"By the way, did you tell Mrs. Hess to remember to tell me about the light in Britingham's shack?"

Kevin had not been surprised that Mrs. Hess had told the sheriff about Jeff and the old shoe. But he knew nothing about a light in the construction shack, and he said so to the sheriff.

"When did she see it?" he asked, fully expecting the question to be dismissed.

"Why do I tell you these things?" Carol asked, knowing that in spite of her frustration with Whitman she would tell him. She had to admit that he had raised some of the right questions and just might, if in possession of the right information, help her to pull the strands of the puzzle together.

So when Carol left with a warning which, translated, meant don't play detective, she wasn't entirely sure she meant it. In some strange and unacknowledged way, the sheriff knew that Kevin Whitman had become her partner in the quest for Britingham's killer.

———

Late that afternoon Kevin decided to get some exercise by taking a walk down to the Milburns and back. The rain had stopped, but the day remained gloomy, and the walk seemed like a better idea than a swim. Dan and Rachel invited him in, and within five minutes Kevin had violated the sheriff's admonition and once again was talking about the case.

It was Dan, however, who brought it up.

"Did I tell you that Rachel saw someone with a flashlight out on the beach later that night we were over at your place for dinner? The night right after the murder, or whatever we're calling it now."

"No. You've been holding out on me, Dan."

"We haven't seen you, and besides we weren't sure it means anything anyway. But late that night—Rachel says it was close to two o'clock—she saw this flashlight playing around out there, over by the Sandersons."

"It's my story, Dan," Rachel interrupted. "If I'd turned on a light, I probably would never have seen it. But we have one of those little night-lights along the baseboard in the hall, and I could see my way to the bathroom. I just happened to look out the window and there was this light, moving around outside in front of the Sandersons' cottage. Somebody was obviously looking for something there. In the dark! Doesn't that strike you as strange?"

"I take it you didn't see who it was?"

"No, just the light dancing around."

"Did you ask the Sandersons about it?' Kevin asked the obvious question.

"We were afraid we'd just have looked snoopy. At first we didn't think anything about it. Larry had probably just left something out there. But it began to bother me. Why would they go looking for whatever it was in the middle of the night? Besides, if it was the Sandersons, why didn't they just turn on their porch light? It'd be a lot more efficient than a flashlight."

"On the other hand," Dan observed, "why should we be making a mystery out of it? There's probably a perfectly simple explanation. This Britingham affair has got us to the point where we're giving even ordinary things a sinister meaning. A dog on the beach, a flashlight in the night—and the night after Britingham was killed at that. Don't you feel a little silly?"

But Kevin wasn't quite so ready to dismiss the episode.

"I think Rachel's got the right idea, though. What if it wasn't the Sandersons? Then we do have a mystery. The mystery of lights where we shouldn't see lights. You see a flashlight on the beach at 2 a.m. the night after the murder. Grace Hess sees a light in Britingham's shack the night of the murder, a light that goes off the next morning. Looks like somebody's prowling around this end of the point at some pretty odd hours. Why?"

"Where did you hear about a light in Britingham's shack? From Grace?"

"No, from the sheriff. While she was lecturing me about the importance of letting her conduct her own investigation. I hate to disappoint the sheriff, but I'd like to talk to Mrs. Hess *and* to the Sandersons. I just don't understand these lights in the night."

And so before returning to his cottage for supper, Kevin Whitman spoke with both of the Milburns' neighbors.

Grace Hess told him what she had told the sheriff, that there had been a light in the shack the night of the murder and that she had seen it go off when she went out with Jeff the next morning. They agreed that Britingham himself had probably been responsible for the light that night, but they both knew he couldn't have switched the light off the next morning, by which time he was already lying dead on Kevin's dock. Both knew that the most likely explanation for the light going out was simply that the bulb had burned out, although Grace wasn't ready to dismiss the worrying thought that vandals might have gotten into the shack.

Kevin knew that the sheriff would test the burned-out bulb theory—had probably done so already. And he seriously doubted that Blue Water Point had been visited by vandals as well as a murderer, all in the space of a few hours.

The Sandersons seemed genuinely surprised when Kevin asked them if they had been searching the beach for something Tuesday night. They had heard nothing about someone with a flashlight, and were adamant that it had not been either of them. They had gone to bed early and had been sound asleep when Rachel reported seeing the light on the beach.

When Kevin settled down that evening to take stock of the day's events and to rationalize his disregard of the sheriff's instructions, he no longer doubted that these lights in the night were connected in some way to Britingham's death. Or that the killer had been using the shack and looking for something on the beach on Mallard Cove.

CHAPTER 38

Under normal circumstances, Dolores Weber would have been at her desk at the Silver Leaf Wine Company at 9:45 on a Monday morning. But the circumstances of Dolores's life had ceased to be normal the previous Tuesday with the death of her boss and lover and the nearly simultaneous discovery of his infidelity. She owed no loyalty to Silver Leaf. More important matters now occupied her attention. So on Monday she had called in sick, and after a leisurely breakfast she had showered, put on a linen dress that she thought showed off her figure to best advantage, and, because she didn't want to work up a sweat, had driven the three short blocks to The Flower Basket. It had not been necessary to leave quite so early, but Dolores wanted the advantage of being there first.

The Flower Basket was not Dolores's kind of place. It had an air of fussiness about it, and its chintz curtains and tablecloths of pink, lime green, and white and potted plants in wicker stands were not to her taste. Dolores was an habitué of coffeehouses, not tearooms.

She took a seat at a table along the wall, where she could watch the people entering the place but not be easily seen by them as they came in. Business was slow. Only one group of three women, all of them considerably older than the woman for whom Dolores was waiting, shared the room with her, and while their conversation was animated, she could not make out what they were talking about. Not that she cared. Her thoughts were focused on the conversation she herself would be having with Emily Hoffman, a conversation that should begin shortly if the clock on the wall was accurate and if her tea partner did not develop cold feet. Dolores didn't think she would.

At precisely ten o'clock the door opened, and the tiny bells above it tinkled brightly, announcing to the lone waitress on duty the arrival of a customer. Dolores watched as the woman entered the room. She was tall, blond, immaculately dressed in a flowered blouse and white slacks, and every bit as attractive as Dolores had expected her to be. In spite of her mission, she had to acknowledge that John Britingham's standards had at least been high. Emily Hoffman, for she had no doubt that's who it was, stood just inside the doorway, looking about. Dolores did not rise to meet her, but she did catch the woman's eye and motioned her to the table by the wall.

Both of the women observed the amenities, but the exchange of introductions and pleasantries could not disguise the awkwardness of the moment or its tension. Emily was torn between a desire to proceed cautiously while she sized up the woman across the table and a need to get quickly to the point of their meeting. She opted for the former approach only because she did not wish to appear too anxious to discover what it was that her companion had of hers. The two women talked about things that mattered to neither of them, skirting not only the issue of whether John Britingham had had in his possession some things belonging to Emily Hoffman but even the fact of Britingham's death. It was Dolores who ended the pretense.

"Look, Mrs. Hoffman, I don't really care all that much for tea, and I suspect that you don't want to spend all morning beating around the bush. Let me show you the things that I believe belong to you."

Dolores fished in the large shoulder bag she had set on the floor at her side and produced a small paper sack. From it she withdrew the earrings, the brooch, and, slowly, for dramatic effect, the panties. She moved the sugar bowl and a bud vase to one side so that she could place these items in the center of the table. Emily watched the performance impassively until Dolores shoved the panties across the table toward her, at which point she glanced quickly around to see if anyone was watching.

"These aren't mine," Emily said in a calm, controlled voice. "I was sure they wouldn't be, but you seemed so sure over the phone that I felt I had to come and look."

"You're quite sure?" Dolores asked. "As I told you, it was your phone number with them that made me think they might be. Can you think of a reason why Mr. Britingham would have had your number?"

"No, no reason I can think of. But these things aren't mine in any event." Emily had not touched any of the items on the table. She was prepared to lose the jewelry; it was valuable, but hardly of heirloom quality. Had the panties been clean, it wouldn't have mattered, but she didn't like the fact that her soiled underwear was in the possession of this stranger, and might soon be in the hands of the sheriff. But she didn't think these items could be traced to her. Moreover, the woman's fingerprints would be all over the jewelry. In spite of her discomfort, Emily felt a surge of relief.

"Well, then," Dolores said, "we may never know whose they are. It probably doesn't matter. I just didn't think it was right that the sheriff should be poking into Mr. Britingham's personal life—or yours."

Emily blushed.

"Like I said, I have no idea why Mr. Britingham had my phone number. I didn't really know the man. I think we met once at a neighbor's cocktail party, but that's all."

"I understand," Dolores said, aware of the irony in Emily Hoffman's lie. Neither of them had really known John Britingham.

As Dolores had expected, Mrs. Hoffman would not wish to linger once she had seen the evidence and decided what to do about it.

"I think I had best be getting back. I appreciate your concern, but it's probably a good idea that the sheriff have these things." Emily folded her napkin and started to push her chair away from the table.

"Mrs. Hoffman, do you mind if I ask you a personal question?" Dolores asked as she, too, prepared to leave. Emily had no interest whatsoever in answering personal questions, but the request was so unexpected and innocuous, and the explanation for it so flattering, that she sat down again.

"I just wondered what your maiden name was. I've been admiring your features and your hair as we talked. You have the genes I wish I had. I just wondered about your family heritage. Scandinavian, I'd guess." It was Dolores Weber at her sweetest, and rarest.

Emily blushed for the second time in two minutes.

"You don't need to envy anyone else her genes," she protested. "You're a very attractive woman. But you're right; my roots are in Scandinavia. My name was Hanson. Both sides of the family came from Sweden."

The smile that flashed across Dolores's face was out of all proportion to the answer to her question.

"Hanson. Yes, I thought it might be something like that. I think you should wait a minute longer. There's something else I'd like to show you."

Emily looked puzzled, while Dolores turned her attention once more to her bag. This time she produced a small object wrapped in tissue paper.

"I wonder if this is yours?" she asked, her voice considerably more matter-of-fact than her mood, which was triumphant. Dolores removed the tissue paper and held in the palm of her hand an elegantly crafted, two-inch long, gold pillbox. She turned it so that Emily could see the lid, on which were engraved in elaborate but clearly legible letters the initials EHH.

Emily Hoffman's face was a frozen mask. She reached out as if to take the pillbox, but then dropped her hand into her lap. She said nothing.

"It is yours, isn't it? It was with the other things, but it is so obviously much more valuable that I thought it deserved special treatment."

"I didn't say it was mine," Emily countered weakly.

"You didn't have to, Mrs. Hoffman. I have a proposition to make to you. You seem to be rather careless with your personal belongings. I'd like to help you. I'll take care of the pillbox; it'll be safe with me—it won't fall into the wrong hands. And you can pay me a fee for looking after it. Not much. After all, it's small. I'd suggest $1000 a month."

Emily didn't blush this time. Her face looked more like chalk.

"That's blackmail," she said between clenched teeth.

"Mrs. Hoffman, let's be civil," Dolores responded in a stern, no-nonsense tone of voice. "I'm trying to help you. Think about it—would you rather I had the box or that the sheriff did? Because if the sheriff had it, I'm sure she'd want to talk to you—and to your husband, of course—about what it means that it was found among Britingham's possessions. And I'm not asking a lot for my services. That's only $12,000 a year, a small price to pay for peace of mind, don't you think? I'm sure not going to retire on that kind of money."

The waitress stopped by their table to ask if they wanted anything else. The two women dissembled, and Dolores accepted the check and handed the waitress a five-dollar bill, telling her to keep the change.

"As you can see, I'm a generous person. I'll be glad to do tea anytime."

"Why don't you just give me the pillbox, and if you'll let me have your name, I'll write you a check for $1000." Emily Hoffman brought her purse around and took out her checkbook.

"That's very nice of you, but I prefer cash. And $1000 isn't really a fair compensation for my services, now is it? I'd like monthly payments, in cash." Dolores hadn't figured out the details for future payments, and the Hoffman woman might, after all, change her mind. Probably not, though—she would be afraid of putting the pillbox in the sheriff's hands, either because she had had something to do with John's death or because it would put her marriage at risk.

"Monthly payments in cash." Emily repeated the words, sounding both miserable and trapped. "Monthly payments for how long?"

"Until the Britingham business blows over and people stop talking about it. One year perhaps, no more than two, I should think. It's hard to say—depends on what happens. And I'd like that first $1000 right away. I'll take it now if you have the cash on you. If not, why don't you run along to the bank and meet me back here in front of The Flower Basket in twenty minutes. I'd prefer our relationship to get off on the right foot, wouldn't you?"

"Of course I don't have $1000 in my purse. And my bank isn't here; it's over in Southport. You're a miserable bitch, do you know that?"

Men had called Dolores that before, but never another woman. At least not to her face.

"I'm sorry you're behaving like this. Please try to pull yourself together." Dolores put the box back in her bag, dabbed at her mouth with her napkin, and stood up. "You just get in your car, drive over to Southport, and be back here with the cash by noon. I don't plan to wait beyond that, Mrs. Hoffman."

And with that, Dolores Weber walked quickly out of The Flower Basket and into the bright morning sunlight.

CHAPTER 39

The knock on the door was tentative, and Kevin might have missed his caller altogether had he not spotted the blue print dress through the window on his way to the kitchen.

"Hi, won't you come in?" he said.

His visitor was Chris Sanderson. Kevin and the Sandersons were not social friends; indeed they barely knew one another. He had exchanged pleasantries with Mrs. Sanderson on a number of occasions, and he knew that the Sandersons were next-door neighbors of the Milburns and that Dan and Rachel spoke well of them. As it happened, he had probably had his longest conversation with them only the day before when he had inquired about the light on their beach the night after Britingham's death. But he didn't think he had ever seen either Larry or Chris at his door before.

"Hello, Mr. Whitman. Nice morning, isn't it? I won't be bothering you but a minute. Larry asked me to bring you this." She thrust a foil-wrapped package into his hands.

Kevin looked skeptically at the package, unsure what it was he was holding.

"It's nothing much, just two fish. They've been cleaned and frozen," Chris said.

"How nice. I was wondering what I'd do for supper, and you've solved my problem. But to what do I owe the pleasure?"

"Mr. Milburn thought you might like them. He's a neighbor, I guess you know. Larry never eats the things—says it's the bones, so I offered them to Dan and he said—oh, I'm sorry, I didn't mean to..."

It was obvious that Mrs. Sanderson was embarrassed, perhaps by the fact that Kevin was not the first person to whom she had offered the fish. He tried to put her at ease.

"It's very kind of you. Which one of you caught them?"

"Oh, I'm afraid we can't take the credit. Larry doesn't fish, if you can believe that. Me either. A friend of ours, Hank Bauer, caught them the other night—actually the night Mr. Britingham got killed. We were playing cards, and when the evening broke up

he left them in our frig. I don't think he meant to, but when I
called he said we could keep them. Anyway, I won't be cooking
them, and it's a shame to let them go to waste."

"If it makes you feel any better, I don't fish either. Always
thought I was the only one around here who didn't. Please sit
down, stay a bit. I'll put these in the refrigerator."

Mrs. Sanderson had not wanted to stay, but she sensed that to
reject the invitation to sit for a few minutes might seem rude. So
she picked the chair nearest the door and waited for Whitman to
return from the kitchen.

Kevin came back with two glasses of ice tea, each with a
sprig of mint. "Is tea okay? I'd just made some up, and the mint is
really good, I think. I was going to say it's the only thing I can get
to grow here, but the truth is it's the only thing I try to grow. I
hope your thumb is greener than mine."

"I doubt it," Chris said. "Thanks for the tea. You have a very
nice place here."

There was something in the woman's manner, Kevin decided,
recalling Emily Hoffman's impromptu visit on the morning of the
murder. But the problem with Mrs. Sanderson was different. It
was less a matter of what she said than how she said it, and how
she sat in her chair and how she looked, as if she didn't think she
belonged in his living room. Kevin had seen it too often, and while
it saddened him, it was something he could understand. Chris
Sanderson was uncomfortable, he thought, because she felt
inferior. Inferior socially and intellectually. She's comparing our
cottages. There would be fewer books at the Sandersons. No music
was coming from the speakers, but Kevin had not put away his
new recording of *The Magic Flute*. Its CD case and several other
CDs spread out on the coffee table would probably say to Mrs.
Sanderson that he had highbrow tastes. She was worrying about
what to say, afraid of committing some social or grammatical faux
pas.

Kevin acknowledged her compliment, but turned at once to
what he assumed was the one safe subject of conversation these
days.

"Do you have a theory about the murder?"

"Oh, no, I wouldn't have any idea. Larry says that work at the
winery just about came to a standstill last week."

"I shouldn't be surprised. It's all everyone seems to talk
about," Kevin said, putting them all in the same boat.

"I know," Chris agreed. "Before he was killed and now—it's the same old thing. He's almost the only thing any of us talked about that night. And we didn't know he'd be dead before morning. It's weird."

Kevin might have chosen a different word to describe it, but at least the Sanderson woman was relaxing a bit more.

"I guess it is," he said. "Weird, I mean. I didn't know the man, but from what I hear, nearly everyone around here had a problem with him. It sounds cruel, but you must be relieved in a way that he's dead."

Chris didn't wish to admit to any such feeling of relief at Britingham's death. She preferred the safer ground of shared grievances prior to his murder.

"It was really such a bad night, everybody complaining about how he'd messed up their lives. It got people to drinking. Heavier than usual. At least nobody had to drive home. I remember saying to Larry how glad I was that Mike could walk and Hank could take the boat."

"The boat?" Kevin wasn't following this meander by the now more loquacious Mrs. Sanderson.

"I'm sorry. I'm just chattering away here. But you're right, about Mr. Britingham being on everyone's mind. We'd been playing cards and talking mostly about him, and a couple of the men had quite a bit to drink. I meant it was just as well that Mike and Bernie and Rose lived right on the point and that Hank had come by boat. He didn't have to take the road back. It can be dangerous with all those curves, especially if, you know, you've had a few drinks."

Kevin had never understood the double standard that accepted behavior on the water that wouldn't be tolerated on the highway. He doubted that drinking and operating a powerboat on Crooked Lake was much safer than drinking and operating an automobile on West Lake Road, but his was a minority view. Concern about the antics of powerboat operators was a major reason why he had limited himself to a canoe, and even then typically used it close to shore. On this occasion, however, he had no wish to bother Mrs. Sanderson with his views on water safety.

"I understand," he said. But Chris, having brought up the subject of the card party and the evening spent talking about John Britingham, still seemed to feel some need to explain herself.

"It was Hank that caught those fish. That's why he had his boat, so he could fish on his way over. Now Mike, he..." Chris stopped in mid-sentence, her face suddenly crimson. "Oh, I'm sorry, Mr. Whitman. I don't know what's gotten into me. You don't know these people, and here I am bending your ear as if it's important. I guess we've just been so wrapped up in this Britingham business. Please forgive me."

"That's silly. There's nothing to forgive. Like I said, I've talked about it a lot, too, with just about everyone I run into. The only difference is that some of the rest of you had real problems with that man. Dan Milburn tells me you and your husband did. And it must have been a constant worry. I've been luckier. And by the way, I do know some of your friends. Mike Snyder especially."

"Well, that's nice. Look, I really should be off now. I didn't mean to stay." Mrs. Sanderson was reverting, before Kevin's eyes, to the self-conscious, self-deprecating woman she had been only a few minutes earlier.

"Sure you won't stay for a refill?" Kevin offered, but his guest had made up her mind and used as an excuse the need to go into Southport on an errand.

They exchanged thanks again for the fish and the ice tea, and Kevin was left to ponder the significance of what he had heard, including the fact that John Britingham wasn't the only person on Blue Water Point who had been drunk or close to it the previous Monday night.

CHAPTER 40

Deputy Sheriff Bridges stood in front of 32401 Lancaster Street, wondering at the sheer size of a city that could produce five-digit street numbers and worrying that he might not have the right address. The woman had given him directions when he'd called to make the appointment, and he thought he had followed them to the letter. But the brownstone walkup didn't look like his mental picture of a house of prostitution. Sam had never visited such a house, however, and he wondered if perhaps the commonplace exterior was intentional, a facade behind which the ladies could better conduct their trade.

The door was opened by a short, well-endowed young woman who favored him with a tentative smile.

"Uh, hello. I'm looking for Miss Starr. Is she in?"

"She sure is. I'm Miss Starr." The smile broadened.

"Crystal Starr?" Sam's doubt showed in his voice.

"Crystal Starr. Come on in."

Whatever Sam had expected, it wasn't this. He was looking at a girl-woman who reminded him of the cheerleaders who had turned cartwheels along the sidelines at high school football games. She had an attractive but not particularly distinguished face under a mop of dark blond hair, which danced as she moved her head. She was wearing a blue skirt that stopped some six or seven inches above the knees, revealing muscular legs. The simple white blouse emphasized her full bust. She wore no makeup or jewelry. And her feet were bare.

"It's Sam, isn't it? You going to just stand there?"

The deputy sheriff of Cumberland County realized that he was staring. He mumbled an apology and followed Crystal Starr, or whatever her name was, into a living room or parlor that was just as much of a surprise as the woman herself had been. Although it was the middle of the day, he had expected drawn drapes and dim light. The dominant color would, of course, be red. But the movies, it would appear, had gotten it all wrong. This room was as bright and airy as a nursery. Marge, his wife of fifteen years, would approve; she had always liked whites and yellows and lots of plants, and this room had them in abundance.

"Drink?" The Starr woman motioned for him to take a seat on the couch and stood poised to take his order.

"No. No thanks, not now. Where are the other—what I mean is, are you alone?"

"Sure. Just you and me. Why? Were you looking for a three-way?"

"I just want to talk." Sam had been going to add 'first,' but thought better of it. It would be a deception, and besides, she wouldn't be interested in sharing either booze or bed with him after he explained his real mission.

Crystal Starr shrugged and took a seat at the other end of the couch, half facing Sam in such a way that he found himself looking at a great deal of well-tanned skin.

"Okay, let's talk. What do you want to talk about? The NASDAQ, that oil spill out in California, the Middle East crisis?"

She's pulling my leg, Bridges thought, his face flushing with unaccustomed embarrassment. He decided he had better get straight to the reason for his trip to the city and his presence on Crystal Starr's couch at noon on a Tuesday in August.

"Do you know the upstate area at all? Like around Cumberland?"

"No, I can't say I do. Should I?"

"Look, Miss Starr, this is going to come as a shock to you, and I don't want you to misunderstand me. I'm not here to make trouble for you, but I'm the deputy sheriff of Cumberland County, and I'm investigating a case. It may be homicide. I have to ask you some questions."

If this announcement came as a shock to Miss Starr, it didn't register on her face. She did, however, tug at her skirt, managing to conceal a bit more of her thighs.

"What does this have to do with me?" she asked in a more business-like voice.

"We're trying to find out what some of the neighbors of the deceased were doing the night he died. You won't know the man who was killed, but we thought you might know one of his neighbors. We're not accusing anybody, you understand, just doing a routine check of who was where." There, Sam thought, that sounds properly professional. It was the next part that was harder.

"I'm inquiring about a man named Alan Hoffman. Do you know him?"

"Why are you asking me about somebody from Cumberland, wherever that is?"

"Because he says he was with you the night of the—the night this man died."

"Alan Hoffman? I may know an Alan Hoffman, but he's from here in the city."

"Same one," Sam said, both surprised and encouraged by the breakthrough. Miss Starr, it appeared, had no hang-ups about confidentiality where her clients were concerned. "He has a place up there as well as down here. So was he with you last Monday night?"

Bridges knew immediately that he had made a mistake. He should have left it to her to fix a date, assuming that they had in fact been together. But he couldn't take it back. He had identified Monday as the crucial night.

"Yes, he was here that night." It was a simple, direct answer. No hemming or hawing, just yes, Alan Hoffman had been with Crystal Starr on the night of the murder. It was too neat.

"How can you be sure? Do you have a book, you know, a datebook where you keep track of who's here?"

"No, I certainly do not. Alan Hoffman is a friend. I don't schedule my friends. He just dropped in."

This attempt to suggest that her relationship with Hoffman had nothing to do with business did not convince Bridges, but it was obvious that his question had annoyed her. She conveyed her displeasure with her body language, uncrossing her legs and moving to the edge of the couch, where she sat, knees together, bare feet planted firmly on the carpet.

"Okay," Sam protested, "I just didn't see how you could remember a particular night."

"Damn it, Sam—Sheriff Sam." She leaned on the word 'sheriff,' underscoring it with sarcasm. "What do you want from me? His favorite position? Look, he slept over. Is that okay? We are consenting adults, you know."

"That's not quite what I meant. I just need to know when Hoffman was here. You know, when he got here, when he left."

This seemed to mollify Miss Starr a bit, and she settled back into the cushions.

"I'm not sure when he arrived. I don't make a habit of checking my watch when company comes. Around midnight, probably a little before, going by what was on TV. And like I said, he slept over. He left after breakfast, around eight."

"You mean he was here all night?" Bridges knew he sounded like a particularly obtuse student, but he had to be sure.

"That's what I said. Right back there in the bedroom. He got up around seven, we had coffee and things, and he left for work."

"Where does he work?" Sam had a nagging suspicion that Crystal Starr didn't know Alan Hoffman as well as she claimed.

"He's with Camber, Phillips and Stein, over near 13th and Commerce. And you want me to describe him, don't you? Let's see. Under six feet, maybe five eight or nine, brown hair, a little gray at the temples, probably weighs 160, 165. He doesn't get much exercise, but he's still got a nice flat tummy. The rest is a secret. Why do you insist on treating me as if Alan is a stranger?"

Because being suspicious is my job, Sam said to himself.

"What do you do for a living?" was what he said to Crystal Starr.

"Oh, come on, you can do better than that. I clip coupons. It beats working."

When Sam fell silent, his agenda of questions exhausted, she put a hand on the cushion between them and walked her fingers back and forth.

"Okay, it looks like we've had our conversation. Now what would you like to do?"

Sam looked at the woman, three feet away from him on the couch and obviously ready to close the distance between them. Those piston-like legs reminded him not only of cheerleaders in general, but also of the captain of the squad whom he had propositioned one night nearly twenty years ago after a few too many beers, only to be rejected. It was a vivid and disturbing memory. Sam looked away from those legs and found Crystal Starr's eyes, which weren't at all like those of the cheerleader he remembered.

She was, he thought, one cool lady, obviously more mature than she had first appeared. There had been no hint of panic when he had identified himself as a police officer. He had expected that it would be necessary to spend a lot of time reassuring her that they weren't interested in what she did for a living, but only in corroborating an alibi for one Alan Hoffman. He had worried about what he would do if she refused to cooperate. But she had cooperated readily and without protest, as if working with the police were an everyday occurrence.

It was all too good to be true, he thought. She knew Hoffman; that was quite clear. But he had no way of knowing whether she had been telling the truth about their spending the previous Monday night together. Wouldn't people like Crystal Starr have had lots of experience in telling lies?

But assuming that she had lied, why this particular lie? Wouldn't she have been more likely to have lied by denying she knew the man? Or by denying that they had spent that night together? The fact that she had confirmed Hoffman's alibi seemed to suggest that she had been telling the truth. But it was all too pat.

"I have to be getting back to Cumberland," Bridges said in a flat, tired voice. "It isn't likely that you'll be needed to testify, but there's a chance. Sorry to have taken your time."

"Not at all, Sam," she said, getting up and offering him her hand. "You're doing your job, and you're really very sweet. If you get down here again, give me a call, and we'll have another conversation."

Crystal Starr gave his hand a squeeze and saw him out the door.

As Bridges walked the two long blocks to the only parking space he'd been able to find, he continued to puzzle over the prostitute's reaction to his admission that he was a police officer and her readiness to talk about a client. She had told him, against all expectations, just what he had wanted to hear. Or was it just what Hoffman wanted him to hear? The more he thought about it, the more it seemed as if Alan Hoffman and Crystal Starr had agreed in advance on the story they would tell the authorities. Hoffman had told the sheriff he had spent the night with Starr; Starr had told Sam the same thing. If Hoffman had indeed spent that night in the brownstone on Lancaster Street, he would have had no way at the time to know that he would need an alibi. This meant either that Crystal Starr was by nature an honest, open, trusting woman or that Hoffman had contacted her since that Monday night and told her to support his story. Bridges doubted very much that Starr was that honest and open and trusting. Which meant that she had told him what Hoffman had asked her to. And it was just as likely to be a lie as the truth, a false alibi as a real one.

Later, as he pulled onto the freeway and began the trip back toward Cumberland, Sam Bridges was feeling both frustrated and smug. Frustrated because of a growing conviction that Hoffman and Starr had conspired to throw sand in the gears of the investigation into John Britingham's death. Smug because it was Sheriff Kelleher who had messed up, giving Alan Hoffman time and opportunity to get in touch with Crystal Starr and set up his alibi.

CHAPTER 41

"Carol? Donegan over in Southport. Do you want to solve your crime?"

The police chief's voice was so loud that Sheriff Kelleher held the phone away from her ear and looked at it as if it were an animate object.

"No, of course not. Do you want to win the lottery?" Chief Donegan's obsession with winning a lottery and his talk about what he would do in retirement with his winnings was a familiar story in the Crooked Lake area.

"So who do you think is sitting in my office right now?"

"What is this, twenty questions? How do I know who's sitting in your office?"

"Guess."

"Damn it, Joe. I'm not sure I'm in the mood for this. So tell me, who is sitting in your office?"

"No offense, Carol. It's the guy you were looking for. Young Britingham. What do you suppose he just told me?"

"Donegan!" The explosion from the sheriff caused Miss Maltbie in the outer office to slop coffee over the mail in her in-box.

"All right, all right. Relax. But I think you're gonna like this. Britingham confessed. He killed his father. How about that?"

The sheriff was both stunned and elated. And instantly skeptical.

"Confessed? He did, huh? What did he say?"

"Well, he just came in and started talking. Said the police weren't going to do anything, so he had to."

Carol was too excited to stay seated. She got out of her chair and began circling the desk, asking questions and trying to think about procedure at the same time.

"Did you read him his rights?"

"We didn't arrest him. He just came in off the street."

"Doesn't matter. You know that."

"Well, I told him you were in charge of the case, that he'd have to tell it to you all over again. I couldn't help hearing him say he'd done it—just blurted it out when he came in. Do you want me to bring him over or do you want to come and get him?"

The sheriff was thinking fast. It'd be the same length of time before she'd be talking to young Britingham either way. If she picked him up, she'd be driving and wouldn't be able to watch him while they talked on the drive back to Cumberland. Of course she could question him over in Southport, but that was foreign turf and she wouldn't be comfortable doing it. She briefly considered contacting Sam and having him collect Britingham, but immediately dismissed that idea; Carol wanted to be the one to meet him, talk with him first, size him up.

"Do me a favor, will you? Have one of your men bring him over. And read him his rights. I mean, don't scare him, just tell him he doesn't have to say anything until he sees me, and I'll take it from there."

And then it was a matter of waiting the half hour for Donegan or one of his officers to make the trip, during which time she would try to plan the questions she would ask the self-confessed murderer of John Britingham.

The young man who preceded Chief Donegan into the office looked very much as the sheriff had expected him to. There was a definite resemblance to the father. She knew that he would be in his twenties, but he could almost have passed for a late teenager— one of those people who would always appear more youthful than their chronological age. Today, he might see that as a handicap. Later, if there were a later, he would be grateful. He was tall, taller than his father had been, but shared the same dark, wavy hair and strong, distinctive features. John Britingham, Jr. was dressed in faded jeans, an Izod sport shirt, and sandals, and sported what looked like a two- or three-day growth of stubble.

After Donegan had left and Miss Maltbie had taken up a seat in the back corner of the office, the sheriff launched into an interrogation about which she was privately, but she hoped not obviously, quite nervous.

"Mr. Britingham," she began, "I suppose there are two big questions on my mind, but first, you understand, you have the right to remain silent and the right to call an attorney."

"I don't want to remain silent. I have to talk about it." The voice was strong and surprisingly deep.

"As you wish. What about a lawyer? You're not from around here, I gather. Do you want me to give you the names of a few attorneys?"

"I don't need a lawyer."

"Why is that? A lawyer would understand the legal implications of what you might say and could advise you." The sheriff was not at all sure that any lawyer of her acquaintance in the Cumberland area would be at home in a matter of this kind, but she felt obligated to say it anyway.

"I don't need a lawyer," Britingham repeated.

Carol studied his face for a moment, frowned, and then picked up the notes she had made while waiting for Donegan's arrival with the man whom she must now begin to think of as the prisoner.

"About those two questions then. I guess what puzzles me is why you're doing this."

"Doing this?"

"Coming to the police. Confessing to a crime—and a very serious crime. Most people would run away, as far as they could. They wouldn't say anything to anyone. We'd have to hunt them down. But you've come to us. Why?"

"I had to. I just couldn't stand it. I really couldn't, you know."

"What couldn't you stand?" Carol was trying to strike a tone that was both official and avuncular.

"That I'd killed him. Killing is wrong, so killing your father—what do they call it?—patricide, I think—it has to be worse. Ten times worse. A hundred times worse. I had no right."

The sheriff watched the young man, looking for some non-verbal clue that might help her better to understand what was going on in his mind. And remembering her conversation with his half-sister, who had told her that the boy was incapable of hurting anyone. No, not incapable of hurting—incapable of killing. And now he was confessing that he had killed, but that the knowledge of his act was unbearable.

"So what do you think will happen now?"

"I don't know. It doesn't really matter. I've got to try to make it right."

The words suggested strong emotions, but Britingham gave no outward sign of emotion. He sat perfectly still. His voice was monotone. His face reflected no inner struggle, much less pain or remorse. It wasn't so much that he was composed, Carol thought, as that he was numb. Maybe the answer to her other question would make Britingham's reason for confessing clearer.

"So you have to confess because killing your father was wrong. Okay, I'll buy that. It's wrong. And in the eyes of the law it's also a crime. Then why did you kill him?"

"Because he killed my mother."

There. He'd said it, said what Carol had half-expected him to say. It was just like Mrs. Carson had said, except she had been convinced that the boy could not have killed his father.

"You killed your father because he killed your mother. Wouldn't it have been the job of the state to punish him? Why did you have to take the law into your own hands?"

"Because they weren't doing anything about it." Suddenly young Britingham seemed more animated. "No one believed he'd done it, and I felt that—I just felt..."

He was groping for words that wouldn't come. Frustrated by his inability to explain, he retreated into confession.

"I did a terrible thing. It was wrong, and I had to tell somebody. You believe me, don't you?"

The sheriff was surprised by the question, then immediately realized that she shouldn't have been.

"Why shouldn't I believe you?"

"It's like you said. You know, that—that people like me don't come to the cops. I just thought—you know, that I had to make it right. But I can't make it right, can I?"

Emotions were now coming to the surface.

"Can I have a Coke or something?"

"Sure," Carol replied and dispatched Miss Maltbie downstairs to the soft drink machine. Funny, mixed-up kid, she thought. Keeps saying he's got to make it right. Wonder how he thinks he's going to do that? She busied herself at her file cabinet, giving Britingham a moment to pull himself together until Miss Maltbie returned with the Coke.

"Let's back up a bit," the sheriff said, resuming her seat behind the desk. "Let's talk about your mother, about what your father did. You tell me he killed her, but we know he was never charged. What I hear is that she drowned in a boating accident. Why do you say he killed her?"

"It doesn't matter anymore, does it?" Britingham's manner and tone of voice said that he'd been asked this question before and that no one had believed him.

"Maybe it does and maybe it doesn't. Tell me anyway."

"There are some things you just know. It wasn't an accident. Or if it was an accident, she didn't have to drown. My mother was a great swimmer. So was my father. She could have made it. Or he could have saved her. They believed him, that's all—never even investigated."

"What would the police have found if they had investigated?" The sheriff assumed that they had investigated and had found nothing to support a verdict other than death by accidental drowning.

"I don't know. Maybe nothing. But he killed her—I know it."

"You were how old when this happened?" The sheriff knew the answer, and she very much doubted that a boy so young would have spotted a crime that a police investigation had missed.

"You think I'm making it all up, don't you? Everybody thinks so, except my aunt. Okay, so I was just a kid. And I wasn't there. But like I said, I know. Not then, I didn't. But later, when I figured it out."

"It was your aunt that gave you the idea?"

"I guess so. Jenny didn't say he killed Mom. She just told me about the fights, and that Mom was thinking of getting a divorce. But she was a terrific swimmer. She taught me. She used to swim all the time, not just in the summer. Most of the women would just paddle around in the water, but she'd do a mile or two every day, with real racing turns and everything. If she drowned, it was because he did it."

The sheriff knew from experience that good swimmers had drowned. The second Mrs. Britingham was probably one of them. But what mattered was what her son believed and what he had done about it. Of his own volition, young Britingham was now explaining himself.

"I'd been thinking about it for a long time. It was a big problem, you know, eating away at me. I couldn't get it out of my mind. It was really messing me up. Finally, I decided to come out here and put it straight to my father, you know, just ask him right out. 'Why did you kill Mom?' I figured he'd be so shocked he wouldn't be able to lie, and then I'd know. But I didn't plan to kill him. I just wanted him to know I knew."

"Why did you change your mind?"

"What do you mean?"

"You say you didn't plan to kill your father but that you did. What made you change your mind?"

"It all went wrong. I just lost my head and—and..."

When the anger Britingham felt toward his father collided with the fact of his father's violent death, he fell silent. It was as if he couldn't reconcile the two.

The desk was now striped with the shadows cast by the afternoon sun through the half-closed blinds. The clock over the door behind Britingham read 2:45, and for the first time since she had begun this interrogation, Sheriff Kelleher found herself looking ahead and wondering how she would bring it to an end. And then what? He would have to be locked up, of course. The thought crossed Carol's mind that she may have been less prudent than she should have been. The young man across the desk from her wasn't just a suspect; he was someone who claimed to have killed his own father. And she'd taken no precautions. The door was unlocked. Her gun—and when had she ever used that?—was still in its holster, and the holster was hanging on a peg on a coatrack on the other side of the room. She hadn't even searched Britingham for a weapon. What if this man about whom she knew so little changed his mind? What if he panicked? How would he react to some unanticipated question or some phantom thought about his mother or father that he couldn't cope with? Why, Carol asked herself, had she been so careless? And what could she do about it now? Certainly not march around the desk and handcuff Britingham.

But this was absurd, some inner voice told her. If she had to use one word to describe the person sitting on the other side of her desk, it would not be 'dangerous.' It would be 'sad.' The sheriff was reminded once again of how young he looked, how young and pathetic. She exhaled slowly and turned her attention to the murder.

"Why don't you tell me about it? About killing your father."

For a brief second she thought she had miscalculated. A look of something close to panic flickered briefly in Britingham's face. But it quickly passed, and he shrugged as if to say, 'What difference does it make?'

"What do you want to know?" His voice was now dull and flat, with none of the animation with which he had invested his explanation of his mother's death. Back to where we started, thought the sheriff.

"Well, I'd like to know where it happened. We've been trying to figure that out. And where you put the—what did you kill him with? Just tell me what happened."

"We met, and we talked," Britingham said. "I told him that I knew about Mom, that there was no point in pretending. And he got mad. He came at me, and we pushed and shoved, and I got mad, too, and I stabbed him. I didn't mean to. I didn't want to do that, but it just happened."

"Where did all this take place?"

"In that shack over by the lake. I'd found he stayed there sometimes, and I'd gone out there to talk to him."

"The shack," the sheriff mumbled, mentally pulling the bits and pieces of information she had assembled into place and trying to fit this one into the mosaic. "What did you stab him with?"

"A knife. It was just lying there, and I grabbed it when he hit me."

"And then what happened?" This was the part that interested the sheriff most, the biggest hole in the puzzle.

"He sort of doubled over and staggered out of the shack."

"And?"

"I don't know. I didn't go after him. What I'd done, it sort of hit me, and I guess I was in shock. I should have tried to find him, but I just sat down on the bed."

Carol looked at Britingham with a mixture of frustration and disbelief.

"That's all? You don't know where he went? How do you know you killed him?"

"The paper said he was found on a nearby dock, dead. People've been talking about it all around here. It looks like he tried to go for help and didn't make it."

The sheriff leaned back in her chair and looked hard at the miserable young man across the deck from her. It could have happened that way, she thought. Britingham knifed, bleeding to death, wandering off somewhere on the point. But some of the pieces were still missing.

"You never saw your father again?"

"No, ma'am."

A first, she thought, this note of formality.

"What did you do then? With the knife?"

"I was going to rinse it off, but there's no water there, so I decided I'd better get rid of it. I heaved it out into the lake."

"Where?"

"Below the shack, through the woods. I was scared. I just threw it away as far as I could."

Not good. The lake drops off fast into deep water in that area. Lots of weeds, too. The knife could be found, but it wouldn't be easy. Carol was rearranging the furniture in her mind. How did this fit with what Doc Crawford had told her? For one thing, the head injury hadn't been accounted for. And how had this badly wounded man gotten from the shack at the south end of the point to a dock hundreds of yards further north? Not under his own steam certainly. And not until several hours after his death.

"What time did you and your father have this confrontation?"

The look of panic crossed Britingham's face again, then disappeared.

"Sometime in the night. I really don't know."

For the first time Sheriff Kelleher visibly displayed frustration.

"Oh, come on, Britingham. I don't need to know the minute, but you can be more precise than that. Was it after dusk? Around midnight? Just before dawn?"

"Sheriff, I'm trying to be helpful. But I can't help it. I'd fallen asleep in the shack before he got there. And afterwards I was scared shitless. It was dark, that's all I know. It could have been anytime between, oh, maybe 9 and—look, I just don't know, but it wasn't light yet."

"You must have some idea whether it was a long time until daybreak or not."

"Don't you believe me?" Britingham started to get up out of his seat, thought better of it, and sat back down. "Why do we have to have all these questions? I've told you I killed my father. Shouldn't that put an end to your questions? You've got your answer, haven't you?"

"Yes and no, Mr. Britingham. I'm doing my job, and my job is to try to keep order in this county and solve our crimes. Happily, we don't have many crimes. This one—yours—is very much out of the ordinary around here. I can't afford just to make an arrest and close the case. I'm expected to tie up all the loose ends, and there are a lot of loose ends here. So if you want to—how did you put it—make it right?—then you'll answer my questions. All of them."

Britingham had been staring off in Miss Maltbie's direction. He turned back to face the sheriff but said nothing.

"So let's try it after the stabbing. After you realized what you'd done. You said you were sitting on the bed. Then what?"

"Nothing. I fell asleep."

"You what?" Carol leaned forward across the desk, incredulity written all over her face.

"I know; it's not what you'd expect. But I was out of it; I mean I really couldn't believe what I'd done. I just sat there, and then I sprawled out on the bed, trying to think—and I fell asleep. When I woke up, it was getting light. I threw the knife away and got out of there."

No matter how mixed up you are, Carol thought, or how tired, you don't visit your father's cabin to confront him with your suspicion that he killed your mother, kill him, and then go back to sleep.

"Why don't you tell me what really happened?"

"But I did!" Britingham practically shouted at the sheriff. "I can't help it if it isn't what you want me to say. It just happened that way. I couldn't cope—I just can't deal with it!"

Sheriff Kelleher had a confession, which by all rights should wrap up the case and spare her heaven knows how many more frustrating conversations with the denizens of Blue Water Point. But it had been a singularly unpersuasive confession. The alleged murder weapon was at the bottom of the lake. Young Britingham had no idea where his father had gone after he'd stabbed him or how he had gotten onto the Whitman dock. Moreover, he had no idea when he'd stabbed his father. In effect, he knew what everyone around Crooked Lake knew, and nothing more.

And at the climax of what would have to have been the most dramatic moment in his life, John Britingham's son had fallen asleep on an old army cot in a stuffy shack where he had just avenged his mother's death. It was possible, but not, Carol thought, very probable. John Britingham, Jr. spent that night safely locked away in one of the Cumberland County jail's four cells, but the sheriff went home to dinner convinced of only one thing: that she now knew who had been using the construction shack on Blue Water Point.

CHAPTER 42

The sun had not yet entirely burned off the morning fog that hung over Crooked Lake, but the forecast was for a sunny if humid day. Kevin had made a decision over his second cup of coffee that he had to reorder his priorities. Not once in the days since he had discovered John Britingham's body on his dock had he sat down at the computer to work on the article he had promised to write for an opera journal. Puccini's heroines had suddenly seemed much less interesting than his own involvement in a murder investigation. Mimi, Tosca, Butterfly—not a word had he written about any of them, and the editor's deadline for a completed manuscript was rapidly approaching. Conscience, more than a conviction that he had anything important to say to what he feared was an aging and dwindling population of opera fans, prompted him to get back to work.

Kevin dutifully assembled his notes and reread what he had written before the Britingham case preempted his attention. He was staring at the screen on his laptop, waiting for a spark of inspiration, when the phone rang.

"Hi, it's Dan. Are you busy or could you come over?"

"What do you think?" Kevin said, relieved that he had an excuse not to do what he had just told himself he had to do. "Have you ever known a time when I couldn't drop what I'm doing? That's why I never publish as much as the university wants me to. What's up?"

"I'm not sure. I just want to show you something."

"Be right there." With no great reluctance, Kevin shut down the computer and set out for the Milburns.

Dan greeted him at the back door. Rachel was baking a pie in the kitchen and waved a flour-covered hand in greeting.

"Get him some coffee, Dan," she ordered, but Kevin vetoed the suggestion, insisting that he'd already had his daily quota of caffeine.

"Let's go out on the porch." Dan led the way through the house.

"What's this all about?" Kevin wanted to know.

"I'll show you." From the porch, the Milburns had an excellent view of the lake in both directions. To the north they could see virtually the entire length of Blue Water Point, and to the south was the sweeping curve of Mallard Cove at the end of the point. The fog had lifted enough so that the far shore was visible for several miles in both directions, although the crown of the hill across the lake was still obscured. No matter how often he stood on this porch, Kevin always found himself thinking that there could be no finer view of Crooked Lake.

Dan led Kevin to the south end of the porch. The Sanderson cottage, with its bed of colorful annuals, was to their right, and it was to the Sanderson property that Dan directed Kevin's attention.

"Do you see their dock?" Dan was careful not to point. For all he knew, Chris might be watching.

"Of course I see it. What about it?" The dock was shorter than Kevin's dock or those of his immediate neighbors because the lake bottom dropped off more precipitously in the cove.

"Do you see that big cinder block on the beach? Larry uses it to prop up the end of the dock so he doesn't have to move the dock in or out when the level of the water in the lake changes. Right now it isn't needed, so it just sits there beside the end of the dock."

Kevin waited. Dan hadn't asked him over to explain how Larry Sanderson raised the shore end of his dock when the level of the lake rose.

"You know how it is when you see things day in and day out. You take them for granted—hardly notice them. That cinder block's been out there on the beach for two or three years. It must be pretty heavy. Anyway, Larry doesn't bring it up and put it under the house when he isn't using it. He just leaves it there. It's always there. Except last week, last Tuesday."

"What do you mean? He moved it?"

"Do you ever get the feeling that something's out of order? Well, I've had it for nearly a week. I couldn't put my finger on it, but it kept nagging at me. I knew there was something different, but I'd be damned if I could figure what it was. Then just this morning it came to me. That cinder block's not the same. I mean it's the same block, at least I think it is, but it's in a different position. I'd gotten used to seeing the holes in it. Even remember seeing a chipmunk pop out of one of them recently. Now, look at it. It must have been turned on its side. No holes showing."

"I don't understand. Why is that such a big deal? Larry probably moved it."

"Maybe, but when I realized it'd been turned over, I realized something else as well. It didn't even register at the time, but now I'm sure of it. That cinder block was missing last Tuesday."

Kevin was still trying to figure why Dan considered this important. Dan was explaining.

"I really am sure about it. The block wasn't there the day you found Britingham, and it was back there but in a different position the next day. After all these months when the block just sits there, it finally gets moved right at the time John Britingham is killed on our point. And what makes it even more interesting, it shows up again just after the night Rachel sees that light out on the Sandersons' beach. Now doesn't that strike you as strange?"

"Did you ask Larry if he moved it?"

"No, and he'd probably have a perfectly good explanation. But what if somehow—don't ask me how—but somehow it's connected to Britingham's death? What if Larry's involved? What would I ask him? Why should I be interested in an old .cinder block?"

"Unless you thought it had something to do with Britingham. I see the problem."

"Do you think it's significant?" Dan wanted to know. "You've been up to your ears in this Britingham business. Does this fit in somewhere?"

"I don't see how just offhand, but it's worth some thought. Why would Larry move the block? You said he uses it to raise the end of the dock when the water level rises. Maybe he—but no, water level's been pretty constant since early spring, and besides, you say the block disappeared for a day and then was back where it'd been before. How about he needed to stand on something?"

"But why move something that heavy when he could use a chair or a stepladder?"

"Do you know if they have a ladder?"

"I'm sure they do. I've seen Larry using it to clean their windows."

"Okay, what about using it for its weight? Maybe they wanted to weigh something down."

"Like what? You'd think there'd be all kinds of things around the house that would be just as good, and easier to move than that block."

"I don't know," Kevin conceded, "but what else could he use the block for? They aren't building anything that I can see. Anyhow, it's back where it was."

"I didn't figure we'd hit on an explanation right off the bat. Just thought you ought to know about it, in case it might be important."

Their discussion soon drifted off to other subjects, and Kevin eventually returned to his cottage to resume work on the article. But he couldn't concentrate on Puccini, and after half an hour of false starts he gave it up in favor of Britingham's murder. He pulled out a yellow pad and moved from the desk to his favorite chair, where he began brainstorming the possible implications of the disappearing cinder block.

Thirty minutes and two pages of scribbled notes later, Kevin found himself back where he had started. He had crossed out everything except for the first six words he had written: "cinder block" and "light in the night." According to the Milburns, Rachel had seen the flashlight on the Sandersons' beach on Tuesday night. And Dan had just told him that the cinder block had unaccountably disappeared on Tuesday only to reappear on Wednesday. Kevin was inclined to be skeptical of coincidences. Odds are, he thought, that the light in the night had something to do with the return of the cinder block.

The more Kevin thought about it, the more convinced he became that Larry Sanderson's cinder block had something to do with Britingham's death. And the more he thought about it in those terms, the more he found himself thinking not about the Sandersons, who would have the best reasons for moving the block and the least need to replace it in the middle of the night, but about others on the point. Hadn't he and the Milburns agreed that if Larry and Chris had been looking for something on the beach they would have turned on the porch light? And hadn't the Sandersons made it clear that they had been sound asleep when Rachel had seen the flashlight on the beach?

If not the Sandersons, who? Kevin mentally inventoried the other inhabitants of Blue Water Point, but it was a frustrating exercise that didn't seem to lead him anywhere. Maybe he should take a break, take a swim. He got up to change into his bathing trunks, and it was while he was going through his ritual of applying sunblock that second thoughts about the Sandersons occurred to him. What if they had not turned on the porch light because they didn't wish to be seen? After all, a flashlight would be much less conspicuous, especially at an hour when the neighbors would be expected to be asleep. And what if they had simply lied about what they did—or didn't do—that night?

Kevin had briefly considered calling the sheriff to share Dan's news about the cinder block. Much as he would have liked to talk to her, to let her know that he was capable of making a contribution to her efforts to solve the Britingham case, calling her did not now seem like such a good idea. What would he tell her? That a common, ordinary cinder block had been moved? That he suspected Larry Sanderson of moving it? He could imagine the sheriff's question: are you suggesting that he killed Britingham? No, he was not suggesting that. He had no reason to believe it, and he was sure that Dan Milburn would scoff at the idea. What was worse, the sheriff would think that he was wasting her time. And she might well have thought just that, for unbeknownst to Kevin, Sheriff Kelleher had been dealing with much bigger developments: the confession by Britingham's son that he had killed his father, and a second murder that very definitely had not been committed by young Britingham.

CHAPTER 43

Sam Bridges tried to ignore the phone on the bedside table, but it kept on ringing. It had been a long day but an emotionally satisfying evening, and Sam had fallen asleep still snuggled close to his wife in their comfortable old four-poster. Now grudgingly awake, he looked at his watch and made a wry face. Twelve-twenty in the morning. The middle of the night, for God's sake. Linda's passionate response to his lovemaking had pushed thoughts of that unpleasant meeting with Crystal Starr from his mind, but now it all came rushing back. What would the sheriff need him for at this hour?

"Sam? Jake Hamel here. Sorry to bother you, but I've got something you ought to know about. I thought it'd be better to call you than the sheriff."

Well, at least it wasn't the sheriff. And better to annoy me than Kelleher, Sam thought. Hamel was local Cumberland police, and he would be sensitive about relations with the sheriff's department.

"I'm over at the Village Garden Apartments. Got a homicide. It looks like rape or maybe attempted rape that went bad." Hamel was trying to sound matter-of-fact about it and not quite succeeding.

"Sounds like your jurisdiction, Jake. Why call me?"

"Let me finish." Hamel began to sound excited, as well he might, considering that homicides were almost as rare in this upstate area as snow in August. Or used to be. Now there had apparently been two in just over a week. "The victim is John Britingham's secretary. Weber's the name. How's that grab you?"

Sam was now wide-awake, and it was his turn to sound excited.

"I'll be damned! Murder. You're sure? Raped and murdered?"

If there had been any trace of irritation in the deputy sheriff's voice, it vanished with Hamel's news that the Britingham case had almost certainly taken an unexpected turn. There was always the possibility that the Weber woman's death had nothing to do with that of her former boss. But Sam knew that Sheriff Kelleher wouldn't believe it for a minute, and neither did he. He'd have to call her at once.

"I don't know about rape," Hamel answered. "It looks like it. But no question about murder. Smothered with a pillow from the looks of things. You want to come out? It's a ground-floor apartment, faces Dunbar Street. Number 18."

"Yeah, I'll be right over. Do me a favor, will you? Leave things just as you found 'em until I get there." Sam sucked in his breath. "What the hell's happening here, Jake? This place is going crazy."

"Looks like it."

Sam quickly dressed, called the sheriff, and having kissed his wife and apologized to her for his abrupt departure, set off for the Village Garden Apartments. When he entered the living room of Dolores Weber's apartment, he was immediately aware of two things, neither of which Officer Hamel had mentioned over the phone. The place was a shambles, and a dumpy woman of indeterminate age was sitting on the couch.

"What happened?" It was not a very astute question, and Bridges felt a little foolish for having asked it.

"You know as much as I do, Sam, but I'd guess the guy that did it ransacked the place, looking for loot."

"You think it was a robbery? What's that got to do with Britingham?"

"I didn't say it's related to your case," he said. "It just seemed kind of funny, her ending up like this so soon after he got killed."

"Like I told you, she was asking for it." It was the lady on the couch, reminding them of her presence, and her tone of voice said even more clearly than her words what she thought of the late Dolores Weber.

Bridges, who had been surveying the room, took a better look at the woman, and Hamel hastened to explain what she was doing there.

"This is Emma Stanton, lives in the next apartment. She's the one that found Miss Weber and reported it."

"What do you mean, she was asking for it?" Bridges was anxious to see the victim, but he also wanted to learn as much as he could before Sheriff Kelleher arrived and took over. This woman obviously had an opinion about Dolores Weber's demise.

"It's what I told the officer here. She had no shame. Always prancing around in the altogether with her shades up. One of those, those—what do you call them?—those exhibitionists. Only this time she got more than she bargained for."

Sam frowned at Emma Stanton. She clearly felt no compassion for the dead woman, only moral indignation over her behavior while she was alive. And her body language reinforced the message of her words. She sat rigid and proper on the couch, her legs tightly crossed under her dressing gown, her arms folded across her bosom as if to declare her disapproval and rejection of the tawdry scene around her. Her face was that of a person who smells a distinctly bad odor.

"How did you happen to find her tonight?" Better get the facts as well as her opinion of Miss Weber, Sam thought.

"It was the carrying on," she sniffed, indignation rising in her voice as she recalled the evening's events. "That music of hers. Noise is more like it. A body couldn't sleep. I pounded on the wall, but nothing happened, so I put on my robe and came over to complain."

"And you saw the man?" Hamel, who had already gone through all of this, was shaking his head. But Sam had to hear it for himself.

"No, just this mess and then her, all naked on the bed. I didn't know a man had been here, not at first, but when I saw she was dead, it just figured."

"How'd you get in? It doesn't look like the Weber woman opened the door for you."

Emma Stanton saw the implied criticism.

"I'm not a busybody, if that's what you're thinking. But I couldn't abide the racket. I knocked, and when no one opened up, I just stuck my head in. The door wasn't locked. Well, soon as I saw this"—she removed one hand from her chest long enough to take in the room with a sweep of her arm—"I came on in and called her name. She had to be in the bedroom—you can see the rest of the apartment from here. Anyway, that's where I found her."

"You said Miss Weber showed off in front of her window. But the blinds seem to be drawn. How do you think she got the man's attention? Maybe he was just a burglar."

The woman sighed in frustration over this lack of imagination.

"I never said she put on a show for some man tonight. Maybe she did, and maybe she didn't. But he'd have seen her sometime and figured she was a loose woman. He came back."

There. That's the way it happened. For Emma Stanton, there would be no doubt, no need to conduct much of an investigation. Of course the man in question would have to be identified and prosecuted, but that was a minor matter. The real culprit was the victim. Dolores Weber.

Bridges was about to ask more about Weber's penchant for exhibitionism when Sheriff Kelleher arrived. Hamel introduced Mrs. Stanton once again, but Carol was more interested in looking at the dead woman than in hearing about her self-destructive behavior.

"You haven't seen her yet?" The sheriff was both surprised by and upset with her colleague.

"I was waiting for you," Sam said without much conviction, and the three of them went on into the bedroom, leaving the Stanton woman on the living room couch.

When Sam Bridges had first met Dolores Weber at the winery, he had been disappointed that she had not gotten up from behind her desk so that he might see what he had been sure was an attractive figure. Now, looking at her body stretched out on her own bed, he knew he had been right; but the sight of her well-turned and well-tanned legs spread carelessly apart on the bedspread only produced a momentary wave of nausea.

The sheriff went over to the bed and gently closed the lids over the eyes that were staring sightlessly at the ceiling. True to his word, Hamel had not touched the body. Beside her on the bed was the pillow that had presumably snuffed out her life. Her face and hands hinted at her struggle, but on the whole her posture on the bed suggested nothing more than restless sleep. Contrary to Mrs. Stanton's report, she was not in the altogether, but her robe was bunched up under her, exposing the panties and brassiere that gave her a modicum of decency in front of the eyes of the three officers of the law. The bedroom, like the living room, was in disarray from her assailant's search for money or whatever it was he was seeking.

It was the sheriff who broke the silence that had overcome all three of them.

"Rape, you say?" It was Bridges who had reported this assumption to the sheriff, but it was Hamel who had first suggested it, and it was the Cumberland policeman who replied.

"Well, like I said, it looks like she put up a struggle. He tries to shut her up; he kills her; he runs away. It sure looks like he tried to rape her. And besides, the Stanton woman's sure that's what it was all about."

"Ah, yes, the woman out there in the living room. Look, let's get her back to her own apartment; tell her I'll be along in a few minutes to talk with her. Jake, why don't you do it? I don't want her eavesdropping. The walls here look thin as paper. Who built these damn apartments, anyway?"

They all knew the local builder, but Bridges and Hamel were sure that no answer was expected. The sheriff had taken charge, and Hamel made no protest. If the truth were known, he was grateful to be relieved of the responsibility. He left to escort Emma Stanton to her own apartment, hoping that nothing of importance would happen while he was gone.

Carol surveyed the room. She was looking at the spilled drawers of the dresser, rather than at Sam when she spoke.

"We'll know soon enough, I'd guess, but I don't think rape was the motive for what we've got here. If he was strong enough to kill her, he was surely strong enough to pull her panties off or at least to break the elastic band. And look at all of this stuff. He was looking for something, and I'll bet it wasn't sex."

The sheriff walked around the bed to where Dolores Weber's pocketbook had been turned upside down beside the table where a reading lamp provided the room's only light. The contents of the purse were all over the floor, a familiar mixture of the personal and impersonal effects to be found in most women's purses. Among the most conspicuous items was a wallet. It had been turned inside out, its deck of credit cards spilled in an irregular row toward the far wall. And there was money. The sheriff wasn't sure how much, but she could see several twenties and some smaller bills without even bending down. It wasn't money that Weber's visitor was after.

"You know, Sam, I'm glad Hamel notified us. This is a helluva lot better than getting the story secondhand from him or Phelps tomorrow. I don't give a damn what that woman next door says, this isn't a sex crime, and I don't think it's even a burglary. Weber had something he wanted. That's why he was here. She wouldn't give it to him, and he killed her. I don't know whether he killed her because she wouldn't give it to him, or because she started to scream and he had to shut her up. But either way, there's a good chance this one does have something to do with the Britingham case."

Carol stepped carefully over the dresser drawers and came around the bed to where Sam was standing by the door.

"What do you know about this Weber woman? Ever hear anything about her?"

"I never met her until..." Bridges began, just as Hamel came back from escorting Mrs. Stanton back to her apartment.

"How about you, Jake?" Carol interrupted. "Know anything about Weber?"

"Not really. You should talk to that neighbor lady. She seems to know a lot about her."

"I'll do that, but how about you? What do you mean, 'Not really'?"

"I never met her. You hear things, though, mostly from guys who work over at Silver Leaf. But it's just guys talking. Not a lot of young women move to Cumberland, Sheriff. People talk."

"You're telling me she's not from around here?"

"I hear she arrived back in the spring, four, five months ago."

"Interesting. What's the talk?"

"You know, the boss and his secretary. You get a good-looking broad working for someone like Britingham—lots of money, all that—well, the guys figure something's going on."

"And you?" Carol turned to Sam.

"Like I started to say, I only met her once, the morning we found Britingham. She seemed awfully cold and business-like." It hurt, even now, to say this, but it was the truth.

"It's like I said, Sheriff," Hamel said. "There's been talk. I mean, why would a looker like her come all the way from California to live in Cumberland?"

Hamel caught himself looking at the body on the bed.

"California?" The sheriff pounced on the word. "How do you know that?"

"She had California plates when she moved into these apartments. Had 'em for about six weeks before she got in-state plates."

Carol smiled, even as she weighed the implications of this news. Jake Hamel had paid more attention to Dolores Weber since her arrival in Cumberland than he had let on.

"For somebody who doesn't know anything about the woman, you've been mighty observant."

"Well, you know how it is, driving around all day in a patrol car. You notice things—especially cars." Hamel had either missed the irony in the sheriff's comment or decided to ignore it.

"I'd talk to that woman next door," Sam suggested. "She seems to know a lot about Miss Weber, or at least she thinks she does."

"So now it's my turn? Okay, I'll go on over. Jake, this is your case, and we don't want to put Phelps' nose out of joint." The Cumberland chief of police wasn't an unpleasant sort, but he could be touchy, as Sheriff Kelleher knew from experience, much more so than Donegan over in Southport. "But I'd be grateful if we could do one more thing—on the assumption that this may have something to do with the Britingham business. I'd appreciate it if you'd look around the apartment here—you and Sam—and see if you can find what it is that Miss Weber's killer was looking for."

"But he might have found it," Hamel protested. "It won't even be here."

"Maybe so," the sheriff replied. "But we can't assume that. If there's a chance that it's here, we look."

"What are we looking for?" Bridges was puzzled.

"I wish I knew."

"You're asking us to look for something, and you don't know what it is or even if it's here?" Deputy Sheriff Bridges didn't usually question the sheriff's judgment, but tonight she seemed to have lost touch with reality.

Carol put a hand on her deputy's shoulder.

"Sam, why don't you and Jake pull the spread over Miss Weber? Gently. Then we'll go out to the living room, and I'll tell you what I think."

Sam was relieved when the body was covered. He'd wanted to do it earlier, but it wasn't his decision.

What the sheriff thought about the object of the search that had left the apartment a wreck turned out to be very little, but it was better than nothing.

"One thing I know. The killer was looking for something small—small enough to put in a purse. He didn't dump the purse just for the hell of it, and he didn't want the money. Maybe he found what he wanted in there with the wallet and the keys and things. But we've got to hope that he didn't. So let's look everywhere. And I mean everywhere. If it was something that important to him, we've got to figure she would know it was important. So she could have hidden it—really good."

"But what? Any idea?" Sam needed to know what he was looking for.

"Yes and no. Something incriminating, I'd guess. A love letter he wished he hadn't written? Something that would be a problem for him if it got into the wrong hands. Use your imagination. Whatever it is, it'll probably look wrong. It won't be hers. It'll be out of place."

Sam was doubtful about searching for an unknown something. Hamel was even more worried about Phelps' reaction when he learned that one of his officers was conducting a search on orders from the county sheriff before he, the chief of police, had even been notified that a crime had been committed. And a very serious crime at that. But it was too late now. Besides, he rationalized, Phelps hated to be bothered at night. As if the criminal element was only active between dawn and dusk.

So the two officers tackled their assignment while Carol knocked on Emma Stanton's door. Her conversation with Dolores Weber's neighbor was brief and considerably less informative than she had hoped it would be. She heard what Hamel and Bridges had heard before her. Then she sought an explanation for the woman's obvious dislike for the deceased.

"How well did you know Miss Weber?"

"Well enough, I should say."

"No, I mean how did you know her? Did you and she talk much? Did she borrow sugar from you, things like that?"

"We spoke once or twice. She wasn't a friendly sort."

"Did she have company a lot?"

"I really wouldn't know. I don't pry, Sheriff."

"No, I'm sure you don't," Carol said, her voice weary. "But as a neighbor, you'd have been sure to see someone coming or going, sometime or other."

"Well, I didn't."

"All right, no company. Just a woman doing provocative things in front of an open window. When did you see her—uh—not fully clothed?"

"Last month. I was coming home with my groceries, and there she was. And again about a week ago. I think it was Tuesday—she just had a towel around her."

"Maybe she had just come from the shower. What were you doing? I mean, how did you happen to see her?"

Emma Stanton thought about it for a moment.

"It was just by chance. I didn't look for her, if that's what you're thinking."

The lady doth protest too much, Carol thought. She was willing to bet a respectable sum that Mrs. Stanton had regularly sought and found excuses to be in a position to observe Dolores Weber, hoping to obtain evidence to support the picture she had already formed of her neighbor. When the sheriff left to rejoin Bridges and Hamel, she knew only that the deceased woman had been careless about drawing her drapes and that Emma Stanton had found that fact deeply offensive to her own moral code.

"Find anything?" the sheriff asked as she closed the door to Weber's apartment behind her. But it was pretty obvious that their search had been unproductive.

"This isn't a big place," Sam said, somewhat defensively. "And there aren't many hiding places, unless, of course, you want us to look behind the wallboard."

"Did you check the toilet tank? The kitchen?"

"Yeah, they're always sticking drugs in the toilet tank on TV shows. We looked. Nothin' there."

"Kitchen?"

"Well, no, we were just getting to that."

"How about the frig?" the sheriff asked. "I know a guy, hates banks, he stores valuables in the refrigerator. Figures they'd survive in there better if there was a fire."

Bridges opened the refrigerator door, and, after a quick look into the crispers and the freezing unit, shrugged and turned up his hands.

"Nope, she didn't hide it here—unless our rapist or whatever he is took it. Damn it, Sheriff, what is *it*?"

Carol ignored this. She was squatting in front of the cupboard under the sink, examining Dolores Weber's liquor stock and finding nothing of interest among the bottles. It was Hamel who made the discovery.

"Hey, look at this." He was peering into the microwave oven, which occupied the counter across from the stove.

They crowded into the corner of the kitchen to see what Hamel had found. It wasn't something the Weber woman had planned to eat. Sheriff Kelleher used her handkerchief to extract an odd assortment of items from the microwave and spread them on the counter. There was a pair of earrings, a brooch, a pillbox, a pair of panties, and a folded piece of paper.

"Do you think this was what the rapist was after?" Hamel asked.

"Murderer, Jake, not rapist. And I don't know. But it's interesting, don't you think? What's this stuff doing in a microwave? I can't imagine Weber keeping her own jewelry in here. Pretty good hiding place, though—can't see a thing through that smoked glass. Our man could easily have missed it. Looks like he did."

The two items that interested the sheriff most were the pillbox and the folded paper. The box bore the initials EHH, and the paper, she guessed, would be a letter. Using her handkerchief once again, she unfolded it.

It was not a letter, after all, but a terse four-word message. "Youl pay for this." Aside from the threatening tone of the message itself, two things about it caught Carol's attention. One was the handwriting. The letters—and there were only fourteen of them—were an odd combination of printing and cursive·script. And there was the misspelling, one L where there should have been two and no apostrophe. It was a crude note. The writer was illiterate or wanted to appear illiterate.

"What do you make of it?" Hamel wanted to know.

"I'm not sure, but I'd like to take these things you found in the microwave, Jake. Phelps isn't going to like this. And I can't say as I blame him. Let me talk to him. I don't want you getting into hot water over this; so let me see if I can smooth things over. Why don't Sam and I get out of here? You'll want to get things going, you know, get the coroner over here, check for prints—you know the drill. All I want now is this stuff she stuck in the microwave. I think I can make Phelps see it my way."

Hamel's anxiety over his chief's reaction to the night's events was rising again, but he was grateful for the sheriff's promise of intercession.

"You going to call him now?"

"Yes, he's got to know. It'll only be harder in the morning."

So Sheriff Kelleher called Cumberland's chief of police and took advantage of his drowsy condition to give him a slightly doctored version of the situation, one that she hoped would spare Hamel the worst of the chief's wrath. Then she and Bridges departed with the strange contents of Dolores Weber's microwave, leaving Jake Hamel nervously awaiting his boss's arrival.

"Know who this stuff belongs to, Sam?" Carol asked as they walked to their cars. "EHH. I don't know about the middle initial—you can do some digging tomorrow. But EH could be Emily Hoffman, our friend Alan Hoffman's wife. In fact, I'd bet on it. Wouldn't surprise me if we had a nasty little triangle here. Two attractive women, a handsome wealthy guy. Real nasty—two of 'em dead."

"You think the Hoffman woman killed Weber?"

"Maybe. The lady next door didn't see anybody, so we may be wrong assuming it was a man. But it doesn't seem likely." The sheriff was remembering Emily Hoffman, sitting on her couch, looking much too delicate for the hard work of smothering a healthy young woman like Dolores Weber. The more likely suspect was Alan Hoffman. But that meant that she was dealing not with a triangle but a four-cornered square, or perhaps two interlocking triangles.

The sheriff slid into her car, started the engine, and flicked on the headlights. The clock on the dashboard announced that it was 2:40 a.m.

"I don't know what to think, Sam," she said before closing the car door. "Let's get some sleep and start over in the morning."

CHAPTER 44

Dorothy Campbell's world was a tightly circumscribed one. She had grown up in Cumberland, and at age 43 still lived in the same house and still occupied the same room that had served as her nursery when her mother had brought her home from the hospital. The room had been redecorated from time to time, but it had remained a sparely furnished, cheerless place, reflecting a colorless personality as much as limited means. Dottie's father had left home, never to return, when she was three, and her mother had never remarried. The two of them had shared the house until her mother's death when Dottie was 27, and the young woman had stayed on, the sole occupant of the unprepossessing clapboard box on State Street.

Dottie regularly walked the mile to work at the nursing home, shopped for groceries at the Food Mart at the other end of State Street, and watched television during virtually all of her other waking hours. There were no books in the house other than an old family Bible, and no papers or magazines other than the occasional tabloid, which she picked up at the checkout line at the Food Mart. It is doubtful that many residents of Cumberland knew Dorothy Campbell, and she was equally unfamiliar with most of her fellow citizens.

But on Saturday, while doing her weekly shopping, she had seen the front page of a three-day-old *Cumberland Gazette*, which occupied a place next to her favorite tabloid in the newspaper rack at the Food Mart. And on that front page she had seen a picture of a man whose face looked very familiar. Inasmuch as no one of Dottie's acquaintance enjoyed any fame or notoriety whatsoever, she leaned over her shopping cart to get a better look at the picture and to read the caption. The man was identified as John Britingham, the owner of a winery over in Southport. He had apparently been found dead the previous day, and the county sheriff's department was investigating. There was an implication that he might have been the victim of foul play. It was interesting, but not as interesting as the adjacent tabloid headlines reporting the sighting of werewolves in Tennessee and the case of a woman who had been impregnated by a creature from a flying saucer. But the story lodged in Dottie's mind because she was sure she had seen the man pictured on the front page, and quite recently. As she paid for her groceries and carried them home, she tried to remember where she had seen him.

If Dorothy Campbell had been even slightly gregarious, she would have heard her coworkers at the nursing home talking about Britingham's death and might have made the connection sooner. But she shunned company, eating by herself at a corner table in the cafeteria, and generally limiting her conversations with staff to matters pertaining to the patients. Her colleagues found her dull and had long since abandoned any effort to draw her out of her shell.

It was not until Tuesday morning, when she found herself again on duty on the second floor, that Dottie put the face on the front page of the *Gazette* together with the face of the man who had inquired about Amos Fielder the previous week. It came to her like a revelation. She was so startled by it that she nearly dropped the tray she was carrying. She had to sit down to control her excitement. She had actually spoken to the man who had been killed! And the night before they had found his body! Dottie was sure it was the same man. It was, she thought, the biggest event of her uneventful life.

For the rest of the day Dottie was giddy with the knowledge that she had spoken to the dead man. She considered sharing this knowledge with other members of the staff, but she dreaded initiating the conversation. They would think she was strange to be excited about a thing like this. So Dorothy Campbell said nothing to anyone until the following morning when, after a night of agonizing indecision, she called the sheriff's office.

There had been no question of her going to the county office building and telling her story in person. She knew her courage would fail her. The telephone would be difficult enough. But Dottie had convinced herself that only she knew who Amos Fielder's visitor had been, and she had to share that knowledge with someone. When she dialed the number which the operator had given her, it was less because she felt a civic obligation than because she needed to be recognized, and this was her first and for all she knew her only chance. It would surely be painful for her, but then at least someone would know, someone who would appreciate her. The sheriff would welcome her information; he wouldn't think her strange.

Dottie dared not make her call from the nursing home desk. There was a pay phone in the corner of the parking lot, and it was to this phone that she went on her coffee break, hoping no one would take notice of what she was doing. In her nervousness she twice dropped her coins, but finally was able to deposit them and dial.

"Good morning. This is the Cumberland County sheriff's office." The voice, a woman's, was pleasant, but Dottie, as if realizing for the first time just what she was doing, very nearly hung up the phone.

"Hello, is anyone there? This is the sheriff's office, Miss Maltbie speaking. Hello."

When she could muster the courage to speak, Dottie's voice was faint, and Miss Maltbie asked her to speak a little louder. It then occurred to the sheriff's secretary that the woman calling might be hurt or that she might be reporting a crime in progress.

"Are you all right? I'm sorry—I can't hear you."

"Yes. I'm fine." The faint voice seemed stronger, but still distant. "I need to talk to the sheriff."

"All right, what shall I tell her it's about?" By speaking more loudly, Miss Maltbie hoped to induce the woman on the other end of the line to do the same.

"It's about that Mr. Britingham, the man in the picture in the paper." Dottie was feeling better. She had crossed a conversational threshold, and now felt that she could go through with it. And the sheriff was apparently a woman. Dottie didn't know that women could be sheriffs, but it might be easier to talk to a woman. Men made her very nervous.

"Please hold the line. I'll call her."

Sheriff Kelleher was on the line in a matter of seconds. Anyone who wanted to talk about John Britingham was guaranteed instant access. Carol, too, had to strain to catch what the woman was saying, and twice asked her to speak more loudly. But she heard the important words.

"I saw Mr. Britingham the night he was killed. He came out here to the nursing home. I talked to him."

"I'm sorry, ma'am. I don't think you told me your name. That would help, and then you can tell me about your conversation with Mr. Britingham."

This request was greeted with silence, and the sheriff had the momentary feeling that she'd lost her—that the woman didn't want to divulge her identity. But then she spoke again.

"I'm Dorothy Campbell. I work out at the nursing home."

"Thank you for calling, Mrs. Campbell." Carol was hugely relieved.

"It's Miss Campbell." It sounded more like an apology than a statement of fact. "What you should know is that Mr. Britingham, the man the paper says got killed, spoke to me at the home that same night. I thought you'd like to know this."

"Oh, yes, Miss Campbell, I do. I'm very glad you called. Who was it he came to see?"

"He wanted to see that old man, Amos Fielder. When he left—I'm sorry—when Mr. Britingham left, not Mr. Fielder—the old man carried on something terrible until Mr. and Mrs. Morgan came. Nurse Parsons had to give him a sedative."

"Morgan? What Morgan would that be?" The sheriff felt her pulse begin to race.

"I don't think I know their names—oh, yes, I do, too! At least hers." Dottie's voice showed some emotion for the first time as she recalled the name. "I think it's Edna. They're from over on Crooked Lake. Amos is the brother of one of them, I think."

"God bless you, Miss Campbell," Carol said to herself, then to her caller. "Was Mr. Britingham a regular caller over there?"

"I don't know. I don't think so, at least I'd never seen him before."

"All right. Now let me ask you a couple more questions. Are you okay, Miss Campbell?" Carol had adopted a solicitous tone, trying to calm the Campbell woman.

"Yes, I think so."

"Good. Now, did you hear anything that Mr. Britingham and Mr. Fielder said to each other?"

"Mr. Fielder can't talk. He had a stroke. But I didn't stay around the room anyway, so I didn't hear anything."

The sheriff cursed under her breath. She was getting greedy.

"Do you know when Mr. Britingham left?"

"I think it was just after Mr. Fielder began to make a fuss. It must have been somewhere around ten o'clock."

"And the Morgans? Did they stay around or did they follow Mr. Britingham?"

"Oh, no. They were there quite awhile. They helped Nurse Parsons calm the old gentleman down."

"Miss Campbell, you've done a very important thing in calling and telling me this. You may have been the last person to see Mr. Britingham alive."

Other than whoever killed him, Carol added to herself. As it happened, she was wrong about that, but she had made Dorothy Campbell's day. Even the sheriff's request for her phone number and address, and her stated intention to visit her and ask more questions, could not dampen the elation Dottie felt as she hung up the phone.

Had anyone else come into the office at that moment, it would have appeared that Sheriff Kelleher was daydreaming. Her gaze seemed fixed absently on the wall across from her desk, and her left hand remained clamped on the phone, now back in its cradle. But Carol's brain was active. It was trying to assimilate the events of the past few days, now including the astonishing revelation that John Britingham and the Morgans had somehow been involved in each other's lives. First it had been the discovery that Alan Hoffman had not spent the night of the crime in his city apartment and, but for a story of dubious value from a prostitute, might have spent it on Blue Water Point. Then there had been the confession to Britingham's murder by his son, a young man obviously burdened by terrible feelings, both of anger and guilt. Most dramatic of all, there had been the violent death of Britingham's secretary and the discovery of evidence that she might have been a blackmailer and could have died because of it. And now this new information.

Carol had had too little sleep and too much coffee. Dolores Weber's death had kept her up much of the night, and she had had to endure a most unpleasant conversation with Cumberland's chief of police over a second breakfast. She shifted her gaze from the wall to the objects spread out in front of her on the desk. She moved her hand from the phone to the pillbox and then to the threatening note. What did any of this have to do with a sick, elderly man who had been upset by John Britingham only hours at most before Britingham's death on Crooked Lake? A sick, elderly man who was related to the Morgans. She recalled her interrogation of George and Edna Morgan the morning of Kevin Whitman's discovery of Britingham's body on his dock. She remembered the distinct impression she had had that Morgan was concealing something and was afraid his wife would give that something away.

There was much too much to do. But the one thing Carol would have to do right away was to drop in, unannounced, on the Morgans. She pushed her chair back, gave some instructions to Miss Maltbie, and five minutes later was en route to Blue Water Point once again. The drive was beginning to lose its allure.

CHAPTER 45

Sheriff Kelleher had been tossing the idea around in her mind for several hours before she finally picked up the phone. For the first time in months she found herself really missing her father, not as a loving parent but as a wise counselor, someone who would provide her with honest feedback when she had a problem. There were too few people like that in the Cumberland area. No, she told herself, there weren't any. At least not any who could help her sort out the complexities of the Britingham case. And each day seemed to bring more complexities. Carol needed to talk with someone. Bridges, of course, was the obvious choice; he was hard working and basically competent. He had followed the case from the beginning, and he knew pretty much what she knew. But he was unimaginative, and what she needed was someone who could, as they were saying these days, think outside of the box.

The phone rang six times before Kevin answered it.

"Hello, Whitman here." He sounded slightly out of breath.

"Oh, I thought for a moment you weren't home. This is Sheriff Kelleher."

"Sorry about that. I was down on the beach." Kevin was surprised by the call and instantly and reflexively anxious about what the sheriff might want of him. "Is there something I can do for you?"

Carol had gone over this again and again and still wasn't sure quite how she ought to put it. But he was now on the line, and she would have to make her request and then improvise her explanation for that request.

"I wonder if I could come over this evening, that is if you don't have plans?"

"Why sure, no problem at all. But what's this about?"

The sheriff plunged ahead with her rationale for a visit, wondering as she did so how it would sound to Whitman.

"Well, it's about Britingham and my investigation, but I suppose you might have guessed that. I don't have any particular reason for talking with you." That didn't sound quite right, she thought. Too negative. "Look, let me be frank. Things are happening awfully fast, but they don't add up. I need to talk with someone, and I thought you might be willing to be a sounding board. You know, let me try some ideas on you, get your perspective on a few things that have been bothering me."

Kevin would gladly have canceled a dinner engagement with the governor to make such an evening possible. He didn't exactly say that to the sheriff, but he made no attempt to disguise the relief and pleasure he felt.

"I'd love to hear what you have to tell me about the case. Really. It's on my mind, too. I'm here all evening. When do you think you'll be over?"

"Is sometime around eight okay? And one more question. Don't I remember seeing a canoe on your beach? Any chance we could take it out? It looks like it'll be a calm night, and I thought it might be a good idea to get away from the neighbors and..." Carol was searching for a way to say it without creating the wrong impression. "I guess I'm tired, and somehow the idea of getting out on the water—well, I thought it might be relaxing. Maybe even inspire some fresh thoughts about the case."

Carol knew that canoe rides were supposed to be romantic, and she hoped that Whitman wouldn't think she had anything in mind except a serious talk about Britingham's murder. But she really did like the idea of taking the canoe out; it had become something of a fixation the more she thought about it. And she had no interest in Whitman, other than as someone who might help her solve the crime. If he misunderstood her suggestion, he'd get over it.

"Good idea, the canoe. We'll do it." Kevin had been delighted with the prospect of the sheriff coming over to talk about something other than his early morning swimming habits. A canoe ride with her was frosting on the cake. "Eight o'clock?"

"I'll be there."

The car that pulled in behind the cottage did not bear the logo of the Cumberland County Sheriff's Department. Nor was the woman who stepped out of it wearing a uniform. Carol had opted for her own car and for blue jeans and a white blouse, and Kevin was both pleased with this signal that their discussion would be informal and impressed by the sheriff's appearance. Why had she chosen a career in law enforcement, he wondered. It wasn't that he considered it an unsuitable job for a woman. Kevin could not imagine himself, day in and day out, dealing with disorderly drunks, trying to put a stop to domestic violence, or, worst of all, scraping the victims of highway accidents off the macadam. Tonight, Sheriff Kelleher did not look at all like someone whose days were filled with just such unpleasant activities. Yet she had come over to discuss a crime that was her responsibility to solve. And she seemed to think he could help her.

"Hello, Mr. Whitman," she said, the hint of a smile tugging at the corners of her mouth. "I appreciate your willingness to take the time to talk with me."

"No problem—I'm looking forward to it." There was an awkward moment when neither of them seemed quite sure who should take the lead. "Would you care for a drink?"

"No thanks," the sheriff replied, and then decided to take charge.

"Look, you probably think it's strange, my suggesting we get together like this. I know I've been suspicious of your role in this business. And critical of your interfering in my investigation. Let's set that aside. I'm sure you've given a lot of thought to Britingham's death, and I want to know what you've been thinking. Everything—no matter how crazy it may seem to you. So let's take that canoe ride."

Carol did not say what she had come to believe, which was that if Whitman turned out to have been the killer, she'd hang a "gone fishing" sign on her door and take a long vacation.

"Sure," Kevin said, and led the way around the cottage and down to the beach.

"Do you want to paddle up front?" he asked.

"No. That way I'd have my back to you; it would be harder to talk. If you don't mind, I'll just take one of those cushions and sit in the bow facing you."

By ten past eight they were drifting along slowly on a very light breeze a hundred yards out into the lake. Kevin used his paddle occasionally to keep the canoe on a course more or less parallel to the shore. Initially, Carol had trailed her fingers in the cool water, watching the receding shoreline, saying nothing.

Her mind should have been on the search for Britingham's killer. But she found herself admiring Kevin's smooth, easy handling of the canoe, and remembering her suspicion when she had first questioned him about the body on the dock that there might have been a woman in his cottage. A fugitive thought crossed her mind: what would it be like to have been that woman?

If her father had been alive, he would be asking her—or obviously making an effort not to ask her—why there were no men in her life and whether it wasn't time to be considering marriage. She considered the fact that she hadn't shared a bed with a man for more than two years. And just as quickly pushed that thought aside, and finally broke the silence.

"This damned case makes me feel like I'm suffocating. Being out here on the water makes me feel—what's the word I'm looking for?—cleaner? That sounds ridiculous, doesn't it?"

"No, it doesn't, not at all. It's funny you should use that word. It's a big reason why I like it up here—on the water, in the water. The city's fine, I like my job, there's a lot going on, but this is special to me. And it is clean."

"Or would be if we didn't have crimes to contend with," Carol said. "That's one of the things about the Britingham affair. It isn't just that someone killed him. Murder's always a dirty business. But everything about the case seems dirty—the things I've learned as I've talked to people, the things that Britingham seems to have been involved in. And other people, too. It's like turning over rocks and having all kinds of slimy things come crawling out."

Kevin considered the slimy things that the sheriff's image conjured up in his mind.

"I know what you mean. For me, though, it's like the plot of one of those good old-fashioned 19th century operas. The music could be powerful, but the plots were pretty wild and unbelievable, all full of vendettas and curses and things like that. Why, I could imagine that Verdi or one of the verismo composers might have—oh, there I go. Sorry."

"No, no. Like I told you, I don't know anything about opera, but it's your field, and if your knowledge of it gives you an angle on this case, I want to hear it. When you talk about vendettas and curses, I'm interested."

"It sounds a bit melodramatic, doesn't it? I guess I'd found myself thinking about Britingham's death and all the hostility he'd stirred up around here, and the analogy just came to mind." Kevin was concerned that the sheriff might think he had been showing off, yet pleased that she was encouraging him to share his ideas about the case, no matter how far-fetched.

There was still light in the Western sky, but it would soon be dark. The powerboats on the lake would be displaying their running lights before long.

"There may or may not have been a vendetta," Carol said, "but it seems to me that most of your neighbors didn't like Mr. Britingham. Your friends, the Milburns, told me as much last week, and I think I'm beginning to fit some of the pieces together. Why don't you give me your slant on some of these grudges against Britingham?"

Kevin had to refocus on the sheriff's question. He'd been watching her, thinking that he hadn't shared the canoe with a woman since before the divorce, and even then Susan hadn't much cared for it. Now a woman was sitting in the bow, inviting him to talk to her about a murder. An attractive woman. The sheriff of Cumberland County.

"I'll try. Where do you want me to start?"

"Let's start with the Hoffmans. I think she was having an affair with Britingham and that her husband may have been onto them. That would give him a pretty good reason to want to get rid of Britingham. What do you know about it?"

Kevin, like the Milburns, had been loath to share mere speculation with the sheriff, but if she, too, thought that the Hoffman woman had somehow been involved with the victim, then there was no longer a reason for reticence. So he told the sheriff about Emily Hoffman's brief visit the morning of the murder.

"You say she seemed upset about what Britingham was wearing when you found him," the sheriff said.

"I'm not sure that's quite the way I'd put it," Kevin said. "It's just that it seemed strange that she was interested in things like that. If she was having an affair with him, that could explain her being upset. But if you've just discovered that your lover is dead, why would you care about what he was wearing?"

"What if Britingham was wearing your husband's sweater?" the sheriff asked. "That could explain her interest in his clothes, couldn't it? She'd be worried that we'd make the connection and that sooner or later her husband would know she'd been having an affair with Britingham."

"I take it you think he was wearing Hoffman's sweater?"

"We'll find out, I'm sure. But, yes, it's a reasonable guess. We know it wasn't Britingham's sweater—not his size, not his style. You tell me Mrs. Hoffman seemed anxious about it. We have good reason to think she was seeing him. It seems to add up. He'd probably borrowed the sweater sometime when he'd gone to see her, sometime when Alan Hoffman wasn't around."

"And that sometime would probably have been that very night, wouldn't it?" Kevin asked. "Otherwise, why would she assume that he was wearing her husband's sweater? People just don't go around wearing other people's clothes, especially when they don't fit. But if she'd seen him in it Monday night, she might well be worried the next morning when she hears he's been killed."

"Which means they were together the night he was killed, right? We don't know that, but it seems probable. He may have been cold and put on something that was handy. If that's what happened, I can imagine that she'd be distressed."

"Are you telling me that you think Alan Hoffman is a suspect in the murder? That would mean he knew that his wife was carrying on with Britingham."

"The thought had occurred to me," Carol said.

"Why do you think Hoffman knew what was going on?" It was a reasonable inference, but hard evidence was better.

The sheriff was looking toward Blue Water Point, where some of the lights were beginning to come on in the cottages that had been disappearing in the twilight. As she watched, a light came on in the Hoffman place, announcing the presence of the wayward wife. Alan Hoffman was presumably in the city. There was no longer any reason for him to take the long nighttime drive back to the lake, as the sheriff suspected he had done the night of Britingham's death.

"We had an anonymous tip about Britingham and the Hoffman woman," Carol said. "It's possible our caller felt obliged to tip off Hoffman as well. Maybe he already knew or had guessed. Anyway, I think he not only suspected his wife. But I also think he may have driven all the way back up here the night Britingham was killed. I think he was right here on this point. No proof, not yet. But I've talked to him, and he's got a problem with that night, no question about it. He's got an alibi, but it looks pretty thin to me."

"So you think Alan Hoffman is your murderer," Kevin observed with just a trace of skepticism.

"Perhaps. It's certainly easier to imagine Britingham being killed by a jealous husband than by any of the other people I've met on this case. Although nobody seemed to like him, and some people might be set off by things that wouldn't bother you or me. Like maybe your neighbor Morgan? Could he have killed Britingham?"

"George Morgan?" If Kevin had any reservations about Alan Hoffman as the murderer, he found it even harder to picture his next-door neighbor in that role. "But how? Britingham was much younger and much stronger. It's inconceivable."

"Maybe so. But could he have been so angry that he might have wanted to kill Britingham?"

"Why would you think so?"

"Remember the day I asked you to leave this investigation to me? Morgan had called, saying you said he ought to talk to me. What did you think he should tell me?"

"I guess I thought he ought to mention his argument with Britingham over the lake steamers and straighten out the matter of when he was up on Tuesday morning. Isn't that what he told you?"

"Yes and no," the sheriff replied. "He told me he'd lied about the time—fudged it, is what he said. Said he'd had to go to the john and then had stayed up, done some chores like burning trash. You people do some strange things before sunup, don't you?"

She didn't expect Kevin to defend his early morning swimming habits again. She wanted to get to her point.

"But he never said a peep about any trouble with Britingham. Never mentioned that Britingham said he was going to go diving, looking for an old boat that had sunk in this lake a long time ago with Mrs. Morgan's aunt aboard. Or that they couldn't stand the thought of him doing it. It was like they saw it as a desecration of a gravesite. Now why do you suppose Morgan didn't mention this?"

Both of them knew the reason: it gave the Morgans a motive for murder.

"If he didn't tell you, how did you find out about it?"

"An employee of the nursing home over in Cumberland saw Britingham's picture in the paper and decided it looked like a man who had visited Mrs. Morgan's brother at the home the same night Britingham got himself killed. Seems there was quite a to-do. This visitor apparently upset the old man, and he carried on until the Morgans got there. Had to give him a sedative. Anyway, this woman called to tell me this, so I went looking for the Morgans.

Talked to them just yesterday. I wanted to find out what possible connection there could be between her brother and Britingham—assuming the man really was Britingham."

"And it was then that they told you about his plans to search for that old steamer?"

"It wasn't easy. They were about as stubborn about not telling me as they were about not wanting Britingham to explore the wreck. She's the one that finally decided they ought to let me know what this was all about."

"I didn't know about the business at the nursing home," Kevin said, "but the rest sounds right. George and Edna haven't said much about their argument with Britingham, but I can believe they'd feel strongly about anyone disturbing *The Commodore*. But kill Britingham over it? Maybe it meant enough to them—just maybe—but I don't see how it would have been physically possible."

"If it's so obviously physically impossible, why all the lies and evasions?" Carol wanted to know. "Why didn't Morgan want me to know he'd been up before dawn that day burning trash? And then this business? If you were innocent of any wrongdoing, would you behave like that? I thought the Morgans were hiding something when I talked to them the first time. And I still don't know whether there's something they're not telling me."

In the fading light Kevin found it difficult to read the sheriff's face. Did she really suspect George or Edna of having killed Britingham?

"You know, we're talking about my neighbors here on the point—good neighbors, too. I'd rather not think they could have killed Britingham."

"Do you mean could have or might have wanted to?" Carol asked.

"I suppose I mean that it's hard to imagine any of them disliking the man enough to want to kill him." Kevin was thinking about it. He had been arguing that the Morgans weren't physically capable of committing the crime, but he knew that several other people on the point could have. "Sure, some of the men might be strong enough to do it, but why? I don't know about Hoffman, but the other problems my neighbors might have had with Britingham don't strike me as grounds for murder. Anyhow, I know these people."

"Ever tune in to the TV news shows and listen to neighbors of people who've just been arrested for a crime? Half the time they say how nice the guy was, what a decent family man, a regular churchgoer. Truth is, we don't really know people as well as we think we do. Don't know what's eating them. Look, I've talked with all of your neighbors, and it's amazing how many of them had a beef with Britingham. You know about Morgan. Then there's Snyder. I'm sure you've heard about the unpleasantness over the Charley's Cup. And Sanderson. There's that flap over his role in the growers' association. What about Hess? She was furious about Britingham's plans to develop Mallard Cove. At least she came right out and told me how she felt about him. I had to pull it out of some of 'em. And you're right, none of your neighbors looks or sounds like a murderer. Not even Hoffman. But I'm willing to bet that one of them is."

The sheriff leaned forward as if to emphasize her point.

"And by the way, you said that some of the men are strong enough to have killed Britingham. Why do you leave the women out? Or Morgan? Britingham was drunk, after all, and I mean very drunk. Is it so inconceivable that an older man like Morgan, or even an older woman like Mrs. Hess, could have killed him? I'm not ready to ignore any of these possibilities, not when they all hated Britingham. And I don't think hated is too strong a word."

"Okay, what if I concede that any of these people, even Morgan, hated him and were physically capable of killing him. We still have to explain the fact that somebody moved his body, and moved it a pretty good distance to get it out to the end of my dock. I can't see either of the Morgans or Grace Hess doing that, can you? So we're left with the younger men—Hoffman, of course, and the guys who were playing cards at the Sandersons. Unless, of course, you've unearthed another suspect I don't know about."

If Carol was really serious about inviting Kevin Whitman into her investigation of the death of John Britingham, she would have to put all of her cards on the table.

"I'm going to share some information with you that isn't public knowledge. And I don't want it to become public knowledge, not yet. I'm sure you understand." She underscored this admonition with what she hoped was an appropriately sarcastic tone of voice.

"You've asked, in effect, if any of your other neighbors are under suspicion. I don't know whether all of the ones we've mentioned should be under suspicion. But they are because they had a grievance, and it would appear that they might have had opportunity. But there is someone else under suspicion, and he's not a neighbor. In fact, he's confessed to killing Britingham, and he's in jail over in Cumberland."

"What?" Kevin's voice registered the surprise he felt at the sheriff's announcement. He immediately rephrased the question: "Who?"

"It's Britingham's son—John Britingham, Jr., who to my great surprise just walked in on Tuesday and gave himself up. Now, what do you make of that?"

"Why, for God's sake, have you been asking me about Hoffman and Morgan and..." Kevin didn't finish his thought. He abruptly stopped paddling, as if to better concentrate on this new development. "You don't believe the confession, do you?"

The silence that followed reminded both of them that sound travels exceedingly well across water. Both lowered their voices.

"I didn't say I don't. But no, you're right, there is something wrong." Carol explained about young Britingham's arrival in the area and his strange account of the fateful evening. She was careful not to dismiss the confession, but she made it clear that this bird in the hand didn't satisfy her.

"Frankly, I don't think he's a threat to anybody else, and I can't imagine him skipping bail. But it would look awfully queer if I were to release a confessed killer. In any event, he doesn't want bail, and he doesn't want a lawyer. He really wants to stay in jail. To be perfectly honest, I don't know quite how to handle it. Do I sound as tired as I feel?"

In the week since the morning they had first met, Kevin had found Sheriff Carol Kelleher to be intelligent, efficient, and, yes, attractive. Now for the first time he also saw her as vulnerable. He wanted to say something comforting, decided it would be inappropriate, and turned instead to a development in the case he had wanted to discuss—and suspected the sheriff would also wish to talk about.

"One thing would seem certain, though, wouldn't it? Whether the boy killed his father or not, he couldn't have killed that Weber woman because you say he was safely tucked away in a cell practically under your nose. So if he's guilty, you've got yourself two killers."

Carol smiled a rueful smile, a smile lost to Kevin because it was now almost totally dark.

"Yes," she said wearily, "there is the matter of Dolores Weber's death."

The occasional powerboat on the lake was now barely visible, only its bow and stern lights announcing its location. Kevin's canoe had no lights, and he realized that in the interest of their safety he should be heading for shore. They had drifted toward the end of Blue Water Point; and had it been lighter, they might even have been able to see the wooded area in which John Britingham had intended to build the cabins which Grace Hess found so offensive. Kevin turned the canoe about and, moving closer to shore, paddled vigorously back in the direction of his cottage. Lights were on in most of the cottages, and voices carried across the water from the vicinity of a couple of beach fires.

As if by tacit agreement, they lapsed into a companionable silence, leaving the conundrum of the Britingham and Weber murders aside for a few minutes in order to enjoy the cool air of the August night.

Arriving back at the cottage, Kevin put his paddle into the lake one more time and drove the bow of the canoe onto shore. The sheriff stepped smartly out of the canoe and turned to pull it further up onto the beach. At the same time, Kevin swung his leg over the gunwale and started to climb out. The sudden movement of the canoe as Carol pulled it forward threw him off balance, and he found himself slipping awkwardly into the shallow water at the canoe's stern. Carol acted quickly, stepping into the water and grabbing Kevin's arm, saving him from an embarrassing but hardly serious fall. The thought flashed through his mind: it's the man who's supposed to rescue the maiden. Yet he didn't mind the sheriff's hand on his arm; he didn't even tense his bicep to make it seem as if he were better muscled than in fact he was. Carol's response had been reflexive. But she maintained her grip on his arm longer than was absolutely necessary. Indeed, she had to will herself to release him.

It was over in a matter of seconds. They laughed together as Carol dumped water out of her shoes and Kevin collected the paddles and tied the canoe to a post. But there was something in their laughter that suggested that they were not only laughing at the situation. Both knew that their relationship had somehow changed.

CHAPTER 46

Sheriff Kelleher was sitting on one of the old overstuffed chairs that Emily Hoffman had pretended to admire only a week earlier. She was sipping coffee. Kevin was on the couch, an untouched highball on the table in front of him. He had changed his water-soaked slacks for a dry pair.

Their discussion of John Britingham's violent death and who might have been responsible for it had nearly come to an end after the canoe had been secured. Kevin had invited her in, but Carol had been uncomfortable about accepting the invitation. She had wanted to raise more questions, hear more of his ideas about the case. But she was now fearful that they would find themselves talking about other things, things she wasn't ready to talk about. In the end she agreed to stay, but only for half an hour. And she declined his invitation to join him in a drink. Of course she needed to be completely sober on the drive back to Cumberland, but she was equally anxious to be in complete control of what she said and did in Whitman's living room, and she wasn't sure that alcohol would be good for her self-control in the circumstances.

It was Kevin who restarted the discussion.

"Let's talk about this Weber woman. Britingham's secretary, right? Sounds to me as if the two deaths are related. I'm not a believer in coincidences."

"Nor am I," the sheriff replied. "Did you know Weber?"

"No, never even heard of her until she was killed."

"She was young and attractive, and it's a reasonable guess that Britingham was interested in her for more than her office skills. We're checking it out, but we already know that he brought her with him from California."

"Would I be wrong to think that maybe Emily Hoffman and this Weber woman were rivals, that they were sharing Britingham?"

"I don't know, but it's not unlikely. I've got a hunch that Weber's the one who tipped us off to Britingham's relationship with the Hoffman woman."

Kevin considered this possibility.

"Which would mean that Weber was so jealous of her lover's affair with Hoffman that she tried to implicate her somehow in his death. Or"—Kevin had another thought—"what if Weber had been so angry with Britingham for two-timing her with Hoffman that she killed him? Not any of the people on this point, not the son, but the man's secretary?"

The sheriff started to raise an objection, but Kevin interrupted, backtracking quickly.

"No, that won't wash, will it?" Kevin leaned forward to pick up his glass and took another tack. "Who do you think killed Weber?"

"Mr. Whitman, I came over to hear your ideas. Why don't you tell me? And why so ready to dismiss the idea of Weber as Britingham's killer?"

Kevin shook his head, and made use of the opening the sheriff had given him.

"I wish you'd call me Kevin. I'll bet there's no rule in the law enforcement book that says you have to stick to last names, even with suspects."

No, there was no such rule, but in this case Carol was reluctant to start down what might be a slippery slope.

"No, of course not. I suppose it's just common practice. But I'll try to remember that it's Kevin. Anyhow, I was asking you about Weber."

"Did you question her?"

"You're still the one asking the questions, aren't you? But the answer is no, not really. My deputy talked to her the morning you found Britingham's body, but at the time we were only trying to learn about his schedule the night before. There was nothing to tie her to his death. In fact it wasn't until the night she was killed that we learned we should have been paying a lot more attention to her—and that she might well have been the one who clued us in to Britingham's affair with Hoffman."

The look on the sheriff's face and the tone of her voice made it clear that she regretted this lapse in investigatory oversight and held herself responsible for it.

"I wouldn't be too hard on myself if I were you," Kevin said. "Who would have imagined that there'd be a second murder?"

"It isn't just her death that makes her role in the case important. It's what we found in her apartment." Carol proceeded to tell Kevin about the contents of Dolores Weber's microwave and the physical evidence in the apartment indicating that whoever had killed her had been searching for something and that it had not been sex.

"I'm almost certain the jewelry belongs to Emily Hoffman," she added. "Initials on the pillbox are EHH, not D-something-W."

But Kevin wanted to talk about the threatening note.

"What was the threat?" he asked, his voice betraying the excitement he felt.

"All it said was 'Youl pay for this.' And it was a crude note. Looked as if whoever wrote it tried to disguise his identity—or hers. The spelling was atrocious. I can't spell worth a damn, and I spotted it right off the bat."

After years of grading student papers, Kevin was thoroughly familiar with spelling errors. Even so, it was hard to believe that anyone could have misspelled any of the four, short, simple words in the note. But he brushed the thought aside.

"I'd be willing to bet it means blackmail." It was an obvious conclusion, and Kevin didn't wait for the sheriff to register her agreement. "You've got a puzzle, though, haven't you? It looks like Emily Hoffman was being blackmailed, which makes her the person most likely to have killed Weber. But I've got the impression you think it's her husband who's most likely to have killed Britingham. So Alan Hoffman kills Britingham because he's discovered that the man was sleeping with his wife. And Emily Hoffman kills Weber to keep her from telling Hoffman about the affair—the affair Hoffman must already know about. If true, that really is the stuff of opera."

The hint of a smile crossed the sheriff's face.

"Complicated, isn't it?"

Kevin's mind was racing on ahead to other possibilities.

"Okay, let's try to simplify it. One killer. And inasmuch as you seem to think Alan Hoffman killed Britingham, that would make him Weber's killer as well. But why? Why would he kill Weber? Let's say you've gotten rid of the other man in your wife's life. Why, then, the other woman in *his* life? Unless..."

Kevin paused as a possible explanation for Dolores Weber's death occurred to him.

"Unless the Weber woman knew he'd killed Britingham. Then she'd be in a position to go to the police."

The smile returned to Sheriff Kelleher's face.

"Or blackmail him?"

"Yes. To put it crudely, she died because she knew too much, and Hoffman knew that she knew it."

"I came here because I was curious about how you saw the Britingham affair," Carol said quietly. "And you're certainly not reluctant to brainstorm it, are you? Do professors typically work that way? Somehow I'd assumed that they'd be more cautious— you know, work their way through a problem, step by logical step. You surprise me. Anyhow, Alan Hoffman couldn't have killed Weber. He was being a very good boy. We have it from the deskman at the Hoffman's apartment in the city that Alan was right where he should have been that night. He was seen in the lobby at more or less the same time we believe Weber was killed. It was the first call I made this morning, and I've no reason to doubt my source."

Kevin was suddenly very uncomfortable. Was the sheriff disappointed in him? Why had she let him speculate on Hoffman as Weber's killer when she knew he couldn't have been?

"I didn't mean that I thought Hoffman had killed Weber," he said defensively. "I was just trying out a two murders-one murderer scenario, and I thought you'd singled out Hoffman as your prime suspect in Britingham's death."

"He's a suspect all right, but I'm not ready to say he's the prime suspect. Remember Morgan. And several of your other neighbors."

"Okay. But even if we accept the idea that Morgan or Snyder or someone else could have killed Britingham, what would they have to do with Weber? With Hoffman there's a connection, if you're right about Britingham sleeping with both her and Mrs. Hoffman. But why would any of these other people have killed Weber?"

Kevin knew the answer to his question: blackmail. But the evidence in the microwave pointed to Emily Hoffman as the blackmail victim, not George Morgan or Mike Snyder or any of his other neighbors. He said as much to the sheriff.

Carol was conscious of the time, aware that the half hour she had given herself had expired. Their discussion had remained safely on the Britingham case. Nothing personal, except of course for Whitman's insistence that she call him Kevin, a request she had sidestepped by not using his name. But she was enjoying their verbal give-and-take. Enjoying it too much, perhaps. She was intrigued by the way his mind worked, liked the way his expression changed, anticipating a new idea. They were talking about the case, but more and more she found herself thinking about Kevin Whitman rather than John Britingham. She knew she had to be going, even if it meant that they might have to resume their discussion another day. Better yet because they would have to resume their discussion another day. Soon.

"Five minutes, Kevin, then I have to be going." There, she'd said it. She was afraid she had sounded like a mother telling her kids they had only a few more minutes of playtime before dinner, but now he was Kevin.

He was pleased, of course, but not anxious to show it. Better to pursue the thought that was taking shape in his mind.

"Okay. I know you've had a long day. But can we go back to the Hoffmans for a minute? You tell me he couldn't have killed Weber. But could the two of them have done it? Not physically, of course, but what if they planned it together and then she did the deed?"

Kevin hurried on, anxious to convince the sheriff that he hadn't completely lost his mind.

"I know it sounds improbable, but think about it. Suppose Hoffman did kill Britingham. I'd guess he and his wife would talk about the man's death—I mean, it would be pretty strange if they didn't, considering it was far and away the biggest news on the lake. And if both of them are in it up to their necks, it would be hard to dissemble, to act like it had nothing to do with them. Somehow they have a crisis of conscience, and it all comes out. They decide it's better to stick together, cover up both the murder and the adultery that was what got Britingham killed. Then Weber enters the picture. She's wise to them and blackmails them. Maybe they're not sure of just what she knows, but they can't take any chances. And this time it's Mrs. Hoffman who draws the short straw. What do you think?"

"I think you have a vivid imagination," Carol said, but she had to concede that as far-fetched as Kevin's scenario was, it couldn't be dismissed out of hand. "All right, it's not impossible, but even if the Hoffmans broke down and confessed to each other, don't you have a problem picturing Emily Hoffman killing the Weber woman? She strikes me as fragile, unaccustomed to hard work. Weber looked much stronger—she was younger, and I'd bet a lot tougher. I just can't imagine Mrs. Hoffman pushing a pillow down over Weber's face and holding it there until she was dead."

"I know," Kevin said, "but when I argued that George Morgan couldn't have killed a younger and tougher John Britingham, you took just the opposite position. Right?"

Carol appreciated the irony.

"Score one for Kevin. Even if you're wrong." She set her coffee cup down, sneaking a surreptitious look at her watch as she did so. She had to bring the evening to an end. "Look, I really do have to be going. Do me a favor, will you? Give some thought to that note we found in Weber's microwave. We've been assuming that she was blackmailing Mrs. Hoffman because of the jewelry—probably found it at Britingham's house or in his office, figured out right away what was going on. But was she blackmailing the husband, too? That's what your scenario suggests, which would mean that the note was Hoffman's and Weber knew he'd written it. But why so quick to assume it was Hoffman who'd threatened Britingham? As far as we know now, any one of several people could have written the note, disguising their handwriting to do it. Anyway, if Weber was blackmailing Alan Hoffman because she knew he had killed Britingham, she must have been one tough cookie. The adulterous wife might have looked like a soft touch, but trying to blackmail a murderer would be pretty risky. So I'd keep looking for the author of that note."

"Yes, and for Britingham's killer," Kevin said.

Carol got up, collected her shoes, and prepared to leave. She hoped she'd given Kevin a reason to get back in touch with her, but she wanted to make sure.

"Sorry to have taken up so much of your evening," she said, not feeling the least bit sorry. "Another favor, if I may. You know I don't know the least thing about opera. But I'm always open to new interests, so I'd appreciate it if you'd suggest an opera you think would appeal to a beginner. Not right now, no hurry, but give it some thought if you would. It doesn't have to have a crazy plot anything like this Britingham affair—just something you think I might enjoy. Okay?"

"Can't think of anything that would give me more pleasure," Kevin said, and he meant it. "I'm always in the business of making converts. And it's been an interesting evening. Glad you suggested it."

He paused for the briefest of seconds, then added, "It's Carol, isn't it?"

It really was time to go.

"Good night, Kevin. I'll be in touch." And she was gone.

She hadn't answered his question, but she hadn't needed to. The small smile, the slight nod of her head, they had answered for her.

The house in which Kevin had been living as a bachelor suddenly looked much emptier than it had over the past several summers. He walked out onto the deck and for a few minutes watched the fireflies as they punctuated the darkness. He reran the evening's discussion in his mind. There were a number of things he had intended to mention and hadn't—the Sandersons' cinder block, Grace Hess's tennis shoe, the small but important changes in Billy and Darrell Keyser's story. There was still much he needed to share with the sheriff—with Carol. He'd call her in the morning.

CHAPTER 47

Friday morning brought sunny skies and a blustery northwest wind to Crooked Lake. Kevin Whitman stood on his dock, admiring the weather and noting the activity on the point. It was one week, three days, and roughly four hours since he had found John Britingham's body in exactly the same place where he was now standing. Kevin had been thinking about what had transpired the previous evening, what had been said, what had not been said. But mostly he had been thinking about the woman with whom he had shared the evening. He very much wanted to call her, meet with her, resume the discussion of the murder that had so completely transformed his summer agenda. But he had resisted the urge to pick up the phone and dial the sheriff's office. Before he did that, he would put in motion a plan that would, he hoped, produce a piece of evidence that might help solve the Britingham case. And impress the sheriff.

He wished it weren't quite so windy, but the sunshine suited his purpose admirably. Billy and Darrell Keyser would not, he knew, be deterred by the lake's choppy surface.

Kevin had experienced a small twinge of guilt as the plan took shape in his mind, but he managed to suppress it without too much difficulty. He would be using the boys, and he would be less than wholly honest with them. But they would see it as an adventure, and if he was right in his hunch, they would have a chance to participate in solving a crime. Even if all went just as he expected, he might have no better idea who had killed John Britingham. But he had to put his plan into action. Now if only the Brocks didn't have some plan of their own which involved Billy and Darrell.

There weren't many people in sight and that was all to the good, although it probably didn't really matter that much. After all, the boys would be doing what they did practically every day. The only difference would be that they would do it a few yards further south along the point, and he, not they, would determine the object of their activity.

Billy made his appearance on the Brocks' porch as Kevin watched. Within a minute, Darrell followed. Neither wasted any time getting into the water; both used the cannonball method from the Brocks' dock. Kevin walked back to the shore, slipped on the sandals he had left there, and headed down the beach to where the boys were swimming.

"Hi!" he yelled. Billy waved, and Darrell ignored him until he announced his intention of talking to them by coming out to the end of their dock. He squatted down and motioned them over to him.

"I'd like your help," he said, getting right to the point. "I lost my watch when I was taking a swim a couple of days ago, and I wondered if you'd give me a hand trying to find it. You look like a couple of good divers to me, and I figure if anyone can get the watch you can." This was a lie. Kevin's watch was not on his wrist, but it wasn't in the lake either. He had taken it off and slipped it into the pocket of his windbreaker. Later it would go into the water so the boys could find it, but not until they had searched the lake bottom for the real object of this exercise. Or objects, for if Kevin had it figured correctly, and if the boys were as good as he hoped they were, they would recover two things: one of them an old tennis shoe and the other a knife.

Ever since his chat with Grace Hess, Kevin had been worrying about that conversation. The woman had been quick to acknowledge that she was the person he had seen with a dog on the beach the morning Britingham had made his appearance, dead, on his dock. She had gone on to confide in him that the dog, Jeff, had found an old tennis shoe and that she had tossed it into the lake. And he hadn't believed her.

It had all been too pat, a plausible story perhaps, but one volunteered, he had come to suspect, to discourage a search for something else. And that something else, he suspected, might be the weapon with which Britingham had met his death. He had no doubt he would find the shoe. Mrs. Hess was too shrewd to be confident that Kevin, or the sheriff, for that matter, would accept the shoe story uncritically. Someone might try to retrieve it, and therefore it had to be there. Kevin assumed that she had tossed an old shoe from her closet into the lake in the general vicinity of the place where he had seen her on the beach, probably disposing of its mate in the weekly trash pickup or in some other way. A white tennis shoe would be much easier to spot among the weeds at the lake bottom than a knife, so its presence would both corroborate Grace Hess's story and bring a halt to a search before a knife was found. *If* there was a knife in the lake, and Kevin had convinced himself that there was.

What if he did find a knife? What would it prove? Not that it was the murder weapon, or if it was, that Grace Hess had killed Britingham. The knife might well have been something she—or her dog—had simply found on the beach. She could not have known there had been a murder, much less that the knife was the murder weapon. Not unless she had killed Britingham. Unlikely, but then why the story about the shoe? Kevin had run these thoughts through his mind over and over again ever since his conversation with the woman. He still didn't know what to believe. But he knew he had to look for the knife. If his hunch was right, the weapon that had been used to kill John Britingham lay on the bottom of Crooked Lake, and not all that far from shore. And in every crime story he had ever read or heard about, searching for the murder weapon was at or near the top of the police agenda. The sheriff would be pleased when he produced it.

It was a good morning for diving, and the Keyser boys were like seals. He was sure they would find the shoe and the knife if they were there, not to mention the watch. He had to be right about just where "there" was, of course, and he had gone over this in his mind many times. His initial uncertainty as to where he had seen the man and the dog, now known to be Mrs. Hess and Jeff, had been replaced by a conviction that they had been approximately in front of the Sullivans' rental property, four cottages down the point. He couldn't pinpoint the exact spot, but he thought the area where the boys would need to dive extended no more than sixty to eighty feet along the beach in that area. Nor did the distance out from the shoreline pose much of a problem. Grace Hess may have kept herself in reasonably good shape, but he doubted that she would have a very good throwing arm. So Kevin intended to put the Keyser boys to work in a rectangular area, which ranged in depth from around ten feet to close to fifteen feet off that part of the point.

"What do we get if we find the watch?" Billy's question startled Kevin, who had been naive enough to think that the excitement of the search would be reward enough. This eleven-year-old had the makings of a shrewd businessman.

"How about a buck apiece?" Kevin hoped that this was a fair offer.

"Sounds good to me," came the reply, and with the arrangement sealed, Kevin said he'd need to tell the boys' grandparents what they were up to. Five minutes later, having secured the Brocks' blessing, he reappeared off their dock in the canoe.

"Okay, let's go," he called out. "We're going down there, just beyond that empty cottage the other side of the Pierces'. I can't be sure, but I think that's where it fell off. You guys use nose plugs? It may be ten feet or more to the bottom."

Kevin remembered that as a kid he had to hold his nose with one hand until he got a nose plug, which had enhanced his mobility under water and enabled him to remain down for what his mother had considered an alarmingly long time.

"Naw, we don't need 'em," Billy answered. The Keyser boys were apparently more nearly amphibious than he had been.

If they had indeed been looking for a watch, the search area would have been further from shore. But it wasn't a lost watch that had prompted the morning's adventure. Kevin doubted that the boys had paid much attention to his swimming habits. If they had, they might have questioned his instructions to begin their search closer to shore than he was accustomed to swimming. His greater concern was that, having been told that the object of their search was a watch, they might fail to see a knife. He decided not to leave the matter to chance.

"I'll bet there's a lot of stuff down there. While we're at it why don't we do our part to clean up this lake? How about another fifty cents for every piece of man-made junk—you know, Coke bottles, beer cans, who knows what you'll find. I'll bet there's an old tire, maybe a piece of silverware. People get careless."

That was as close as Kevin wished to come to suggesting that they keep an eye open for a knife. The strategy was a risky one. If the boys found things in this area, they could decide they were onto a good thing and expand their zone of operations and hence their claim on his wallet. In any event, it was worth it if they produced the knife.

Billy and Darrell were soon diving and resurfacing with the cheerful abandon of youth, while Kevin tried to hold the canoe in place against the breeze and keep the boys working in something resembling a systematic pattern. It was, in the beginning, an unproductive search, and Kevin began to worry that they would lose interest in the absence of success. Darrell was the first to find something. It was only an old soft-drink can, but the boys acted as if they had discovered treasure.

It was some fifteen minutes and three assorted beverage cans into the search when Billy popped to the surface, waving a tennis shoe over his head. He swam over to the canoe and added it to the small pile, now worth two dollars, at Kevin's feet.

"How do you suppose someone lost a shoe out here?" Billy asked, still breathless from his exertions.

"Darned if I know," Kevin replied disingenuously.

Billy wasn't keen on a further discussion of the matter, and quickly rejoined his younger brother in the search for the missing watch, which was still safely in the pocket of the windbreaker. Kevin was pleased to have recovered the shoe, but until the knife lay alongside it in the bottom of the boat, he wouldn't know whether Mrs. Hess had told him the truth or not. Could he be sure even then? But he knew such speculation was premature. He shifted his attention to the shore; there were a few people in view, but no one seemed interested in two boys in the water and a man in a canoe. Grace Hess was not among these people. She could not possibly see Kevin and the boys from the vicinity of her cottage, and Kevin had gambled, quite safely so far, that she would not choose to take a walk along the beach at this hour of the morning.

It was getting on toward lunchtime, and Kevin was beginning to worry that Alice Brock would call the boys in and that perhaps he had been wrong about Mrs. Hess. The loot in the canoe was now worth $6.00, Kevin having decided to give Darrell the benefit of the doubt and count a piece of metal the origin and purpose of which were impossible to determine. It was Billy once again who made the critical dive.

"Hey, look at this!" This time there was an excitement in Billy's voice that had been lacking following the drink cans and the shoe. He had come to the surface at the outer limits of the area Kevin had blocked out in his mind for their search. Darrell, by mutual consent, had been working the waters closer to shore.

"Have you found the watch?" Kevin shouted.

"No, it's a knife," Billy spluttered as he swam toward the canoe. Kevin made a conscious effort to suppress a satisfied smile, adopting instead a frown that said he couldn't imagine why there should be a knife on the lake bottom off Blue Water Point. When

Billy reached the boat, he grabbed the gunwale with one hand and held aloft his trophy.

"Can I keep it?"

"I don't think that'd be such a good idea, do you?" Kevin had no intention of letting Billy Keyser keep this particular knife, even if the Brocks didn't mind, which they would. "It looks dangerous to me."

As a matter-of-fact, it did look dangerous. And it was obviously not the typical piece of lake bottom detritus. Kevin took the knife from Billy, examined it briefly, and laid it down with the other junk the boys had recovered. He didn't want to appear too interested in the knife. Not now, not with Billy hanging on to the canoe and Darrell coming up alongside the bow to see what his brother had found. But Kevin was excited. The knife was fairly long and relatively new, and the blade was sharp. The absence of algae indicated that it had not been on the bottom long. It didn't look like the typical kitchen knife.

It was time to bring the game to an end.

"Still no watch. Can you spend another ten minutes?" He asked in his most casually hopeful voice. "If we don't find it now, maybe we can try again another time."

"Sure. We'll get it for you." Billy was disappointed about the knife, but he wasn't about to admit defeat over the watch. He pushed off from the canoe, swam off a few yards, took a deep breath, and headed once again for the bottom. Darrell followed suit.

Kevin maneuvered the canoe around and paddled a few strokes in the direction of his own cottage. When the boys were both submerged, he fished the watch out of his pocket and dropped it over the side. He made a mental note of the spot, estimating the distance from the shore and using a tree stump as a point of reference. He hoped he would see his watch again.

There was no need to worry. Both boys tended to do their diving in the vicinity of the canoe; as it moved, they moved. It took less than Kevin's 'another ten minutes' before Darrell came up with the watch. There was some justice in this, he thought, in view of the fact that Billy had produced the shoe and the knife. While Darrell was jubilant, Billy, undoubtedly still unhappy after being told he couldn't keep the knife, revealed himself to be a poor loser.

"Big deal," the older brother said as they gathered around the canoe. "You'd already been over that area. How'd you miss it?"

It was less a question than a putdown, and Darrell wasn't having any of it.

"You're just sore 'cause you didn't find it. All you got was some old junk."

Kevin intervened to restore brotherly love, feeling not a little guilty about his role in the affair.

"Hey, no quarrels. You both did great. Let's go to shore and settle accounts."

And they did. Billy and Darrell Keyser headed home for lunch richer by $3.50 each, and Kevin made his way back to the cottage with a few items for the garbage can and two for somewhat closer scrutiny. And to get in touch with his partner in the Britingham investigation, Sheriff Carol.

CHAPTER 48

The sheriff was in the process of finishing a rather tasteless tuna fish sandwich when the office intercom buzzed.

"It's that man Whitman on the line again," Miss Maltbie said. "Says he has to see you. Not just talk to you, see you."

Carol thought she detected a note of criticism in her secretary's voice. But that was absurd. She had said nothing about her whereabouts the previous evening, and Kevin had never visited the office. The problem was in her own mind, and reflected her own confused thoughts about the man who had started it all by reporting his discovery of John Britingham's body.

She had been half expecting his call, and she both welcomed it and dreaded it.

"Hello, Sheriff Kelleher here. What's up?"

"Hi. I thought we were dispensing with the formal stuff." Kevin effected a chuckle. "Anyhow, I need to see you. I've got something you ought to see, and I've got an idea I want to try out on you. How about lunch?"

"At two o'clock? County employees eat early. Anyway, I'm just now finishing my lunch, right here at my desk. What is it I should see?"

"I'd rather show you. Can we meet somewhere this afternoon?" Kevin would come to her office if necessary, but his preference was somewhere away from the phone and the secretary and what he assumed would be countless interruptions. The sheriff disappointed him.

"Well, of course. Why don't you come on over to the county office building. I'll be here all afternoon—unless another murder calls me away. Is two-thirty too soon?"

It wasn't, and half an hour later Kevin was sitting across the desk from the sheriff. His first thought on entering the room had been that while she looked good in her uniform, he preferred her in mufti. His second was that the room itself was a surprise. He had expected a drab office with standard issue furniture, mostly bare walls, and the occasional reminder that its reason for being was law enforcement. But he had been wrong. Potted plants were everywhere. The pictures which had been used to decorate the walls were not originals, but they were bright and colorful and in good taste. The incongruity of all this upbeat cheerfulness in an office devoted to apprehending the doers of bad deeds was not lost on Kevin. He decided that Carol Kelleher was indeed a rather special person.

"I've been thinking about last evening," Kevin began. "I mean our discussion of your case. We talked mostly about the Hoffmans. I thought you'd zeroed in on him as the most likely suspect in Britingham's murder, and then the Weber woman's death seemed to point the finger at them as well. But don't you think we ought to be casting the net a bit wider?"

"Listen to yourself, Kevin." The sheriff had thought a lot about the matter the night before and decided that she'd go with his given name. But at the moment she wasn't so sure it was a good idea.

"'*We* ought to be casting the net wider?' *We?* I appreciate your suggestions, but this is still my investigation. If I blow it, it'll be my ass in a sling, not yours—not ours. And I haven't forgotten that there are other people who could have killed Britingham, not to mention Weber. Weren't you trying to tell me just last night that those other people—your neighbors—couldn't be murderers?"

"Point well taken." The last thing Kevin wanted to do was push their relationship back onto more formal ground. He knew the knife would restore his credibility, so he dispensed with the preliminaries and produced it from the grocery sack he'd brought with him, laying it carefully on the desk.

"And what is this?" Carol asked as she leaned forward to examine the knife.

Kevin proceeded to tell her about his conversation with Grace Hess, his reservations about her story, and the diving expedition with the Keyser boys. As he did so, he watched the sheriff's face carefully for an expression of interest and approval.

"Of course I don't know that this is the weapon that killed Britingham." The demurrer seemed in order; Kevin didn't want the sheriff to think he was too smug about what he had done.

"Let's see now," Carol said. "Are you telling me you think it was Hess who killed Britingham?"

Kevin knew that this was a logical inference. He hadn't searched for the knife because he'd suspected Grace Hess of the murder. He'd simply been puzzled by her story about Jeff and the shoe, puzzled and curious. And he still had trouble picturing her as a murderer. Not to mention someone strong enough to put the body on his dock.

"I really don't know what to think. But whether she did it or not, I'd be surprised if she didn't throw this knife into the lake just a few cottages below my place. Why would she do that?"

"Let's say she did. You seem pretty sure of it, but there's no proof, not yet. Anyway, let's assume that Hess is responsible for the knife in the lake. Why? Maybe she saw it on the beach and figured it was dangerous to leave it lying around like that. Maybe she's not environmentally friendly, so she tossed it into the lake rather than into her recycling bin. Who knows? Well, I intend to find out. I'll talk to her. Anyway, we don't even know if the knife has anything to do with Britingham's death. There's probably a lot of stuff on the lake bottom, stuff lost by boaters and fishermen."

Carol knew she was reacting negatively and that it wouldn't be what Kevin wanted to hear. And she really was grateful for his help. After all, her officers had turned up nothing in what she suspected had been too perfunctory a search.

"Look, I'm glad you found the knife," she said. "There's a chance you're right, I suppose. I'll get on it right away. Anything else I ought to know?"

Kevin reported the problem of the light in Britingham's shack and the mystery of the disappearing and reappearing cinder block on the Sandersons' beach. He also related the Keyser boys' revised version of what they'd seen the night of the murder.

If Carol had had reservations about the importance of the discovery of the knife, she was even less excited about these other revelations. She remembered her own conversation with the boys and was still skeptical of Kevin's source. For all she knew they'd have yet another version of that night's events when she talked with them again. And she would. She factored the information about the light in the construction shack into her knowledge of young Britingham's use of it; that probably explained the light, but she'd question him further. As soon as Kevin left. As for the cinder block, it seemed to her that he was so wrapped up in his role as self-appointed private investigator that he was forgetting the old axiom that the simplest explanations for things are usually the best.

But Carol was again careful not to dismiss what Kevin had to tell her. Not only might it be relevant in some way not yet clear, but it also gave her an excuse to sustain a dialogue which she very much wanted to continue.

"What do you make of these things? The cinder block business, for instance."

"Well, they've started me thinking about the south end of Blue Water Point, down around his shack. Even the boys' story has Britingham—or maybe his killer—heading down that way during the night. And who's down there that's involved with Britingham? Mrs. Hess for one. And the guys who work for him— three of 'em playing cards that night practically next door to his property. I'm not saying any of these people knifed Britingham, but we know that Hess and Sanderson had a bad relationship with him. And Snyder, too—he was part of that card party. Or that other guy who was playing cards with them, Bauer—the men seem to think he's in a funk and that it's related to Britingham."

"I know," the sheriff said, her voice weary. "Britingham's enemies, everywhere on Blue Water Point. Maybe it was a gang killing—the Blue Water Point gang."

Kevin had no reason to suspect any of these people, nor did he have a theory as to how any of what he was telling the sheriff would unlock the mystery of Britingham's death—and he said so. And then quickly he turned to the other reason he had come to Cumberland that afternoon.

"One other thing," he said. "That threatening note you found at Weber's place. I'd like to see it, and I was hoping you'd let me accompany you while we went through Britingham's files."

The sheriff's eyebrows rose perceptibly.

"Why would you want to do that?" she asked. "We've already gone through everything in his office and at his house. It was one of the first things we did. What do you think we should be looking for?"

"It's the handwriting—something which would match the note in the microwave. I think I might be able to help you find it."

"Anything is possible, I suppose, but I thought we'd agreed that whoever wrote that note had deliberately disguised his handwriting. Or hers. Why do you assume we'd find a similar specimen of someone's handwriting at Silver Leaf? Or at the house?"

"No," Kevin said. "We didn't agree that the handwriting had been disguised. Maybe you believe that, and maybe it's true. But what if it isn't? Anyway, you asked me to give some thought to the note, and I've been doing just that. You believe it was written by Hoffman, that he threatened Britingham because he was fooling around with his wife."

Kevin held up his hand as the sheriff started to object.

"Okay, you think he *may* have written it. But there are other possibilities. Anyway, even if Hoffman wrote it, doesn't it make sense to look for a possible handwriting match? I'll bet your people searched Britingham's files last week, before you found the note. And because you think whoever wrote it disguised his handwriting, there's no need to go through the files again. But we don't know whether the note writer disguised his handwriting, do we? What if he didn't? Wouldn't it be nice if we—sorry, if you— could identify the writer of that note by locating another specimen of his handwriting? Or hers."

This is certainly a different Kevin Whitman, Carol thought, not the diffident man with whom she had spoken the morning of Britingham's murder. More like a bloodhound hot after some scent. It was an interesting transformation, but she found herself resisting his theory. She got up and crossed over to her file cabinet, where she extracted a file.

"Here," she said, handing him a paper from the file, a paper carefully encased in a glassine envelope. "This is the note you wanted to see. And by the way, so you don't think I'm hopelessly incompetent, you should know we did check for prints. Weber's are all over it, of course. And Britingham's. It's pretty badly smudged—I doubt we'll be able to get any match except theirs. Anyway, doesn't it look like a calculated effort by the author to conceal his real hand?"

Kevin looked at the four-word message. It was as the sheriff had said, legible but not neatly written, certainly a bad example of penmanship—or pencilship. And there was that misspelled word.

"Maybe."

"Maybe? Who spells 'you'll' like that?"

"You'd be surprised. Look, I've had lots of experience reading papers and exams, and I'm convinced we're a nation of lousy spellers. A lot of people don't know how to punctuate. My students are always writing 'it's' with an apostrophe when they mean the possessive, not the contraction. And vice versa. I correct that one on student papers all the time. Sorry to sound pedantic, but..."

"Okay," the sheriff interrupted, "let's assume for purposes of argument that whoever wrote the note wasn't trying to disguise his handwriting. Maybe he was just marginally literate."

"No, I don't want to make that assumption either. Bad penmanship and poor spelling don't make a person illiterate. Some of my best students have been poor spellers. My wife, too."

Kevin quickly amended that to ex-wife, anxious that the sheriff should know that Susan was now very much part of his past.

"Look," he plunged ahead, "I've been asking myself some of the same questions you must have been asking. Who was the note intended for? Who could have written it? It seems to me that there are only two possible answers to the first question—Weber and Britingham. Take Weber. What if she'd killed Britingham and someone knew it? Couldn't that explain the note?"

"You're not suggesting it was Weber who killed Britingham, are you?"

"No. I don't think the note was intended for her, or that she killed Britingham. But the note was in her possession, and in the end she did pay for it, whatever 'it' is, just like the note writer threatened. So it's a possibility that can't be dismissed.

"But it's the idea of Britingham as the target of the note that makes most sense. Someone could have been threatening him, telling him he'd pay for some misdeed. There seem to have been plenty of those. And because Weber was his secretary—and probably his lover—she could easily have found the note at his office. Or even at his home. Did your men find any of her prints out there?"

"Oh, yes, lots of them. Doesn't mean that they were lovers, but it makes it more likely."

"Then there's the other question," Kevin said, anxious to make his case for the search for a handwriting match. "Who wrote the note? There's Hoffman—your candidate. But what about X? Think about it. Weber finds the note, thinks she recognizes it because of the handwriting. It reminds her of something she's seen, probably at the office but maybe out at the old Keighly place. Maybe Britingham even showed it to her, you know, pulling his macho act."

"If he did, then Weber might not have had to make the handwriting connection—maybe Britingham simply told her who had threatened him."

"Well, yes, that's possible," Kevin agreed, "but she's dead so there's no way you're going to find out who she decided to blackmail—unless there's a handwriting match."

"Other than Emily Hoffman."

"Right. And it could have been any number of people. So let's see—which of the people you've been investigating might have written something that Weber could have seen in the course of performing her secretarial duties? Or visiting Britingham? Which of them might be X?"

Kevin waited, but the sheriff outwaited him, so he began to tick off the names on the list he had put together that morning.

"Of course anyone could have written to Britingham at some time or other, even someone like George Morgan, telling him in writing what he told him in person—to leave that wreck alone. But I'm thinking more specifically about people like Grace Hess. She'd taken steps to prevent Britingham from building on that property next to hers, and there's a good chance she'd have notified him in writing of what she was doing, or that he would have received a copy of some form she'd filled out and filed with the county. And then there are several people you've been questioning who are Silver Leaf employees—Larry Sanderson for one, and Bernie Carlino, and that other man who was playing cards at the Sandersons that night Britingham was killed, Hank Bauer. They'd all have things on file, various forms, requests for leave, you know, the sorts of things that would make up a personnel file. And Sanderson had probably written to Britingham in his capacity as spokesman for the grape growers.

"There could be others, but the point is there are people besides Alan Hoffman you might want to think about. And that's why I hope you'll let me go with you to look at the files in Britingham's office."

The sheriff leaned back in her chair, a smile on her face.

"What have I gotten myself into? I ask you to think about the case, share your ideas with me, and now this. You ever been deputized? Well, you have now, and I hope I don't get my tail in a sling for it. I'll send Bridges down to the winery, and you can go with him. No point in doing Britingham's house—it's clean as the proverbial hound's tooth. I very much doubt you'll find anything at the office either, but I guess it can't hurt."

It was an hour later that Kevin met a conspicuously unenthusiastic Sam Bridges at the winery. No one had moved into

Britingham's office; it remained, at the sheriff's request, exactly as Bridges had found it the previous Tuesday.

"You know, Mr. Whitman, this is going to take awhile. And I'm not even quite sure what we're looking for," Bridges said, waving a folder. He leafed through the papers in it and tossed it to one side of the desk. "This is really going to be a needle-in-a-haystack search, you know."

The man was clearly unhappy. All that driving back and forth to the city had been bad enough, but at least it had a purpose he could understand, and it had paid dividends. The business of going through Britingham's files for a second time seemed downright silly.

"Look," Kevin said, "why don't you let me do it? It was my idea after all. If you want to do something else, just give me some time with these files, then you can come back and close up the office."

The proposal was tempting. It didn't take two of them to do what they were doing, and the sheriff had apparently given Whitman some kind of authority. Sam wasn't quite sure how much discretion he had, but he was bored and frustrated, and he really wanted to get out of the stuffy office. He made his decision.

"Okay, I've got to run downtown." He looked at his watch. "I'll be back at five-thirty, give or take a few minutes. Don't go until I get here, and let's leave the files like we found them."

After the deputy sheriff's departure, Kevin tackled the files with an enthusiasm he had rarely experienced when confronted with a batch of student papers to grade. It was nearly an hour later that he found something that, to his eyes at least, looked promising. It was tucked away in a folder, which lacked the typed tab with which most of the folders in the file cabinet were labeled. In its place was the unhelpful label "SLS," handwritten in red ink.

The folder contained four pieces of paper. Two were letters, typed and bearing recent dates. One of these was on Silver Leaf letterhead and the other bore the name of a company of which Kevin had never heard. The third appeared to be an invoice. And the fourth was a handwritten note on a sheet of paper from the kind of tablet available at most drugstores and widely used by kids in school.

The fact that the note was handwritten made it worth a second look. The second look was initially discouraging. The note was in the form of a short list. The words stayed within the lines on the tablet, and nothing appeared to be misspelled. But whoever had written the note had shifted erratically between cursive and printed letters; it was the first thing Kevin had come across in which the handwriting looked at all like the note found in Dolores Weber's microwave, so he continued to study it. And as he did so, he began to see small idiosyncrasies that reminded him of the other note.

When Sam Bridges returned, as he said he would, at five-thirty, Kevin was in the process of closing the bottom file drawer. He told the deputy sheriff that his search had been inconclusive. As a report on the results of his perusal of John Britingham's files, it was not dishonest, but neither was it entirely straightforward.

"That's what I figured," Bridges said. "Sorry it was a wasted afternoon."

Kevin wasn't so sure it had been time wasted. He felt confident that the sheriff would be interested in the contents of the "SLS" folder, which with some difficulty he had managed to stuff into his pocket. With any luck, they might be closer to a solution to the week-old puzzle of who had killed John Britingham.

PART VI

LAKE TRAGEDY

CHAPTER 49

Southport was rarely the scene of a traffic jam, not even on its busiest day. At nine o'clock on this particular Saturday evening in August, there was no traffic at all. Kevin Whitman stopped dutifully at each corner, however. He did so because he was a law-abiding citizen, but his meticulous observance of the law was also due to the fact that Sheriff Carol Kelleher was sitting beside him in the Toyota.

Two young couples were standing on the sidewalk in front of the ice cream parlor, and one lone figure could be observed across the square, heading up Vine Street. The neon sign in the window of Jack's Tavern advertised a regional beer and the fact that Jack's was open for business. For all Kevin knew, the place was packed. But no one could be seen entering or leaving, and even with the car window rolled down he could hear no music or other sound coming from the tavern. The lights inside the local drugstore went out just as he made the turn and headed toward the east lake road.

The street lamps that bathed the village in a pale yellow-green light thinned out as the car approached the intersection. Kevin turned north, and while the speed limit was a moderate 45, he kept the car at village speed so as not to miss the cottage that was his destination.

Sheriff Kelleher was unaccustomed to sitting in the passenger seat while someone else did the driving. She liked to be behind the wheel, in control of the car. Tonight she was not in control of the car, and, she feared, not even in full control of the investigation into the violent deaths of John Britingham and Dolores Weber. Forty-eight hours earlier she had asked Whitman for his advice on the case, and before that evening was out had shared information with him which a more prudent officer of the law would probably not have divulged. Just yesterday she had allowed him to go through files in Britingham's office. And tonight she was riding shotgun for this man who had talked her into going along with a crazy plan to coax a confession from someone he was convinced had killed Britingham and his secretary.

She had listened patiently the previous afternoon while Kevin told her what he thought had happened. Initially she had simply listened politely. Twenty or so minutes later she had become constructively skeptical. In the end she had acknowledged that his theory was intriguing, and arguably as persuasive as the one that had been taking shape in her own mind. The problem, of course, was that there didn't appear to be any really hard evidence—no smoking gun, as the media would put it. She didn't see how she could prove ownership of the knife. There were no witnesses to the movement of the cinder block. The handwritten list from the winery files didn't look to her nearly as much like the note in Weber's microwave as it did to Kevin. And the testimony of the Keyser boys would clearly have to be taken with a grain of salt.

She had decided that Kevin might be onto something, but that she didn't have enough to confront the man, much less to make an arrest. And then for the better part of an hour she had listened while Kevin presented and defended what he referred to as plan B. Plan A called for the sheriff to bluff it out with the suspect, hoping he would crack, at which point he would be taken into custody. Plan C was business as usual, an ongoing investigation which would hopefully turn up evidence on which to base an arrest. Kevin agreed with the sheriff that plan A was premature, but argued that plan C could not be counted on to produce new evidence and that it was necessary to bring some pressure to bear.

"So, why don't you let me be the one to talk to him?" Kevin had suggested. "I'm not the law, which ought to make it easier. And I think I have an angle, a way to get the conversation off the ground."

They had kicked plan B around for a while, with Kevin inflating the prospects for its success and minimizing the dangers it posed, while the sheriff juggled a host of conflicting emotions. In the end Carol had given her consent, with the stipulation that she go along in order to be on hand, just in case something went wrong—something that might jeopardize the investigation or something that would put Kevin at risk. She wasn't sure which was her greatest fear.

From the turnoff at the Bauer cabin, there was no way to tell whether anyone was at home, although Kevin had been assured that Hank would be there. He eased himself out of the car and stood at the edge of the gravel surface next to the hollyhocks, looking down at the roof of the cabin and beyond that at the dark waters of the lake. Carol hunkered down in the front seat, readying herself for a vigil she didn't look forward to.

What a damn fool I am, she was thinking, playing Lestrade to Whitman's Holmes, or Japp to his Poirot. She had long been an avid reader of mystery stories and, like untold numbers of other readers, had been amused at the ease with which these great fictional detectives had run circles around the police. But the Britingham case was not fiction, and Kevin Whitman was no Holmes or Poirot. He's a professor of music, for God's sake, a bright but inexperienced amateur for whom Britingham's death is a great midlife adventure.

"Don't do something stupid," Carol whispered as she leaned across the front seat and pulled the car door quietly shut. She wished she could be sure Kevin would not do something stupid. The whole thing was stupid.

Kevin carefully felt his way along the guardrail at the edge of the pull-off and down the steps. The outside light above the door had not been turned on. Perhaps Bauer had credited his visitor with night vision. Or, in spite of his assurances, he may simply have decided he did not want to talk with Kevin after all.

It had been no easy task getting him to agree to the meeting. Larry Sanderson had known what he was talking about when Kevin had inquired about Bauer.

"He's been hurt, real bad, and he's as stubborn as a mule. A couple of months ago he was the easiest guy in the world to know. He'd talk at the drop of a hat. Loved to talk baseball."

Kevin had found himself waiting for Sanderson's next cliché. It came even faster than he expected.

"Now he shuts up like a clam when you mention it. I never saw a guy change so fast. I wouldn't bet you'd get much out of him."

Nor was it yet clear that he would. He hadn't told Larry the truth about his reason for wanting to talk with Bauer, and he didn't intend to tell Bauer either, not at first. Kevin had decided to resort to subterfuge, and before he was through with it he was going to make a rash promise without first consulting Gary McFadden.

McFadden was a colleague of Kevin's at the university, and a good acquaintance if hardly a close friend. They had served on committees together, and they often found themselves at the same table in the faculty club. McFadden was a sociologist and a specialist in the sociology of sports. He had done a book on the

problems professional athletes experience when slowed reflexes
and injuries force them into retirement or what Gary called 'real
life.' So when Kevin told Bauer over the phone that a friend was
writing a book based on the lives of athletes who didn't quite
make it to the big time, and that he might want to use the Southport baseball player as one of his case studies, it wasn't exactly a
lie. Kevin had convinced himself that Gary would find the idea
irresistible and that his own promotional skills would be sufficient
to guarantee Hank Bauer's inclusion in such a book.

It had taken a phone call of nearly ten minutes duration, during which Bauer had almost hung up on him twice, to get a very
tentative 'maybe' and an agreement to meet and pursue the matter.
And now he was standing at the ex-ballplayer's door, feeling both
a little guilty that he had not been honest with him and anxious
that he might never be able to steer the conversation to the real
reason for the meeting. Kevin rapped sharply on the door.

The man who opened the door bore little resemblance to the
man he had pictured in his mind. He knew that Bauer would be
older than Sanderson or Snyder by several years. But he had
expected a more vigorous looking man, still trim and muscular.
After all, his bat was sorely missed in the Silver Leaf softball
team's lineup. What he saw instead was a man who carried neither
his height nor his weight well. His shoulders were rounded, as if
he had just set down a heavy weight, and his gut was conspicuous
over his belt buckle. The ill-fitting clothes and balding head
competed the picture—Hank Bauer was clearly over the hill, and
the downward slide had begun before his recent troubles. At least
the physical part of it.

"Mr. Bauer. Hi, I'm Kevin Whitman. Good of you to see
me." Kevin tried to make it sound like a cheerful, upbeat greeting.
He half expected the door to be closed in his face.

But Bauer stepped aside and let him into the tiny cabin. He
didn't shake hands, but he did invite Kevin to take a seat and
offered him a drink. Whether the offer of a drink was a friendly
gesture or simply an acknowledgement that Bauer himself was in
need of a drink, Kevin couldn't be sure. The presence of an
uncapped bottle of whiskey and a partially filled glass on the table
next to the couch suggested that the latter explanation was
probably correct.

Hank Bauer had done some housecleaning since the sheriff's
visit, so Kevin had no way of knowing that the cabin was unchar-

acteristically neat. But no amount of dusting and dishwashing could conceal the fact that it was a drab and dreary place. The one lamp that was lit could not have more than a 60-watt bulb and did little to dispel the gloom. Kevin wanted to ask if he couldn't turn on the room's other lamp, but didn't. If Bauer wanted to sit in the semi-dark, that was his business.

Kevin accepted the offer of a drink, although he didn't particularly want one. It was unlikely that he would be asked to leave until he finished it, and if he nursed it carefully he could perhaps exercise some control over the duration, if not the content, of their conversation. He had expected to be questioned further about the book and about the interview which McFadden would want to arrange, the book and interview about which Kevin's colleague knew absolutely nothing. But Bauer took no conversational initiative.

Kevin found this disconcerting. He had anticipated some resistance to his idea, and he had concocted a positive, ego-building strategy for dealing with it. Instead he found himself launched into a monologue, which sounded, to his ears at least, not terribly convincing. Bauer listened impassively. It was impossible to tell whether he was giving the idea any serious thought or merely being patiently polite. Kevin's highball was half-gone. He would have to try another tack.

"From what my friend tells me," he said, adding to the fiction of McFadden's interest in people like Bauer, "some players simply walk away from their sport, pay it no more attention. For others it remains a lifelong love. You'd be in the second category, from what I hear. I wish I were. Of course, I wasn't good at my game like you were. I was what they call good field, no hit, except I wasn't even a very good fielder. Barely earned one varsity letter my last year in high school. There was a time when I followed baseball, especially the Yankees, but by the time I'd been out of school a few years I'd forgotten just about all I knew. Never even read the box scores anymore.

"I ran into a guy not long ago who made me regret I'd lost touch with the game. We were at a meeting, just sitting around having a friendly drink. There was a TV set going, and there was a game on. The Yankees were playing. We weren't watching, but something the announcer said must have caught this guy's attention, because out of the blue he pops this baseball trivia question.

"'Bet you don't know who was the Yankee first baseman Lou
Gehrig succeeded and who was the one who succeeded him when
that disease took him out of the lineup all those years later.' Of
course I didn't know, and this guy never told me. Some other
people came up right then, we got to talking about something else,
and he went off without ever telling me who those first basemen
were."

Kevin thought he detected a spark of interest in Bauer's face.
It was a gamble, but Kevin was guessing that a man named Hank
Bauer, with a reputation for detailed knowledge about baseball
facts and figures, would be likely to be especially well informed
about the Yankees. And the story was true, all but the last part of
it—his companion had provided the answer to his own question.
Kevin was willing to bet that Bauer could, too. If he was wrong, it
was doubtful that he'd learn anything about Britingham's death
from Hank Bauer.

"Like I said, I never did know much about such things, and I
forgot most of what I did know. Now you, you're different. I hope
you can tell me who those two first basemen were. It's been
bothering me that I don't know."

"Wally Pipp," Bauer said, his first words in almost ten minutes. "And Babe Dahlgren."

"Pipp and Dahlgren. I don't remember either name. Want to
tell me about them?" Careful, Kevin thought. Don't press your
luck.

"Not much to tell," Bauer replied, still reticent. But the ice
had been broken, and he seemed willing, if not anxious, to talk.
"Pipp was pretty good. Probably would have had a long career
with the Yankees if Gehrig hadn't come along. Dahlgren was just
a journeyman, though. The Yankees didn't find a good replace-
ment for Gehrig for years. Never did find his equal, never will."

"That's remarkable, Mr. Bauer. I mean, how do you remember things like that? We're talking about—what?—sixty, seventy
years ago, even more?"

"I guess people remember what's important to them," he answered with a shrug, as if to say it was no big deal.

"I hear you don't like to talk about baseball. That's too bad.
I'd love to talk baseball with you—play catch up for all the years
I've missed. It seems to me if I knew the things you know, I'd
want to talk about them. What happened?"

Bauer looked down at his shoes for a time without answering the question. When he looked up, he spoke with more emotion than he had at any time since Kevin's arrival.

"I don't want your friend, the guy who's writing this book, to get into it. It's personal. But somebody made a fool of me, about baseball I mean, and it just didn't seem like it was much fun anymore. I still think about it; I just don't want to talk about it."

"Or play it either, I understand."

"Yeah."

"It sounds like you think people won't respect you. But you're wrong. You say somebody made a fool of you. I'll bet what he did was make a fool of himself. And I'd also bet the man who made a fool of himself was that conceited ass Britingham." The time had come, Kevin decided, to take the plunge. "Would I be right?"

Bauer's silence was as eloquent as an affirmative response.

"I thought so. Nobody around here with an ounce of decency would try to make you look foolish. Friends don't turn on a man. But Britingham, he comes in here, from what I hear, all full of himself, and starts running everyone down. He did it to Mike Snyder and Larry Sanderson. I understand they're friends of yours, so you know what I mean."

Kevin thought it would be wise to put the brakes on a bit, so he entered the proper demurrer.

"I suppose I shouldn't speak badly of the dead, but no one I know has a good word to say about that man. You shouldn't let him beat you like that. Anyway, he's dead. It's over."

Kevin almost literally held his breath. He knew it was Britingham who was responsible for Bauer's funk, but the man hadn't admitted it to him. Denial was still possible, in which case this conversation might come to a dead end.

"How do you know Larry and Mike?" This question, as it turned out, took them quickly to Kevin's real agenda.

"We're neighbors over on Blue Water Point. I don't know either of them all that well—Mike better than Larry, I suppose. But they've told me about their problems with Britingham."

"You're the man who found his body, aren't you?" Bauer asked. Kevin had assumed from the beginning that Bauer might have known this. After all, his name had been in the local paper and on the radio, and he figured that by now there would be people from all over the area, people who wouldn't know him from

Adam, who would be casually dropping his name in their discussion of the murder. In fact, he suspected that Bauer's reason for acceding to his request for a meeting had as much to do with curiosity about his discovery of Britingham's body as it did with an interest in being the subject of a book.

"Right. I couldn't believe it. I knew he was pretty unpopular, so maybe I shouldn't have been surprised that somebody had done him in. But I sure was surprised to find him on my dock. It gave me quite a start."

The conversation had now taken the critical turn. Kevin was trying to strike the right tone, balancing the shock he would be expected to feel with the absence of sorrow or regret which would presumably mirror Bauer's own feelings. It was now clear from his host's more animated expression that he was genuinely interested in what Kevin had to say about the crime.

It took Kevin a few minutes to recount the morning in question. He carefully avoided speculation, concentrating on providing a factual account of what he had seen and done. Bauer seemed particularly interested when Kevin mentioned that he had seen Mike Snyder just before he had taken his swim. For much of the story, he had listened without comment, but when Snyder's name came up, he interrupted.

"Do you think they suspect Mike?" The question carried a note of genuine concern. It was easy enough to see why Mike might be suspected, given his physical proximity to the place where Britingham had been found, plus the widely known episode of the fishing competition.

Bauer's question provided an opening, and Kevin took advantage of it.

"They might have suspected him, I suppose, except for the fact that somebody else had confessed to killing Britingham."

Bauer's reaction was transparently one of disbelief. He leaned forward, his jaw working.

"Who is it?"

"I don't know that I'm at liberty to say," Kevin replied.

This was obviously unsatisfactory from Bauer's point of view. He started to protest, but then a thought occurred to him which propelled him out of his seat and over to the whiskey bottle.

"Wait a minute," he said in a voice suddenly tense with suspicion. "How do you know this? I didn't hear any announcement that somebody's been arrested."

"The sheriff who's investigating the case was talking to me, asking more questions about what I'd seen that morning. She mentioned that she'd had a confession. I guess she was trying to tie the loose ends together." It was, to say the least, an oblique reply to the question.

Bauer was no longer the passive listener he'd been for the previous half an hour. He sat down, then got up again, as if to get something, only to change his mind and sit back down. His questions came in rapid-fire order.

"She tell you who confessed? Did she say when she's going to give out the story? Is it someone you know? I mean a neighbor or…"

"Or what?" Kevin wanted to be the one asking the questions.

"I don't know, I was just wondering, you know, which of the people that didn't like him did it. It was someone like that, was it?"

"If you mean was it someone from around here, the answer is no," Kevin said quietly. "I guess it'll be out soon anyway, so I might as well tell you. It was Britingham's son."

Hank Bauer was having a great deal of difficulty absorbing this news.

"His son? I don't understand."

"I'm not sure I do either. It seems Britingham had a son, lived out in California. Apparently he came east weekend before last, had a confrontation with his father, and killed him. That's what he told the sheriff when he gave himself up. Just a young man, too. Can't be more than 20-something from what I hear."

"My God, that's awful. Why'd he do it?"

"No idea." Kevin finessed the question, and returned to the tragedy of patricide. "In the eyes of the law it probably won't matter why he killed him. I almost feel sorry for the kid. The old man's dead, and nobody's mourning, but the son probably gets put away for a long time, maybe life. It doesn't seem fair."

"God, no, it's not fair!" The words were strong, but the voice was faint, barely more than a whisper. "Do you think he really did it?"

"I wouldn't know, Mr. Bauer. What do you think?"

"I mean why would he confess if he didn't do it?"

"Do you think he didn't do it?" Kevin tried to keep his tone conversational when the temptation was strong to use his voice as a drill to bore into Bauer's mind and expose whatever thoughts were going through it at the moment. For the first time since arriving at the cabin, Kevin found himself thinking about the sheriff, sitting up there in the car, and wishing there were some better way of communicating in an emergency. In the movies he would have one of those small transmitters hidden on him somewhere so the sheriff could hear all that was being said. But this wasn't the movies. It was a rural backwater, and that kind of equipment didn't seem to be standard issue. Carol would be chewing her nails, wondering what was going on, hoping she could hear him if something went wrong. Kevin had assured her that nothing would go wrong.

"I don't know," Bauer finally replied weakly. He covered his face with both hands and contemplated the floor though his fingers.

"I don't know either, but I'll tell you what I think, Hank." It was the first time Kevin had used Bauer's first name. "I don't think young Britingham killed his father. I think he hated him, just like a lot of people around here did, like you did. I've heard a rumor that the boy's mother was drowned and that the son thought his father was responsible for her death. Anyway, he might have wanted to kill him, and he might have become so distraught that he became confused about it, but I don't believe he did it. Do you want to know what I think happened?"

Kevin waited until Bauer nodded.

"You understand that I don't know anything for certain. But I think I've figured out most of it." Kevin took a sip from the now lukewarm highball he'd been nursing. His heart was beating faster. He hoped the sheriff hadn't fallen asleep in the car.

"A week ago last Monday night Britingham came to Blue Water Point in the late evening to visit a woman he'd been seeing. I think you may have heard of her. She's a neighbor of Mike Snyder's and mine; name's Hoffman. I think he had a lot to drink. When he left her cottage, it would have been around midnight, maybe after. He headed for that construction shack of his—have you heard about that? It's down at the south end of Blue Water Point, not too far beyond the Sandersons' cottage. I don't know whether he was going to get his car and drive home or just sack out there in the shack. It doesn't much matter, because he never made it.

"Somewhere along the way he left the road and cut down toward the beach, probably to avoid a light someone had left on out back of their cottage. It could have been at the Sandersons, because a card game was just breaking up. I heard about the game from Mike, and Chris Sanderson mentioned it, too. I think you were there. Am I right?"

Bauer nodded again without looking at Kevin.

"Anyway, maybe Britingham ducked around the house to the beach· because he saw somebody leaving the Sandersons. We'll never know. But what he didn't know, and we do, is that the beach wasn't deserted. When the card party broke up, everybody went out the back way because they lived on the point and the road behind the cottages was the easiest way back home for them. Everybody but one. You came by boat, I believe, so you were on the beach, probably untying your boat and getting ready to shove off from the dock and head home. It was pure coincidence that Britingham came along at just that time, wasn't it?"

Bauer made no reply. This time he didn't even nod.

"Like I said, Hank, I'm just telling you what I think happened. You'll have to tell me if I've got it right or not. I think you and Britingham met there in the dark. Only it's never totally dark, is it, and you saw each other. I don't know whether Britingham recognized you at first, but I'm sure you knew who he was. After all, he'd done a terrible thing to you, and you remembered him— his voice, his face—even in the middle of the night, even when you hadn't expected to run into him. I'd guess the two of you had words and then something happened. Let's say he took a swing at you. He'd been drinking, and he was always pretty belligerent anyway. You defended yourself, of course. You had a knife with you. In fact you'd used it to clean the fish you'd caught that evening. In the melee he got knifed. Like I said, it was probably self-defense.

"But it was a bad knife wound. And I think Britingham lost his balance and fell. I'd guess he hit his head on that cinder block Larry keeps at the end of his dock. Anyway, the knife wound, the head injury—one or the other or both were fatal. To make matters worse, in the confusion, with all that flailing around, you lost the knife. So now you had two problems. You had a dying man you'd just stabbed. You couldn't leave him there on your friend's beach. And you couldn't find the knife.

"You had to get Britingham away from there, even if it meant looking for the knife later. I think you dumped him into your boat, along with the cinder block. I'm not sure why you took the block, but I can think of a couple of reasons. Those blocks are porous, so you figured it might have blood on it. And you couldn't be sure of getting the blood off in the dark just by splashing water on it. So you took it with you. Then there's another reason. You had to get rid of Britingham, and maybe the cinder block gave you an idea: tie it to him and dump the body overboard somewhere out in the middle of the lake on the way home.

"But something happened to change your mind. Maybe you worried that the rope would break, or that the block wouldn't be heavy enough to do the job. Anyway, you decided to dump the body somewhere else on the point, so that when it was found no one would have reason to suspect your friend Larry Sanderson. Or any of the people who'd been playing cards there."

Kevin had been nervously watching Bauer for some show of anger, some sign of denial. He had not expected to talk so long without interruption. But there had been nothing. Hank had simply sat and listened.

"I think you came back the next night," Kevin continued. "You had to bring the cinder block back, and you had to find the knife. This time you had a flashlight with you, but it didn't do you much good, did it? The knife wasn't there. You hoped no one would have seen it, and the odds were in your favor because the Sandersons aren't beach people. But it was gone, and you must have been worried sick about the knife.

"That's more or less what I think happened. Why don't you tell me your version?"

"What do you want me to say?" Bauer asked, his voice dull and dispirited.

"It isn't what *I* want you to say. What do *you* want to say?"

"Why are you accusing me of killing Mr. Britingham?" It was a weak rebuttal, less a denial than a stalling tactic, an effort to keep Kevin talking and thereby avoiding the moment when he would have to defend himself.

"I think you see the problem, Hank," Kevin said gently. "There's a young man sitting in the jail over in Cumberland because he claims he killed Britingham. If he did, I think we can assume that he'll go to trial and be convicted and serve a long sentence. But if he didn't, it would be a terrible miscarriage of justice if he went to prison. I think we can agree on that. And the police aren't likely to pursue other suspects very vigorously when they have a confession, now are they? Of course they just might, and that would mean that they might be after your friend Snyder. Or they might go after a man whose wife was supposed to be sleeping with Britingham. He'd have a pretty good motive, too, wouldn't you say? And the body was found down that way, near their cottage.

"It just looks to me as if a lot of innocent people could be badly hurt before this is over. I've told you what I think happened. I don't think you meant to kill Britingham. My guess is that he provoked you, and you killed him in self-defense. That's manslaughter, not murder."

Kevin left it to Bauer to come to the right conclusion. He thought of him as a basically decent man who had been goaded beyond his limit. He hoped he would do the honorable thing.

The time had come to leave. It was not, Kevin thought, his responsibility to wheedle a confession from Bauer. He had planted a seed, and it might take time to sprout. Nothing Bauer had said raised a doubt in Kevin's mind about his reasoning. And what Bauer had not said only confirmed his conviction that this was the man who had killed John Britingham.

He rose to go, but stopped at the door. The moment of maximum danger had passed. It had not been necessary to tell Bauer that the sheriff was waiting just outside, much less to holler for help. He thought he could let the other shoe drop.

"By the way, I know you must be familiar with the death Tuesday of a woman named Dolores Weber. She was Britingham's secretary. The sheriff's office hasn't had much time to work on that one yet, but I think it's likely that she was killed by the same person who killed her boss. I don't think you meant to kill her either, but she had something you needed, something that might focus police attention on you in their search for Britingham's killer. You were afraid she'd give it to the police. In fact, I think she threatened to do just that if you didn't pay her. She blackmailed you, didn't she?"

Kevin didn't expect a reply, and he got none.

"I'll tell you what I think she had of yours. It was a note threatening Britingham. Of course it wasn't signed, but you were afraid the handwriting would give you away. You worried about it because you'd prepared a list of equipment for the Silver Leaf softball team for Britingham, and it would be a simple matter to compare the two. Weber wouldn't give you the note. She probably started to scream, and you smothered her.

"You've been terribly unlucky, haven't you? You lost your knife when you killed Britingham, and you didn't get the note when you killed Weber. You can't be a very happy man, Mr. Bauer. You have my sympathy."

Kevin opened the door but paused for one final word.

"Don't forget about the book. When this is over, my friend will be in touch with you. I hope you'll see him. And when you want to talk baseball, I'm a good listener. I really am."

It had been a harrowing hour. And a depressing one. Kevin experienced an enormous sense of relief as he slid into the car and closed the door. He reached across the front seat and pulled the sheriff to him, locking her in a tight embrace that surprised him as much as it surprised her.

They quietly disengaged, their thoughts about what had just happened unspoken. Kevin turned the key in the ignition, maneuvered the car out of Bauer's small turnoff, and headed back toward Southport. Neither spoke for several minutes, until finally, as they headed north on West Lake Road, Carol began to ask the inevitable questions. Kevin reported the essentials: Bauer had not confessed, nor had he behaved in a threatening manner, but everything about the way he had reacted said he was guilty, a beaten man. It would only be a matter of time before he gave himself up. Kevin then lapsed into silence, and the sheriff did not pursue it further.

It was a clear, beautiful night for the trip back to Blue Water Point where the sheriff had parked her car. But Kevin took no pleasure in the drive. He was thinking about the sad man who had almost certainly killed two people within the past two weeks. They had died because they weren't as decent as he was. The term 'tragedy,' he mused, had been debased by overuse and misuse. But this case had all the markings of a real tragedy. Kevin felt no sense of vindication when he got home. It had been a bad night's work. Except, of course, for that impulsive hug, that moment that told both Kevin and Carol that they had very probably solved John Britingham's murder—and perhaps much more.

CHAPTER 50

On the morning of the twelfth day following the discovery of John Britingham's body on his dock, Kevin Whitman once again found himself up and about much earlier than he wanted to be. This time, unlike that other traumatic morning, he knew very well why he had had trouble sleeping. He had awakened to a feeling that something was wrong, and almost immediately that something became the vivid memory of his meeting with Hank Bauer.

By 6:10 he was sitting on the deck, still in his bathrobe, hands wrapped around a cup of steaming black coffee. A front had passed through the area overnight, and the temperature had taken a plunge. Can't be more than 50 degrees, if that, he thought, which means that the day's high would probably not go much above 70. The lake, usually becalmed at this hour, was in motion, with a brisk breeze out of the south pushing modest waves from right to left across Kevin's line of vision. He felt no compulsion to take a solitary swim.

Kevin found himself reviewing what had happened in Bauer's cabin to see if his impressions of the night before would stand up in the light of day. When he first sighted the boat, it barely registered on his consciousness. Someone was fishing. Someone was always fishing. A bit later, perhaps as much as a minute later, he again became conscious of the boat. It was still way out in the middle of the lake and a bit further to the north. It was obviously moving with the morning breeze in the direction of the upper end of the lake. Kevin watched the boat absent-mindedly as it continued its drift northward.

The realization that something wasn't quite right dawned slowly, so that the boat was almost directly across from the Snyder cottage before Kevin began to pay it more serious attention. It looked empty, and it seemed to be rather low in the water. His commonsense told him that the boat's occupant was probably bending over, doing something with his line. He relaxed in his chair, only to lean forward again for a better look when it occurred to him that he hadn't seen anybody in the boat at any time since first noticing it.

The binoculars were on the mantle over the fireplace. He retrieved them and adjusted the focus until the boat came clearly into view, now so close it could have been only twenty yards offshore. There was no question about it: the boat was unusually low in the water, the gunwales only half a foot above the lake's surface. It had obviously shipped water. And it was almost surely empty.

There was no one else in sight to lend a hand, so Kevin decided to take the canoe out and see for himself what was wrong. He discarded his robe, pulled on a sweatshirt and an old pair of wash slacks, and launched the canoe.

The breeze was favorable, and Kevin was a good canoeist. The fishing boat was drifting slowly up the lake, but he applied his paddle in steady, powerful J-strokes, and within a few minutes had closed the distance between himself and the boat sufficiently so that he could tell that it was indeed unoccupied. A little less than a minute later he came alongside and grabbed the boat near the bow.

Not only was there no fisherman, but there was also no evidence that anybody had been fishing. Damn thing must not have been tied securely, he thought. Probably came loose in the night and had simply drifted with the current.

It would be easier to tow the canoe behind the fishing boat, he decided, provided he could start the motor. And provided he could get most of the water out of the boat. He found an old coffee can tied to a strut supporting one of the seats, obviously something the owner used for bailing. Kevin held on to the boat with one hand and bailed as rapidly as he could with the other. After a couple of minutes the water level had been reduced to a point where he felt confident he could risk moving from the canoe to the fishing boat. He climbed carefully into the larger boat and used the canoe's bowline to tie them together. He pushed the starter button on the motor; it coughed a time or two and then, to his relief, caught. It was going to be easier to get the boat to shore than he had thought.

As he headed back toward his own dock, Kevin poked around the boat, looking for something that might identify the owner. The registration number was on the hull, of course, and the owner would be easy to trace. But he was curious, so he went through the pockets of an old denim jacket, now soaking wet, which was tucked under a seat. Finding nothing there, he turned his attention to an oilcloth packet, rolled and tied, which lay under the jacket on the bottom of the boat. When he unrolled it, he found himself looking at four tools—a Phillips screwdriver, an adjustable wrench, a combination bottle and can-opener, and a long bladed knife. The knife looked brand new. It also looked very familiar.

Kevin suddenly thought he knew whose boat he was driving, and the thought produced a physical reaction close to nausea. If you fish a lot and have just lost the knife you use to clean your fish, you would want to replace it right away, and you would naturally choose a knife like the one with which you were familiar. But perhaps he was wrong. After all, there must be dozens of people around the lake who owned knives like the one he was looking at. But he could not put down the premonition of tragedy. In spite of the early morning hour and a reluctance to raise the noise level, Kevin gave the engine more throttle.

Having pulled the two boats well up onto the beach, Kevin hurried up to the cottage to place a call to the sheriff. As he reached for the phone, he suddenly remembered that it was not yet seven o'clock. How would the sheriff react to his story? Did he know it was Bauer's boat? What evidence did he have? Last week it had been a body on his dock. Today it was a boat drifting past Blue Water Point. Kevin put the phone back in its cradle. This was no time to make himself look unnecessarily foolish in Carol's eyes. He doubted that she would be amused if it turned out that the boat belonged to one of hundreds of other boat owners on Crooked Lake. Maybe he should do a bit of sleuthing before bothering her.

Kevin drove directly to Bauer's cabin. Hank's car was parked exactly where it had been the night before, and Kevin felt the first real stirrings of doubt. What if Bauer were home and surprised him while he was prowling around? Maybe he should simply knock on the door. But what explanation would he give for his presence if Hank should answer it? No, he'd first check the dock. If the boat was there, he'd turn around and go home. If it wasn't, he'd try the door.

He descended the steep steps until he reached a place where the dock came into view. The boat was gone. Several things had been taken out of the boat and left on the dock, including two fishing poles, a net, a tackle box, oars, and a life jacket. Kevin's heart began racing. The scene before him did not constitute proof that the boat he had rescued was Bauer's, but it shifted the odds in favor of his theory.

Half an hour later Kevin was back at his cottage and on the phone with Sheriff Kelleher. She was alarmed enough by the implications of his report that she had agreed to give top priority to identifying ownership of the boat and trying to locate Bauer. When Kevin went back down to the beach, he found Mike Snyder examining the mystery boat.

"You finally getting yourself a real boat?" Mike asked.

"I'm afraid not. No, this was just drifting out there this morning, no one in it, so I went out and pulled it in." Kevin knew he shouldn't be telling Mike that he thought Hank Bauer was Britingham's killer; it wasn't official, and it was possible that it wasn't even true. But he had to ask him about the boat.

"Tell me, is there any chance this could be your friend Bauer's boat?"

"Hank's? Why on earth would you think it might be his?" Snyder was puzzled by the question, but he squatted down, looking more closely at the boat. When he straightened up, he looked bewildered. "By gosh, you may be right. It's a common make, lots of 'em on the lake. I don't remember all of the registration number, but I do remember those three sevens in a row. And it's got the extra electric motor, like Hank's. But I don't understand. You just found it adrift?"

"Little over an hour ago. And when I went over to Bauer's place to see if his boat was gone, it was. He'd left most of his gear—poles, net, tackle box, life jacket, even the oars. It's a puzzle, that's for sure." Unfortunately, Kevin was thinking, it might not really be that much of a puzzle.

"Jesus!" In spite of his deep tan, Mike suddenly looked almost pale. "The life jacket was still there? Oh, my God. He couldn't swim."

Now it was Kevin's turn to be shocked.

"Couldn't swim? But he lived right on the lake."

"Hank's always been afraid of the water as long as I've known him. He never set foot in the boat without his life jacket. Only felt safe when he had it on. I can't understand why he'd go out without it. Maybe somebody stole the boat." Mike was grasping at straws.

"We ought to be finding out pretty soon. The sheriff's looking for him," Kevin said.

Mike leaned against the cottonwood tree. He was clearly shaken.

"I still don't get it. What made you think it might be Hank's boat?" he asked.

"I hate to say this, Mike, but I've had a hunch that it was Bauer who killed Britingham. And I think there's a good chance that he's committed suicide."

Mike Snyder closed his eyes and slumped to the ground on the beach.

When Sheriff Kelleher arrived at the Whitman cottage shortly before ten o'clock, she could say for a fact what Kevin had suspected and Mike had all but confirmed: the boat which Kevin had rescued was indeed registered in Norman Bauer's name. She had not, however, been able to produce the missing man or anybody who had seen him that morning. Kevin shared Mike's information that Bauer was a nonswimmer. This, coupled with the fact that the man's life jacket had been left on his dock, led almost immediately to talk of drowning and to the dreaded prospect of dragging the lake for a body. Kevin knew that the sheriff must be thinking about, and probably regretting, her acquiescence in his attempt to coax a confession from the man. They both knew that they would not, in all probability, be having this discussion had he not confronted Bauer with his suspicions the previous evening.

But it was a length of yarn the sheriff discovered in the fishing boat that more than anything else turned their uncomfortable suspicions into depressing near certainties. Kevin had missed it, and when Carol noticed it she initially paid it no attention. It looked very much as if Bauer had snagged some article of his clothing when climbing into or out of the boat. But the sheriff had a faculty of storing away small bits of seemingly useless information for future reference, and one such piece of information was that the sweater Britingham had been wearing when his body was discovered had a run in it. It had begun at the point where the sweater had been ripped by the knife with which Britingham had been mortally wounded, and it ran nearly halfway around the garment near the pocket line. When she spotted the piece of yarn in the boat, it was wet and plastered against the side of the boat. She absent-mindedly gave it a tug, only to find it caught under the brace that fastened the bench seat to the frame of the boat. Only then did she take notice of the color and remember Kevin's theory that Bauer had moved Britingham's body by boat the night he had been killed.

To prove that the length of yarn had once been part of the sweater Britingham had been wearing would require much more than eyeball identification. But the sheriff was virtually certain that, barring a coincidence too rare to be credible, John Britingham had been in Bauer's boat the night he had borrowed the sweater and met his death on Blue Water Point. Kevin's theory, which had looked promising the previous afternoon and which Kevin at least believed had been strengthened by Bauer's behavior the previous evening, now looked even more compelling. Carol was prepared to believe that Hank Bauer had indeed committed suicide.

Suicide or not, Bauer's death became official the following afternoon, when a fisherman found his body just a little over two miles north of Southport. Within an hour the coroner had rendered his preliminary verdict of death by drowning.

CHAPTER 51

It is doubtful if the Crooked Lake grapevine ever worked more effectively than in the 24 hours following the discovery of Hank Bauer's body. By late afternoon on Monday, only infants and adults who had remained closeted in their homes and failed to answer their phones did not know that the legendary local athlete had drowned. But only a handful of the area's residents had any inkling that Bauer's death had closed the Britingham case, and four of them were sitting in Kevin Whitman's living room.

Sheriff Kelleher had called earlier that afternoon and told Kevin that she wanted to stop by for the drink she had declined the night of the canoe ride. She had some news she wanted to share with him, and it was, after all, the end of a particularly difficult week. Dan and Rachel Milburn had dropped by unannounced some ten minutes before the sheriff arrived, and so it was that at six o'clock on a Monday evening in late August the Milburns and the sheriff were sharing a drink with Kevin and discussing the denouement to the summer's biggest story.

Kevin explained for the benefit of Dan and Rachel how he had arrived at the conclusion that Bauer had probably killed Britingham. It hadn't been one thing, but many. The fact that he had come to the Sandersons by boat. That he had a knife on him. That the Keyser boys had seen Britingham disappear in the direction of the Sanderson cottage in the middle of the night. That the cinder block was missing the day after the crime, together with his theory about the reason for its disappearance. That someone had been looking for something on the Sandersons' beach the next night, something that in all probability was the knife. That the knife—Kevin was now simply taking it for granted that it was *the* knife—had been found in the lake where Grace Hess had presumably thrown it. He gave her golden retriever, Jeff, full credit for discovering the knife and carrying it off so that Bauer couldn't find it.

And then, of course, there had been the threatening note which had been found in Dolores Weber's microwave and the similarities between the handwriting on that note and on the equipment list for the Silver Leaf softball team which Bauer had drafted for Britingham. On Friday he had seen this as the clincher. Now the sheriff also had a piece of yarn that was very probably from the sweater Britingham had been wearing the night he was killed.

"It's mostly circumstantial, you understand, but it adds up. And he had a motive. His friends say he was devastated by the way Britingham had humiliated him."

"We'll get a professional opinion on the yarn and the handwriting," Carol said. "And there may be fingerprints, of course. But I think Kevin is right—Bauer's almost certainly our man, for both killings."

"I'm impressed," Rachel commented, "but I haven't heard anything to explain how Britingham got onto your dock."

Kevin started to say that this was the one loose end they hadn't tied up, but Carol interrupted him.

"I told you I had a reason for coming over, other than to drink your beer," she said. "You know I'd given a lot of thought to Alan Hoffman and his little lies. Well, I decided not to let him off the hook. I called him at his office this morning, told him we'd gotten Britingham's killer, but that we were considering an obstruction of justice charge against him. It was mostly bluff, but it worked. He said he and his wife had had a sensitivity session of sorts, but that it didn't work out like he thought it would. They'd both owned up to their affairs, hers with Britingham and his with that prostitute down in the city. Trouble is, she seems to have decided that their marriage is a bust, said she was going to get a divorce. Anyway, once she knew what he'd been doing and I'd told him we'd identified the killer, he didn't see any reason not to tell the truth.

"And the truth ties up the biggest loose end. Alan Hoffman was on Blue Water Point the night Bauer killed Britingham, just as we suspected. He was hiding out in the bushes, spying on his wife. That's what he says, and I believe him. He never did see what he came to see, but when it began to get light he decided he'd better get the hell out of there. He wanted to wake himself up for the drive back to the city, so he went down to the lake to splash some water on his face. And what does he see? Even tripped over him, he says. It's Britingham, stone dead on his beach.

"Hoffman says he almost lost it right there. Can't say as I blame him. But he pulled himself together, figured with everything that'd been going on he couldn't afford to have the body discovered on his property. So he dragged Britingham to Kevin's dock—pulled him through the water, in fact, because it was easier to move the body that way. Besides, he had this idea it would look like Britingham had climbed out of the lake onto the dock."

"Did he say why he picked my dock?" Kevin wanted to know.

"He probably would have used the Morgans' dock, but someone in their cottage had apparently been awake not long before he found Britingham, so he thought it would be safer to put him on the next dock. That would be yours."

"Why do you suppose the body was on Hoffman's beach in the first place?" It was Dan's question.

"I've tried to put myself inside Bauer's mind," Kevin said. "He would have wanted to get the body away from Larry Sanderson's cottage—to protect Larry and himself. And Mike Snyder tells me they'd been talking that evening about Britingham's alleged affair with Mrs. Hoffman. So it figures that when he started thinking about a place to dump the body, he thought of the Hoffmans. I doubt he was consciously trying to frame Hoffman, but he probably figured it would give the police ideas."

"And it would have, if Mr. Hoffman hadn't moved the body," the sheriff observed ruefully. "But there's another loose end, probably not all that important, but it still bothers me. I'd like to see if I can't get your neighbors, the Morgans, to tell me what their secret is. I'm sure they're hiding something."

Kevin's face broke into a smug grin.

"Let me tell you what I think, and after you've talked with them, you can tell us if I'm right. I think George was up early that morning, and that he must have seen the body out on my dock. He would have been naturally curious, so he went out to take a look. Heaven knows what his first reaction was when he saw it was Britingham. But I'd bet his second had to do with Britingham's visit with Edna's brother at the nursing home that night. It's my guess that Britingham took an old keepsake letter from Amos Fielder—a letter written by Edna's aunt before she was drowned in that accident on the lake a long time ago. And I think George thought so, too. He would have been afraid the letter was on Britingham, where your people would find it. And that would have aroused your suspicions of the Morgans. So he went through Britingham's pockets, and he did find the letter. Then he burned it—it would have been damp, so he had to put some other stuff in the fireplace with it. That's why I saw all that smoke coming out of their chimney when I took my infamous swim."

Dan looked skeptical.

"Seems a bit far-fetched, don't you think?" he asked.

"No more so than Britingham's body getting moved all around that night," Kevin said.

It was Rachel, who had said nothing for quite some time, who brought the discussion back to the tragedy of Hank Bauer.

"Suicide is such a terribly sad thing," she said. "I wonder why he didn't take his chances in court. The way you describe it, neither killing was premeditated, and the one was probably self-defense. Isn't it likely he would have had a good chance for early parole?"

Kevin looked at the sheriff, but she busied herself with her drink, deferring to him.

"You may be right, although we don't really know whether he killed Britingham in self-defense—never will. But I don't think Bauer saw it that way. I didn't know him, but he struck me as a person who just couldn't face the thought of jail. I think he thought his life had already been ruined—first by Britingham's cruel brand of one-upmanship, then by those two deaths, which must have weighed heavily on his conscience. What was there to live for? Years in a prison cell, even if he didn't serve a full sentence? He was an outdoor man, remember, not a reader or a thinker. He must have seen prison as the ultimate indignity, and boring beyond our imagining. I think he decided that it was best to end it now, before it got any worse."

"You make him sound like as much of a victim as Britingham or that Weber woman," Rachel said.

"In a way I think he was."

"So does it still remind you of opera?" Carol asked, her face wearing a smile for one of the few times in over a week.

"Oh, yes," Kevin replied. "When we were talking the other night, I was thinking of some of those twisted plots from 19th century opera. But now I'm reminded of a much more recent 20th century work. It's called *Peter Grimes*. An Englishman, Benjamin Britten, wrote it. This man Grimes, a fisherman, is something of a misfit, and he's indirectly responsible for the accidental deaths of two young apprentices. In the end he's driven to commit suicide— he takes his boat out to sea and drowns himself."

"I'll be damned," Carol said.

"Life imitating art," Rachel Milburn observed.

———

It was sometime later, and the Milburns had departed. The sheriff had agreed to Kevin's offer of another drink and a quick supper of bacon and eggs, and they were in the process of tidying up the kitchen.

"There's one piece of good news in all of this," Kevin said. "Gloria Snyder's coming back. They're going to give it another shot. I think Mike was really shaken up by Bauer's death. He's convinced that if Hank hadn't been drinking that night he'd never have pulled a knife on Britingham. I think he believes he could have done the same thing given the condition he was in. Mike's really scared about what the booze is doing to him. He's going into a program, and I think he's serious about straightening himself out.

"By the way," he added, "I've wondered why you never seemed to zero in on Mike as a prime suspect in Britingham's murder. I'm glad you didn't, but he had as good an opportunity as anyone, plus a motive. And if anybody was strong enough to do it, it would have been Mike."

"I never ruled him out, you know," Carol said. "But I figured Snyder was the one suspect who had something more important on his mind than his quarrel with Britingham—the breakup of his marriage. I'm not sure that's very good logic, but I guess it's as good as your gut feeling that he just couldn't kill anybody."

They drifted back into the living room and chatted casually about the case, bringing it to conversational closure.

"What have you done about young Britingham?" Kevin wanted to know.

"It wasn't as hard as I thought it might be," Carol said. "I think a few nights in jail had planted some doubts in his mind about what he was doing. He didn't exactly retract his confession, not in so many words, but he didn't argue when I released him. He'll stay around until we've officially wrapped this up, then probably go back to California. I gave him some money to tide him over—probably shouldn't have done it, but, damn it, I feel sorry for the kid."

"You're an old softy," Kevin said, "my kind of sheriff."

It was shortly after ten o'clock when Carol had the evening's last word on the people who had been affected by the late John Britingham.

"Got another piece of lake gossip for you," she said. "Grace Hess had a letter from Britingham's daughter, offering to sell her that property on the cove once the estate has been settled. And at a very good price. I don't have to tell you that she's elated. So some good things have come out of this affair, wouldn't you say?"

Oh, yes, Kevin thought, and it wasn't Grace Hess he was thinking about.

It was close to 10:30 when the sheriff got to her feet and started to say good night.

"Look, it's late; it's been a long day—a long two weeks," Kevin said. "Do yourself a favor, will you—stay here. Your case is closed, so you really don't have to be up at daybreak. We can do bacon and eggs again in the morning, or pancakes if you prefer. Okay?"

Carol blushed, hesitated, then sat back down.

"Now that you mention it," she said, "I'm exhausted. I like the offer."

Kevin joined her on the couch, putting an arm around her. This time the hug lasted much longer than it had several nights earlier.